GUN SHY

ALSO BY BEN REHDER

Guilt Trip
Flat Crazy
Bone Dry
Buck Fever

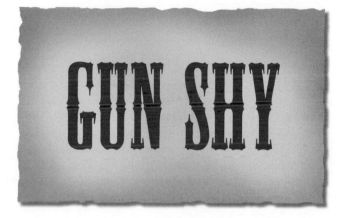

GUN SHY

BEN REHDER

ST. MARTIN'S MINOTAUR/NEW YORK

This is a work of fiction. All of the characters, organizations, and events portrayed in this novel are either products of the author's imagination or are used fictitiously.

GUN SHY. Copyright © 2007 by Ben Rehder. All rights reserved. Printed in the United States of America. No part of this book may be used or reproduced in any manner whatsoever without written permission except in the case of brief quotations embodied in critical articles or reviews. For information, address St. Martin's Press, 175 Fifth Avenue, New York, N.Y. 10010.

www.minotaurbooks.com

Library of Congress Cataloging-in-Publication Data

Rehder, Ben.
  Gun shy / Ben Rehder.—1st ed.
    p. cm.
  ISBN-13: 978-0-312-35752-8
  ISBN-10: 0-312-35752-4
    1. Blanco County (Tex.)—Fiction.   2. Marlin, John (Fictitious character)—Fiction.
  3. Gun control—Fiction.   I. Title.

PS3618.E45G86   2007
813'.6—dc22

2007007890

First Edition: May 2007

10 9 8 7 6 5 4 3 2 1

This one's for Phil,
Toni, Samantha,
and Benjamin.

ACKNOWLEDGMENTS

SPECIAL THANKS TO Lieutenant Tommy Blackwell (retired from the Travis County Sheriff's Office); Lampasas County Game Warden Jim Lindeman; Martin and JoAnn Grantham; John Grace, assistant criminal district attorney, Civil Division, Lubbock County; Judi Youngblood, program specialist, Victim Services Division, Texas Department of Criminal Justice; John Kelso with the *Austin American-Statesman*; and Beverly Villarreal, forensic specialist, Texas Parks and Wildlife Department.

I owe Trey Carpenter an ongoing debt of gratitude.

Thanks also to Becky Rehder, Jo Virgil, and Frank Campbell for the color they added to the manuscript.

Much appreciation, as always, to my early readers—Mary Summerall, Helen and Ed Fanick, and Stacia Hernstrom—and to my copyeditor, India Cooper.

Jeff Abbott and Maggie Griffin have both been good friends and wise advisers from the beginning.

Ben Sevier and Jane Chelius should probably have their names on the cover of this book, but they're gracious enough to let me keep it for myself.

Last, thanks to Don Gray for his input on the Guatemalan sand crab, Steve Cauley for his expertise on postmodern furniture design, and Kerry Hilton for his patented line-dancing techniques.

All errors or distortions of reality are my own.

PART ONE

An armed society is an at-risk society.

—Brady Campaign to Prevent Gun
Violence Web site

In fact, guns deter gun violence.

—National Rifle Association—Institute
for Legislative Action Web site

You can convince anyone of anything if you just push it at them 100 percent of the time.

—Charles Manson

SATURDAY, JUNE 20
NATIONAL WEAPONS ALLIANCE RALLY
HOUSTON, TEXAS

FIFTY-TWO YEARS AGO, at the tender age of nine, Dale Allen Stubbs fell head over heels in love. He simply couldn't help himself. The object of his affection was slender and hard, blessed with understated curves that begged for the caress of his young hand.

It was a bolt-action Remington .22 given to him by his grandfather Atticus Stubbs on Dale's birthday. Christ, what a gun! Oil-finished walnut stock. A twenty-inch barrel with the same blue-black sheen as a raven's wing. A true thing of beauty. Stubbs' palms were sweaty with anticipation the first time he cradled that marvelous weapon. For the first week or so, he actually slept with it, the barrel rising up between his legs, little Dale having no understanding of the Freudian implications.

Now, half a century later, the white-hot love affair continued, though Stubbs was by no means monogamous. He'd amassed an arsenal over the years, nearly fifty weapons in total—handguns, rifles, contemporary black-powder muzzleloaders, antique flintlocks and muskets—all housed inside twin burglarproof safes, with a certified fire-protection rating of more than sixteen hundred degrees. Had to protect his babies, you know.

Of course, like a father with many children, he had his favorites. His Winchester Model 70, a pre-1964 specimen, chambered in .375 H&H Magnum. His L. C. Smith side-by-side twelve-gauge with rear oval lock plates, manufactured in 1898. Monogram grade. Extremely rare. And the centerpiece of his collection—a pair of Colt Model 1849 pocket percussion revolvers, inscribed to Major C. Smith.

Yes, he loved each and every one. A lot. More than his six-bedroom home with its state-of-the-art security system. More than Dexter, his five-thousand-dollar bird dog. More than his brand-new fully loaded Chevrolet crew-cab pickup. Yes, even more than sex—with Margie, his wife of twenty-five years, or with Tricia, his twenty-four-year-old secretary, who captured Stubbs' heart when he discovered that she carried a snubnose .38 in her handbag.

The only thing that maybe, just maybe, stirred Dale Stubbs' passion more than guns was speaking to other people who held the same convictions he did. Preaching the gospel of Truth gave him a sense of satisfaction more profound than dropping a charging Cape buffalo (which he had done on three separate occasions).

Now, as he strutted onto the dais, preparing to address a crowd of four thousand—true patriots, every last one of them—Stubbs was feeling an all-time high. Adrenaline flowed through his heart like water through a hose. The audience rose to its feet, clapping and cheering wildly.

It was amazing, really, he thought. A simple country boy had managed to reach dizzying heights, turning his fondness for guns into not just a lucrative career but a higher calling. He was making a *difference* in the world, by God. He was president of the Texas chapter of the National Weapons Alliance, the most powerful lobbying organization in the world. As such, he *lived* for moments like this.

As the applause slowly ebbed, Stubbs adjusted the microphone. The opening line of a speech was always the most important one, and Stubbs was up to the task. Using the deepest, most charismatic voice he could muster, he said, "I wanna welcome y'all to Houston . . . where great Americans still recognize the value of freedom!"

The crowd went berserk.

Right on cue, thousands of red, white, and blue balloons dropped from the rafters. Someone backstage cranked the music to a deafening level. Men in Stetsons proudly waved flags and banners. The pandemonium lasted a full minute. Stubbs simply waited, beaming, enjoying every last moment of it.

Finally, just as the auditorium began to settle down, a buxom blond girl wearing minuscule shorts, a tight NWA T-shirt, and a cowboy hat yelled, "We love you, Dale!"

"I love you, too, sweetheart," Dale replied cheerfully.

That elicited a booming round of good-natured laughter, followed by more hearty applause.

"In fact, I love *all* of you," Stubbs continued, taking the microphone in hand like a television evangelist. "Each and every one of you is a soldier in the battle to keep our great country strong."

Another eruption, almost as long as the first. He expected it; he'd carefully crafted his speech to draw reactions at key moments. You had to control the audience, just as you controlled your pacing and your content. Sometimes, though, you needed a little help, and that's why Stubbs had asked one of his assistants to plant the blond girl in the third row. Just a little parlor trick to get him off on the right foot. Now Stubbs raised one hand, palm outward, and the audience grew silent. It was as impressive as Moses parting the Red Sea.

"It's apparent that we're all in a great mood this morning, and for good reason. The National Weapons Alliance, I'm proud to say, is stronger today than it has ever been. Granted, we've faced treachery on many fronts in the past decade. In the nineties, a weak-minded and short-sighted president attempted to usurp the power of the American people."

Boos all around. Stubbs nodded sympathetically.

"More recently, misguided cities and counties, and even a few states, tried to sue the gun manufacturers out of existence. But were we daunted or discouraged or defeated? No sir! We did what our daddies would've done. We persevered! We fought back, using the second most effective weapon we have: our God-given right to vote. From state capitals around the nation, all the way to Washington, our voice was heard as one—and that voice said *the right of the people to keep and bear arms shall not be infringed!*"

The audience sprang to its feet. A standing ovation! Quoting the Second Amendment was always a surefire winner. This outbreak was the longest one yet! Stubbs basked in the glow and waited for the calm before he proceeded.

"Now we are in a position to ensure liberty for generations to come, for our children and our grandchildren. We have a friend in the White House—a great man who understands that we, the common citizens, must always remain vigilant as we stand guard against tyranny. He's one of us, my friends, and you have yourselves to thank because *you put him there!*"

Applause for ten seconds. About what Stubbs had expected because, let's face it, the president did have certain flaws. His intelligence was questionable. His diplomatic skills were suspect. He was often nervous and clumsy in front of a camera. Plus, to get picky, he didn't even have a gun rack in the truck he used on his ranch. What kind of message did that send? Ah, well, you did your best with what you had, and one of Stubbs' jobs was to make the NWA's strengths appear indomitable.

"But, as we have all learned over the years, we cannot become complacent. We cannot rest on our laurels and our accomplishments. The antigun zealots and the liberal media are quick to jump on even the smallest crack in our armor. Take the incident last month in Springfield, Massachusetts, where one of our members—Zelda Grimby, a retired algebra teacher—mistakenly thought her postman was a burglar and shot him in the groin. Did the reporters mention that Zelda was fully licensed to own a handgun? No, they did not. Did they mention that Zelda lived in a high-crime area? Somehow they overlooked that. They focused solely on the fact that the mail carrier lost a testicle, and the second one was badly damaged. Yes, it's unlikely that he'll ever father children, but"—Stubbs paused for effect, then came back stronger than ever—"I'd say that's a small price to pay for a strong and well-armed republic!"

Wild cheering proved that Stubbs was right. He had the audience eating out of his hand. Time to wrap this up and get out on a high note. Move on to the barbecue and a cold beer.

"The point is, we must keep up the good fight, and that is the reason we are all here today. We have gathered to show our unified support for a man who, with our help, will be elected the next governor of the state of Texas. I'm speaking of a man who will push to fully expand our Second Amendment rights, making it legal for law-abiding citizens to carry a concealed weapon anywhere in Texas without a permit. I'm referring to a good friend of mine by the name of Congressman Glenn Andrew Dobbins!"

This was the moment the crowd had been waiting for. They quickly began a chant: *Daw-bins! Daw-bins! Daw-bins!* They waved placards and hand-painted signs. Khaki-clad men kissed khaki-clad women with joyous exuberance. Somewhere in the back, someone played "Deep in the Heart of Texas" very poorly on a trombone.

After a minute, Stubbs tried one of his usual settle-down gestures, but even that didn't work. He simply had to wait it out, and he didn't mind at all. If this was any indication, the NWA's candidate was a shoo-in come November. Finally, after nearly two minutes, the ruckus began to subside.

"Unfortunately," Stubbs said, "Congressman Dobbins was unable to join us today. But as you know, this is only the first of many rallies to be held in the next few months. Fort Worth. San Antonio. Midland. Abilene. Not Austin, thank you very much."

Stubbs waited for the chuckles that line merited, and he was amply rewarded. No, Austin, the liberal bastion of Texas, would not be hosting an NWA rally. No way. Not a city that had more anti-gunners than the remainder of the state combined. The rest of Texas—that's where the NWA intended to spread its message.

"In fact, two weeks from today," he said, "on Independence Day, we'll be convening in the heartland of our state . . . in Blanco County, just outside Johnson City, and I know Congressman Dobbins intends to be there to thank each of you for your support. Because make no mistake—it is you, the rank and file, the front-line troops—who are the backbone of our organization!"

Pure pandering, but they ate it up. Audience members slapped each other's backs and exchanged high fives.

"Speaking of the Blanco County rally," Stubbs said, switching to a folksy delivery for a moment, "I have a very special announcement to make, and this just tickles me to death." He paused again to build the drama, studying the crowd with what was meant to come across as genuine affection. "We've been holding the location of the rally back as a surprise, and now I can share it with you."

A buzz was starting to build. This was going to be big, Stubbs had no doubt of that.

"I'm pleased to say that it will take place at a ranch owned by—hold on to your hats, friends!—none other than our newest spokesman, star of our latest radio and television ads, country music superstar Mitch Campbell!"

The audience responded with an outburst unlike any Stubbs had ever seen or heard. Even the gleeful cheers for Dobbins paled by comparison. Stubbs did his best to speak over the uproar.

"Mitch Campbell, I think we'd all agree, is a fine representative for the NWA. His smash-hit song 'My Cold, Dead Hands' has brought in a quarter million new members nationally in the last six months alone!"

Was anyone even listening at this point? It was hard to tell above the melee.

"Mitch offers a powerful new voice for responsible gun ownership!"

Lusty female shrieks ascended to the heavens.

"He is a man of ethics!"

Men whistled and stomped and shot imaginary pistols into the air.

"A man of virtue!"

An overweight woman near the front swooned and cracked her head on a speaker assembly.

"A man of strong moral fiber and good old-fashioned Christian values!"

The hall was now a full-on madhouse.

"The kind of man the NWA can be proud to call its own!"

The crowd had taken up a new chant—*Campbell! Campbell! Campbell!*—and Stubbs knew, without question, that the NWA was about to enter its golden age.

2

TWO HOURS BEFORE Mitch Campbell pumped a two-hundred-grain .45-caliber slug into an innocent man, he was in bed, struggling with a massive hangover, trying in vain to remember the names of the naked twin sisters sleeping next to him.

Too much whiskey. Too much cocaine. Too much of, well, whatever those pills were that had made the rounds last night. Mitch hadn't planned for the party to happen—he'd only invited a handful of his new friends over—but these things had a way of snowballing, everybody wanting to rub elbows with the hottest male vocalist on the country charts. By midnight, the house had been crawling with people. Mitch knew he should've thinned it out and toned it down, but damn, where was the fun in that? Hell, he'd *earned* it, hadn't he? Sixty shows in seventy days, and now he deserved a little R&R, right?

But, Christ, this morning he was paying the piper. His brain throbbed like he'd just had cranial surgery. His mouth tasted like a hamster had camped out in it overnight. His memory of the evening's festivities reminded him of one of his trendy music videos: lots of quick cuts and fades, vignettes that lasted mere seconds, bathed in shadow. He had fragmented flashbacks of nude people in the hot tub. White lines on the glass-topped coffee table. Sucking tequila out of some babe's navel. Had it been one of the twins?

Kathy and Kelly? Lisa and Leslie? Something cutesy like that, he was pretty sure. The girls were still snoozing, or passed out, really, one on either side of Mitch in his king-sized bed. He propped himself on his elbows, trying to ignore the drumbeat in his skull, and surveyed the room.

Three pairs of boots and jeans were scattered on the floor. Panties. Blouses. He looked for telltale condom wrappers—expecting two or three—but spotted none. Was that a good sign or a bad one? Had he gone in completely unprotected, not even a thin layer of latex between him and a paternity suit? Or had he managed to control himself this time, to refuse the bounty that was so lovingly offered?

It brought back a recent conversation with Joe Scroggins, his manager.

"You cain't keep humpin' everything on two legs, Mitch," Scroggins said with that harsh East Texas twang Mitch still hadn't gotten used to. Sounded so damn ridiculous.

Mitch laughed. "Wanna bet? I take vitamins."

"What I mean is, you shouldn't."

"Why the hell not?"

"Damn, son, you're a *country* star, not a *rock* star. I know the ladies love you and all, but take it easy on the one-nighters, will ya? You got a image to maintain. No more buckle bunnies."

"But I—"

"Besides, you're getting married, remember?"

"Yeah, I guess."

"And dope, too. Steer clear of that shit. Nothing stronger than beer, ya hear?"

"Ryan Buckley does it," Mitch pointed out. "Sleeps around *and* gets high."

"Now, see, Ryan Buckley is an entirely diff'rent product. He's the bad boy of the industry. Why d'you think he wears a black hat?"

"Well, then, maybe I should get a black hat. Maybe we should shake things up a little and—"

"Too late. You're white hat all the way. You're supposed to be *wholesome,* Mitch. All-American. God-fearing. The boy next door, 'cept better looking. You're lucky they even let you keep the goatee."

"What about this whole gun gig? The boy next door carries a gun?"

Scroggins shook his head, like a father dealing with a slow child. "Down here they do. As far as country fans are concerned, ain't nothin' more American than guns. Ain't you been paying attention?"

"I still don't understand why I can't just be myself," Mitch whined.

"You do that," Scroggins replied, "and we'll both lose a got-damn fortune. That what you want? Hot one week, out on your ass the next?"

So, yes, all in all, it had taken some getting used to, this whole hat-wearin', boot-scootin', gun-totin', good-ol'-boy act. That's because Mitch Campbell's real name was Norman Kleinschmidt, and he'd been born and raised in Middlebury, Vermont. His father was a highly paid industrial chemist, his mother a stay-at-home mom. Back when he was known as Norman, he'd never shot a deer, roped a calf, or chewed tobacco. He'd never done the two-step, and he didn't know the first thing about tractor pulls, stock-car races, bass fishing, or any of that other redneck crap.

Norman, in fact, had attended private prep school, followed by four years at Dartmouth, where, between pot-smoking parties and Ecstasy-induced orgies, he occasionally went to class. His grades were appalling, but generous donations to the school by Norman's exasperated father ensured that he wound up with a degree. After graduation, Norman worked on Wall Street for two years. Wore a thousand-dollar suit every day. Made big bucks. Absolutely hated it. Assholes everywhere.

What he needed, he decided, was something a little more creative. A career where everyone wasn't so damn uptight. So, to his parents' dismay, he switched gears and signed on at an advertising agency as a junior-level copywriter. Here, he thought, he could use his brain and his sense of humor. This would be fun and rewarding and glamorous.

His first assignment was to write a thirty-second television commercial for a feminine-hygiene spray called Spring Mist. The project brief specified that the spot should feature "two middle-aged Caucasian women" who were having a "genuine and frank discussion" about "neutralizing feminine odor, not just covering it up."

Holy Christ.

Norman left for lunch, had five Manhattans instead, and decided not to return.

Two days later, stoned out of his gourd on some outstanding herb, listening to a group called Canker Sore, it finally dawned on him. Of course! It had been so obvious all along. He had never enjoyed anything more fully than the garage band he'd had in high school. They called themselves Pus Bucket, a mixture of rock, neo-punk, and fusion. As far as talent went, they were plenty loud. Norman *did* have a voice, though. Despite his cushy and privileged upbringing, Norman always managed to sound as hauntingly poignant as Kurt Cobain or Alanis Morissette.

I'll write some new songs! he thought. *I'll cut a demo!*

And so he did, ignoring the fact that the odds against making it in the music industry were astronomical. Norman got hold of some wicked meth and wrote ten songs overnight. When he finally had a clear head, he narrowed it down to the best three: "Sweet Love Weasel," "Say Hello to Woody," and "Binge and Purge."

Then he hired some awesome session players, and they were in the studio three days later. The recording went flawlessly. He felt certain he had genuine platinum on his hands. The next day, Norman sent press kits—a CD, a bio, and a head shot—to two dozen producers, record-label heads, and managers. Norman was feeling giddy as he dropped the promotional packages into the mail.

Then reality set in.

A month passed. Nothing. Two more weeks. Not a word. Norman made some calls, but he couldn't get past the iron wall of front-office stooges and peons.

Two months later, finally, a response! A man named Joe Scroggins had scribbled a note across the bottom of Norman's head shot: *You got a face for Nashville. Ever written any country?*

Country? Norman thought. *Sappy songs about broken hearts and beer joints? Fiddles and steel guitars? You gotta be fuckin' kidding me.*

He tossed the note in the garbage can.

Another month passed. Norman sent out more press kits and got nowhere. He was being completely ignored, and it pissed him off. *Don't these fuckwads recognize talent when they hear it?* he wondered. He should do the music industry a favor, he thought, by tracking these jerkoffs down and putting a bullet into each one of their heads.

That's when he decided to write a country song after all. A catchy little ditty about guns. It started out as a joke, really, just goofing around on his acoustic guitar. Something he noodled around with to make himself feel better. It was full of black humor and bitter revenge fantasies. He mailed it out for no other reason than to give all those assholes a piece of his mind. Nobody could possibly take it seriously.

Nobody, that is, except Joe Scroggins. Joe heard something more. He had a vision. He saw the potential for this tossed-off novelty song to become an American classic.

"It's a winner," Joe said over the phone, "but it needs help. Maybe a bit of redirection."

"What do you mean?" Norman replied, a little stunned. A little stoned, too. Was this guy for real? The song was mostly a gag. Still, Norman decided it wouldn't hurt to play along.

"I'm thinking it needs to be a tad more patriotic and a bit less, well, homicidal."

"Yeah?"

"Instead of hunting down record producers, for example, make it terrorists. Then you'll have something."

"Terrorists?"

"Got-damn right. They's big right now. Now, I don't mean come right out and say 'Let's all kill Mohammed' or some shit like that. Ya gotta be subtle. And pro-USA. Wrap a flag around it, as they say. Guns are what make us strong. Guns prevent crime and keep our country safe. That sorta thing."

"Anything else?"

"Change the Kalashnikov to a Remington or a Colt. American-made product. Now I realize that'll gum up your rhyme scheme, but I think it's for the best. Just rework that whole section. And down in the chorus, where you're talking about writing epitaphs in blood—make it something about the Constitution instead."

"You serious?"

"As a swollen prostate."

Norman had never been to Nashville, so, three days later, he decided to fly down and present the revised lyrics in person.

Joe read them twice and said, "Damn, boy, now we're getting somewhere."

"You like it?"

"Got-damn, I love it. This could be huge. The time is right for this kind of message. 'Mericans are nervous, maybe a little scared. The world's in turmoil. Song like this makes 'em feel safe and secure. Like we're all in it together, ready to kick ass and take names."

Norman couldn't help himself. He was starting to get excited by the prospect. Country music? Really? Who would have guessed?

"One other thing," Joe said. "You're gonna need a new name."

"What?"

"And a dialect coach."

"Seriously?"

"No offense, son, but you talk real funny."

Norman laughed. "*I* talk funny?"

"Glad we agree. And I notice you got a little hitch in your gitalong."

"A what?"

"A limp, son."

"Oh, that's an old snowboarding injury."

"Snow what?"

"Snowboarding."

"The hell's a snowboard?"

"It's, um, kinda like a surfboard, but smaller. You ride it. On snow."

Joe gave him a puzzled stare. "Well, forget that crap. Cowboys don't snowboard. Anyone asks, you done that riding a bull."

3

AFTER HE ROUSTED the girls and herded them out to their car, Mitch woke himself with a shot of bourbon and two scorching lines of crank. It was a fond farewell of sorts, because Mitch had made a big decision. Next week he'd start to go straight. Cold turkey. No alcohol, no drugs. The women, too. No more whoring around. Stay true to Sheryl, because that's what the conservative crowd in Nashville expected.

It would be worth it, because, when it came right down to it, Mitch knew he was the luckiest man on earth. He'd stumbled ass over teakettle into good fortune, and he wasn't going to blow it by doing something stupid, like so many of the other rising male vocalists.

No drug bust on national television, like Clyde Crawford, who was currently serving eighteen months in Huntsville.

No indecency charges, like Taylor Burrell, who propositioned an off-duty cop in a rest-stop men's room.

Nothing like that was going to happen to Mitch Campbell.

He would *not* fuck up his career. He would *not* throw it all away.

* * *

Looking back on it all, as Mitch would do so many times in the future, it was probably the psilocybin that did it. Just an innocent-looking mushroom that he found in a plastic Baggie when he was cleaning up. A leftover from the party.

Yeah, he knew exactly what it was, and sure, he was tempted.

But speed was one thing, even Ecstasy, and 'shrooms were something completely different.

On the other hand, it was a really small mushroom. Not much bigger than the kind you'd find on a pizza. Nothing much to worry about. Right? It would be kind of fun to take a quick trip before setting out on the path of the straight and narrow.

He took the mushroom out of the bag and squeezed it between his fingers. Not as squishy as he expected. Held it to his nose. Smelled fine.

Okay, what the hell.

He popped it into his mouth, chewed it up, and chased it with an ice-cold Corona.

This'll be fun, he thought.

The walls were melting.

He didn't like looking at his hands, because his fingers had turned into little sausages.

A two-hundred-pound poodle was eyeing him from the corner, and Mitch didn't even own a dog.

Somewhere in the deepest recesses of his brain, he was aware that he'd made a rather large mistake. Paranoia was setting in.

He went back to his bedroom and locked the door. Unplugged the phone. He'd stay right here until this thing blew over.

His clothes had suddenly turned radioactive, so he stripped them off.

He lay on the bed and felt himself sink three feet into the mattress. It was made of pudding.

Snakes were hanging from the light fixture.

He closed his eyes. Saw nothing but colors—hues and shades that hadn't even been invented yet.

Time passed. Three minutes? Three days?

His pillow began to speak to him. Scary things!

Don't you hear that? it screamed. *Someone is outside your window!*

Mitch resisted. The pillow had a well-deserved reputation as a liar. Treasonous bastard. But what if it was telling the truth this time?

Then there *was* a noise. Definitely.

Mitch pulled himself out of the pudding, trotted nimbly across the carpet, and pressed his back against the wall. He slowly sidled next to the window. Ever so cautiously, he craned his neck around the jamb, peeked between the blinds, and . . .

OHMYGOD!

A dark-skinned man was lurking not three feet from the house!

Mitch pulled his head back. Had he been seen? He didn't think so. He was breathing heavily. His heart was thumping wildly in his chest.

Why was this man on Mitch's ranch? Was he an assassin?

Mitch summoned up his courage and risked another look.

OHMYGOD!

The man had a gun in his right hand!

Mitch dropped to the floor and crawled across the carpet. He knew exactly what to do. Call the cops! *There's a murderer loose!*

He lifted the phone and dialed 9-1-1.

Nothing happened! There was no ringing, no dial tone.

Mitch assessed his situation with steely resolve. There would be no help. He was on his own. He'd have to survive on wits and cunning.

Then, out of the haze, he remembered something. A certain gift from his new friends at the National Weapons Alliance. Tucked away in his nightstand drawer.

Rodolfo Dominguez thought America was the great country. Only ten days had he been in Blanco County, and already, so much opportunity! Plenty of labor for the man who wanted it. Some of the work was hard. Digging the holes. Clearing the brush. Hauling the rock. But Rodolfo did not complain. How could anyone ever complain in a land such as this one?

Today, and for the week to follow, he had the easy job. Prepare the wealthy man's hacienda for the large fiesta. Tend the gardens. Rake the leaves. Mow the grass. Trim the trees. It was not really the one-week job, but Rodolfo believed he could make one week of it, for how often did a man earn ten dollars every hour? What a large amount! There would be plenty to send home to his family.

This morning he was killing the weeds. Spraying them with the strong liquid. Tomorrow they would be brown, and he would pluck them from the soil by the roots.

Spray-spray.

He chuckled to himself. These Americans. So silly. Did they put the weed killer in the simple bottle? No, they did not. The liquid was called WeedBlaster, the funny name, so they put it in the container shaped like the gun. It did not look like the real gun, but like the child's toy, what they call the squirt gun. Made from the hard, black plastic.

He never understood America with the love for the guns, but he had to say he was having the good time. Pulling the plastic trigger, shooting the weeds. His *amigos* would not believe he was paid for such labor.

He was working on the west side of the house, where it was shady and cool. As the sun rose, he would move to the north side, and in the late afternoon, the east side. That was how he had always done it, as his father had taught him. Avoid the sun. Stay cool. Work long. Earn the money.

He was near the window now, where he had found many of the dandelions.

Spray-spray.

Suddenly, Rodolfo saw something strange. Inside the house, a man behind the window. A naked man. Was this the owner, the famous singer? Rodolfo did not know.

Rodolfo was confused. He raised his head and smiled. He waved. The man did not smile back. He had the angry look on his face. Or the frightened look. Then he did raise his hand, but not to wave, no.

Madre de dios!

He had the gun. The real gun!

Rodolfo was more confused. He wanted to speak to the man, but Rodolfo had very little English.

He tried to smile again.

Then Rodolfo heard the large roar, the window exploded, and he felt the hot pain in his chest.

Rodolfo staggered backward and fell with his back against a tree trunk.

Perhaps America was not the great country after all.

Dale Stubbs' secretary was doing interesting things to him with a bottle of strawberry-scented personal warming lubricant ("A break-through in pleasure!") when his cell phone rang.

He figured it was his wife calling, wanting to know where the hell he was. Thank God for caller ID. He groped for his phone on the nightstand while Tricia gamely continued with her endeavors. It wasn't his wife. This was a call he'd have to take.

He answered by saying, "How you doing, superstar?"

That's when things took a horrible turn.

If Tricia had been above the sheets, rather than under them, she would have seen Dale Stubbs' expression change from consternation to disbelief to abject horror.

"Oh, God," he said.

"You like that, sugar?" Tricia murmured, softly enough for only him to hear.

"Oh, God," he repeated.

"I guess so," she purred.

"Oh, God, no!" Stubbs shouted, sitting up suddenly.

"What, too hot?"

4

JOHN MARLIN—THE game warden in Blanco County, Texas, for more than twenty years—was always a big hit at social gatherings, chiefly because he had such colorful stories to tell. It came with the territory. He regularly witnessed unbelievable human behavior in the woods and on the water, most of which involved stupidity, ignorance, drunkenness, or folks just plain being weird.

Like the two teenagers who decided to propel a canoe around a small lake with a gasoline-powered leaf blower. They said they'd originally planned to use an electric model, but the extension cord wasn't long enough.

Then there was the man who drove his truck into a rain-swollen Miller Creek. He and his passenger managed to get out safely, but since the driver had forgotten his bottle of Wild Turkey, he dove back in to retrieve it. He drowned for his troubles.

Over the years, Marlin had encountered a man hunting in a chiffon evening dress, a group of naked college girls painting a fishing shack, a ninety-year-old widow with four pet skunks, and a drug smuggler who used imported Mexican deer as living suitcases.

He received some amusing phone calls, too.

One man, who must have been a former city dweller, called and said, "There's a bunch of deer along the road near my house. I think they got loose."

"Got loose from where?" Marlin asked.

"Wherever you keep them at night."

So Marlin wasn't surprised when a woman phoned his office at the sheriff's department on Tuesday morning and said, "Ever since my husband and I moved here from Dallas, I've had a problem with deer in my yard."

"Yes, ma'am, we do have a lot of deer around here," Marlin replied.

"They eat all my plants," she whined. "Destroyed my pansies this spring. And now, my petunias? Gone. Same with my hydrangeas. Don't even get me started on my rosebushes."

I won't, thought Marlin. "Sorry to hear that."

"Well?" she said. "What're you gonna do about it?"

"Uh . . . what am I going to do?"

"We sure didn't move to the country to be disturbed by a bunch of wild animals. You have to do something. You *are* the game warden, right?"

"Yes, ma'am, but there's really not much—"

"I have an idea. There's a deer-crossing sign right in front of my house. I want it moved."

"Um. How would that help?"

She let out an exasperated breath. "Well, duh. They wouldn't cross there anymore. Problem solved."

An hour later, Darrell Bridges, the sheriff's dispatcher, buzzed and said, "Another call, John."

"As good as that last one?"

"It's Ken Bell. Sounds a little upset. Line two."

Ken Bell was an old-timer who lived on Cypress Mill Road, where he'd purchased one hundred acres after World War II. Marlin pressed the flashing button and said, "Mr. Bell, how you doing, sir?"

A pause, followed by, "Not so good, John." The eighty-three-year-old did indeed sound distressed.

"What's going on? Are you hurt?"

"Aw, hell, I'm fine. It's just that I done something foolish, and now I got myself into some trouble, I guess."

Marlin wondered how much trouble an octogenarian could get into, especially one who'd had hip-replacement surgery not four months ago. "Okay, well, why don't you tell me about it and let's see if I can help?"

"Lemme ask you something. It legal to shoot somebody who's been poaching on your property?"

Uh-oh.

"I'm not liking the sound of this, Mr. Bell. What happened?"

The rancher took a deep breath and said, "I was just now driving the ranch and I saw this feller hunkered down against a tree. He was tucked away real good in some brush, along that fence line that separates my two pastures. Dang it, I shoulda just called you, but . . ."

"What'd you do?"

"You know I cain't get around like I used to. He was maybe sixty yards away, acrost a gully, so I couldn't get up close. I honked, but the sumbitch didn't budge. Completely ignored me."

"You sure he was poaching?" Marlin rarely received poaching calls in June. Most poachers were after deer, and at this time of year, the deer were still in velvet, growing their new antlers for the mating season in the fall.

"I was using binoculars, and yeah, I could see a rifle barrel sticking up beside him, like he'd leaned it against the fence."

"Okay, what happened next?"

"Well, I kept on with the honking, and he just sat there, up against this tree, like maybe he thought I couldn't see him or something, even though he was wearing a white shirt. So then I rolled my window down and hollered at him. Told him to come on out, 'cause I saw him, but he didn't."

"So you drove home and called me?" *Please say that's what you did,* Marlin was thinking.

"Well, I was getting right pissed off by then," the old man said. "You know I've had my share of poachers. So I sorta took matters into my own hands."

This was getting worse by the minute.

"I had my shotgun with me . . ."

Oh, Jesus.

"So I decided to pop him with some birdshot. Hell, at that distance, it shoulda just stung him a little, maybe left a welt or two. I figured that'd be enough to show him I meant bidness and send him on his way. So that's what I done. Loaded up and let loose. Next thing I know, the boy tips over on the ground and don't move a lick. Like I kilt him. I was a little shook up by it, so I double-checked my shells. Well, shit. I feel like a horse's ass, 'cause it wasn't birdshot I was using. It was buckshot. Double aught."

Marlin sat up straight. "Mr. Bell, don't say anything more, okay? Just hang tight. I'll be there shortly, and so will an EMS crew."

The old man's voice was thick with grief. "I believe it's too late for that. I kep' an eye on him for ten minutes and he ain't never even twitched."

Sabrina Nash wasn't above using her boobs as weapons, figuratively speaking, if that's what it took—just as she'd done two decades ago on prime-time television. Granted, she was forty-three years old now, but her breasts were still quite formidable when she wanted them to be. All natural, thank you very much.

She'd kept herself up nicely. Worked out. Ate right. Battled the effects of gravity by wearing properly supportive undergarments. When she cinched those suckers together and put 'em on display, look out! It was still quite a spectacle.

Frankly, she felt as ridiculous about doing it now as she had back then. Honestly, wasn't it all kind of silly? Shouldn't two adults be able to speak intelligently, rationally, one on one, about an extremely important issue, without sexuality coming into play? Yeah, sure, in some fantasy land. But here in the real world, she had to use every possible advantage. The stakes were just too high. Who would know that better than she?

Of course, for today's appointment, she had to maintain some modicum of discretion. There was, after all, her audience to consider. Just one man, but a very important one. He'd be dressed conservatively, in an expensive, well-tailored suit, no doubt—probably summer-weight wool—so she should also be appropriately attired.

"Appropriate" didn't necessarily rule out sexy, though.

She wanted contemporary, but not flashy. So she had chosen cuffed wide-leg pants, white, woven from cotton sateen. Topped them with a wrap jacket the color of chocolate. It offered a moderate amount of cleavage, and the years had taught her that it would not go unappreciated. Like the others, he'd sneak peeks when he could. His demeanor would be all business, but his eyes would rove when the opportunity presented itself. As a result, he'd be more inclined to give her what she wanted.

How crazy was that?

It was just a sad, sick fact that attractive people were treated differently than "average" people—not just in Hollywood, but anywhere. Research had proved it, and her own experience had borne it out. Didn't mean this meeting would be a success, but it wouldn't hurt to try.

For now, she waited. She sat in a leather chair in the outer office, thumbing through magazines. *Time. Newsweek. Texas Monthly.* A few others. No hunting magazines, she noted. Nothing overly macho or fueled by testosterone. A good sign.

Sabrina glanced up and, for the second time, caught his receptionist watching her surreptitiously. The desk placard said the young lady's name was Rita Summers. Couldn't have been older then twenty-one, twenty-two. She had the kind of personality one might describe as "buoyant." Smiled a lot. Had a singsong lilt to her voice. She was a cute little thing, too. Wavy brunette hair. High cheekbones. Good body. Immaculately made up and accessorized. Her boss had selected a looker, and that, in Sabrina's opinion, was another good sign.

Sabrina and Rita made eye contact a third time.

"I'm sorry," Rita said, "but I recognize you. I just want to say—I think you're fabulous!"

Sabrina had been afraid of that. She didn't enjoy being recognized. Her past . . . well, it was a little embarrassing. She dreaded these conversations, because they usually ended with something awkward like "So . . . what happened to your career?"

"Thank you," Sabrina said, offering no more, hoping to nip it in the bud. No such luck.

"I watch your show in bed every night!" Rita gushed. "On TV Land! It is sooo funny!"

Sabrina knew it wasn't fair to judge, but right now she had Rita's IQ pegged at about eighty. Ninety if the test included questions about shoes. Anybody who could enjoy the show, especially after it had aged for twenty years, couldn't possibly be all that intelligent.

"Thank you," Sabrina said again. She dropped her eyes down to her magazine. *Just ignore her. Maybe she'll get the hint.*

"I always wondered," Rita said. "Did they use trick photography or something?"

Sabrina raised her head, because it would've been rude not to. "Excuse me?"

"I mean, I've never seen anyone so flexible. Why, just last night, you touched both heels to the back of your head! Can you still do that?"

Sabrina glanced at the outer doorway. It was tempting to make a break for it. She smiled instead, and said, "I'd be afraid to even try."

Rita giggled. "My boyfriend wanted me to give it a shot, but I said, 'No way, mister. Not unless you want me to pull a muscle.' And he said . . . well, I won't tell you what he said, but it had to do with pulling a different muscle. You know how men's minds work."

Sabrina couldn't believe she was having this conversation. Not here. She nodded and continued to smile.

"Anyway, I just wanted to say I'm a big fan. The show is really great."

Sabrina was thinking, *Are you kidding? It was nothing but sexist pabulum. I was young and stupid. I'm embarrassed to have my name associated with it.*

Instead, she said, "That's very kind."

Then Rita said, "I don't want this to be awkward or anything, but I also want to say I'm really sorry about what happened to your son."

There it is, Sabrina thought. The other reason she didn't like speaking to strangers. Because some of them knew the full story. When they brought it up, it made Sabrina extremely uncomfortable—and, sometimes, emotional. "I appreciate that."

"It sounds like he was a very special boy."

"He was." By now, Sabrina had a lump in her throat.

Rita opened her mouth again, but before she could speak, her telephone chirped. She answered it, listened for a moment, and said, "I'll send her right in." She turned to Sabrina and offered her widest smile yet. "Seriously, it's been a real pleasure meeting you. The governor will see you now."

A second young woman appeared at Rita's elbow and cheerfully escorted Sabrina down a maze of hallways, past offices and conference rooms, straight to the office of the highest elected official in Texas.

As it turned out, the governor was a skilled and crafty peeker. But he was absolutely no help at all.

5

SIX DAYS EARLIER, Red O'Brien had an ulterior motive when he said, "First thing the Nazis done was take away ever'body's guns. Disarmed the civilians so they couldn't fight back. That's a genuine fact. I read it on the Innernet."

Red's best friend and longtime trailermate, a three-hundred-pound bruiser named Billy Don Craddock, said, "Uh-huh," and kept thumbing through the current issue of *Bustin' Out.*

No concern for our country, thought Red. *Just like your average American citizen. Nobody pays attention to the important stuff. One more reason everything's going to hell in a handbasket.*

Red paused for a moment to scan the bank of video monitors mounted on the wall. Absolutely nothing going on, as usual. Never was any excitement around here. For three months now they'd been working as night-shift security guards at an Austin company called Advanced Technologies, Inc., and not once had there been a reason to spring into action.

There was never anybody lurking in the shadows.

Nobody creeping down the hallways.

No one ever broke through a window, wearing a mask and gloves, with a diabolical plan to steal valuable corporate secrets.

Yeah, the job was easier than building rock walls or erecting fences or hanging drywall, all of which was Red's usual type of work, out in Blanco County where he lived. Here, they'd thumb through magazines, maybe go into somebody's office and do what they called surfing the Web, which was everything Red had heard and more. But still, sitting on your ass wasn't all it was cracked up to be. The boredom could wear on you.

He longed for the day when he could Mace somebody full in the face, cuff 'em, and haul 'em downtown, where Red would be showered with praise from uniformed cops. Until then, he was earning an easy eleven dollars and forty-three cents an hour, and all he had to do in return was stay awake, which was often a challenge.

So he propped his feet on a desk and continued with his monologue. "See, they had what they called the 'desirable' people, which was the Nazis themselves, and the 'undesirable' people, which was the Jews, the Gypsies, the Po-locks, and such. They wouldn't let the undesirables have guns. Now, say what you want about the Jews, but I'd say that ain't right, taking their weapons like that. Besides, where's the threat, because I imagine your average Jew is about as handy with a handgun as he is with a hockey stick. Anyway, point is, if you're gonna make it okay to have guns, then you can't just say one particular group should be excluded. 'Cept maybe the towelheads. Ever'body hates them nowadays."

Billy Don grunted in reply, unwilling to pull his eyes off this month's pictorial of "hot and saucy" pizza-delivery girls.

As usual, Billy Don was about as tuned in to world events as your average kindergartner. Sad, but the big man wasn't the sharpest knife in the drawer. A few weeks ago, Billy Don had said, "Hey, Red, how come it always rains after a drought?" And he hadn't been kidding. Hence, Red felt it was his moral duty to share his knowledge with Billy Don, to fill him in on the way things really worked in the world. Red figured it was the least he could do for a friend.

"We got a lot of politicians," he said, "mostly what they call lib'rals, who'd do the same damn thing. Take the guns away from the common folk, regardless what it says in the Constitution. Strip us all bare so we won't have a chance to defend ourselves."

Billy Don finally glanced up from the magazine. "Defend ourselves 'gainst what?"

Red lowered his voice, as if a squad of men in riot gear might be hiding in the next room. "Hell, if we ain't careful, from the guv'ment itself."

Billy Don, always skeptical of Red's theories, frowned. "Why would the government want our guns? Ain't they got enough?"

That was a question Red had never been able to figure out entirely, so he paraphrased the explanation he'd heard so many times himself: "It's just in their nature. Power is the greatest amnesiac, ever'body knows that. 'Fore you know it, you got a tyrant running around, telling ever'body what to do."

Billy Don did not appear concerned, or even interested. "Government ain't after our guns," he muttered, his eyes back on the magazine.

"Oh yeah, then why'd that game warden take my thirty-aught-six last year? Explain that!"

"Because you was shooting deer off the highway."

"Okay, yeah, maybe, and because they want to disarm the citizenry! They don't want us to be free, and guns is what keeps us safe from despots!"

Red figured a ten-dollar word like "despot" might impress Billy Don, but the big man wouldn't budge from the pizza girls.

So Red tried another approach. "Guns, if you wanna know the truth, is a lot like that magazine you're looking at."

"How you figure?"

"You hurting anybody by reading it?"

"No sir, but I ain't exactly reading."

"It gonna turn you into some sorta sex freak?"

"Hell no!"

"Then what's the problem?"

"Ain't got no problem."

"You sure as shit do, because they's plenty of folks who'd like to toss all your nudie magazines into a pile and have themselves a little weenie roast."

Billy Don scowled suspiciously. "These magazines is mine. Ain't their bidness."

"Hey, you don't have to tell me, bubba. All I'm saying is, we got rights as American citizens, but sometimes we have to stand up for those rights."

Billy Don rolled up the magazine and tucked it safely inside his official security guard jacket, which was large enough to serve as a circus tent. "How d'we do that?"

"Well," said Red, "for starters, ain't no better way to protect your First Amendment rights than by protecting your Second Amendment rights."

"Which is what, exactly?"

"The First Amendment says you got the right to read all the nudie magazines you want without anyone buttin' in."

"Yeah?"

"Yeah. And the Second Amendment says you can own as many guns as you want without nobody trying to take 'em away. Not even the guv'ment."

"I think I hearda that one."

"Makes sense, don't it?"

"I guess."

"You want to defend your rights, don't ya?"

"I sure do like my magazines."

"All right, then," said Red, finally reaching the point of the conversation. "That means you'll do what I'm gonna do and become a card-carrying member of the National Weapons Alliance."

Red reached into his pocket and came out with two NWA membership applications. "Don't cost but twenty bucks a year," he said, "and that entitles you to an official NWA decal, a key ring, and a pinup calendar featuring hot babes with assault rifles."

The truth was, Red *did* feel strongly about gun ownership, and he'd been meaning to sign on with the NWA for years. Lately he'd come up with another reason for joining, though, and Billy Don, to Red's amazement, figured it out in no time.

"Oh, I get it. This is about your song, ain't it?"

"Do what? No! No, this is about—"

"This is about the rally out at Mitch Campbell's place! Red, I'm tellin' ya, there ain't no way he's gonna record that song you wrote."

That was another thing Red had been doing in his spare time as a security guard. Writing a song. He thought it had turned out pretty good, too. "This ain't about my song, but since you mention it, why the hell wouldn't he? It's the perfect follow-up to 'My Cold, Dead Hands'!"

"You think guys like Mitch Campbell get their songs from strangers they meet at gun rallies?"

"It could happen! What the hell do you know about the recording industry?"

"More than you, from the sounds of it."

"Hey, I got a cousin that works for RCA!"

"Yeah, as a janitor."

"He hears things! He says songs come from all over. You think guys like George Strait and Brad Paisley write all their own songs? Hell, no! They get 'em from other folks—people who got a way with words."

Billy Don snickered. "Like you?"

Red didn't like being made fun of. Not by a guy who hadn't finished eighth grade. "You know what? Forget about it."

"I'm trying."

He picked up an application form and pulled a pen from his pocket. "You can sit there and play with yourself, but I'm gonna join the NWA. And I'm gonna go to the rally and meet Mitch. Then you'll see."

"Better strap a pillow to your backside."

"What for?"

"You start pestering Mitch Campbell at that rally, they gonna throw you out on your ass."

6

"DAMN, WE GOT bees everywhere!" said Trent Faulkner, one of the paramedics who'd responded to the call.

John Marlin and Chief Deputy Bill Tatum, riding together in Marlin's state-issued Dodge Ram, had met Ken Bell at his front gate, where they'd waited sixty seconds for the ambulance they'd heard in the distance. Then Bell had led the small caravan to the southeast quadrant of his ranch. Marlin had asked the elderly rancher to return to his home and wait, then he and Tatum and the EMTs had hoofed it across the small ravine.

Faulkner had shimmied under the fence, and now he was standing near the body, which was sprawled on its side, legs near a cedar tree, torso beneath a large flowering plant that was appropriately known as a "bee bush." There was no hurry; they all knew that from the horrible smell, which they'd noticed from twenty yards. The flies, too. Swarms of them. *Not a fresh kill.* But Faulkner had to make it official. The paramedic was pulling latex gloves onto his hands, swatting at the occasional honeybee that veered too close.

"Just leave 'em alone," Tatum said. "They won't bother you."

"Easy for you to say," Faulkner replied. "I'm allergic, you know." Then he knelt and checked for a pulse. "Guy's been gone for a good while. Man, oh man, he's ripe. Want me to flip him?"

"Yeah, go ahead," Tatum replied.

Faulkner gently rolled the body face up.

The victim was a slender Hispanic male, mid- to late twenties, dressed in scuffed Red Wings, faded khaki work pants, and a white short-sleeved T-shirt thick with dried blood on the chest. His bloated face bore the blisters and discolored striations of putrefaction. On Marlin's side of the fence, a deer rifle was leaning against the third strand of wire, its barrel abutting a fence post, pointing harmlessly toward the sky.

"How long's it been, you think?" Tatum asked. "A couple days?"

"Yeah, maybe three or four at the outside," Faulkner said. "Lem'll have to narrow it down."

Lem Tucker, the medical examiner for Blanco County, would be called to the scene, along with Henry Jameson, the forensics technician who served a five county area in the sparsely populated region west of Austin.

Faulkner lifted one of the victim's arms, then lowered it back to the ground. "Rigor's come and gone. Plus, this blood on his shirt is— Ow! Son of a bitch!"

The paramedic sprang to his feet and scurried away from the bush, holding a gloved hand to the side of his neck. "Little bastard got me." He shot a glare at Tatum.

The chief deputy shrugged and said, "On the other hand, you never know what an angry bee will do."

Marlin stifled a smile.

"What were you saying?" Tatum asked.

"The blood ain't fresh, that's all. Mickey, we got any eppy?"

The other EMT said, "In the ambulance."

Faulkner dropped to his belly and crawled back under the fence. "I'd better scoot. If I don't get a shot real quick, my lips'll swell up like that Lara Croft girl. My daughter loves her. What's that gal's name?"

Marlin shook his head.

"That actress," Faulkner said.

"Thanks for coming out, Trent," Tatum said. The paramedic's work was done.

"It'll come to me," he said, as he and Mickey walked away.

Marlin and Tatum stepped closer to the fence and stared at the body, ten feet away. For the time being, they'd treat the area as a crime scene, until they could determine exactly what had happened.

"Guess he managed to shoot himself?" Tatum asked. He was half a foot shorter than Marlin, but stout, with enormous biceps. He rested his forearms on the top strand of barbed wire, and the fence sagged under the weight.

"Sure looks that way," Marlin replied.

Attempting to cross a fence with a loaded rifle was a fairly common way to do some major damage to yourself. It wasn't all that difficult to snag the trigger on one of the fence's barbs, especially if you crossed the fence first, then pulled the rifle toward you by its barrel. Incredibly stupid, but Marlin had seen it before.

Tatum said, "He must've been slumped against that cedar tree."

"That's what Mr. Bell said."

"So he's crossing the fence, he accidentally shoots himself, then he sits down and leans against the tree until he dies."

"That'd be the theory."

"And he stays that way for several days, until Bell comes along and knocks him over with some buckshot. He tips sideways into the bee bush."

"Good news for the old man. Least he didn't kill anyone."

Marlin began to study the terrain on the other side of the fence. There were several cedar trees in the area, and the shaded ground was covered with a reddish-brown mulch, a natural compost of decomposing bark, small branches, and berries. Even so, Marlin eventually spotted what he was looking for. "There's the spatter."

Tatum looked where Marlin was pointing. It took him several seconds to see the blood, even though it was only ten or twelve feet away. A cone-shaped grouping of blackened, elongated drops—none larger than a dime.

"Good eyes," Tatum said. He nodded toward the body. "I don't suppose you recognize him?"

"Kinda hard to tell in that condition," Marlin replied. "Judging by his clothes, I'm guessing day laborer."

"That's what I was thinking. Probably a wetback."

A bee buzzed around Marlin's head, then disappeared. "In twenty-four years," he said, "I think I've busted three illegals for poaching. None of them in June."

Illegal aliens generally went out of their way to avoid calling attention to themselves. Fear of deportation.

"Kinda strange," Tatum said.

Forty miles away in Austin, Detective Paul Hebert was appraising a different corpse when he said, "Yeah, this one's weird, but I had a stiff in a seafood plant that tops it."

"A seafood plant?"

"Yeah, back in Harris County."

Hebert was smoking a cigarette, being real careful, flicking the ashes into his breast pocket. Even so, the crime-scene guys would bitch when they got there, but fuck 'em. At this point in his career, what did Hebert care? "I ever tell ya about that one?" he asked.

Hebert's third partner, thirty-five-year-old Ramon Arriaga, shook his head. Hebert liked to tell stories—he had plenty, from thirty-four years on the force—and Arriaga always seemed to enjoy listening.

So Hebert said, "Okay, the night manager at the plant calls it in, says he thinks he's got a body in the crab tank. He *thinks*. Sheesh."

"When was this?" the younger detective asked. He was leaning against a wall, waiting patiently, chewing on some of that nicotine gum. Gave up smokes two months ago. Which meant Hebert, unless he wanted to be an asshole, couldn't light up in the car. Ramon was fairly new, but he was okay, so Hebert didn't raise too much hell about the nonsmoking situation. They weren't supposed to smoke in the cars anyway.

"Shit, ages ago, when I was still in Houston," Hebert said. "Early eighties. Couple of years before Vince called it quits."

Vince was Hebert's first partner. Retired now, living in a condo in Little Rock, of all places. Hebert was about eight months from doing the same. Definitely not Arkansas, hanging out with a bunch of banjo strummers, but Jesus, somewhere decent.

"Anyway, yeah, we get there, and the manager's right. Body in the tank. Well, what's left of a body, because these are live crabs, hundreds of 'em, and—"

"What kinda crabs?"

"What kind? No fucking idea. Just crabs, that's all I know. Big ones. Anyway, let me tell you, those boys are meat eaters."

Ramon made a face.

"So we pull the guy out, then start trying to ID him. His face is mostly gone, fingertips eaten away. We're getting nowhere. Next day, the ME says the stiff ain't got no gunshots, no stab wounds, no head trauma, nothing. Tox screen says he was drunker than Cooter Brown, but not enough to croak."

"So how'd he die?"

"That's what *we* was wondering. Turns out, he was still alive when he went in the tank. The crabs killed him."

Ramon snorted, as if he thought Hebert was pulling his leg.

"Serious," Hebert said. "Long story short, he was dating some gal who worked at the plant. She split up with him, broke his heart. He offed himself by jumping in with the crabs. We found a note in his trailer."

"That's some sick shit."

"You're telling me." Hebert took a long drag. "This one, though. Runs a close second, as far as the oddness factor."

"Think it's the owner?"

"I imagine so."

"Maybe we should just run his prints."

"We'll know soon enough."

What they had was a dead man in a gun shop, a small place owned by a man named Wilber Henley. Earlier, the customer who'd found the body said Henley was born in Austin, moved to Abilene for a few years, then moved back to Austin in '98.

"Sounds like you knew him pretty well," Hebert said.

"He knew everything about guns. I mean *everything*. That him under there?"

"Could be. He have any tattoos, scars, or distinguishing marks under his clothes?"

The guy gave Hebert a funny look. "We wasn't *that* close."

Now Hebert pondered the situation. Finding someone dead in a retail establishment wasn't unusual. Not at all. The *way* this guy died was what put this one over the edge. Judging by the marks on the chest and wrists, he'd been zapped with a stun gun, then handcuffed.

So then he was at the killer's mercy. *Most killers, what would they do next?* Hebert wondered. Hell, they're in a store loaded to the fucking rafters with guns. Why not use one of them? Too loud? Okay, there was a whole case full of knives, too. Just plant one in the guy's sternum and be done with it.

Uh-uh. Not good enough, apparently.

What this weirdo had done was plaster the guy's head with stickers. Bumper stickers, from right here in the store. Dozens of them, each with a wise-ass message.

KEEP HONKING, I'M RELOADING

INSURED BY SMITH & WESSON

DON'T SHOOT TO KILL, SHOOT TO LIVE

GUN CONTROL MEANS BEING ABLE TO HIT YOUR TARGET

From the crown of his head down to his neck, the guy looked like a friggin' mummy. Suffocation. Hebert could tell you right now, that's what killed the guy.

This thing had been personal. Hate came through, loud and clear. Anger. Rage. Hebert was willing to bet the killer had known the victim.

Problem right now was, they couldn't ID the guy, what with the stickers all over his face. Hebert knew better than to just yank them off. Trace evidence. Fibers, hairs, maybe some prints under there if they were lucky. So Hebert and Ramon had to wait for the crime-scene techs to do their job, and then for the ME's guys to cart him off to the morgue and remove the stickers.

Hebert had an idea. While they were sitting on their thumbs, they might as well have some fun. He handed his Polaroid camera to Ramon. "Get a shot of me with this guy, will ya? I wanna send a copy to Vince. Remind him what he's missing."

7

LUNCHTIME, AND DALE Stubbs was fondling his secretary's magnificent breasts—perfect C cups—but things weren't happening as they usually did. His little soldier was being stubborn. Wasn't ready for battle.

"What's wrong, baby?" Tricia Woodbine asked. They were in a hotel room not far from the NWA offices.

"Lot on my mind," Stubbs said.

"Is it me?" she asked.

"'Course not."

"Wanna talk about it?"

"Does the pope read *Penthouse*?"

"You don't have to snap at me."

"Sorry."

She rearranged the pillows and propped herself up on one elbow. "Sugar, I want to be here for you. If something's bothering you, I want you to share it with me."

He kissed her on the forehead. Girl wasn't all that bright, but she was plenty sweet. "Just thinking about the rallies," he lied. "A million little details. Don't worry about it."

The truth was, he hadn't slept well in several days, and the reason was painfully obvious.

He was nervous.

Hell, more than nervous, he was scared. Yeah, scared, he'd admit it—and it had been so long since he'd been gripped by that particular emotion, it took him a while to recognize it for what it was.

What have I done? he wondered.

Two days earlier, when Stubbs had arrived at Mitch Campbell's ranch—after completing a four-hour drive in three hours—the first thing he said was, "Son, I can't even begin to tell you what a monumental fuckup this is."

Campbell's face, when he'd opened the door, was as white as a deer's rump. Stubbs noticed that the singer's eyes weren't quite right. Terrified, sure, but there was something else. It was the pupils—they were humongous. Drugs?

"I know," Campbell said, his voice high-pitched with fear. "I don't know what happened! I was at the window and there was a guy with a gun and so I shot and then I realized it wasn't a gun after all and ohmygod what are we gonna do if—"

Stubbs stopped him with a raised hand. "Deep breaths, son. Deep breaths."

Now Campbell—who came across as a macho hombre in his videos—appeared to be crying, and it filled Stubbs with disgust. Stubbs had spent quite a bit of time with Campbell in the past six months; they'd played golf, drunk whiskey, talked business. They weren't best buddies, but Stubbs felt he'd spent enough time with the man to size him up. Stubbs' assessment? Campbell was a solid citizen, a decent enough fellow, though a little too slick and packaged for Stubbs' tastes. A drugstore cowboy who liked to pretend he'd seen his share of rodeos.

Campbell hadn't, however, shown signs of being a sniveling wimp, as he was now revealing himself to be. Stubbs had to wonder: *Is this the next generation? Is this who I'll be leaving my country to when I die? Is this the kind of person who will carry on the legacy of freedom?* It was damned disturbing.

"Please—can you help me?" Campbell blubbered.

That was the big question, wasn't it? Stubbs had pondered it thoroughly on the drive. He'd always been proud of his ability to remain cool under fire, so he'd calmly and rationally mulled every possibility, weighing his options, which were few.

This wasn't just a catastrophe for Mitch Campbell, this was an unmitigated disaster for the National Weapons Alliance. Everything the NWA had struggled to accomplish in the past decade—the revocation of the assault weapons ban, new concealed-carry laws in a dozen states, the fending off of lawsuits against firearms manufacturers—it was all at risk.

If the anti-gunners learned that the NWA's star spokesman had gunned down an innocent man . . . Christ Almighty, it would be a media bloodbath. The NWA would be a laughingstock. Even the fence-sitters—people who had no firm opinion on gun laws—would side with the liberals on this one. Simply put, the Second Amendment would take the most severe blow it had ever suffered in its glorious history.

Stubbs had already decided that he'd do everything he could to prevent that from happening. He'd throw himself on the grenade, if need be. Take one for the team. Put himself in jeopardy in a major way, if that's what it took. But right now, he needed to determine what, exactly, he *could* do.

"Have you called anyone else?" he asked.

"Not a soul, I swear!"

"Is there anyone else on the ranch? Anyone in the house?"

"It's just me."

"Okay, then. Let's see what we're dealing with."

Campbell closed the door behind him and trotted around the western side of the massive ranch house. Stubbs followed at a slower, more deliberate pace. Hell of a nice place the boy had. Big. Expensive. Brand-new home with a pool and tennis court around back. High on a hill with fifty-mile views. The ranch itself had to be a couple thousand acres. A large herd of Brangus cattle. The nearest neighbor was a good mile away or farther.

When Stubbs rounded the corner, he saw a blue tarp covering an unmistakable shape against a tree. Work boots were sticking out from one end. Campbell was cowering nearby, visibly shaking.

Stubbs pulled the tarp away, and what he saw caused him to stare for several seconds in disbelief. Not at the body—some Mexican guy—but at the object *next to* the body.

"You thought that was a real gun?" Stubbs had difficulty disguising his disdain.

Campbell's lower lip was quivering. "It all happened so fast!"

Stubbs tapped the "weapon" with the toe of his boot. A plastic bottle of weed killer, shaped like a gun out of some corny sci-fi movie. The Mexican had presented a danger, all right—to dollarweed and toadflax. It was all so damn ridiculous, Stubbs wanted to return to his truck and hightail it home. But he had to stay. Not for Campbell's sake, but for the good of his brothers-in-arms around the nation. He had to press forward.

"He die against that tree or did you move him?" Stubbs had watched enough episodes of those crime shows to know you had to be careful how you moved a body around. Something about the way the blood settled.

"That's where he was."

"Any idea who he is?"

"J. B. said something about hiring a gardener. To get the place ready for the rally on Saturday."

J. B. Crowley was Campbell's ranch foreman. Like a lot of "gentleman ranchers" in Texas, the singer needed a genuine ranch hand to run the place for him. Not a big surprise.

"Where is he now?"

"On vacation. His son's out of school and—"

"When's he coming back?"

"I don't know. He just left yesterday."

"He usually hire wetbacks?"

"Wetbacks?"

"Illegal aliens, son. From Mexico."

"Yeah, I think so. The ones we've had out here, they're always talking Spanish."

Stubbs contemplated the possibilities. If a wetback disappeared, it was likely that the cops would think he'd gone home to Mexico or moved on down the highway. They wouldn't look for him too hard.

Stubbs bent over and patted the corpse's pockets for a wallet. Found one, removed it, and checked for ID. Nothing. No credit cards, either. The man was almost certainly a Mexican, but Stubbs couldn't take that as a given. Wasn't worth the risk. He wiped the wallet with a handkerchief, then slipped it back into the dead man's pocket.

"You expecting anybody out here anytime soon?"

"A film crew is coming on Thursday. For a chili commercial."

"When are they setting up for the rally?"

"Friday. What're we gonna *do*?"

Campbell's voice was filled with panic and as shrill as a schoolgirl's.

Stubbs had had enough. "First you're gonna stop your goddamn whining and act like a man," he snapped.

The singer stared at his feet.

"We'll get through this," Stubbs said, "but it ain't gonna be easy. It's time to cowboy up and do what needs to be done. If you can't handle it, you need to tell me right now."

To his credit, Campbell rubbed his nose with his wrist and said, "I can handle it. Whatever we gotta do, I can handle it."

"All right, then." Stubbs gazed at the horizon and continued to contemplate the situation. "We'll need to replace the window glass and hose down the lawn. That his old truck out front?"

"Must be. I mean, I don't know for sure. But yeah, it's gotta be. Nobody else is here, and it's not mine."

The way Stubbs figured it, there were two choices:

Number one, he could try to make the body disappear and hope nobody ever went looking for the man. That was risky, Stubbs knew, because a corpse wouldn't be an easy thing to hide or destroy. Fishermen and hunters found dead people all the time; they floated up from watery graves or got dug up by hungry scavengers. Even cold-blooded murderers who carefully plotted their deeds had a tough time getting rid of the biggest, ugliest piece of evidence against them. Stubbs wasn't stupid enough to think he possessed skills they didn't.

That left option number two.

Move the body, and make it appear that the man had been killed somewhere else. Deflect the attention away from Mitch Campbell, and therefore away from the NWA. If and when the cops approached Mitch, he'd simply deny that the man had ever set foot on his ranch.

Stubbs figured if he was really lucky—if he thought things through and kept a cool head—he might even be able to make the whole thing look like an accident. A hunting accident. Things like that happened more often than people realized. Just ask Dick Cheney.

Sabrina Annabelle Nash had not been born beautiful. In fact, the first thing her father said to her mother was, "Damn, Lurlene, you been sleeping with Winston Churchill behind my back?"

As Sabrina entered the first grade, she looked like any other skinny schoolgirl growing up poor in the windswept oil town of Andrews, Texas, where people spoke with clenched teeth to keep the grit out of their mouths.

Sabrina had blond hair and green eyes, and, like most of the kids in her neighborhood, she wore hand-me-downs that carried the lingering odor of unrefined petroleum. By the time she turned eleven, however, she started to receive comments from fawning adults.

"Why, aren't you just as cute as a spotted pup."

"If you was any more precious, you'd have to be twins."

"I could just eat you up with a side of biscuits."

In the seventh grade, despite Sabrina's protests, Lurlene Nash entered her daughter in a county-wide beauty pageant. Sabrina, to her own surprise, brought home the title of Li'l Miss Fossil Fuel, which earned her a crown shaped like an oil derrick and five cases of commercial-grade transmission fluid.

The years passed, Sabrina continued to blossom, and by the time she graduated from high school, most of the remarks were made by the roughnecks she served as a waitress.

"Gal, you got more curves than a barrel of snakes."

"Hell, I'm gonna buy you an ice cream cone just to watch you eat it."

Most of the time, Sabrina simply ignored them.

Then came a bright spring day in Sabrina's nineteenth year, when one customer at the diner—a graying man in a dark suit—stared just a little too enthusiastically. Somehow, this creepy stranger's blatant ogling was worse than the oilfield workers' clumsy flirtations.

"Take a picture," Sabrina snapped at the man. "It'll last longer."

"Pictures," he said, nodding. "That's exactly what I had in mind. Head shots."

Head shots! Sabrina thought. *What sort of pervert is this guy?*

So she dumped a basket of fried catfish in his lap. The deluxe dinner, with hush puppies and a corncob on the side.

To Sabrina's embarrassment, it turned out that "head shots" didn't mean what she thought. It also turned out that the man was an agent. A film and television agent. From Los Angeles. Sabrina had heard a lot of lame lines in her time, but this guy had a business card to back it up, along with photos of himself hobnobbing with big stars like Richard Grieco and Molly Ringwald.

After the man explained the situation and finished wiping the tartar sauce from his thighs, Sabrina said, "I'm really sorry. You sure don't look like an agent."

In truth, she had no idea what a Hollywood agent was supposed to look like. Not this guy, because he struck her as a local—maybe a sales manager at a used-car dealership. He was wearing snakeskin boots with his suit, along with a gaudy silver-and-turquoise belt buckle. His drawl was worse than her own.

"Haven't been home for twenty-five years," he said. "Had to come back for a funeral. My mother."

"Oh. That's a shame."

"Hey, you never know," he said. "Could be the end of one act and the start of another." He stuck out his hand. "Name's Willie Ray Thurston. Folks call me Buddy."

BYRON GLADWELL DESPISED being Harry Jenkins' boss. Not solely because the political cartoonist was physically intimidating and verbally abusive, but because Harry had a knack for distorting virtually anything you said or did into some exaggerated desecration against mankind or the planet we inhabit.

Gladwell considered himself rather progressive and moderately liberal, but compared to Harry Jenkins, he was a regular David Duke. Gladwell's opinion—or anyone's, for that matter—was never quite enlightened or forward-thinking enough to suit Harry.

Drive a gas guzzler? According to Harry, you were a polluting monster who ought to be hung from your scrotum. Harry had converted his Volvo to run on natural gas, but on most days he rode his bicycle to work, his ponytail flapping in the breeze.

Ever eat a hamburger or wear leather shoes? You murderous bastard! Animals, in Harry's view, had as many rights as you and I. He proclaimed that if cows had the right to vote, they'd probably exercise it more regularly than humans do.

Hand out a memo? For God's sake, man, think of the trees! Couldn't you have sent this thing out by e-mail? What are you going to do for an encore? Lay waste to the rain forest?

Speculate innocently on a coworker's sexuality? A hate crime! You self-righteous bully! Perhaps you have latent tendencies of your own that you'd rather not discuss, you insensitive homophobe.

There was a long list of topics Gladwell would never broach with Harry Jenkins: abortion, capital punishment, baby seals, third-world clothing factories, campaign finance reform, civil rights, immigration, racial equality, military spending, nuclear energy, water-collection systems, the endangered red-necked sapsucker, global warming, whaling, Medicaid, Social Security, fur, socialized medicine, tax reform, welfare, police brutality, mass transit, school prayer, even Daylight Savings Time.

And gun control, of course. For obvious reasons.

Don't even get Harry started on that one. Not unless you wanted to see his eyes shine with anger and his face turn beet red.

Harry's position: Nobody should own any type of firearm for any reason at any time. Period. No rifles, no pistols, not even an air gun. A slingshot, under Harry's rule of law, would require a background check and a five-day waiting period. And if you didn't share Harry's opinion on the matter, well then, my evil friend, you were nothing but "an irresponsible cretin with phallic insecurities."

Which made this current conversation particularly ticklish. Gladwell was grateful Harry had been working from home lately, and they were speaking by phone. That way, Harry couldn't see that Gladwell was nervous, sweating profusely, despite the assertiveness training course he had taken last month.

Stay on message, Gladwell said to himself. *Don't let him intimidate you.*

"I can understand your stance, Harry, I really can," he said soothingly, choosing his words oh so carefully. "You're not just a cartoonist, you're an artist. A visionary. You have a message to deliver, and we certainly don't want to stifle your creativity. But, unfortunately, I think this one crosses the line. In my opinion. For what it's worth."

"Don't be a fucking wimp, Byron."

Gladwell chuckled, acting as if the remark had been delivered in jest, rather than with blatant insubordination. "Harry, I—"

"Pussy."

"I wish you wouldn't—"

"Pantywaist."

"If it were up to me—"

"It *is* up to you, Byron, so have some balls and start acting like it. Run the damn thing."

Gladwell could feel an urgent churning in his lower bowels. Every time he had a confrontation with Jenkins—something he avoided rigorously—he wound up with gastric distress. It was the price he paid for supervising a temperamental, self-righteous Pulitzer Prize winner. A man who, Gladwell hated to admit, was a genius. A man whom the managing editor wouldn't fire if Jenkins paraded into a board meeting wearing a tiara and a thong bikini. He was that important to their readership. As always, Jenkins had to be handled delicately.

So Gladwell said, "This particular cartoon, Harry . . . well, don't get me wrong, I can certainly appreciate the incisive commentary, but I'm afraid not everyone shares my sensibilities. Frankly, I'm concerned that a great number of our readers would be legitimately offended."

"Fuck 'em."

"It's not that simple. Darn it, this thing borders on pornography. There, I said it. I'm not ashamed. I think there's a good chance you've probably gone too far this time."

Gladwell studied the image on his computer screen—the file Jenkins had e-mailed an hour ago. It showed a caricature of Dale Stubbs, the president of the Texas chapter of the National Weapons Alliance, kneeling in front of gubernatorial candidate Glenn Dobbins. You couldn't actually *see* fellatio being performed, but that was the undeniable implication. In the caption, Dobbins was saying: *So, Dale, I guess this means I have your full endorsement.*

It wasn't surprising. In the past few months, Jenkins' offerings had become more vindictive and mean-spirited, skewering the right wing with reckless abandon, but all of it done with a certain unevenness that seemed to match the cartoonist's mood. His behavior swung wildly from surly to melancholy, from morose to bellicose. Gladwell had no idea what was bothering Jenkins, but it was a cause for concern.

"What did Terry say about it?" Jenkins asked. Terry being the aforementioned managing editor.

Gladwell was reluctant to answer, but he did anyway, trying to keep some tone of authority in his voice. "I haven't shown it to him, and I don't plan to. This is my own call, and I stand by it. I would appreciate it if you would—"

"You're a turd, Byron, you know that?"

Fourteen years, Gladwell thought. *I've been putting up with this for fourteen years.* "That's uncalled for."

"A turd covered with pubic hair."

"That's a twisted thought. I'm concerned about you, Harry. I really am."

"Are you gonna run it, or are you gonna be your usual candy-ass self?"

"It's vulgar and crass."

"God damn it, are you gonna run it or not?"

"It's tasteless and offensive."

"Yes or no, you spineless wuss?"

"It's obscene and sophomoric."

Jenkins didn't reply.

"It simply doesn't meet the standards of this newspaper."

Still nothing. Maybe, for once, Jenkins was going to succumb to Gladwell's wishes without an epic struggle.

"I'm doing you a favor, Harry, really. I know you have a lot of anger about this issue, but trust me—this is just too much. It could hurt you professionally."

The line was silent.

"Harry?"

A secretary passed by Gladwell's open door, and he took the opportunity to say, "Harry, I'm tired of your smart mouth! I want you to show me some respect!"

There was no reply, of course, because, as Gladwell knew, Harry had already hung up.

* * *

The vice president of recruitment for the Texas chapter of the National Weapons Alliance was a suspicious man. Once burned, twice shy, as they say. Only natural, because the anti-gun zealots—or "the kooks," as he called them—were so damn sneaky.

Ten months earlier, in a debacle that had embarrassed and discredited the NWA and other gun-rights organizations, a man named Leroy Haynes had purchased a .357 at a gun show in Longview, Texas. Not a big deal, in and of itself. After all, upwards of six million guns changed hands across the nation every year.

The problem was, Haynes was a convicted felon—an armed robber, recently paroled—and he had been sent to the show by a renegade group known as the Society of Nonviolent Americans to Control Handguns (SNATCH). Their objective was to prove how easy it was for criminals to obtain weapons due to the so-called gun-show loophole.

They paid Haynes five hundred dollars for his participation, then sent him in with a tiny video camera hidden in his hat. He strolled in, purchased a gun from a *private collector*, not a *dealer*, and was back outside in ten minutes.

Of course, the SNATCH crew was waiting in the parking lot, giddy with triumph. They quickly converted the footage to a digital file and e-mailed it to all the major television news outlets, network and cable.

As expected, everyone except Fox aired it, and the anti-gunners had a good laugh all around. Did the pompous liberal anchors mention that fewer than two percent of convicted criminals obtained their guns from gun shows—a statistic proven by three federal studies? Nope.

What they *did* do was use phrases like "cause for alarm" and "a black eye for the gun lobby" and "evidence of a gaping hole in our national gun laws."

All in all, it really sucked.

Now it appeared that the kooks were up to another one of their despicable tricks.

Not twenty minutes ago, a recruitment representative had brought in a membership application that was so narrow-minded and ignorant, it simply could not be authentic. The alleged applicant— one Mr. Red O'Brien of Johnson City, Texas—had not only completed the form, he had included a rambling essay intended to convey his "vision for America's future."

The nearly illegible scrawl read:

Dear Mr. President Dale Stubs:
I want to join the NWA because I am concerned with what our country is becomming. Its gotten so a fully-armed white man can't hardly walk down the street anymore without being the object of scorn and ridecule. Just because we like guns and honor the amendment, that makes us somehow evil? I don't understand that and I want to do something to help. For starters I want my rifle back from the game warden that confusscated it! Outside of poaching, my criminal record is very short, and I don't pose a danger to nobody that don't deserve it. But how am I suppose to defend myself and my loved ones if I can't have my guns? Well I think we all know the answer to that question. The goverment wants our guns so we won't complain when they give all our jobs to the Mexxicans. So we can't do nothing when they raise the taxes to pay for all "those people" on welfair. So we can't march on Washinton to protest two gay people of the same sex getting married. So we can't shoot camel jockeys for being such assholes. I see a time comming when common country folk might have to rise up and form our own societey. Free from Nazis, fashists and the like. Modesty aside, I propose that I would make a good candidate as some sort of offiser with the NWA not just a member. Please review my credentials and let me know as soon as possible. I look forward to joining your club and making things right.
Yours in freedom,
Red O'Brien

P.S. Billy Don would make a good offiser too, only he won't cough up the money to join. Something to keep in mind in case your short on leadership type people.

The VP of recruitment had gone over the application and the essay three times, and with each reading he became less concerned and more amused.

Such a desperate, transparent ploy. He could just hear the kooks crowing, *See what type of person is allowed into the NWA! See what kind of hatred and bigotry they engender!*

But he was way ahead of them this time. He wasn't about to fall for it.

He swiveled his chair, poised his hands over his computer keyboard, and set about the delicate task of composing the first rejection letter in the history of the National Weapons Alliance.

9

ANOTHER FUNNY THING about being a game warden: Plenty of civilians, especially those who didn't hunt or fish, had no real grasp of what a game warden was.

The average citizen didn't realize that a game warden was a fully commissioned Texas peace officer, with the power to enforce any state law, not just those pertaining to hunting and fishing.

John Marlin once pulled over a driver whom he suspected of poaching. It turned out the man had stopped on the shoulder of a quiet county road not to hunt but to take a leak. He was thoroughly intoxicated, his floorboard littered with empty cans of Pabst Blue Ribbon.

"Looks like you've had some beer tonight," Marlin said, shining his flashlight into the vehicle.

"Jus' a couple," the man replied.

"A couple dozen?" Marlin asked.

"A couple dozen what?"

"Beers."

"No thanks, I've already had some." The man grinned, and Marlin could smell the alcohol. "Don't tell the cops, 'kay?"

Marlin played along. "No, sir, I won't. But I am gonna ask you to step from your vehicle and complete some field sobriety tests for me."

The man's brow knitted with confusion. "Wha' for?"

"Because I have reason to believe you're driving under the influence of alcohol."

"But you're a game warden."

"Yes sir, I am."

The man snorted. "Come on. You can't bust me for DWI. I'm not *that* drunk."

"I'm afraid I can."

"No shit?" He stared at Marlin for a few seconds through bloodshot eyes. Then he said, "In that case, I wanna change my answer."

When he staggered from the vehicle, he threw up on Marlin's shoes.

The building that served as the Blanco County morgue had previously been a Dairy Queen. The walk-in cooler that used to contain chicken strips and corndogs now housed the local dead. Most people, especially the cops, saw the humor in it—perhaps more than they should have. On several occasions, Sheriff Bobby Garza, a man with a fine wit of his own, had had to ask his deputies to refrain from referring to the corpses as "Dilly Bars."

Now the morgue was holding an as-yet-unidentified Hispanic male. The man on Ken Bell's ranch had not been carrying any form of identification in his worn leather wallet. Just seven dollars in singles, a prepaid telephone card, and a handful of snapshots. No credit cards, no driver's license, nothing that provided a name. For the time being, he was listed as Juan Doe.

Late Tuesday afternoon, as the autopsy was wrapping up, Marlin drove to the morgue to meet Garza and Bill Tatum in the parking lot. It wasn't mere curiosity on Marlin's part; the sheriff, who had become a close friend of Marlin's over the years, had asked for his assistance in the investigation. Marlin had played a key role in several major cases in the past—homicides, burglaries, missing persons, drug busts—and he enjoyed helping out when he could.

Now Garza and Tatum emerged from the building, and the expressions on their faces said they weren't satisfied. Marlin stepped from his truck, his eyebrows raised, and Garza said, "You're gonna like this one." The sheriff was grinning, but there was a determined set to his handsome, square jaw.

"Let's hear it."

"Lem says the time of death was probably sometime between midnight on Saturday and noon on Sunday. But it most definitely was not an accident."

"No?"

"Absolutely not. Oh, they staged it real well. Placed his hands on the rifle afterward to leave prints. They even fired it with his hands wrapped around it to leave residue. There was a spent shell in the chamber of the rifle. Somebody went to a lot of trouble on this one."

Marlin could already feel the buzz that came with the beginning of an important case. "How do we know?"

"Care to hazard a guess?"

Marlin was becoming more and more curious, and he knew the sheriff was enjoying himself, doling out the information a little at a time. Apparently, Garza had something solid—something unusual—that he was about to reveal.

Marlin said, "The lividity told you something? The body was moved?"

Garza said, "You have a keen mind, John. Anyone ever tell you that?"

"My fifth-grade teacher."

"You're a natural investigator."

"Thank you. So I was right?"

"Sorry, no, but it was a good try. The lividity—well, Lem said it looked about right. I mean, Christ, talk about a screwed-up crime scene. After Mr. Bell peppered the guy, we had no way of knowing the body's original position. Yeah, Bell said the guy was leaning against a fence post, and Lem says he can't dispute it. He probably was."

So Marlin said, "Okay, let's hear it."

"Three things. First, there weren't any powder burns around the wound or on the clothing. Close-range shot like that, there should be burns, don't you think?"

Marlin agreed that there should.

"Second," Garza said, "Lem found some glass in the wound. He—"

"Wait. Did you say glass?"

"Yeah, silica. In powdered form, basically, from the rifle blast. Lem found it under the microscope. We're talking tiny fragments that attached to the bullet as it passed through a window."

"He was shot through a window."

"Yep."

"So he was moved."

"Without a doubt. Henry's gonna follow up on that and tell us exactly what kind of glass we're dealing with. Windowpane, automobile, whatever. Would be a big help in narrowing down what kind of crime scene we're looking for."

"What's the third thing?"

The impish grin returned to Garza's face. "You know, I just have to admire the guy for trying something this outrageous. The spatter you saw at the scene? We don't know where that blood came from yet, but it damn sure wasn't human."

Marlin looked from Garza to Tatum and back. "You're kidding me. Animal blood?"

"That's what Henry says."

"What kind of animal?"

"He's working on that, too."

Marlin could hardly believe what he was hearing. "That took some balls."

"Might've worked, too, if we'd bought into the accident angle."

"Which you didn't, of course."

"I look like a dumb hick to you?"

"Well, not the 'dumb' part."

"Touché."

"What about the rifle?"

"Too old. Serial number leads nowhere."

"Okay, so what next?"

"We've gotta figure out who this guy is. We won't get anywhere until we get an ID. Lem found some more money stuck in his boot. About three hundred bucks—some of it in pesos—so we're pretty sure he's an illegal."

Illegal immigrants rarely opened bank accounts. They lacked

the proper documentation to do so, or the language barrier intimidated them, or they simply didn't trust anyone else with their money.

"I'll run his prints through AFIS," Tatum said. "And I'll send the prints and a photo to the Mexican consulate in Laredo."

Standard procedure in a case like this one. If it involved a dead immigrant, you covered your ass and notified the consul.

"And let's subpoena the records on the phone card the guy was carrying," Garza added. "In the meantime," he said to Marlin, "I've got an exciting job for you. Wanna knock on some doors?"

Paul Hebert was supposed to be making some calls, following up on forensics, but he was flipping through a glossy travel brochure instead. It showed attractive people playing golf, hiking through forests, tanning by the pool. They wore snappy double-knit polo shirts and crisp khaki shorts. They had perfect teeth and well-coiffed hair.

Hebert had a whole stack of brochures in his desk drawer: Phoenix, Las Vegas, San Diego, St. Petersburg. A dozen more. Every so often, he'd take one out and see if it spoke to him. Scan the photographs and see if the vibe felt right. Occasionally, he'd narrow the choices down by dumping a brochure in the trashcan. In three months, the plan was, he'd be down to just one. Then he'd pack whatever he could cram into his '98 Chrysler and head out. Sell the house, the furniture, his dead wife's diamond ring. Some extra cash to make a fresh start. With that and his pension, he should be fine.

Retirement, the way he looked at it, should be like an extended vacation. No worries, no stress. What he wanted was booze and broads—and plenty of both. Maybe near a lake or an ocean, if he could swing it. Or even the mountains. Denver was a distinct possibility. Rain all the time would suck, he decided, so just like that, Seattle went into the garbage. That was easy. Only fifteen to go.

Ramon Arriaga stuck his head into Hebert's office. "You talk to Bindlemeyer yet?"

Bindlemeyer was the crime-scene tech working the case. Good man. Detail oriented. Had a nice bass boat, and he'd invited Hebert on a fishing excursion just last month. Hebert didn't know jack about fishing or boats, but that trip had hooked him, so to speak, and he intended to learn a lot more in the coming years. It was relaxing to get out on the water, shoot the shit, and drink beer all day.

As for the current case, Bindlemeyer had identified the corpse as Wilber Henley, as expected, and now he was working on the back sides of the bumper stickers, seeing if he could come up with any prints.

"I was just gonna call him," Hebert said, still thinking about boats. *There's an idea,* he thought. *I wonder what it would be like to live on a houseboat? Fish for dinner every night.*

"Wanna hear something interesting?" Ramon asked. "Henley took a collar for selling a gun illegally, but the charges were dropped."

Hebert snuck a peek at his watch. Nearly seven o'clock, and this kid would probably want to keep after it until the wee hours. Hebert figured Henley would be just as dead in the morning.

"Yeah, when?" He let out a big yawn, a signal that it wouldn't hurt to shut it down for the night.

Ramon glanced at a document in his hand. "Let's see. Uh, seven years ago."

"Where?"

"Right here in Austin."

"Seven years."

"Right."

Hebert made a face meant to express doubt. He didn't want to come right out and say, *You're chasing your tail, kid. That's a dead end.* Instead, he said, "Long time ago."

Ramon didn't get the message. "Looks like he cut some kind of deal to testify in another case. Think I should check it out?"

Hebert had to wonder if he was being hasty. He shouldn't make snap decisions. Sure, Seattle was rainy, but it was nice and cool up there.

10

"THIS DARN REMOTE'S acting up again," Nicole Brooks said, thumbing it with no effect.

She was stretched out on Marlin's couch, her feet in his lap, enjoying one of his patented foot massages. Her long auburn hair was pulled back, her face bare of makeup—and still, she was achingly beautiful. Gorgeous, funny, intelligent. What more could a guy want?

"Oh, really?" Marlin replied, playing along. He could stare at her high cheekbones for a solid hour. They were that amazing.

"Seriously," she said, trying to suppress a grin. "I think the batteries are dead."

What is it with satellite television? Marlin wondered. It seemed every time Nicole surfed the channels, one of the home-shopping networks was hawking a diamond engagement ring. It was happening again on Tuesday night after dinner.

Isn't this a fabulous stone, folks? An elegant radiant cut with superb clarity and a platinum setting. I guarantee, this one will take her breath away. And right now, with our easy payment plan . . .

Nicole frequently used the opportunity to have a little fun. Made Marlin squirm by pretending the remote had gone on the fritz and she couldn't switch channels. But he knew she only teased him to make him blush. They'd talked vaguely about the future before, in serious terms, and she'd revealed herself to be a smart, cautious lady who wasn't prone to rush into things.

They'd been dating for a little more than a year, beginning just weeks after she'd moved to Blanco County, and they'd settled into a comfortable pattern. Once or twice a week, she'd spend the evening at his place. On Saturdays—if it wasn't deer season, his craziest time of the year—he'd load up his dog, a pit bull named Geist, and spend some time at Nicole's small home in the southern tip of the county.

Of course, all of that was out the window if either of them was working. She was a deputy with the sheriff's office—now working alongside her cousin, fellow deputy Ernie Turpin—and that meant her schedule was as prone to unexpected late nights as Marlin's was.

He reached for the remote, saying, "Give it here. I'll get it to work."

"Maybe I'm just not hitting the right buttons."

Oh, you're hitting the right buttons.

He rolled his eyes and changed the channel. Then he decided to test the waters. "Be careful what you wish for. If a guy showed up with a ring, I can just picture an independent lady like you running in the opposite direction."

She laughed. "Hmm. You may be right. Depends on the guy, I guess."

"Does it?"

"Yeah. Like, say, Tom Selleck. For him, I'd probably hang around. Or George Clooney."

"Wimps."

"Ha! Somebody's jealous."

"What if the ring was a cubic zirconia?"

She gave him a look. "I'm surprised you even know what that is. You been doing some research?"

Now he *did* blush. "I'm a worldly guy. I hear things."

He set her right foot down and started massaging the left. She had a small mole on the instep, and a gold ring on the second toe. She wore size seven shoes. Her nails were painted a light shade of blue. She let out a sigh of contentment that pierced Marlin's heart.

He'd never felt more at ease with a woman. Check that: He'd never felt that he and a woman were better suited for one another. The same interests. The same love of small-town life. Similar politics—on most issues. She was easygoing, just as he was, quick to see the lighter side of things.

In their time together they'd only had one sour moment, sparked by a piece of mail, of all things. His renewal form for the NWA. She'd called him an ignorant redneck, and he'd laughed it off as if she'd been joking. He figured a man and a woman couldn't be completely alike or it would get boring. Besides, they'd made up later in a way that made it worthwhile.

No, he wasn't the type to rush, either, but he wasn't going to dawdle. He knew from experience that when you find a woman like Nicole—

His thoughts were interrupted by a graphic on the TV screen: BLANCO COUNTY HOMICIDE. The anchor was saying that the sheriff's office was investigating the murder of an unidentified Hispanic man. Details were sparse. Garza had withheld several key facts—standard procedure in any homicide investigation—and it was still too early to release a photo to the media. Not until they'd tracked down the next of kin. Marlin hoped somebody would hear the news and come forth with a name. They needed somewhere to start, because so far they had nothing.

The "exciting job" Garza had asked Marlin to do was canvassing a small subdivision—thirty or forty homes on one-acre lots—that shared a fence line with Ken Bell's property. Marlin had gone door to door, asking questions, and come up empty. Nobody remembered hearing any shots in the past few days. Nobody had seen a slender Hispanic man carrying a rifle.

When the short news report was over, Nicole said, "No hit on the guy's prints?"

"Nothing."

"Think he's an illegal?"

"That's what we're guessing."

"No ID, I guess?"

"Nope."

"You should ask around at the Git It & Go tomorrow morning."

Marlin had already planned to arrive there at daybreak, but he said, "Good idea."

They sat through the weather report: Highs near ninety-six. They hadn't had rain in thirty-six days, and there was no chance of it in the five-day forecast. Typical Texas summer. Hot, sweaty, and dry as a bone.

"You tired?" Nicole asked.

"Not really."

"Well, then. Can I interest you in rubbing a few other body parts?"

"What? Yeah, sure."

Nicole laughed. "Boy, you don't sound very enthusiastic about it. Where are you?"

"Sorry."

"We shouldn't have watched the news, huh? Sorta ruined the mood."

"Yeah." He turned the volume down and sorted his thoughts. "The thing that bothers me is, the guy probably traveled hundreds of miles up from Mexico—and you know how bad the crossing can be. They drown in rivers, die in the desert, suffocate in trailer cars. All for a shot at what we have. Then he finally gets here, home free in the land of opportunity, and what happens? He gets killed."

"Welcome to America."

"That's about the extent of it."

Neither of them spoke for several moments. The sportscaster was interviewing Augie Garrido about the recent College World Series. The question—Marlin knew this even with the sound turned down—was: Would the Longhorns be back in Omaha next year? Right now, the answer to that question didn't seem all that important. Garrido wouldn't answer it directly anyway. He'd say something Zen-like about challenges and life experiences and building character.

Nicole finally said, "Before my parents moved to Seguin, my dad was a deputy in Webb County. This was back in the sixties. The sheriff down there was this big, mean redneck—tough as leather, hard on crime, all that sort of stuff. Which is what people around there wanted. Anyway, the first month on the job, my dad got a call about a body on a ranch on the Rio Grande. This place was something like sixty thousand acres, forty miles from the nearest town. It was the middle of summer, way over a hundred degrees. What they figured was, this poor guy had crossed the border, run out of water, got desperate, and ended up drinking from a cattle tank."

Marlin knew where this story was headed. He'd heard tales just like it countless times. In fact, he'd once dated a woman whose family had made a similar crossing when she was young, and had barely made it across with their lives.

Nicole continued: "That, of course, was a big mistake. The water was contaminated, and the guy starts vomiting. Dehydration sets in, and there's not a damn thing he can do. He just curled up under some scrub brush and died. Not unusual, unfortunately, but here's the sick part. The sheriff shows up with a shovel and starts digging a hole. My dad says, 'Aren't we gonna take him in?' The sheriff says, 'You know how much it costs the county to bury one of these guys?'"

Mitch Campbell winced at the sound of his own voice.

Howdy, folks, Mitch Campbell here. You know, next to singing songs, there's nothing I like better than getting out on a sunny autumn afternoon and hunting a few quail with my dog, Buster. Hunting is one of America's finest pastimes, a time-honored heritage passed down from father to son—but it could be just a memory if gun-control advocates get their way. You see, there are some people who believe that all firearms—including shotguns and sporting rifles—should be outlawed. Well, call me old-fashioned, but I believe in the United States Constitution, and I intend to defend my Second Amendment right to bear arms. That's why I joined the National Weapons Alliance, and I hope y'all will do the same. As a member of the NWA, you'll be standing up for—

In bed, Mitch managed to uncurl from the fetal position long enough to reach for his stereo remote and cut the commercial off. He couldn't bear to hear any more. He hated the phony Southern accent, the pretense that he was some sort of rugged outdoorsman. Even the dog, Buster, was the figment of some anonymous copywriter's imagination.

Mitch Campbell was a total fraud, as carefully marketed as a Mercedes-Benz or a bottle of women's perfume. But one thing was excruciatingly real, and it had haunted Mitch for the past two days.

He was a murderer. He'd shot a man right through the chest. Mitch kept telling himself that the drugs were to blame, but he couldn't help feeling that he was somehow responsible for what had happened. After all, drugs or no drugs, the end result was the same. And what had Mitch done? He'd acted like a coward and covered the whole thing up. Gutless! Spineless! He wasn't sure he'd be able to live with himself.

It was too late now to come clean, to give an honest account of what had really happened. The cops would call it murder. A Mexican was dead, and Mitch would not only be ruined, he'd be looking at life in prison. No more gold records. No more country-music awards. No more parties with comely twin sisters.

Speaking of parties, there was one other truth these events had made abundantly clear, and Mitch was finally willing to admit it to himself. He had a substance-abuse problem. A major one.

Yes, with the tour and everything, he'd been drinking a lot in the past six months—every day, really, usually starting before noon—but he hadn't thought much about it. He'd wake up late feeling crappy, have a stiff Bloody Mary or two, and everything would be fine. Then there'd be beer throughout the day, and whiskey at night, after the show. Drugs, too, mostly cocaine. Not a lot, but more than could charitably be called "recreational usage." Now it was obvious that those indulgences had come with a price.

He hadn't had a beer, a shot of whiskey, or a line of coke since Sunday morning, and no hangover in the history of hangovers could compare with the way he'd been feeling since then. Withdrawal symptoms, that's what it was.

He couldn't sleep for more than an hour at a time, and his fitful slumber was marred by grotesquely unsettling dreams. He had no appetite, and when he did eat, he couldn't hold it down. Not crackers, scrambled eggs, or even oatmeal. His fingers trembled and his eyelids twitched. His head pounded and his small intestine rumbled like a sluggish drainpipe. His breath was sour, his sweat carried a stagnant fungal reek, and his tongue tasted like a hunk of rancid pork. He was pale one minute, flushed the next, and his heart thundered irregularly in his chest. He could actually *feel* each beat throughout his body, as if the valves and arteries and ventricles were struggling to meet the demands placed on them.

In short, he was all but crippled by his ailments. In two days, he hadn't answered the phone, hadn't had any guests, hadn't even left the house—and because of that, he still hadn't done what Dale Stubbs had told him to do. Just one chore, and he couldn't summon up the energy or the fortitude to get it done.

He hadn't replaced the broken window in his bedroom.

The curtains rustled in the breeze; the blinds rattled against the frame; mosquitoes and wasps buzzed in and out at will. His air conditioner ran nonstop as an endless wave of cooled air pushed from the house. At least it hadn't rained.

Now, regardless of how he felt, he had to get on the ball. He'd been tracking the news, and it wasn't good. Dale's little plan hadn't worked at all. A hunting accident? Yeah, right. Even the small-town cops out here in Blanco County had been able to see right through it. They were calling it a homicide and asking the public for help.

Worse yet, J. B. would be back soon. He'd see the untended lawns, the weedy flowerbeds, the oak trees thick with dead limbs and ball moss, and he'd wonder why his hired worker hadn't shown up. Eventually he'd hear the news about a murdered illegal alien, and then he'd figure it out. Fortunately, the cops hadn't given a photo to the media, probably because they hadn't been able to identify the man yet. J. B. would ruin all that, and then the cops would come poking around. Mitch had to get ready to face reality.

He'd thought about calling Stubbs, asking for help, but Stubbs had said they should keep the calls to a minimum. Less for the cops to latch on to. Which meant it was all up to Mitch. He'd have to make a trip to Austin for replacement glass. Tomorrow. He'd do it tomorrow. Right now, he'd clean himself up. Start to get his act together.

He forced himself off the mattress and staggered into the bathroom, where he studied himself in the mirror. A horrible sight. Bags under his eyes. Three days' worth of beard. He cut himself seven times while shaving. He brushed his teeth and his gums bled profusely. The mouthwash burned like some sort of acid.

The warm water of the shower was a blessing, and he let it pour over his scalp until it ran cold.

He nearly fell over as he struggled to get dressed.

He sank to the floor, thinking, *I can't do this. No way.*

The very idea that he could successfully repair the window in his current condition was completely implausible. His hands were clumsy and weak. His knees were wobbly. His head spun when he remained standing too long.

There *was* a solution, though. An obvious one. He tried to put it out of his mind, but it was no use.

All I really need, he figured, *is a drink. Just a good stiff shot to get me through the night. Maybe a couple more in the morning. Something to steady the nerves.*

He was merely being practical. Facing facts. Without alcohol, he was screwed. With alcohol, he'd be back to his old self. He could rally his motor skills and take care of business. It was the sensible thing to do. Not that he was giving up on sobriety, no. He'd go straight as an arrow after he'd put this whole messy business behind him.

Mitch rose from the floor, headed down a long hallway, past the study and the living room and his office, and made his way to the recreation room. He checked the bar and his spirits plummeted. Nothing. Not a single damn bottle. Now he remembered: He'd poured it all out on Sunday, part of his new pledge to sobriety. How stupid was that?

He lumbered into the kitchen and yanked the fridge open. Surely there'd be a stray beer or wine cooler in there, tucked in the back. He rummaged behind a jug of orange juice and a carton of expired milk. Wrong again. The party on Saturday night had cleaned him out.

Mitch leaned against a cabinet, shirtless, and slowly slumped to the floor. He couldn't drive into town for booze, he had no doubt of that. He simply couldn't handle such an enormous challenge.

Then he had a thought. A nasty one, but the only alternative available to him.

Jesus, am I really that desperate? he wondered.

The answer came quickly: *Yes. Yes, I am.*

He clambered off the floor and went through the laundry room into the three-car garage. He flipped the lights on. There, against the near wall, were three full garbage bags, waiting to be carried to the rolling cart down at the front gate. The trash from the party.

If this isn't rock bottom, he thought, *I can definitely see it from here.*

He untied a bag and dumped the contents. Bottles clattered and rolled across the concrete floor. The smell of cigarettes and stale beer was overwhelming—but Mitch found it intoxicating rather than nauseating.

He dropped to his knees and grabbed a Budweiser bottle that still had an ounce at the bottom. Without a moment's hesitation, he lifted it to his mouth and drank. It was hot and flat and *oh Holy Jesus* it tasted wonderful!

He smacked his lips and grabbed another bottle.

11

SABRINA'S PHONE WOKE her at 2:04 A.M.

She fumbled for the lamp beside her bed, then managed to answer on the fourth ring. No rush, really, because she already knew exactly who was calling. No doubt in her mind whatsoever.

She was proven right when a tentative voice said, "Brina?"

"Damn it, Harry," she said. "We talked about this. You said you wouldn't call this late."

"What, did I wake you?"

"It's two in the morning. What do you think?"

"Yeah, sorry about that."

"Most normal people are sleeping right now."

"Ah, but remember: You always said I wasn't normal."

The line was silent for several seconds, until Harry said, "Sorry. You alone?"

Sabrina self-consciously ran a palm across the cool, empty space in the bed beside her. "None of your damn business."

A pause. Then: "You're right. Sorry for asking."

"No, you're not."

"Right again, I'm not. But if there's someone with you, please tell me, so I can go swallow a quart of bleach."

"Don't tempt me."

"I'll do it, by God."

"Make it a gallon. The kind with the spring-fresh scent."

He laughed, and it tugged on her heartstrings like a puppy on a leash. She wanted to be angry with him, to punish him for all the bitter feelings she had accumulated in the past seven years, but she couldn't. After all, it wasn't his fault. As much as she felt like blaming him sometimes, it wouldn't be fair.

The divorce, though; he *was* completely responsible for that, without question. She'd asked for the split-up, but only after he'd made it clear through his actions that she simply couldn't remain married to him.

People respond to tragedy in their own unique ways; his was smoking pot, drinking scotch like tap water, and screwing everything on two legs. "It was either that or Prozac," he said on the final day at her attorney's office. Not a joke, either. His therapist had recommended the antidepressant, advice that had gone unheeded. "You know how I feel about the pharmaceutical companies," Harry offered as an excuse. "Greedy bastards."

That was six years ago, even though it seemed more like six months. Sabrina found the rapid passage of time hard to believe.

"I was calling about your meeting," he said now. "Please tell me it went well. I need some good news."

"I wish I had some."

"*Sonofabitch!* What the hell did he say?"

She had long ago grown used to Harry's outbursts. "That we need to talk to Pardons and Paroles."

"Did you tell him you already have, several times?"

"Yep."

"And?"

"Didn't help."

"Did you tell him he'd better toughen up on crime or Dobbins is gonna whip his butt?"

"He didn't seem real concerned with my opinion. He's still leading in the polls."

"The man is a douche bag."

"Then why did you vote for him last time?"

"Because the alternative was another douche bag who wanted to give tax breaks to his rich buddies."

Sabrina sighed. "Can we not do this right now?"

"Do what? Converse like mature adults?"

"Drag up all this hideous stuff for the thousandth time. I'm just so . . . tired."

The line went silent again. "I'm tired, too, Brina. And the hearing is less than a week away now."

"I know."

"We can't give up. Ever. If there's one thing that still bands us together, it's that. Right?"

"Yeah."

"If we don't do it, who will?"

"You don't need to give me a pep talk, Harry."

"Maybe not," he said somberly, "but sometimes I have to give myself one."

It had been a long time since Sabrina had heard Harry so despondent. She wondered if he'd been drinking.

"You okay, Harry?" she asked. "You don't sound so good."

"I'm . . . yeah, I'm fine. Thanks for asking."

"You sure?"

He laughed, but it sounded forced. "Well, honestly, no. I've been having the dream again."

Now, doing a complete one-eighty, she wanted to comfort him—but she had no idea where to even start. How could she provide solace for another when she couldn't find any for herself? All she could say was, "It came back?"

"Yeah, the same one. We're driving, almost to the spot where it happened, and I start telling myself not to swerve. Just whatever you do, don't swerve. But you know what? I swerve every damn time."

A long silence.

"Maybe you should move." Harry was still in the same house, where the three of them had lived. Sabrina didn't understand how he could stay there.

"You know I can't. Too many memories."

"Some of them bad."

"Yeah."

"Maybe you should talk to someone about it."

"I am. I'm talking to you."

"That's not what I meant."

"Yeah, I know."

She said, "It wasn't your fault. You have to *know* that."

She could hardly hear his reply, which was, "Thank you, Brina. I appreciate it."

She wished she had more to offer, but she could only remain silent. "I've got to get some sleep," she said finally. "I have a meeting in the morning."

"With who?"

"Pardons and Paroles. Who do you think?"

This time, Harry's chuckle was genuine. "Oh, really? You're a stubborn old bitch, you know that?"

"You're wrong about that, sweetie. I'm not so old."

At 3:00 A.M., on the outskirts of Austin, a seventy-two-year-old insomniac named Roland Nichols was in his garage, preparing for the morning ahead. If things went as planned, he was going to lodge a .177-caliber pellet firmly in the hindquarters of an aging, half-blind dachshund named Schotzie.

The Griffins, two doors down, owned the miserable little beast, and the Griffins themselves were equally objectionable. They had loud dinner parties on their backyard patio. They left their garbage cans on the street for several hours after the trash had been collected. Their yard was weedy. Their snotty twelve-year-old made unkind remarks about Nichols' hairpiece, probably repeating things his parents had said.

But the dog was the worst of it.

The Griffins had the infuriating habit of allowing Schotzie to wander unchecked—despite a county leash law that forbade such transgressions. It was an outrage. Where was their sense of responsibility? Didn't they understand the personal liability inherent in owning a pet?

Just after sunrise every morning, the arthritic creature would begin his slow waddle from lawn to lawn, lackadaisical, carefree. He'd occasionally stop to lick his genitals or to raise a gimpy leg and squirt a few feeble drops onto a mailbox post. Then, when the mood struck him, he'd hunker down, legs quivering, and leave a grim, dry stool in the middle of some unlucky neighbor's property.

More often than not, Schotzie chose to relieve himself on Nichols' immaculately maintained lawn. Three times in the past ten days, Nichols had discovered Schotzie's disgusting deposits marring an otherwise unblemished carpet of St. Augustine. Now, despite the overabundance of patience Nichols had exhibited, he'd had enough. He'd been pushed, damn it, and now it was time to push back.

So Nichols had retrieved the pellet rifle from the closet in his bedroom. He'd bought it two years ago to discourage a raccoon that had been raiding his garbage can, and he'd quickly discovered it was equally effective on roaming pets. Since then, he'd popped a Pomeranian, nailed a Newfoundland, and blasted a basset hound.

Now I'm going to drill a dachshund. He chuckled to himself.

All in all, it seemed like a reasonable solution. A slap on the paw, so to speak. If that didn't work, then he'd explore other, more extreme options.

A well-placed kick, if he could coax the mutt close enough.

Maybe a slingshot loaded with a ball bearing.

And yes, perhaps even hamburger meat laced with rat poison—the same tactic he'd used on that persistent feral cat that had hung around his house last summer. Purely a worst-case scenario for Schotzie, but one that Nichols wouldn't hesitate to employ if the dog didn't respond appropriately to his other measures.

But first, the rifle needed a quick once-over. The last time out, when Nichols had dispatched a birdfeeder-raiding squirrel in his backyard, he'd noticed that the rifle wasn't operating as smoothly as it should. Somewhat stiff. A few drops of oil should do the trick.

He retreated to the workshop in his garage and flipped the lights on. Then he hit the button to raise the overhead door; a little fresh air would be nice. The streets outside were still and dark.

Nichols plopped onto a stool and set about his work. At first, he merely oiled the trigger axis pin and the bolt spring guide, the safety and the cocking lever. Then he decided, what the heck—he'd strip the whole thing down and give it a good cleaning. So he went after it with a screwdriver; fifteen minutes later, he had an assortment of small parts on the workbench in front of him.

He was so intent, so focused, he never even heard the unexpected visitor until he said, "You realize, don't you, that guns are the worst evil we've ever introduced into our society?"

Nichols glanced up and saw a man—tall, athletic, with a ponytail— standing in the entrance to the garage. Nichols was startled, but he tried not to show it. It was a habit ingrained in him from years in his chosen profession: Never let 'em see you sweat. Besides, this guy looked more like an artist or a professor than a parolee.

"Pardon me?"

"Guns are the worst plague mankind has ever thrust on itself," the man said. "Worse than drugs, pornography . . . even disco." He smiled at his own joke, but there was something unsettling about it.

"Do I know you?" Nichols asked. He rose to his feet, still holding the stripped skeleton of the rifle.

"We've met. Several years ago. What is that, an air gun?"

"Yeah, a Benjamin Sheridan," he replied, thinking: *Who is this? Some nutty neighbor out for a late walk? And now he wants to chat when I've got important things to do?*

"Ah, yes," the man said. "What most people would regard as a toy. But did you know that thirty-nine Americans were killed by BB, pellet, and paintball guns between 1990 and 2000? Thirty-two of those victims were children. That's according to the U.S. Consumer Product Safety Commission."

Oh, great, Nichols thought. *One of those guys.* "That's okay," Nichols said. "I don't have kids."

"Maybe that's for the best."

Nichols was starting to get creeped out. Something weird was going on here. "I'm Roland Nichols," he said. "Who are you?" He was hoping a name would jog his memory, which wasn't as reliable as it used to be.

The stranger evaded the question. "I know who you are. Former assistant district attorney for Travis County. You hold the record for the highest conviction rate in county history. Well done, I must say. Unfortunately, toward the end, you got a little lazy."

Nichols abandoned all attempts at civility. "Listen, pal, I don't know who the hell you are, but—"

The man stepped closer. "Seven years ago. A man killed a boy and you filed manslaughter charges on him. Not murder, but *manslaughter.* Honestly, Roland, is that what they taught you at law school?"

Nichols' stomach did a somersault. A family member seeking revenge? Was that what this was about? If so, it could mean serious trouble. The door to the interior of the house was ten feet away. He might have to make a run for it. Slam the door behind him. Go get some real firepower. "I want you to leave. Right now." His voice sounded shaky and weak. Not forceful and commanding, like in the old days.

"I will. But first, you need to pay for your incompetence."

"You're crazy!"

"Well, now, I won't argue with that. Four out of five therapists agree, when you have to bury a nine-year-old, it does a little something to your faculties. Kind of tweaks the ol' psyche. Puts you in a really bad mood. Trust me."

The man turned toward a collection of tools hanging on a pegboard mounted on one wall. Screwdrivers, vise grips, socket wrenches, pliers.

An axe. Oh God.

Nichols' knees were suddenly weak. His hands were trembling.

But the man ignored the axe and gestured toward the workbench. "What's that there? Gun oil?"

Nichols didn't reply. He was feeling trapped; he could never make it to the door. He was too old, too slow. The stranger was younger, stronger, and too close.

"That's an awfully big bottle. You must own a lot of guns, huh, Roland?"

"A few."

"Yeah, I bet you do. You ever think about the carnage they cause? The misery, the pain, the suffering?"

"Owning a gun is my right as an American!" Nichols croaked, attempting to bolster his courage. *And if only I had one in my hands right now,* he thought.

The stranger shook his head with impatience. "Oh, come on. Not that Second Amendment crap? Can't you read, Roland? It refers to the *militia,* not to the common citizen."

"The Supreme Court says —"

The man slapped his palm down on the workbench, and Roland

jumped involuntarily. "The Supreme Court has been very clear on this matter! *U.S. versus Miller* in 1939! Ever hear of that little gem? They ruled that 'a well-regulated militia' refers to the National Guard, not to you or me or any twisted bastard who wants to carry a pistol."

"That's not right. *Miller* said—"

"It is right! And the Court has affirmed that ruling twice—in 1965 and 1990. Aren't you familiar with any of this stuff?"

"What about *U.S. versus Emerson?*" Nichols squeaked.

"Ha! A renegade decision by a rogue judge!"

The stranger was delusional, Nichols concluded. *Emerson* was the most comprehensive examination of the Second Amendment ever undertaken by any court, anywhere. By now, though, Nichols was afraid to speak.

"Guns kill people, Roland. That's all they do." Now the stranger actually sang: "Ain't good for nothin' but put a man six feet in a hole." He smiled. "You gotta love the classics."

Out on the street, a car passed. Nichols was tempted to wave, to signal for help, but the vehicle came and went too quickly. Now the stranger came even closer, just on the other side of the workbench. "As far as I'm concerned, there's only one gun that has any value at all."

He removed something from his pocket and held it for Nichols to see.

A stun gun.

Nichols swallowed hard. Was this man really going to attack him? Right here in his own garage?

The man triggered the stun gun, and it crackled with a sharp, ominous snap. "The good thing is, it's nonlethal." He let loose with a wry chuckle. "Well, normally."

When the stranger rushed him, Roland Nichols didn't even put up a fight.

PART TWO

State militias were viewed as a counterbalance to the federal army, and the Second Amendment was written to prevent the federal government from disarming the state militias.

—Brady Campaign Web site

Anyone familiar with the principles upon which this country was founded will recognize this claim's most glaring flaw: In America, rights, by definition, belong to individuals.

—NRA-ILA Web site

Get your facts first, and then you can distort them as much as you please.

—Mark Twain

12

"JESS, I KNOW heem," the man by the name of Ignacio said. He held his thumb and forefinger an inch apart. "Thees much. Juss a lee-tle."

Dawn, Wednesday morning. Three dozen day laborers were scattered behind the Git It & Go convenience store, the unofficial pickup spot for day laborers. Men would cruise up in trucks, offering a hard day's labor—clearing brush, laying bricks, hanging drywall—for eighty or ninety dollars a day.

Marlin recognized some of the faces. Illegal aliens who had lived in Blanco County, off and on, for several years. Many of the men were skittish, casting uneasy glances Marlin's way, wondering, no doubt, what had brought a uniformed government employee into their midst. He'd smiled at a knot of them earlier and given a small wave. *"No problemo."*

They smiled back, but they couldn't hide the mistrust in their eyes.

Ignacio was the only person who'd answered when Marlin asked if anyone knew English. Certainly there were others who could speak the language—at least to some degree—but those who could were usually hesitant to admit it to authority figures. Ignacio probably had a green card, hence his willingness to come forward.

"*Quién es?*" Marlin asked. The state required him to take four hours of rudimentary Spanish every year. Not much. He figured he knew just enough to bungle it entirely.

Ignacio studied the photograph again. "Rodolfo."

"Rodolfo?"

"*Sí.* Jess."

"Rodolfo what?"

"*Que?*"

"Do you know his last name? *Apellido?*"

"Don' know. He very quiet. Talk very leetle."

"Where does he live? *Donde es Rodolfo's casa?*"

"Ciudad Acuña."

A good lead, but not what Marlin meant. "What about here in Texas? *Donde es Rodolfo's casa en Blanco County?*"

Ignacio shrugged. "Don' know."

"Who does he usually work for? Do you know that?" In an effort to help Ignacio understand, Marlin found himself speaking more loudly than usual, which was, of course, ridiculous.

Ignacio grinned sheepishly. "*No comprendo.*"

Marlin struggled to remember the words. "*Donde es trabaja recientemente?*"

"Oh! He say he work at beeg ranch."

"Okay, good. *Bueno.* Which big ranch?"

"Don' know."

"Nearby?"

"Don' know."

Marlin pointed to the other men around them. "*Conocer Rodolfo?*" He'd asked: *Do these men know Rodolfo?* Or he hoped that's what he'd asked.

Ignacio made a gesture with the photo, meaning, *Do you want me to show it to them?*

Marlin nodded vigorously. "*Por favor. Muy importante.*"

Ignacio went from group to group, speaking at a rapid clip that

Marlin couldn't follow. The responses were shrugs, shaken heads, and Spanish too rapid for Marlin to understand.

After he made the rounds, Ignacio returned and said, "He maybe have a small truck. Blanco."

"He lives in Blanco?"

"No, the truck ees blanco. White."

"Toyota? Ford? Mazda?"

"Don' know." Ignacio made an upside-down U with one hand. "It has cover in back."

"Covered, like a camper top?" Marlin asked.

"*Sí*, jess, the camper."

Something clicked into place. Marlin could see the truck in his mind's eye—because he'd spotted one matching that exact description very recently. On Cypress Mill Road. "An old truck?"

"Jess, old."

Marlin asked several more questions, but he'd gotten all he was going to get. A good start. He pulled a ten-dollar bill from his wallet, but Ignacio was already backing away, shaking his head.

"*Muchas gracias*," Marlin said, extending the money.

Ignacio waved him off. "*De nada.*"

Dale Stubbs' secretary, Tricia Woodbine—former homecoming queen at Baylor University—had several weaknesses that, a mere two years out of college, had placed her on the brink of financial ruin.

For starters, quite literally, there was the grande mint mocha chip Frappuccino she bought on the way to work every morning. Four bucks a pop. A thousand bucks a year, when you added it up. Given her income, she realized she should put a stop to that irresponsible habit immediately—but oh my God, the stuff was like an instant orgasm in a cup.

Her Starbucks tab was a drop in the bucket compared to her wardrobe. The finest Anne Klein dresses. Perky skirt-and-blouse combinations from BCBG Max Azria. Shoes from Via Spiga, Jimmy Choo, and Marc Jacobs. An assortment of exquisite French lingerie that hugged her body like a drunken uncle at a family reunion. She knew her extravagant tastes were a huge part of the problem, but what was the solution? Shop at Dillard's or, heaven forbid, JCPenney? As if. She couldn't bear to be spotted anywhere less than Nordstrom.

Top it off with jewelry and makeup, hair and nails, a decent cell phone plan, happy hour three times a week, a newish car, and a respectable place to live, and not only did the ends refuse to meet, they'd never even been introduced.

Tricia considered turning to her parents for help, but since her father—irony of ironies—was a well-respected financial planner, she couldn't bring herself to admit to her indiscretions.

So she fixed the problem—temporarily, at least—the way many hapless Americans did. With credit cards! She gleefully slapped all her debt onto plastic and never gave it a second thought. Until the bills started coming in. Every single month! She currently owed six thousand on a Visa. Eight on a MasterCard. Ten-five on a Discover card, five months overdue, and the dedicated folks in accounts receivable weren't pleased about that at all.

Tricia was stymied. Baffled. Confused. Was being an adult supposed to be this difficult? Was she really expected to make do with her pittance of a paycheck? It seemed she was, and yet she had no idea how to go about it.

Thus, she considered it kismet when, back in May, two men approached her in the Neiman Marcus parking lot and remarked on the nice weather they were having.

She agreed.

Then they told her that, with a little effort—nothing illegal, mind you—she could earn a rather large sum of cash.

She thought about it for about two seconds. Then she said, "I'm listening."

Before work on Wednesday morning, she drove her three-year-old BMW out to Plano, a suburb to the north of Dallas. The car's air conditioner had crapped out the day before—yet another expense for the credit cards—and it was not a comfortable journey. Rush hour was in full swing, and at each traffic light the bitter smell of exhaust filled the air.

She took Preston Road, past strip centers and convenience stores, then pulled into a sprawling apartment complex that the builders, in a fit of inspired creativity, had named Preston Pointe. She'd decided on previous visits that Preston Pointe looked like an okay place to live. No, it didn't have the amenities of her current apartment—a large pool with a waterfall, a hunky security guard tooling around in a golf cart—but it was reasonably clean and well maintained. Perfect for students, or for young couples on a budget.

She parked behind Building D and took a moment to touch up her lip gloss. Then she ascended the stairs to the second floor and went to the door of apartment 2203. Once again, she was struck by how ordinary it appeared.

A welcome mat read WELCOME, PARDNER! WIPE YOUR BOOTS! A pair of running shoes was pushed to the left of the mat, a thriving potted plant to the right. Props, all of it. And it worked. From the outside, the apartment was as anonymous as every other unit in the complex.

It was clever, really. The perfect cover.

Nobody would have suspected that the apartment was actually a clandestine field office for a left-wing organization known as SNATCH.

The name still made her giggle. She couldn't believe they'd actually named themselves SNATCH. And the funniest part: They seemed to have done it with no trace of humor at all. Weird people.

She knocked twice, waited three seconds, then knocked twice more. Just like the other times. All this subterfuge still felt a little silly and awkward, like the first time she'd given a blowjob in high school; she played along, but she kept wondering if she was doing it right.

A few seconds later, she heard a soft voice say, "Who is it?"

"Heather Locklear." Her code name. That part she liked. She figured it was because she bore a striking resemblance to the lithe, beautiful actress.

"Password?"

"Kevlar."

The door swung open, and a stern-faced red-haired man waved her in. She didn't know his name because he was a total grump and had never offered it. Or maybe it was because she was an outsider, merely a freelancer hired to complete a single job. She sensed that

the members of SNATCH looked down on her, because her participation in their little scheme was based on money rather than moral
outrage or smug self-righteousness.

Truth be told, she didn't really care if these nuts respected her or
not. From what she'd seen, they were as far off the deep end as Dale's
bunch. Besides, there was her damned air conditioner to consider.

The grump closed the door and tapped his wristwatch. Condescending as hell. "You're late."

"Sorry. Traffic was a real bitch. Everyone drives like a retard in this
city."

He gave her a glare and said, "Please make an attempt to be on
time in the future. Dieter values punctuality."

Dieter, she thought. *Get real.* No way was that his real name. It was
obvious that none of them—Dieter or the redhead or any of the
other unnamed minions she'd seen on past visits—wanted her to
know their actual identities. They were like a bunch of school kids
play-acting as spies. Like she even cared.

Today, though, the apartment was quiet. Nobody at the three
computers that rested on a long table in the living room. Nobody
monitoring the bank of four televisions, each tuned to a different major news channel. For the moment, it appeared things were slow in
the wacky world of guerrilla liberalism.

With no further discussion, the redhead led her down a hallway to
the bedroom on the right. He knocked—three quick raps, probably a
signal of some kind—and from behind the door came the reply:

"*Eintreten!*"

Puh-leeze. What was that—Dutch? German? As corny as some old
black-and-white movie.

"You have ten minutes," the redhead murmured. "He's on a tight
schedule today."

Then he opened the door.

She stepped into the room—and there was Dieter, sitting behind
his desk, dressed the same as always. A turtleneck shirt, even though
it was summertime. A small hoop in his left ear. And the topper, so to
speak: a beret, which would have been laughable if he didn't look
kind of cute in it. Yeah, okay. She kind of liked him in a this-guy-is-all-
wrong-for-me sort of way. He had charisma or something. Or maybe

it was his piercing brown eyes. She wondered if he'd notice the short skirt she'd worn today. The high heels.

"You look hot," he said.

Wow! He did notice! And he was so blunt about it. He'd never paid her a compliment before. He was usually as uptight as the rest of them, getting right down to business without any small talk. "Thank you," she said, self-consciously smoothing her skirt.

He frowned. "No, I meant you've been perspiring."

"Oh. Yeah. My air conditioner is, uh—"

"Have a seat."

She sat.

The office was utilitarian. A metal desk with a computer and stacks of paper on it. Three metal filing cabinets. Nothing else. No art on the walls, no framed photographs. No personal effects of any kind. Tricia gathered that Dieter and his crew moved frequently, so it was impractical to get too comfy.

He placed his elbows on his desk and steepled his fingers. "Well?"

This was the part she'd been dreading. She shrugged. "Still nothing."

He sighed heavily. "That's very disappointing."

"I'm sorry."

"You've had six weeks."

"I know, but as far as I can tell, there's nothing to fi—"

"Impossible!"

Tricia jumped. Dieter had never raised his voice before.

He took a deep breath, composing himself. He was counting to five. She could see his lips move. "I apologize," he said. "But if you're asking me to believe that the NWA runs an honest operation, well, I'm afraid you haven't been digging hard enough."

He raised a hand and counted three fingers, one by one, as he spoke. "Bribery. Kickbacks. Illegal campaign contributions. Those are their standard practices. They are circumventing the will of the American people through graft and corruption, and we intend to prove it once and for all. You, my sweet, are supposed to be helping us with that."

Tricia wasn't sure she'd recognize evidence of a kickback if it jumped up and bit her on the left tit, but she'd been doing her best.

Going through files. Listening in on conversations. Asking delicate questions. She'd gotten nowhere. "I'm sorry, Dieter, it's just that—"

"What methods have you been using?"

"Methods?"

He arched an eyebrow. "You *have* been sleeping with him, no?"

She crossed her legs and tried to appear offended. "That's really none of your business."

"Maybe not. But a woman with your attributes—we feel that you'd have a greater chance for success if you were to commit yourself wholly to the project."

He leered at her, and it made her feel dirty. She decided to change the subject. "There is one thing . . . I'm not sure if it's important or not."

He waved a hand in an impatient let's-hear-it gesture.

"Okay. Mitch Campbell—you know who he is, right? Well, Mitch called him late on Sunday morning. And Dale kind of freaked out, you know? Dropped everything and drove right out to see him. Two hundred miles. And he wouldn't tell me why."

To Tricia, it didn't seem relevant—what could the country singer have to do with anything?—but Dieter appeared interested.

So she continued. "Ever since then, Dale's been acting . . . I don't know, kind of strange."

"Strange how?"

"Distracted. Grouchy." *Can't get it up.*

Dieter swiveled in his chair and stared at the blank wall, drumming his fingers on the desk. Several moments passed. Tricia began to wonder if the meeting was over. Was he expecting her to leave? It wasn't always easy to tell with a guy like Dieter.

Then he pivoted abruptly and punched the intercom button on his phone. "Bring me the Interloper 3000."

There was a long pause, then the voice of the redhead: "Uh, are you sure? That seems kind of—"

"Bring it to me!"

He punched the button again, then fixed Tricia with a hard gaze that made her squirm. "Unfortunately, I believe it's time to resort to Plan B."

"Plan B?" she asked, hoping for some elaboration.

"Yes, Plan B," he said, and no more.

Then they waited. A long time. She was nervous. What the hell was Plan B? They'd never discussed anything called Plan B—but she was afraid to ask. He was still staring at her.

"Is that patchouli oil you're wearing?" she asked.

He nodded.

"Nice." *If you like the smell of stagnant bong water.*

"Thank you."

Tricia looked around the office. "I could bring you a Pottery Barn catalog if you wanted one," she said. "Warm this place up a little. Even just a throw rug would work wonders. Maybe a new lamp."

Dieter didn't reply.

Finally, the redhead reentered the room, handed Dieter a small black box—some sort of electronic device, no larger than a deck of cards—and quickly departed.

Dieter held the box with reverence, as if it were a videotape of the president snorting cocaine and banging hookers. "Ah, yes, the Interloper 3000," he said. "Quite handy. Risky, yes, but it could be the solution we've been looking for."

Tricia didn't like the gleam in his eye. "What does it do?"

He placed it delicately on the top of his desk. "It records phone calls." Then, by way of explanation, he added, "We have friends at Radio Shack."

Recording phone calls? Tricia wasn't sure she wanted to betray Dale so flagrantly. It was one thing when she was simply reporting what she had seen and heard, but to tape Dale's private conversations . . . that was like selling secrets to the Canadians.

"I've never been very good with electronic thingies," she said, purely as an excuse. "Like, there are some features on my cell phone that are a total mystery."

"This is really simple to operate. It's automatic. You don't have to do anything."

"But won't he see it?"

"It plugs in at the PBX."

"See, you've lost me already."

"Relax. I'll show you exactly how it works."

"Isn't recording calls illegal and stuff?"

Dieter huffed, as if the law were nothing but a troublesome impediment. "If you want to get technical, yes—but you would be amply compensated."

Tricia knew that if she agreed, she'd be crossing a serious line. Up to now, she hadn't done anything that was strictly illegal. Unethical, maybe, but not illegal, as far as she knew. So she asked the most important question of all.

"How ample are we talking about?"

13

CYPRESS MILL ROAD, in the sparsely populated northeast portion of Blanco County, was a typical two-lane country blacktop. Lots of twists and turns. Poorly marked. No shoulders. Mostly paved, but a little rough in spots. Nothing much of interest on either side. Barbed-wire fences. An occasional trailer or ramshackle pier-and-beam home. Rusted metal outbuildings. Small herds of cattle bedded in the shade of oak trees, seeking refuge from the withering summer sun.

Follow it far enough, and the road would eventually hook up with Farm Road 962, which continued east into Travis County and crossed the Pedernales River west of Austin.

But if you traveled just three miles east of U.S. Highway 281, Cypress Mill Road passed the entrance to Ken Bell's ranch. Somewhere in that three-mile stretch—that's where Marlin had subconsciously noted a small, white, older-model imported truck with a camper top. In fact, he'd seen it twice—coming and going from Bell's place.

Years as a game warden had ingrained in Marlin the habit of noticing any empty vehicle parked on a quiet roadside. Passing by, his eyes would automatically scan the adjoining woods, searching for signs of poachers.

The day before, as he and Tatum had responded to Ken Bell's call, something about the truck had made him pay it little heed. Now, as he rounded a bend just past Cottonwood Creek and saw the truck— still parked in the right-of-way—he remembered what it was. There was a For Sale sign taped to the rear window of the camper top.

The sign was what had made Marlin remember the vehicle, but it was also what had made him dismiss it as having any connection with the dead man on Bell's ranch. He'd concluded that someone living nearby had simply parked the truck along the road to expose it to potential buyers. After all, there was a mailbox a mere thirty yards away, and it had been easy to assume that the owner of the mailbox—a green one, with a National Weapons Alliance decal on the side—also owned the truck. Marlin wondered if that conclusion had been hasty.

He parked his Dodge Ram well behind the truck—a battered Nissan with Texas plates—and climbed out. He kept to the pavement as he approached, even though the grassy right-of-way wouldn't have held any footprints.

He hoped to see a broken window, maybe some blood on the door—an indication that he'd discovered the original crime scene— but no such luck. Both windows were rolled up tight, and the windshield was whole and undamaged.

He peered inside. The vinyl seats were worn and split, but the cab was relatively clean and free from clutter. A small ice chest rested on the passenger-side floorboard. A twenty-ounce Coke bottle, empty, sat in a drink holder between the seat and the stick shift. A Jesus figurine hung from the rearview mirror.

Marlin moved to the rear. The bed of the truck, beneath the camper shell, was crammed with gardening equipment and supplies. A lawn mower and a weed trimmer. Shovels, hoes, and rakes. Pruning shears, hedge clippers, and a chain saw. An inverted wheelbarrow. Six bags of mulch. An assortment of hand tools for working a flowerbed. Plus, a bedroll and a small duffel bag.

Marlin returned to his truck and lifted the radio handset. "Seventy-five-oh-eight to Blanco County."

Static, then: "Blanco County, go ahead seventy-five-oh-eight."

"Darrell, I need a ten-twenty-eight."

"Go ahead."

Marlin gave him the plate number, and then he waited. In less than a minute, he'd know the name of the registered owner.

The gardening tools told him he was on the right track. Rodolfo was a day laborer. It made sense that he might invest in some necessary equipment.

When Darrell came back, though, the owner wasn't named Rodolfo. Far from it. "Junior Barstow owns that truck, John."

Just that quick, with five simple words, Marlin's spirits began to deflate. He resisted the urge to say, *You sure?* Instead, he said, "Can you run a twenty-nine?"

"Already did. Negative." *Not stolen.*

Not what Marlin had expected. It appeared to be the wrong vehicle. What now?

"Darrell, let Bobby and Bill know I'm en route, will ya?"

Another day, another goddamn bureaucrat, Sabrina thought. Until she actually met Marcus Roark. He wasn't what she had expected at all.

She had worn a basic pencil skirt that showed off her nicely toned legs. Medium heels. Above, a well-tailored plum-colored faux-wrap top that was tasteful yet flirty. Of course, her push-up bra—that miracle of modern engineering—was doing its job masterfully.

It didn't matter. She could just as well have worn a suit made from Saran Wrap, or, on the other extreme, a dress fashioned from a potato sack. Because Roark, much to Sabrina's dismay, appeared to be gay.

A photo on the wall behind his desk showed Roark and an attractive blond gentleman, shoulder to shoulder, both smiling, with the Golden Gate Bridge looming in the background.

A second photo: the same blond man, sitting in a recliner, holding a cat. Wearing a floral-print silk shirt. The man, not the cat.

A third photo: Both men again, seated, leis around their necks, gaudy sunglasses, sunburned faces, the whole bit. Apparently on a cruise ship, sipping tall, frosty drinks with a pineapple wedge on the rim of each glass.

The wall featured more photos of other handsome, well-groomed men—solo, in pairs, in groups—in a variety of exotic and domestic settings. There was only one woman in any of the shots, and she appeared to be in her seventies. Roark's mother, probably, because he had her cheekbones.

So much for the power of cleavage.

Roark said, "I'll be frank with you, Miss Nash. I'm not sure what I can do for you. You've already spoken to other members of the board. From what I've heard, you've also met with the governor."

Roark was pointing out, without a lot of subtlety, that he was aware that she'd gone over his head. It wasn't an encouraging way to start the conversation, but she plowed forward anyway.

"Please call me Sabrina. And to the contrary, you can do a lot for me. You can make sure my son's killer stays in prison. You can send the message that when a child dies from gun violence, it's simply unacceptable. Did you know that guns are the second leading cause of death for people under the age of twenty in the U.S.?"

"Actually, I did, but—"

"And for every child that dies, four are wounded. Our kids aren't safe in their homes, in their neighborhoods, or in their schools. It's an epidemic—a worse problem than polio was in the first half of the twentieth century. I'm asking you and the board to help me do something about it." Sabrina wondered if her delivery had sounded rehearsed. At least she'd remembered all her lines.

Roark spread his hands on his desk and appeared to choose his words carefully. "You have to understand: We're not here to set policy or make any sort of statement about social ills. We simply review cases on an individual basis and determine if we think the inmate is ready to be released back into society."

"But your decision is discretionary."

"Yes, it is. And the factors we take into consideration are the seriousness of the crime, the inmate's criminal history, time served, his behavior in prison, that sort of thing. But politics don't enter into it. Even if we wanted to send some sort of message, that's simply not our job."

That was the thing about these government types: They had an answer for everything. And it was always the wrong one. "I just want to make sure Jake isn't forgotten," Sabrina said softly. "He's the victim in all this, and I want everyone to remember that."

Roark nodded noncommittally.

Sabrina added, "Duane Rankin is a very sick man. Surely that's obvious to everyone involved. He's dangerous. I'm looking for some assurances that the board isn't actually going to release him."

Roark shook his head. "You know I can't give you that. Besides, we haven't even made our decision yet."

She continued to push. "Which way is the board leaning?"

"I can't tell you that, either. That sort of information is confidential."

Sabrina was suddenly very tired. It hit her that way sometimes, like a sail collapsing in the absence of wind. Momentum gone, energy depleted, spirits becalmed.

She heard Harry: *We can't give up. Ever.*

But she was the one doing all the fighting, wasn't she? What was Harry doing, really? She stoked that thought into anger and propelled herself forward with it.

"Jake was born with Down syndrome, Mr. Roark. It was a mild case, so he was lucky, if you want to call it that. Even so . . . it was a struggle. For all of us."

Roark opened his mouth to speak, and Sabrina knew exactly what he was going to say: *I've seen the files, Miss Nash. I'm familiar with the case.*

But he changed his mind and simply said, "I'm sorry."

"You shouldn't be. Jake wasn't. Besides, to be blunt, I'm not looking for pity or sympathy. I just want you to know all the facts—to hear it from me—because reading a stack of paperwork doesn't cut it. Your files can't tell you everything you need to know about Jake."

Sabrina's voice had risen, and she wondered if she'd crossed the line. She'd given Roark an excuse to glance at his watch and let her know his time was limited. Then he'd say that he only had time for issues that were specifically relevant to Duane Rankin's potential release. He'd tell her she'd have her chance to speak at the formal hearing on Monday, by which time, she feared, they'd have already made up their minds.

Except . . . he didn't say those things.

Instead, he leaned back and nodded, indicating that she should continue. It caught her off guard. The man was willing to listen? She was stunned. She proceeded quickly.

"We moved to Austin when Jake was two, after Harry was offered the job at the *Statesman.* I was thrilled, because I knew what kind of city Austin was. Everyone is so . . . accepting. It felt like a good place to raise him, and I didn't need to be in L.A. anymore because I'd already decided to retire from acting. One year after we got here, Jake was diagnosed with leukemia. Children with Down syndrome are twenty times more likely to get leukemia than other kids. Did you know that? Most people don't. Jake was in and out of treatment for months. Chemotherapy, bone marrow transplants, the usual routine. He beat it, and he never complained once—and I mean not ever. He was such a happy boy. Just a total joy. When he was old enough for first grade, we had enough money to send him wherever we wanted. A private school, a specialized facility. But, well . . . have you heard the word 'inclusion'?"

Roark said, "Educating all kids, with or without disabilities, together."

"Exactly. That's what Jake wanted, to be like all the other kids, so that's what we did. Sent him to a public school."

"How did that work out?"

Sabrina took a moment to consider her answer. "Reasonably well, I guess. The teachers were . . . accommodating. Very supportive, for the most part. But even so, they couldn't give Jake the individual attention he needed. He couldn't always keep up. I tried to teach him some things myself, but he wasn't much interested in learning from his mom, and frankly, I wasn't very good at it. So we hired a tutor. Well, nothing formal. Our neighbors had a son, Matt, who was in college. Really smart kid, and he was a natural teacher. Matt would spend an hour with Jake every day, and it made a huge difference. They became close, which was nice, Jake having a friend like that, because some of the kids at school made fun of him. Or they'd comment on his appearance. You know how kids are. His ears were misshapen, so they'd tease him about it. They'd mimic the way he talked. But you know what? He laughed about it. He said they were the ones with the problem, not him. That's just the way Jake was. Can you even imagine that—going through life, knowing you're different than everybody else, and not letting it get to you? Would you have the strength for that?"

As soon as the words left her mouth, Sabrina realized her faux pas. Roark was a gay man, and she'd just implied that he couldn't understand ostracism, ridicule, and the lack of social acceptance. Huge mistake. She became flustered. "I'm sorry, I—I didn't mean to say—"

"It's okay."

Her eyes strayed to the photographs, and then back to Roark's face. He didn't look angry.

"Miss Nash, may I give you some advice, between you and me?"

Sabrina nodded.

"When you speak at the hearing . . . forget all those facts and figures you recited earlier, and don't ask us to make an object lesson out of Duane Rankin. Just tell us about Jake—exactly the way you're telling me today."

After she left, Marcus Roark attempted to concentrate on other matters, but his eye kept wandering to the Duane Rankin file. He kept hearing Sabrina Nash's tale.

Down syndrome.

Leukemia.

The shooting.

It was heartbreaking.

Okay, he'd spend just a few minutes going through the file again, to ensure that he understood every nuance of the case.

What it told him was this:

Duane Rankin had, to this day, steadfastly maintained his innocence. Since his incarceration, he'd been a model inmate. Took correspondence classes. Worked in the prison library. Not a single disciplinary problem.

But . . .

Duane Rankin had stalked Sabrina Nash. A classic case. He'd met her through her next-door neighbors, the Mergenthalers. The Mergenthaler boy was named Matthew, classmates with Rankin. Had to be the same "Matt" that had been Jacob's tutor. Duane, apparently, quickly became obsessed with Sabrina. Arrested twice for trespassing on Sabrina Nash's property. Arrested a third time, for unlawful entry, when he entered through a rear window and left an erotic poem on Sabrina's pillow. Confessed to it. Served six months.

After the shooting, when detectives searched Rankin's apartment, they found that Rankin, after his release, had taken up right where he'd left off. He'd shot more than four hundred photos of Sabrina Nash with a zoom lens. In many of the pictures, her husband had been cut out with pinking shears. In his testimony, Rankin admitted to staking out the Nash residence on at least twenty different occasions.

Then, the night of the shooting. A patrolman spotted a dark blue or black truck—one similar to Rankin's—speeding on Loop 360. He began to pull it over but was called to an accident a mile away. He later learned that the accident occurred when a dark-colored truck, like the one he'd been following, had fired a shot through the rear window of Sabrina Nash's vehicle. The bullet missed the occupants and exited the opposite window, flying harmlessly into the night, but the shot caused Harry Jenkins to swerve. He lost control. Jacob was killed.

Rankin admitted to purchasing a gun illegally. A .22. *Just for target practice,* he'd said. *But I didn't shoot at Sabrina. I would never do that to her.*

He had an alibi. Claimed he was with a young woman, but she flatly denied it.

End of file.

14

MITCH WAS RIGHT back where he started, in bed, with a hangover bad enough that it could've been construed as punishment from the gods. He contemplated the day before him.

Oh, Christ, I gotta go get window glass.

He slowly lifted his head, testing it, seeing how bad it was. Okay, not quite as severe as the day before. His mouth tasted like an ashtray, but overall, his condition was manageable. He'd been through worse, many times. He could function, if he focused.

The phone rang, and it pierced his brain like an ice pick. He hadn't been answering the phone, but he couldn't keep avoiding all his calls. He wanted to, but he couldn't. He grabbed the handset and said hello.

A voice he didn't recognize said, "How's it going, Norm?"

For a few seconds, it didn't register. Then Mitch thought: *Norm?* His parents still called him Norman, when they were alone, but everybody else knew him as Mitch. *How's it going, Norm?* This was not a good sign. He hadn't heard *Norm* since prep school.

"Wrong number," he said.

"Dude, that accent sounds pretty good. You've got everybody fooled. Hell of a job. That drama class you took must've paid off."

Drama class? This was getting worse by the minute. Mitch tried to act confused and laugh it off. "Sorry, buddy, ain't no Norm here."

"That's right, keep it up. Otherwise Mitch is down the tubes, huh? Nobody wants a country star who used to get stoned before lacrosse practice. And I know the NWA wouldn't want a spokesman who used to worship Tupac. Doesn't exactly fit their image, does it? Might cause a bit of a PR problem."

Mitch's stomach was binding into a tight knot. "You must be smokin' something yourself, 'cause I got no idea—"

"You used to be a scrawny little pothead, and now you're this big, corn-fed superstar. A genuine American hero. Kudos, dude. You've got the world by the balls."

Mitch swallowed hard. He and Joe had always known this was a possibility. What to do? Cave in? Ask him what he wants? Or deny it completely? "I'm gonna hang up now," Mitch said.

The man laughed. "I don't blame you, Norm. I imagine this is all kind of a shock. But I'll be back in touch real soon. Shit, you and me, we've got a lot of catching up to do."

Mitch eased the handset into the cradle. His head was throbbing. His throat was parched. *He'll ask for money next time,* he thought. He slowly hoisted himself out of bed and checked the caller ID. Blocked.

Why now? he wondered. *Why does this have to happen right now?*

"The great thing about giving a story to the media," Chief Deputy Bill Tatum said, "is all the helpful leads you get. One guy called to tell me it was Jorge Campos."

John Marlin frowned. "Who's Jorge Campos?"

"Used to be the goalie for the Mexican national soccer team," Bobby Garza said. "Big celebrity down there. He's an assistant coach now, I think. I guess he decided to give up all that fame and fortune for odd jobs here in the States."

They were in the conference room at the sheriff's department, drinking coffee, deciding what to do next. Marlin had already told them what he'd learned from Ignacio: that the body was possibly that of Rodolfo, last name unknown, from Ciudad Acuña. He might have owned a small white truck with a camper shell, much like Junior Barstow's. He might've been working recently on a large ranch. The question: Was any of it accurate?

Tatum said, "Another goofball was absolutely certain it was Ricardo Montalban. I don't know why I even bothered, but I said, 'No, this guy's much too young, plus Ricardo Montalban is dead.' He said, 'Yeah, I know, I heard about it on the news last night.'"

"Except he's not dead," Garza replied.

"Montalban? He's not?"

"Nope. Still going strong."

"Really? I thought he was dead."

Marlin said, "Maybe we should track down Tattoo. See if he can shed any light on this."

"That little guy, on the other hand, *is* dead," Garza said. "Committed suicide, if I remember right. A long time ago."

"Huh. Well, then, I guess he won't be very helpful."

Garza leaned forward, getting serious. "Okay, I spoke to Henry, and he sent a blood sample to the state lab in Austin yesterday afternoon. They conducted a little test called immunodiffusion—species identification, basically—and what we now know is the blood spatter at the scene was from a deer. Good old-fashioned venison."

"Wouldn't be so hard to get," Tatum said. "Shoot one. Find a fresh carcass on the side of the road."

"Keep going," Garza said. "What happened next? How did he create high-velocity spatter? It's not like he could just drip some blood around and make it look authentic."

"Maybe he took the carcass—or part of it—back to the scene," Marlin said. "Then he shot through it."

"Great minds." Garza smiled. "I already had Henry try to replicate the spatter by doing exactly that. Didn't match our pattern at all."

"Maybe the carcass wasn't fresh enough," Marlin said.

"Yeah, there are about a million variables that could change the outcome. The type of weapon used, the firing distance. But Henry tried it several ways and here's the problem: Each time he shot, he ended up with scattered fragments of deer flesh and hair, not just blood. At the scene, all we had was blood."

"Twenty-three years as a cop," Tatum said, "and I think this is the weirdest conversation I've ever had."

"Let's talk about glass, then," Garza said. "Henry says it came from a basic household-type single-pane window, so if we can find a house with a broken window, we might just have our original crime scene. Assuming they haven't replaced the glass."

Tatum said, "I'll check with repairmen in the area. Get a list of recent customers."

"If it were me," Marlin said, "I'd want to stay off the radar. I'd fix the window myself."

"That means a trip, most likely, to the Home Depot in Marble Falls," Tatum said. "A lot harder to track."

"Does that store have video cameras?" Garza asked.

"No idea. I'll check it out."

"Maybe there'll be a record of the transaction. See if they can pull recent sales of window glass."

"Won't do much good if he paid cash."

"We don't have a lot of options at this point."

"True enough. I'll get on it."

"What about Ernie? You send him back out there?" Garza asked.

Deputy Ernie Turpin had spent the previous evening, until sundown, scouring the crime scene. He was hoping to find a footprint, a tire track, anything that might tell them how the body had been moved onto Ken Bell's ranch.

"Yeah, along with Nicole," Tatum said. "But with the drought, that damn caliche's like pavement right now."

"Just tell them to keep looking, and not just on the main road. Have them spread out and check all the little back roads and trails. Maybe the killer came in on an ATV, or maybe a horse. He damn sure didn't carry the body in there by hand."

"I wouldn't think so."

"Where are we on the phone card the guy was carrying?"

"That remains to be seen. Problem is, the company that issued it is based in Mexico, and I have no idea whether they'll honor our subpoena or not. Then there's the question of where to send the damn subpoena. I've talked to three different people and gotten three different answers. Finally, I just faxed it to one of them and they're supposed to get back to me. Don't hold your breath."

"We really need to ID this guy. That calling card . . ."

Tatum nodded. "I know. It's our best lead. Meanwhile, based on what John told us, I'm gonna send a copy of the photo and the prints to Acuña. Maybe the guy has priors."

"That'd be a nice break. I'll put a BOLO on the truck. In the meantime, John, can you talk to Junior? Let's make sure that truck's his. Maybe he loaned it out or something."

"Will do."

"Then can you expand your canvass a little? Talk to every landowner within, say, a one-mile range. We've gotta figure out how this guy got onto Mr. Bell's property. Somebody had to've seen something."

Red O'Brien hurried from his mailbox, bounded through the front door of his mobile home, and said, "Okay, fuckwad, got any smart-ass comments now?"

He waved an envelope at Billy Don, who was stretched out on the couch, munching a bag of Funyuns, watching a rerun of *Hogan's Heroes.*

"Electric bill?" Billy Don asked.

"What? No. Oops, wrong one. This one here." Red thumped the envelope for emphasis, just to rub Billy Don's nose in it a little. There, in the upper left-hand corner, was an embossed logo: National Weapons Alliance. Beneath that, two muskets, crossed like swords.

"Fast, huh?" Red crowed triumphantly, plopping down into his worn recliner. "Anybody answers an application that quick, you just *know* they got plans for me. I wouldn't be surprised if they want me to head up a new chapter right here in Blanco County. Sorta get folks organized in this area. If you play your cards right, I might still need an assistant. You know, someone to fetch coffee and doughnuts while I'm holding important meetings." Red cackled with glee and said, "Ain't you got anything to say, big man? Cat got your tongue?"

Billy Don remained silent, save for the crunching of his deep-fried snacks.

Red grabbed a fillet knife off the cable-spool coffee table and slit the envelope open. "It's a damn shame you won't be able to make it to the rally," he said, chuckling. "Members only, you know. Gotta keep out the riffraff. Be a lotta nice ladies in attendance, I'm sure. Cold beer. Good food. Oh, and did I mention that Mitch Campbell will be there? Well, of course he will! The whole damn thing's being held on his ranch! Fancy that. Imagine li'l ol' me hanging out with a country-music superstar, telling him all about the song I wrote. Who woulda thought that was even a possibility? Me, that's who."

Crunch, crunch. Billy Don was pretending not to listen.

Red pulled the one-page letter out of the envelope and unfolded it. He couldn't resist one last stab. "Someday, Billy Don, you're gonna learn to trust me. Sure, I've had a few misfires in the past, but this time, ain't nothin' gonna stop me. You should know that by now."

Billy Don offered a guttural grunt, which could mean anything from "You're right" to "My underwear's riding up."

Finally, Red let his eyes fall to the letter. "Dear Mr. O'Brien," he read aloud, unable to keep the pride out of his voice. "Thank you for your interest in the National Weapons Alliance. It is obvious that you've put a great deal of thought into the challenges facing responsible gun owners in today's world. We at the NWA are equally concerned with ongoing threats to the Second Amendment. Unfortunately—"

Red stopped reading. Over on the couch, the munching came to an abrupt halt.

Unfortunately?

Red knew that nothing good ever followed that word. People said things like "Unfortunately, he forgot to set the parking brake" or "Unfortunately, my penis still burns when I urinate."

"What's it say, Red?" Billy Don asked.

Red scanned the next sentence, and he couldn't believe what he was reading. Not only couldn't he believe it, he wasn't quite sure he understood it. "Unfortunately, we feel that some of the unique ideologies you expressed in your application might lead to your ultimate dissatisfaction with the NWA."

"Ideologies?" Billy Don muttered. "What's a ideology?"

Red continued: "After all, our agenda deals solely with firearms ownership, and does not delve into issues such as immigration, terrorism, race relations, or the sanctity of marriage between heterosexual adults. Might we suggest you investigate other, more politically oriented organizations, perhaps one that embraces an archconservative view such as yours? That's one of the great things about our country:

There are plenty of platforms from which one can voice his opinion, be it moderate, mainstream, or otherwise. Best of luck to you."

"Archconservative? The hell's all that mean?" Billy Don asked. "You understand any of it?"

Red released the letter and watched it flutter to the floor. "It means they don't want me in their damn club."

15

TWO MONTHS AFTER young Sabrina Nash met Buddy Thurston, the Hollywood agent, he called her at work.

"I got you an audition."

She could barely hear him above the din of the diner. "What? You're kidding." He'd taken some photos of her, but she'd never expected to hear from him again. It all seemed like such a lark.

"Friend of mine is the showrunner on a sitcom that just got greenlighted. Working title is *Holy Roller*. It's about a nun who lives in Venice."

It was the lunchtime rush; Sabrina had six full tables. "Uh, that sounds interesting, Buddy, but I don't speak any Italian."

"Not *that* Venice. The one in California. You know what *that* place is like, so obviously the nun would have her work cut out for her. She spends her time skating around the boardwalk, helping people with their problems. See, people around there won't come to church, so she takes the religion to them. Runs into all sorts of weird characters in the process."

"She, uh, skates?"

"Clever, huh? Wants to blend in. Be hip, you know?"

Sabrina wasn't an expert on television programming—far from it—but it sounded sort of bizarre. "So . . . I'd be a nun?" She didn't know much about Catholics, either. They went to mass. They confessed a lot. They ate little crackers and drank red wine. That summed up her expertise on the subject.

"Well, no, you'd be playing the other starring role. The nun's sister. They're roommates, living in a small apartment. Their landlord is a gay Jewish man who wants to be a fashion designer. Your boyfriend is a lovable idiot who's a professional surfer."

"Boyfriend? So my character isn't a nun?"

"Uh, no. Just the one nun."

"What is she, then?"

"A dancer."

"Really?" That part, Sabrina would admit, sounded intriguing. "Like, what, a ballerina? A chorus girl?"

A pause. "An exotic dancer."

"You mean a stripper?"

"Well, yeah. But her sister's a nun! So you can see the possibilities for humor. I've read the pilot. Funny stuff. Sort of a clash between values."

A customer was waving to Sabrina, signaling for more coffee. The manager, behind the counter, gave her a hurry-it-up gesture. This was all so ridiculous. Just up and go to California? Try to become a star? Girls from Andrews, Texas, didn't do things like that. Girls from Andrews became waitresses or bank tellers or grocery clerks, and they married quiet, hardworking men who sometimes lost a finger or a toe out in the oilfield. They raised their children and kept a clean house and didn't chase crazy dreams that would only end in failure and disappointment.

"I don't know, Buddy. I appreciate all the trouble you're going to, but I'm not an actress. I've never even been in a school play."

"So you'll take a few lessons."

"But—"

"Believe me, it's not a problem. Think Farrah Fawcett can act? Or Bo Derek? Think Suzanne Somers has an Oscar in her future? Just be yourself, you'll be great."

Then there was the whole idea of playing a stripper. Not that Sabrina would ever get the role, but if she did—if somehow the planets lined up right or the producers were taking drugs and couldn't see that Sabrina was completely unqualified and wholly incapable of carrying it off—her mother would have a stroke.

"A stripper, huh?"

"That a problem?"

"I don't know."

"If it is, now's the time to tell me."

"Is she . . . uh, does she . . ." Sabrina was having difficulty voicing her concern.

"What?"

She spat it out. "Is she a slut?"

"No, no, nothing like that. Well, okay, yeah, maybe a little. But it's not like you'd be dancing around a pole. There won't be any scenes inside the club. You'd have to wear tight T-shirts, short skirts, a bikini now and then, things like that. Just look gorgeous. It's no worse than anything else on TV. Trust me."

"I do, Buddy. But I just don't know."

She heard him take a patient breath. "There are plenty of girls out here—thousands—who would kill for this role. Hell, they'd kill just to audition. But my friend saw your head shot and fell in love. He wants to meet you."

Sabrina had a disconcerting thought. "I'm not sleeping with him! I've heard how things work out there and—"

"No, of course not. It's not like that. I promise."

She hesitated.

"Worst case," Buddy said, "you fly out, give it a shot, and you don't get the part. What's the harm? You make a little vacation of it, meet a few celebrities, go home happy."

Sabrina was starting to think it might be an exciting adventure. She'd never been to California. Heck, she'd never even been outside of Texas.

So she said yeah, why not, she'd go.

She left four days later.

Her first day in Hollywood, she actually met Scott Baio.

The second day, she got the part.

Six months later, despite scathing reviews, *Holy Roller* rocketed to the top of the ratings, and Sabrina Nash was the hottest commodity in the entertainment industry.

Seventy-two-year-old Junior Barstow was slicing the skinned carcass of a four-foot blackneck garter snake into small segments when John Marlin rapped on the open front door of Barstow's double-wide. The sagging trailer wasn't Barstow's residence, it was the main showroom for the Snake Farm & Indian Artifact Showplace, of which Barstow was the proud sole proprietor.

Uninformed tourists traveling Highway 281 south of Johnson City viewed the place as just another cheesy roadside attraction. In reality, Barstow possessed a massive collection of exotic and indigenous snakes that was the envy of many reputable zoos and nature centers, and his extensive display of Native American artifacts—from common arrowheads and rare Clovis points to hand axes and centuries-old pottery—drew curious archaeologists and anthropologists from all over the Southwest.

Not that Barstow made a living on the Showplace alone. He was also a taxidermist and a butcher of wild game. Squatting beside the trailer, a decrepit Blue Bell ice cream truck—paint peeling, no wheels—provided cold storage for deer carcasses during the hunting season.

"Hey there, John," Junior said, looking up from the cutting board. "Come on in."

Marlin stepped inside. "How you doing, Junior?" The walls of the trailer had been removed, so the interior was one large room. Hundreds of small glass cases, each with a snake or two inside, were carefully arranged throughout the space. There were cases on countertops, on desks, on shelves that reached to the ceiling.

"Having a little snack. You hungry?"

Near the cutting board, a skillet bubbled with hot oil. Next to that, a bowl of flour. Marlin had always wondered what Junior did with a snake when it went to that great field of plump mice in the sky. Now he knew.

"Thanks," he said, patting his stomach, "but I had a big breakfast."

"Suit yourself," Junior said, holding a shiny chunk of gray meat in the air. "*Thamnophis cyrtopsis ocellatus.* Fancy name for a common little snake like this, ain't it? Damn tasty, though. Even raw."

Junior popped the piece of flesh into his mouth, and, as he chewed, Marlin tried to keep his stomach from cartwheeling.

"Listen, Junior, I got a question about your Nissan truck."

Junior said, "Already sold it. Whatcha need another truck for?"

"When'd you sell it?"

"Last week. Thursday, I think. Bought it for five hundred about a month ago. Didn't really need it—already got my own truck—but I couldn't pass up a deal like that. Sold it for eight. If I'd known you wanted it—"

"Who'd you sell it to?"

"Spanish guy."

Bingo. It had to be Rodolfo. Marlin didn't point out that *Spanish* people were from Spain. Junior, like a lot of old-timers, tended to refer to Hispanic people as "Spanish," simply because they spoke that language. Which was akin to calling a U.S. citizen "English."

"You remember his name?"

By now, Junior had picked up on the fact that Marlin's interest had nothing to do with buying the truck. "Not off the toppa my head. Why? What's up?"

"Part of a case I'm working on. It's important. Was his name Rodolfo?"

Junior squinted hard, thinking. "You know, I think it was. That sounds about right."

"Did you get a last name?"

"'Fraid not. Just signed the pink slip. He wasn't here but about five minutes. Never even test-drove it."

In Texas, a private individual could sell a vehicle by merely signing the back of the title. The buyer then had twenty days to file the proper paperwork and officially transfer ownership. Rodolfo apparently hadn't completed that chore yet. Chances were, he never would have; not if he was an illegal alien.

Marlin removed a folded piece of paper from his breast pocket, a blow-up of one of the photos from the man's wallet. "This the guy?"

Junior studied it. "Yep." Then he frowned. "I ain't in trouble, am I? He been poaching in my truck?"

"No, it's not that. You seen the news lately?"

Junior squinted again, then his eyes went wide. "This the boy they found on Ken's place?"

"Yes, sir."

He took another look at the photo, then passed it back. "Damn shame. Wish I had more to tell ya. He didn't speak much English."

"But he could speak some?"

"A little."

"Did he say where he lived?"

"Nope. Like I say, he wasn't here but a few minutes. We didn't get into a lot of small talk. When he left, he turned south, toward Blanco, if that's worth anything."

Probably not, Marlin thought. Rodolfo could've been driving to a job site, or to Highway 290 on his way to Austin for the supplies Marlin had seen in the back of the truck.

On the other hand, the truck might finally yield Rodolfo's full identity, if they could find the title, a driver's license, or any other document with a name on it. He'd call Garza and give him a progress report. Then he'd return to the scene and wait for a tow truck to move the vehicle to the sheriff's department. Safeguard any evidence—forensic or otherwise—that might be found inside. One step at a time.

16

"HEY, BILLY DON," Red said. "I got a idea."

"Forget it."

"Would you stop that?"

"Stop what?"

"Saying 'forget it' before I even tell ya what the idea is."

"Force of habit. Based on nothing except the quality of some of your previous ideas."

"It's annoying as hell. Plus, it's bad manners."

"Yeah, right. You're gonna teach me about manners?"

"You could use a few lessons in that area, you know. Besides, just shut up and listen, will ya? You don't have to worry, because this idea don't involve you at all."

"My favorite kind."

They were in Red's trailer, in their usual spots: Red in the ratty recliner, Billy Don sprawled out on the couch. Red rarely sat on the couch anymore because the springs were shot. Billy Don's sheer bulk had taken all the play out of them. It was like sitting in a damn bucket, the way the couch swallowed your ass when you sat down. Red had no use for it.

On the other hand, the recliner—which Red had officially declared off-limits to Billy Don—was still a comfortable place to watch football, drink beer, take a nap, or daydream about a better life. A life, say, in which Red was a revered songwriter, known far and wide for his way with words and colorful personality. Like Willie Nelson, sort of, but without the pot. No, Red wasn't ready to give up just yet—not when he had a surefire number-one smash tucked away in his back pocket, just raring to go.

Screw the NWA, he thought. *Who needs 'em?* He'd think of a better way to get his song into Mitch Campbell's hands. He already had something brewing, though maybe the idea wasn't all that brilliant. Just a place to start.

Red ignored Billy Don's last comment and said, "What I oughta do—tell me what you think—is send Mitch Campbell a strip-o-gram."

Billy Don stared at him.

"You know," Red said, "like people sometimes get on their birthdays. The gal sings 'Happy Birthday' while she's getting nekkid. Only instead, she'd sing my song. When she was done, she'd give him a cassette with the song on it. Clever, huh?"

"That's the idea?"

"It's *one* idea."

"Real smart. I think that's how Alan Jackson got his big break. Sent a hooker to some Nashville hotshot."

Red took a deep breath. "You don't have to get all smart-ass on me. I'm serious about this, and if you were any kind of friend, you'd quit teasing me and try to help out."

Billy Don didn't answer, which was standard when Red chastised him. The big man had delicate feelings.

"Okay," Red added, "I'll admit that the stripper's not such a great way to go about it. But I gotta come up with something unique. I'm sure people are throwing songs at Mitch all the time. What I need is something unusual, something creative. Something that will make him actually listen to my song."

Neither of them spoke for several minutes, until Red had another brainstorm. "Hey, maybe I could call and leave the song on his answering machine. Then he'd *have* to listen to it."

"He's probably unlisted."

"I imagine he is. He's famous and all."

"You got his phone number?"

"Well . . . no."

"Know anybody at the phone company?"

"No."

"Got any way whatsoever of getting his number?"

"No."

"Then why are we even talking about it?"

Billy Don's attitude was starting to piss Red off. "Okay, fine. Instead of shooting my ideas down, why don't you come up with one of your own?"

Billy Don swung his large feet off the couch and sat up straight. "No problem. You want a idea, I got a idea. Remember that boring movie we watched last weekend? The one with Robert De Niro?"

"Robert Duvall," Red corrected him. It was called *Tender Mercies*. One of Red's all-time favorites. Billy Don had given it a thumbs-down because there hadn't been any explosions. "What about it?"

"He played a musician in Oklahoma," Billy Don said.

"Texas."

"Had a problem with drugs."

"Booze."

"Lived with that divorced lady."

"Widow."

"I think it was Jessica Lange."

"Tess Harper."

"She owned a café."

"Motel. With gas pumps out front."

"And remember those kids in the truck?"

"It was a van."

"Whatever. Point is, those boys had a band and they'd wrote a couple songs of their own. And when they wanted Robert Duvall's help, they didn't come up with some sorta gimmick. They didn't send no strippers or pester him on the phone or nothing like that. They just went right up to him and talked to him, man to man. Told him who they were and what they were doing."

Red paused for a second, thinking, *Maybe Billy Don's on to something here.* "Sounds like a waste of time."

Billy Don grunted. "Well, you want my opinion, that's the way you oughta do it. Hell, Mitch Campbell lives right down on Cypress Mill Road, everybody knows that. Just go out and see him. Talk to him like a normal person. Worth a shot."

Red mulled it over. That approach was so damn simple, it just might work. There was only one other problem he could think of. "What if he's got a big gate or something? What if he's got body-guards or Doberman pinschers? What if I can't get in?"

Billy Don went back to a prone position, his thinking done for the afternoon. "Well, if that's the case, yeah, you're shit outta luck. But you won't know till you try, will ya?"

The restaurant where Dale Stubbs met Congressman Glenn Dobbins for lunch was a little too citified for Stubbs' tastes. Linen napkins. Crystal stemware. Dim lighting. Some kind of hippie flute music in the background. And along came a light-footed waiter who clasped his hands and said, in a near whisper, "Hello, gentlemen, my name is Quentin, and I'll be your server today." Big smile. As if they were on the brink of a glorious long-term relationship. Queer as a cucumber sandwich.

Then the menu. Goddamn train wreck. Sure, you could get grilled lamb loin with roasted shallot sauce, creamy polenta, fennel-mint puree, and marinated white bean relish, but just ask for a goddamn chicken-fried steak and watch Quentin's eyes glaze over. Ain't happening, my friend. Didn't really matter. Stubbs wasn't all that hungry anyway. He asked for "anything made of beef and a cold domestic beer."

He'd debated flying down from Dallas for what, in essence, would amount to a ten-minute conversation, but this was much too important to discuss over the phone. There was too much at stake. Stubbs' butt, for one thing. The entire political agenda of the NWA, for another.

Because, much to Stubbs' dismay, the cops in Blanco County hadn't fallen for it. They'd declared the wetback to be a homicide victim. No, it hadn't made the news in Dallas, of course, but bright and early this morning, Stubbs had read all about it with sweaty palms on a Web site for a small newspaper called the *Blanco County Record*.

Dead Mexicans, it appeared, were front-page material out in the boondocks. Stop the presses! Chico kicked the bucket! And he had help!

The cops were asking for information. Looking for witnesses. Wondering if anybody knew this poor dead spic. An unfortunate turn of events, yeah, but not all that unexpected.

It made Stubbs realize that he might not be able to contain this thing himself. He might eventually need the resources that the congressman could bring to bear. So Stubbs, like it or not, would have to fill him in.

The congressman cut a pork medallion in half with his fork and said, "So. You said it was urgent. What's up?"

Dobbins had a head full of silver hair, a few deep wrinkles around the eyes, but otherwise, he didn't look so different than he had forty years ago, back when they'd attended Southern Methodist together. Dobbins was nothing but your garden-variety good-old-boy, really, but, like Stubbs, he had the charm and the smarts and the savvy to rise to the top. He knew exactly how the game was played. Hell, he'd become a master at it.

Stubbs leaned over the table, which was in a corner, away from eavesdropping ears. "You and me've been through a lot, ain't we, Glenn?"

Dobbins chuckled. "That's the God's honest truth."

"We got ourselves into a tight spot a few years back with that, uh, shooting. But we both did what needed to be done. We're both willing to . . . make certain sacrifices for the greater good."

Dobbins nodded thoughtfully. "Absolutely."

"Well, I hate to spring this on you right now. The timing is horrible. But we've got another situation on our hands."

Dobbins paused with a fork full of green apple and dried apricot chutney. "Tell me."

Stubbs took a gulp of his beer, then spilled the entire story. Dobbins didn't interrupt or show much of a reaction. He simply listened. When Stubbs was finished, Dobbins said, "This could've been handled differently. Dammit, you should've called me right away."

"I didn't want to trouble you with it."

"Fuck that. My future's at stake here, you know. Everything we've both worked for."

"I think it'll be fine. But I wanted you to know, just in case."

Dobbins sat silently for several moments. "You keep a lid on this thing, you hear me? Just like before. Do whatever you need to do. And keep me posted, goddammit. I can't afford for things to go bad."

They're already bad, Stubbs thought.

17

BACK IN HIS office at the sheriff's department, Marlin looked up a phone number, dialed it, and got no response, not even an answering machine.

Next, he pulled a tall, thick book off a shelf. He'd gotten it from the tax appraiser's office, and it was a very handy item on those rare occasions when he needed it.

The book contained large foldout maps with plats and parcel numbers for every tract of land in Blanco County. Some of the maps contained hundreds of plats, others contained just a few—it all depended on the size of the properties represented on a particular map.

Marlin could take a given parcel number, plug it into the county tax rolls on his computer, and seconds later have the owner's name, mailing address, and phone number. A parcel number never changed, even when a property sold, so it was the easiest way to obtain up-to-date information.

In his day-to-day operations as a game warden, Marlin seldom referred to the book, because he already knew most of the county's ranchers and owners of larger hunting tracts. In this case—dealing with numerous owners of smaller properties, as he knew he would be—it would surely prove helpful.

He flipped through the pages until he found the map containing Ken Bell's ranch, on the south side of Cypress Mill Road. The ranch—one hundred acres of rolling hills and gently sloping valleys dotted with live oak and juniper, mountain laurel and redbud, cypress trees standing tall along the creek banks—was reduced to a plat no larger than Marlin's palm.

He laid the open book on his desk and grabbed a pencil from a drawer. According to the legend at the bottom of the page, one mile was equal to ten inches. He marked the crime scene on Ken Bell's property as a center point, then drew a loose circle with a ten-inch radius. By his count, the circle encompassed all or part of ninety-four parcels. This was going to be a bigger job than he'd thought.

Directly to the east of Bell's ranch was Shady Hollow, the subdivision Marlin had canvassed the day before. Thirty-two tracts in total, and Marlin had already spoken to twenty-six of the owners. These people were the closest to the crime scene, but none of them had reported hearing a shot. What Marlin needed was somebody who had *seen* something.

Subtracting the twenty-six from the day before left sixty-eight properties, the bulk of them in another subdivision, Wildflower Creek, to the west of Bell's ranch, two tracts over. Marlin was familiar with that neighborhood, and he knew it contained quite a few empty tracts. At least half of them were unsold, or the absentee owners hadn't built on them yet. That would reduce the target number quite a bit. All in all, he estimated there were forty owners he'd need to speak to. Enough that he'd tackle the job by phone, rather than in person.

He was making a list of the relevant parcel numbers when a soft voice said, "Hey, good-lookin'."

Marlin glanced up and saw Nicole standing in the doorway to his office, holding a large bottle of water. Her auburn hair was pulled back in a braid, her face still flushed from the summer heat, her khaki deputy's shirt speckled with perspiration.

"Hey, yourself. When'd you get here?"

"Just now. We're taking a quick break for lunch, then right back to it."

"Any luck?"

She blew the bangs out of her face and sat in the lone chair in front of Marlin's desk. "Absolutely nothing. If I didn't know better, I'd say the body was brought in with a helicopter. We haven't found a footprint, a trampled weed, nothing. Nor do I expect to. Ground's like rock. It'd take a jackhammer to leave a mark out there." She fanned herself with one hand. "Heard you found the victim's truck."

Marlin shrugged. "Well, I didn't find it, it was there all along, but we hadn't picked up on it yet. Henry's going through it right now. Maybe it'll tell us something."

She nodded and took a big drink of water. "God, this AC feels good. Mind if I take my shirt off?"

That was another great thing about Nicole: a playful sense of humor. But she was discreet, too, and never made that type of remark when someone might overhear. The other deputies were well aware that she and Marlin were seeing each other, but nobody commented on it.

"You do that," he replied, "and it's only going to get hotter in here."

She gave him a campy wink. "Better wait till later, then." She noticed the map on his desk. "What're you working on now?"

"Potential witnesses."

"Widening the net, huh?"

"For what it's worth. Seems like anybody that knows anything would've come forward by now. Can't hurt to check, though."

She leaned forward in her chair to get a better view of the map. "That's a lot of people."

"It's not so bad. Plenty of those lots are vacant. Can you imagine covering an area that size in the middle of Austin? You'd be talking about tens of thousands of people."

She smiled. "Good reason not to live in Austin."

Marlin's direct line buzzed. When he answered, Phil Colby said, "We still on for lunch?"

"Definitely. Twenty minutes?"

"Works for me. And I've got 'em, in case you were wondering. Three to look at."

Marlin felt his face getting warm. "Okay, excellent."

"Melinda says these are the most popular styles."

"Good."

"But she has a lot more to choose from if you don't like 'em. I think you will, though. They look good to me. Of course, what the hell do I know about it?"

Colby was waiting for Marlin to comment, so Marlin said, "Let's talk at lunch, okay?"

"Can't talk?"

"Nope."

"Let me guess. Is she standing right there?"

"Yep."

Colby laughed. "Oh, this is too perfect. Put her on the line. Let me tell her what's on the agenda for today. Maybe she'll want to join us."

"Funny."

"Loosen up, bud. You hear about the guy who went to a psychiatrist and said, 'I'm a teepee, I'm a wigwam, I'm a teepee, I'm a wigwam'? The shrink said, 'Relax, you're two tents.'"

Marlin laughed and said, "I'll see you at Ronnie's." When he hung up, Nicole was staring at him.

"You okay?"

"What? Yeah, why?"

"You look flushed."

"Just a little warm in here."

She appraised him for a few more seconds, then returned her attention to the map. "What's this here?" She was pointing to a small star Marlin had drawn on Cypress Mill Road.

"That's where the truck was parked."

"And who's this?" Now she was pointing to the plat directly beside the star. The forty-seven acres between Ken Bell's ranch and Wild flower Creek. The landowner whose mailbox had an NWA decal on the side.

"Man's name is J. B. Crowley," he said, "and I'd sure like to talk to him. I knocked on his door about thirty minutes ago, after the truck got towed in. He wasn't home. I left a note. I just tried to call him."

"You know him?"

"Never met him. According to the tax rolls, he bought the place sometime last year. Before that, he didn't own any property in Blanco County. Either he rented, or he's new around here."

Nicole continued to ponder the map in silence. Marlin followed her eyes, and he could see that she was focusing on the large property due north of Crowley's place, on the other side of Cypress Mill Road. More than two thousand acres. He didn't need to access the records to identify *that* property.

Nicole reached out and touched the plat. "Mitch Campbell's ranch, right? You gonna talk to him?"

Marlin didn't know the answer to that question yet. Granted, a small wedge of Mitch Campbell's property fell within the circle he'd drawn. But Marlin knew that Campbell's home—the one that had set so many tongues to wagging with speculation and gossip when it was being built—was well to the rear of the large ranch, and the entrance to the ranch was a quarter mile west of the gate to Bell's place. Anyone coming or going from Campbell's would not have driven past Rodolfo's old truck sitting on the roadside. Marlin seriously doubted that Campbell or any of his guests would have any information to share.

Marlin shrugged. "Possibly. He's not real high on my list right now."

"But this is your big chance. I figured you'd want to meet your fearless leader."

He looked at her. Joking? She was smiling, but there was no warmth in it.

"My *fearless leader*?" he said.

"Yeah, the leader of the gun nuts. Isn't he your hero?" She clutched a hand melodramatically to her chest. "And he's such a handsome young buck. When he struts around in his tight Wranglers, my heart just goes pitter-pat."

She wasn't smiling now. In fact, her face was tense.

"Are you pissed off about something?" he asked.

"You gonna talk to him or not?"

"I don't know yet. If I need—"

But she had turned and was walking out the door. "Bunch of macho bullshit," she said.

"Nicole?"

She continued down the hallway.

"Nicole?"

Marlin was baffled. *What the hell was that all about?*

18

SABRINA NASH LIVED in a loft in downtown Austin, a small two-bedroom place she'd found six years ago, after the divorce. Fortunately, she'd gotten in at the right time. Lofts had been all the rage for the past several years, but as far as she was concerned, the only difference between a loft and a condo—other than the open floor plan—was the price. It was all marketing. "Loft" sounded, well, loftier. People paid more for them. Not that condos were cheap; anything in the city center was expensive these days, given Austin's unabated growth. Even homes in the suburbs were selling for twice what they would've brought ten years ago. Software designers and salespeople and account reps flocked here from California and Arizona and who knew where else, and they didn't bat an eye at prices in the mid six figures. Property values skyrocketed, and taxes went right with them.

In the fourteen years Sabrina had lived in Austin, she'd seen a lot of changes for the worse. Crime had become a serious problem. Traffic was a nightmare. Pollution was now a genuine concern, with a dull haze hanging over the skyline on "ozone action days." What had once been widely regarded as the nicest city in Texas—a funky ultra-liberal college town with a personality all its own—was losing its unique identity. It was becoming a land of strip malls and tract homes, a smaller version of Dallas or Houston. A Starbucks on every corner. A Home Depot over here, a Target over there, a McDonald's out near the street for easy drive-through access. Anywhere, USA.

Sabrina had thought about returning to West Texas. Her mother was still in Andrews, still living in the same small home Sabrina had grown up in. But Sabrina couldn't leave Austin. She couldn't bring herself to stray that far from Jake's grave. Maybe someday.

She was in a better mood now after her meeting with Marcus Roark, and she'd run a few errands on her way home, including a stop at the supermarket. She'd just come through the front door when the phone rang.

"Sabrina, it's Byron Gladwell."

Harry's boss. Nice man, though a bit of a shrinking violet. She'd met him on several occasions over the years—various parties and charity events—but they'd never spoken on the phone. "Oh, hi, Byron, how are you?"

A pause. "Uh, freaking out a little, to be honest. Listen, I hate to bother you with this, and I don't mean to be an imposition . . ."

"Yes?"

"Do you have any idea where Harry is?"

"Um, no, but I talked to him late last night. Early this morning."

"Yeah? Did he sound a little, well, insane?"

Sabrina let out a laugh. "Not any more than usual. Why? What's going on?"

"I'm having a tough time tracking him down. We had a disagreement about his work yesterday, and I haven't heard from him since. Lately he's been acting kind of . . . I don't know . . . erratic. In my opinion. Nothing to be concerned about, I'm sure."

Duane Rankin, Sabrina thought. *This ordeal has Harry tied up in knots.* Obviously, he hadn't told Gladwell about the hearing on Monday. Just like Harry to keep that sort of thing to himself. Sabrina debated telling Gladwell what the problem was, but she decided against it for now.

"He miss a deadline?" she asked. She knew from sixteen years as Harry's wife that, in the newspaper business, nothing was as critical as a deadline. If Gladwell was in a panic, Harry must have missed one. Which would be a first.

"I guess you haven't seen today's paper. I had to scramble to fill his space. Now I'm starting to worry about Sunday's edition. You know how important Sunday is."

She did indeed. Harry always saved his best work for Sunday. "I'm sure he'll be in touch." She knew she didn't sound convincing.

"If you hear from him, please have him call me, will you?"

"Of course."

They hung up, and Sabrina immediately dialed Harry's home number.

He refused to own a cell phone, because the mining of tantalum—an extremely valuable ore used in the manufacture of capacitors for mobile phones and other high-tech devices—was financing a bloody civil war in the Democratic Republic of Congo. The violence was bad enough, Harry said, but miners were illegally plundering protected national parks for tantalum. In the process, they were destroying habitat for the endangered mountain gorilla—and to make matters even worse, they were killing the great apes for food. Horrible stuff, and your average American didn't know a thing about it.

Harry knew, though. He knew, and he acted on that sort of information, and that was one of the things that set Harry apart. Sabrina had always respected him for his strong convictions, even though she didn't always agree with them.

On the other hand, sometimes Harry was so ardent in his beliefs, he became a real pain in the ass. Rational discussion became impossible; he'd refuse to even listen to the other side of a debate. He'd categorically dismiss every word or thought that came from someone who held an opposing view.

The Harrys of the world would never be a part of the solution. They were too unwilling to meet with their enemies, to open the lines of communication and find a middle ground. "Compromise" was a dirty word, as sour on their tongues as the taste of defeat.

Harry, just like his counterparts on the far right, was fearful that the smallest acquiescence would be his undoing, that he'd lose everything he'd battled so hard to accomplish. He wouldn't budge an inch, and when your opponent was equally dug in, nobody made any progress at all.

That was Harry. As ornery as a West Texas mule.

Like this recent skirmish with Gladwell. As Harry's phone rang, Sabrina wondered what *that* was all about. She had to chide herself when she realized she was thinking, *Whatever it was, it was probably Harry's fault.*

And for Harry to miss a deadline? Amazing, because nothing was more important to Harry than his cartoons. That eight-by-eight space was his soapbox, his chance to shine a light on all that was wrong with the world. Other than seven years ago, when he'd taken a leave of absence following Jake's death, nothing had ever silenced the pen of Harry Jenkins. Not illness, not holidays, not travel.

She replayed the late-night telephone conversation with Harry in her head. Had she missed something? He'd made a few cynical re-marks, had come across as his typical strident self. Was he in worse shape than it had seemed? With his personality, it was hard to say.

Answer the damn phone, Harry.

Mitch Campbell's ranch had a gate, all right. An eight-footer, con-structed from fancy wrought iron, with a likeness of a longhorn bull in the center of it. On either side of the gate was a massive limestone wall running for about thirty feet down the fence line, with a large Texas star crafted from sandstone in the center of each wall. *Beautiful work,* Red thought. *Somebody made a fortune on the masonry.* To the left side of the driveway, Red noticed, was one of those electronic giz-mos, like a telephone keypad, where you punch in a code to get through.

"What the hell do we do now?" he asked.

He and Billy Don were in Red's ancient truck, parked on the shoulder just past the gate. It was three in the afternoon, not a cloud in the sky, and the AC was struggling to keep up with the heat. Red had always heard that musicians slept till noon, so he had waited un-til a decent hour to come calling. Now it appeared that it was futile anyway.

Billy Don swiveled in the passenger seat and peered through the rear window. "Don't see a mailbox nowheres."

"He's probably got a big box at the post office. For all his fan mail."

Red was starting to wonder why nothing ever seemed to go right for him. He felt he was a reasonably intelligent person. He had ambition. Drive. The guts to take a chance now and again. He had great ideas all the time, but they never quite panned out, as if bad luck and bad timing conspired against him. As a result, he lived in a dilapidated mobile home that was hardly fit to serve as a weekend hunting cabin. He drove a 1972 Ford pickup held together by Bondo, rust, and baling wire. He could barely make his bills, and his diet consisted primarily of deer he poached from the roadside and varmints he trapped in his backyard. It was depressing as hell, really. This wasn't the kind of life he'd envisioned for himself when he dropped out of high school.

"Wanna hang around for a while?" Billy Don asked. "Maybe we'll catch him coming or going."

Red let out a sigh. "Hell, for all we know, he's up in Nashville or out in L.A. We could be here for days. Let's just go on home."

"You sure?"

"Yeah." Red didn't want to put any more effort into this fiasco. It was a pipe dream. A wild goose chase. A castle in the sky. He'd been foolish to ever get his hopes up. What chance did he have to become an authentic hero, like Mitch Campbell?

He wrapped a sweaty hand around the steering wheel and started to make a U-turn, but he glanced in his rearview mirror and saw a vehicle approaching. He waited for it to pass by.

But the vehicle, a shiny midnight blue Ford Expedition, didn't pass by. It slowed and pulled into Mitch Campbell's entrance, stopping in front of the keypad.

"That's gotta be him!" Billy Don squealed. "Hurry up, Red! Go! Go!"

Red was suddenly stricken with a case of nerves. His hands were quaking, just as they did before he poached a big buck. "Come with me."

"What?"

"Come with me. I might need your help."

"Really?" There was astonishment in the big man's voice at being asked.

"Yeah. In case I start to screw up."

Billy Don nodded, his face serious. "Okay. Okay. You'll do fine. Got your cassette?"

Red patted his breast pocket. "Right here."

"Then let's do this thing."

They simultaneously popped their doors open and piled out—just in time to see the SUV pulling through the gate. Billy Don hollered and waved his arms frantically, but the vehicle receded onto the ranch, the driver obscured by windows that were tinted pure black. Red stood on the hot asphalt and watched the gate swing shut.

And that was that.

He was too damn late. He'd come *this* close, and he'd blown it by jacking around. He yanked the cassette from his pocket and dropped it onto the roadway. He raised his foot, ready to stomp the song to smithereens, and that's when Billy Don said, "Hold on a sec."

The Expedition's brake lights had come on. The SUV came to a stop, then began to slowly reverse. The gate swung open again, and the SUV backed past it, until it was outside the fence.

Red picked his cassette up off the ground.

"Do it, Red!" Billy Don hissed. "Get moving!"

The Expedition was idling in place.

Red began to walk toward it, certain the SUV would pull forward again and leave him in a cloud of dust.

It didn't.

Red was ten yards away. Then five. Then he was right next to the driver's window, trying to see through the smoky glass. "Mr. Campbell? That you?"

Nothing happened. Red fidgeted with the cassette in his hands. He felt stupid talking to a man he couldn't see. "I was wondering if I might have a word with you. I know you're busy and all, but—"

The vehicle lurched slightly as the driver shifted into park. Then the window began to slide down . . . and Red saw the familiar face of Mitch Campbell. He was wearing a feed-store cap, a black T-shirt, and sunglasses. But it was him. It was definitely him!

Red was wishing he could remember what those boys in the van had said to Robert Duvall. Too late now. He'd have to make it up on his own. "How you doing, sir? It's an honor to meet you. Me and Billy

Don is big fans of your music. Far as I'm concerned, you're an American legend."

Mitch Campbell didn't reply. He didn't smile or nod or acknowledge Red's presence in any way.

Red noticed a case of expensive whiskey riding on the passenger seat. An open can of beer was lodged in a cup holder built into the dash. There were three empties on the floorboard.

The silence was awkward. Red didn't know what to say.

Billy Don was right behind Red now, and he muttered, "Talk to him!"

So Red said, "Mr. Campbell, I know you must get a lotta people shovin' songs at ya, and I hate to bother ya with this, but I've got one here that would be just perfect for you. Now, I ain't a professional songwriter or nothin'—"

Billy Don cleared his throat. "He's selling himself short, Mr. Campbell. It's a real fine song. Patriotic as hell. Gives me chills ever' time I hear it."

Red felt himself flushing with pride. "I made a demo," he said, holding the cassette up for inspection. "Sung it myself. I ain't much of a singer—"

"This time he ain't lyin'," Billy Don said, and they both laughed.

When their chuckling petered out, the uncomfortable silence returned. Mitch Campbell still had not spoken. Behind those dark glasses, he seemed to be inspecting them both—looking down at Red's ratty boots, studying Billy Don's grungy overalls, eyeballing the decrepit Ford truck sitting on the right-of-way.

Then, finally, the singer opened his mouth, and Red expected him to say something like "Sorry, but I already have plenty of material," or "You'll have to speak to my manager," or possibly even "Y'all beat it before I call the cops."

What he said instead was, "Either of you guys ever replace a broken window?"

A broken window?

For a moment, Red was confused by the odd question. Here he was, pitching a song, and Mitch wanted to talk about windows. The worst part of it was, neither he nor Billy Don had ever replaced broken glass. Sure, they'd *hung* plenty of windows. Hundreds of them. Doors, too, and cabinets. They'd installed drywall, ceramic tile, electrical wiring, sinks and countertops, all sorts of shit. They'd framed out entire houses, done plenty of roofing—both shingle and metal—and laid enough brick to cover ten football fields. But replacing broken glass? Nope. Never done it. Not once.

So Red was somewhat surprised when Billy Don stepped forward and said, "Hell yeah. Plenty of times. Need some help?"

19

RONNIE, A QUIET man who made some of the best barbecue in Texas, was busy at the cutting board, but he gave a quick salute when Marlin came into the restaurant. The place was about half full, mostly men in pairs and trios. Marlin waved back, then headed to the rear of the dining area, where his best friend, Phil Colby, was waiting at an isolated table with a sly grin across his face. They'd known each other since they were boys, and they were closer than most brothers. They could read each other better than they could a Blanco County map. Which, in this instance, wasn't necessarily a good thing. Marlin was ready for it.

"Damn, check you out," Colby said. "Don't think I've ever seen a look quite like that before. Sort of a cross between constipation and flat-out terror."

Marlin pulled a chair out and sat down. "That's right, go ahead, get it out of your system."

"I'm just saying, I've seen cheerier faces at a funeral. On the corpse."

"Good one."

"I've seen guys taking paternity tests that weren't as nervous."

"Uh-huh. You about done?"

Colby seemed to be searching for other lines, then said, "Yeah, I guess so. You gonna eat?"

There were no waitresses. Customers placed their orders up front, and then watched as Ronnie sliced generous slabs of brisket or pork loin or several other delectable meats. But, for the first time in his life, Marlin was at Ronnie's without an appetite. His stomach was doing flips. Colby, on the other hand, already had a chopped-beef sandwich in front of him.

"I might just skip lunch today," Marlin said. Before Colby could reply, he added, "And I don't need any smart-ass comments about it."

Colby held both hands up in surrender. "Touchy. You're taking all the fun out of this."

"The fun'll come later. Let's just see what you got."

Colby reached into his shirt pocket, removed three small white cardboard boxes, and placed them reverently on the tabletop. "Okay, all kidding aside, just let me say this. You are making absolutely the right move. I think it's fantastic. You know I only want the best for you, because I love you like a third cousin, twice removed."

"Stop, or I'm gonna get all weepy," Marlin said.

"All right, then. On with the festivities."

Colby opened the first box and dumped a marquis-cut diamond ring into his palm. After a moment's admiration, he read some handwritten notes on the outside of the box. He kept his voice lower now. "This one's just over a half carat. Melinda says it's a VS1, K in color, whatever that means."

Melinda was Colby's semiserious girlfriend, whom he'd been dating for more than a year. Sweet lady, and a savvy businesswoman. She owned a thriving jewelry store in west Austin, and she'd agreed to send some samples home with Colby—after, of course, Colby had sworn her to secrecy. She and Nicole saw each other frequently, when the two couples got together.

"Nice," Marlin said. He took the ring from Colby's hand and held it low, over the table. Being discreet. He didn't want a lot of gossip flying around town.

"Kinda pointy on the ends," Colby commented. "That's the thing I noticed."

The stone shimmered in the light. "You're right," Marlin said. "I mean, it's beautiful, but doesn't it seem like it would get snagged on her clothes?"

"That's exactly what I said to Melinda. She said it's not usually a problem."

Marlin turned the ring, studying it from several angles, then he handed it back. "Okay, good. What else?"

Colby glanced around the restaurant, to make sure they weren't being watched, then he emptied the contents of the second box into his palm. "This one is called a princess cut. Exactly half a carat. It's a VS2, color is I."

Marlin knew right off he didn't like it. It was a square, with beveled edges. Looked clunky and utilitarian. Marlin thought diamonds should look more elegant than this one did. He gave it a quick look anyway, then passed it back.

"No?" Colby asked.

Marlin shook his head.

"Okay," Colby said, "this last one's your basic round stone. Classic, Melinda says. Bigger than the others. Nearly a carat."

Colby removed the ring from the box and, just like that, Marlin immediately knew it was the one. The stone sparkled like morning dew at sunrise, refracting the light, casting magnificent shades of blue and red and green across the tabletop. Colby was still talking, but Marlin didn't hear any of it. He was picturing the ring, with its slender gold band, on Nicole's finger. He started to perspire, but his heart thrummed with an excitement he had never felt before.

"If this is the style you like," Colby was saying, "she has a bunch more like it. Different sizes. You know—smaller. Less expensive."

"This is the one I want." The words seemed to come of their own accord.

Colby grinned at him. "Yeah?"

"Yeah." Marlin couldn't ignore the fact that he was feeling a little light-headed.

"Okay, then. She says she'll sell it to you at cost, but it's still kind of pricey."

"I don't need a discount."

"Yeah, well, she knew you'd say that, and she says you're getting one anyway."

"What do I need to do? Go by the store?"

"Nope. When you're ready, just call with your credit card number and it's all yours. In fact"—Colby produced a velvet-covered jewelry box—"she sent this along, just in case."

He opened the velvet box and inserted the ring into the display slot. He snapped it shut and offered it to Marlin. Then Colby said, in a voice like a television announcer, "It's a big moment, folks. Will he or won't he? Will the hopelessly single game warden accept true love into his heart, or will he doom himself to a lifetime of loneliness and—"

Marlin snatched the box from Colby's hand. "Christ, give me a break. And thank you, by the way."

Colby nodded. "Good choice. You're a wise man." He flipped the top bun off his neglected sandwich and picked up a plastic bottle of barbecue sauce.

Marlin stuffed the velvet box into his pants pocket and switched gears. "You know a guy named J. B. Crowley?"

Colby squeezed the bottle, but nothing came out. "Yeah, I met him once. Major asshole."

"Where'd you meet him?"

"Feed store. Parked his truck right in front of the loading ramp and acted like a jerk when I asked him to move it." He squeezed the bottle again, but the tip was apparently clogged.

"Know where he works?"

"No idea," Colby said, clamping the bottle with both hands. The clog finally loosened—and barbecue sauce jetted out, splattering across Colby's plate and all over the table. Little orange drops of sauce everywhere.

Like blood, Marlin was thinking. *Just like blood.*

Before returning to his office, he drove to his house and removed a single-shot .22 from the gun safe in his closet. Next, he used pliers to pull a bullet free from its casing, creating, in effect, a blank. Then he went to the kitchen and squirted half a cup of ketchup into a small bowl. He mixed water into it—a few drops at a time—until the viscosity was about right. It didn't need to be precise; this was just a trial run. Henry would conduct more extensive testing later, if Marlin's theory proved valid.

He grabbed a small funnel, the bowl, and the rifle and exited through the back door. His pit bull, Geist, was drowsing in the shade, and her tail thumped against the dry grass.

Marlin loaded the rifle, then, pointing it toward the sky, he held the funnel over the muzzle and poured a generous amount of the ketchup mixture straight down the barrel.

It would be a hell of a mess to clean up—he'd likely have to disassemble the entire rifle—and he hoped it would be worth it.

"Here goes nothing," he said.

Geist raised her big head and watched expectantly.

Marlin began to lower the rifle barrel, but he kept it above horizontal, so the contents wouldn't spill out. He aimed at the upper trunk of a massive live oak tree and pulled the trigger.

Immediately he knew that a small piece of the puzzle had fallen into place.

"I can't believe you're such a dumb-ass," Red whispered. "You had to open your mouth and screw everything up."

"How hard could it be?" Billy Don replied, repeating what he'd said several times in Red's truck as they'd followed Mitch up to his enormous ranch house.

"But I don't know what the hell I'm doing!"

"That's never stopped you before."

They were in the bedroom now—Mitch Campbell's actual bedroom, for Chrissakes!—preparing to tackle the job. Mitch, so far, hadn't been much of a host. Hadn't said much. Not real friendly. He'd led them into the house, muttered something about the window getting broken during a party on Saturday night, and retreated to another part of the house, leaving Red and Billy Don alone to do the job.

Mitch had left behind a sack of supplies he'd gotten at the hardware store: window putty and a putty knife, a small plastic bag filled with glazier's points, linseed oil for the window frame, a thin paintbrush for applying the oil, and fine-grit sandpaper. The sheet of glass that had been in the back of the Ford Expedition was now leaning against a wall.

"Shoulda just been honest," Red said, holding the putty knife, tempted to smack Billy Don upside the head with it. He was daunted by the task in front of them. If they didn't get it just right, Mitch would never be willing to hear Red's song.

But Billy Don wasn't listening anymore. He was running a hand along the empty window frame, studying it, making *Uh-huh* and *Yep* sounds, as if he'd seen this sort of thing a thousand times. An old pro. "It'll be a cinch," he pronounced.

"You think?" Red wanted to believe. Oh, how he wanted to believe!

"Trust me. Piece of cake. Won't take but ten minutes."

Two hours later, they were done.

Billy Don, with putty all over his hands, stepped back to admire their work. "What'd I tell ya? Not too shabby, huh?"

Red couldn't believe it. It actually looked pretty damn good. Not perfect, but acceptable. The putty was a tad thick in places, because the new glass hadn't fit as well as it should have, but that wasn't their fault. Overall, yeah, it was a success. They'd done good. The apprehension Red had felt earlier was being pushed aside by excitement. "Well, then, hell—let's clean up and go tell Mitch."

After a few minutes of wandering and calling out, they found him at the other end of the house, in a recreation room that was larger than Red's entire trailer.

Red stood in the doorway, in awe. This place was better than the old Friendly Bar in Johnson City! A nine-foot pool table over here, an old-time Wurlitzer jukebox over there, three refurbished pinball machines against one wall. To the rear was a full-length bar with half a dozen bar stools lined up in front. All sorts of dead animals—exotic creatures that Red couldn't identify—were mounted on the walls. The far wall was one big mirror, which made the room seem even larger.

Over in one corner, Mitch was sitting on a black leather couch, unaware of their presence, staring at a humongous projection television that was tall enough to crowd the ten-foot ceiling. More like a miniature movie theater.

This is what it's like to be a success, Red thought. All the toys a man could want, and then some. Rich as hell, women falling all over you, not a worry in the goddamn world. Red could only dream he'd have it as good someday.

"Mr. Campbell, sir?"

Mitch jumped at the sound of Red's voice. The singer had been watching a twenty-four-hour news station, and now he clicked the huge TV off.

"Didn't mean to startle you," Red said, "but we're all done."

Mitch stood and, to Red, he seemed somewhat unsteady on his feet. Maybe because of the glass of booze in his hand. "Excellent!" he called out. "Everything go all right?"

"Well, the putty—"

Billy Don cut in. "Needs to dry, but it looks good as new."

"That's what I like to hear!" Mitch gestured toward the bar, spilling an ounce or two from his glass. "You guys come on in and get something to drink. Cold beer, whiskey, whatever you want."

Red couldn't believe his ears. This wasn't the same Mitch Campbell he'd met earlier. This guy was friendly, outgoing, fun-loving—the same man Red had seen on TV interviews and award shows—and he was inviting them in for a drink. This was the break Red had been looking for his entire life!

He darted for the bar before Mitch could change his mind.

20

ANSWERING MACHINES. MARLIN kept getting answering machines. That, or no answer at all. Understandable, since it was late afternoon on a workday. He'd only spoken to eleven live human beings, and none of them had had anything to offer. He'd been leaving messages for all the others to call him when they returned. He'd tried the feed store, too, with no luck.

Then, near the bottom of the list, he got something that had potential. A widow named Buell, a woman in her seventies, lived on three hundred acres to the east of Ken Bell's ranch, on the other side of the subdivision named Shady Hollow. Marlin knew her well; he'd gone to school with her son, a good man who was now a cop in Houston. After hearing the update on her son's thriving career (he'd made captain last year), Marlin asked if she'd heard any shots recently. He didn't tell her why he was asking.

"You know, I did hear one the other day," Mrs. Buell said. "I noticed because there ain't as much shooting around here nowadays, with all the new houses and everything. Used to be, you'd hear shots all the time—mostly twenty-twos, people plinking tin cans. Then during deer season, out come the big rifles. That's what I heard, let's see, I guess it was Sunday evening. A rifle. Or a big handgun."

Sunday evening. Rodolfo was already dead by then. So the shot Mrs. Buell had heard could've been the one that was fired to create the blood splatter—if Marlin's theory was valid.

"You remember what time it was?"

"About seven o'clock. I was pulling laundry off the line. Wanted to get it in before dark."

"Which direction did it come from?"

"Maybe northwest. Hard to tell."

Ken Bell's place was to the west.

"How close?"

"A mile at the most. Or closer. Maybe in Shady Hollow. Some of those folks hunt over there, even though they ain't supposed to. Hell, you know that."

"Just one shot?"

"Yep, just the one. Maybe I shoulda called it in."

"Let me ask you something else. Did you go anywhere over the weekend?"

"Sure. I go for groceries every Sunday afternoon."

"Did you notice a white truck parked on the shoulder?"

"I did, with two men hanging around it. I thought maybe they were broke down till I saw the For Sale sign in the back."

"What time was this?"

"Probably a little after five. On my way home."

"This was a couple of hours before you heard the shot?"

"Right."

"What'd these men look like?"

"Well, I wasn't paying much attention. One was older—maybe sixty or so. Lotta gray in his hair. Didn't see the other man very good. Just his back."

"Do you know J. B. Crowley?"

"Who's that?"

"He owns the place right there where the truck was parked. To the west of Mr. Bell."

"Never met him."

"Ever seen him, maybe when he was opening his gate?"

"Nope. That his truck?"

"We're looking into it. What were these two men doing, exactly?"

"Well, not much. Just standing beside the truck. I figured they was thinking of buying it."

"Was there another vehicle there?" If the men were random passersby who'd stopped to inspect the truck, they'd have been driving.

"Didn't see one," Mrs. Buell said.

Sheriff Bobby Garza appeared in Marlin's doorway. "Henry's ready for us," he mouthed.

"Thanks, Mrs. Buell. You've been a big help."

Harvey Shore—one of the original pioneers of shock-jock radio, now relegated to afternoon drive time—said, "A lot of people think all of you guys are scumbags."

"Yeah, I know."

"Bottom feeders."

"I don't listen to that crap."

"Some of the biggest names in Hollywood call you a parasite, a leech, a lowlife."

Rhonda Bowman, Shore's sidekick, chimed in with, "Doesn't that bother you?"

Casey Walberg had heard it all before. He adjusted his headphones and said, "What do I care what they think? A man doesn't have the right to earn a living?"

Shore said, "Yeah, but they say the way you do it, earn your living, is pure evil. They hate the paparazzi. They talk about a special place in hell for you."

"Some people say that about you, too."

Shore snorted out an ugly laugh. "Yeah, they do. Good point. You know what I say? Screw 'em all. Really, who gives a rat's ass?"

"Exactly. Hey, with celebrities, it's the price they pay for fame. What they should worry about is when we start *ignoring* them. Then you'd see their attitudes change, I guarantee it. Suddenly they'd be whining, like, 'Where are all the cameras? Doesn't anybody want a picture of *me*?' Bunch of friggin' prima donnas. Besides, I don't see what the problem is. We take pictures of you, Harvey, and you never whine about it."

"Hey, you wanna waste your film on my ugly mug, go right ahead. Free country."

"You are *not* an ugly man, Harvey," Rhonda interjected. "Quit being so hard on yourself."

"Hear that, Casey? She said 'hard on.' But yeah, I'm ugly, and I have a penis the size of a cocktail wienie. I'll admit it. Last night I was with this broad and she said, 'Who you gonna please with that little thing?' I said, 'Me.'"

Rhonda giggled. "Oh, Harvey. That's terrible."

"But let's talk about some of your work, Casey. What was the first really big picture you got? The one that got you started?"

"Justin Timberlake in a swimsuit with his junk hanging out."

"Wow. Big stuff."

"Uh, not literally."

"Good one. I heard about that shot. How much you get for it?"

"A couple bucks. Enough to get me started. Bought some new lenses."

"It takes a lot of equipment, huh?"

"I've got about fifty grand tied up."

"That's some big dough. Whattaya earn in a good year?"

"Well—"

"Just ballpark it for me."

"I make a living."

"What, a hundred grand? Two hundred?"

"How is that your business, Harvey?" Rhonda asked. "Give the poor guy a break."

"Half a mil?"

"I do okay," Walberg said.

"I bet you do, you sneaky bastard. Spend all your time following hot actresses around, waiting for their tits to pop out. Without you, I never woulda guessed Katie Holmes wears a nipple ring."

"Glad I could help."

"What a weird life you must lead."

"It can be pretty dull, really. Lotta waiting around. You can spend a week or two trying to get one shot."

"Sean Penn ever take a swing at you?"

"Not yet, but there's always hope."

"I'm always wondering how you get the really tough shots—the weddings, baptisms, crap like that. No matter how they try to duck all of you guys, there's always photos."

"Lotta times, someone tips us off. Like—this is just an example—a jeweler might tell me George Clooney bought a diamond ring. Then a waiter might tell me he's got dinner reservations for Friday night. You put two and two together, you can sometimes figure out where and when it's gonna happen. You can always get the info for a price."

"You gotta pay those guys?"

"Everybody wants a piece of it, yeah."

"Why doesn't that surprise me? I got a tip for ya. I'll be fondling myself tonight in the shower. That worth anything?"

"About a buck fifty."

"Smart-ass. Remember who you're talking to."

"There's not a big demand for cocktail wienies."

"Tell me something I don't know. I live with that fact every single day. So what's going on in Texas? I hear you're flying down there tomorrow."

"Uh, no comment."

"Seriously, who ya chasing? Who the hell's in Texas? Sandra Bullock having a lesbian affair or something? Matthew McConaughey growing pot in his basement?"

"Don't start rumors, Harvey," Rhonda said. "Matthew McConaughey is a nice boy."

"Just a vacation," Walberg said.

Shore snorted again. "Yeah, right. I don't trust you for a minute."

"Would I lie to you, Harvey?"

"Of course you would. In a heartbeat. That's why everyone thinks you're vermin."

"I'm afraid I don't have much for you," Henry Jameson said, and Marlin heard a unified sigh from Bobby Garza and Bill Tatum.

It was five o'clock, and the investigative team—minus Nicole and Ernie, who hadn't returned yet—had gathered in the interview room. Jameson was giving an update on his initial processing of Rodolfo's truck.

"A vehicle that old," Jameson continued, "I expected to find all kinds of junk in the cab. But whoever owned it before Junior kept it pretty neat. Either that, or they gave it a really good cleaning recently, probably right before they sold it. Part of the problem is, everything's vinyl. The seats, the flooring. No carpet anywhere, which means trace evidence was hard to come by. I did find various hairs and fibers, but again—with a truck that old—I can't tell you whether any of it will prove useful. Could be ancient stuff. If some of it's new, great—except we don't have anything to compare it to."

"What kinds of fibers?" Garza asked.

"Hard to say. Clothing, probably. I'll be sending it all to the lab in Austin."

"Any prints?"

"From the interior, yeah, a couple. But, just by eyeballing them, I think they're all from the victim. There were a few places—the steering wheel, the stick shift, the door handle—where I'd normally expect to find prints, or at least smudges. They were completely clean."

"Like somebody wiped 'em down?" Marlin asked.

"Probably. From the bed of the truck—all those tools and supplies in the back—I've got plenty of the victim's prints, plus a lot of unknowns. Could be from people who worked at the store where he bought all that stuff. Or from other customers. Or even employees at the places where all those items were manufactured."

"Let's run 'em through AFIS anyway," Garza said.

"Of course."

"Any blood?" Marlin asked. It would be helpful to know if the body had been transported in the truck.

"Nope. But the body could've been wrapped in a tarp or blanket."

"I don't suppose you found any ID?" Tatum asked.

Jameson shook his head. "Sorry. Apparently, the guy hadn't really made himself at home in it yet. I found a receipt for an oil change in the glove box, but that was Junior's. There was one thing that might help: a small scrap of paper with four numbers written on it. Six-seven-nine-one. It was down between the seats. You might want to check with Junior and see if it was his. It did have the victim's prints on it, so we know, at least, that he handled it at some point."

"Six-seven-nine-one," Marlin repeated. "Like a date? From 1991?"

"Well, maybe. But there weren't any dashes between the numbers. I'll make copies and you can draw your own conclusions. Lord knows you don't want me interpreting evidence."

"Anything else?" Garza asked.

Earlier in the day, Marlin had told all of them about his experiment with the ketchup in the rifle, and Henry would eventually run some tests of his own, but that was low priority at the moment. Proving how the splatter was created wouldn't get them any closer to the killer.

"That's all I've got," Jameson said. "I'll let you know if I learn anything from the prints."

"Please do," Garza said. "As soon as you can."

The forensic technician excused himself, and Garza turned to Tatum. "Bill?"

The chief deputy grimaced. "Nothing yet on the phone card. Still waiting on the records. I'll keep hammering away at 'em. Meanwhile, I sent the victim's photo and prints to the PD in Acuña, but struck out. He wasn't in their system. They didn't know the guy."

"Anything with the broken window?"

"There isn't anyone local who specializes in windows, so I've been talking to general repairmen, carpenters, that sort of thing. No luck so far. Then again, the killer could've called someone from Austin or San Antonio, and if he did, that's a much bigger pool to draw from."

"How big?"

"The Austin phone book alone has several hundred listings for glass repair. San Antonio has even more. Here's what I'm recommending: Let's let Ernie and Nicole finish out the evening at the crime scene. If they don't find anything by end of day, there's probably nothing to be found. Then, first thing in the morning, I'll team up with them and start making calls."

Marlin felt obliged to offer his opinion. "I still think he'd fix the window himself."

"Could be," Tatum said, "unless he isn't much of a handyman. Ever replaced broken glass?"

"Yeah, I have, and you're right, it's kind of tricky. But I bet it would be easy to find instructions on the Internet. Or he could've asked for instructions at the store."

"Maybe. It'd be a real pisser if he hasn't even done anything about the window yet. Maybe he just boarded it up or covered it with a tarp. Or worse, what if the original crime scene is someplace where the killer doesn't care if the window stays broken? Someplace that can't be connected to him."

Garza said, "If that were the case, wouldn't he have left the body there, too? Why this big cover-up? I'm guessing the crime scene is the killer's home. Or the victim's. If it happened anyplace else, we'd likely have heard about it by now. That means he'd fix the window."

"Makes sense," Tatum conceded. "Which brings us back to the Home Depot in Marble Falls."

"Right. You were gonna talk to them about video cameras."

"I did, and they do run video at their store. Here's the problem. They don't cut glass for customers anymore. None of the stores do. They still sell standardized sheets of glass, but not much of it, because the glass almost always has to be cut to fit the window. That would mean our guy would also have to cut the glass himself, or—a lot more likely, in my opinion—he would've gotten the glass, cut to size, directly from a glass company. Less of a hassle."

"I agree with that," Garza said. He looked at Marlin.

"Me, too. He might've started out at Home Depot, then moved on. But you're right, I can't imagine him trying to cut the glass himself. Just replacing the glass is tough enough."

"Which makes our job easier, really," Tatum said, "because the repair companies are basically the same people who sell cut glass. So we'll ask about service calls to this area, or any customers who might've just bought glass. Again, though, we're screwed if he paid cash."

"But let's make the calls," Garza said.

"Will do."

Garza turned to Marlin. "Anything for us?"

Marlin recounted his conversation with Mrs. Buell—the gunshot she'd heard and the two men she'd seen.

"She's sure it wasn't a firecracker?" Tatum asked.

"I'm betting she can tell the difference. Her two sons hunt out on her place. She hears a lot of shots."

"She give you a direction?"

"To the northwest, but she wasn't positive. You know how sounds bounce around in the hills."

"Has possibilities, though," Garza said. "Time of death was sometime from midnight Saturday to noon on Sunday. You have to figure the killer freaked out for a while, then he had to come up with this whole accidental-shooting scenario. Plus, he had to move the body—without being seen—onto the ranch. This thing with the two men is interesting. A lot easier to carry a body when you've got a guy on each end."

"Then again," Marlin said, "it might've just been somebody looking at the truck."

"Could be. I guess you haven't reached Crowley yet?"

"Nope. I've called three times. I've been trying the feed store, too, but Mike hasn't answered either." Mike Winters, the owner of the feed store, would likely know where Crowley worked.

"Think Crowley's involved?" Tatum asked, addressing nobody in particular.

Marlin said, "Wouldn't be real smart, leaving the truck right there along his own fence line."

"Killers aren't generally known for their IQs," Garza said.

"True," Marlin said.

"If nothing else, maybe he saw something. Hell, everything took place right around his property."

"What do we know about him?" Tatum asked.

Marlin shrugged. "Very little. Looks like he moved to Blanco County about a year ago."

"From where?"

"Don't know."

"What's he do for a living?" Garza asked.

"Don't know that, either. I do know that he's an NWA member, because he had a decal on his mailbox."

"Well, let's track him down. Find out what he knows. While you're at it, go ahead and run a CCH. See if he's—"

Garza was interrupted by a knock on the door. Darrell Bridges poked his head into the room and said, "Sorry to interrupt, but I figured y'all would want to know. I've got a Mexican gal on the line who's trying to track down her brother. She's worried because she hasn't heard from him lately. Says his name is Rodolfo Dominguez."

21

SEVERAL YEARS BEFORE Mitch Campbell topped the country charts—long before Glenn Dobbins had designs on the Texas governorship or Dale Stubbs became a key player in the National Weapons Alliance—a chain-smoking beautician named Patty Jo Martin decided to enroll her twelve-year-old son in the Boy Scouts. It was a desperate ploy by a woman at wit's end. Freddie, after all, was what several healthcare professionals had diagnosed as a "troubled child," and what her live-in boyfriend, a plumber named Dick Angerman, had labeled a "worthless punk."

In his bedroom, Freddie heard part of the conversation through the thin walls of the mobile home.

"You kidding me?" Dick sneered. "They ain't never gonna take him."

"God knows, Dickie, I don't know what else to do."

"That kid's Scout material like you're a Dallas Cowboy cheerleader."

"Well, fuck you, too, sweetheart. You ain't exactly Troy Aikman, case you was wondering. Thing is"—there was a pause, and Freddie knew his mom was sucking on a Marlboro—"they say he needs discipline."

"Bring him in here. I'll give him discipline."

"This Scout thing might be good for him. They always look so cute in their little neckerchiefs. Maybe he'll make some friends." Freddie could hear the aggressive scritching of an emery board across his mother's fingernails. "Maybe he'll build one of them wooden go-carts. Something to keep him busy."

"Military school—that's the solution. None of them damn baggy jeans down there, I guarantee it."

"You gonna pay for it?"

"Hell no."

"All right, then."

"Whatever. Shit, if it'll keep him outta my hair, I'm all for it. But don't be asking me to run him all over town. That's all on you. Now whyn't you run make me some nachos?"

So, the following weekend, Patty Jo loaded Freddie into her aging Firebird and dumped him at his first troop meeting, where he was issued an ill-fitting khaki uniform and a copy of the venerated Boy Scout handbook.

Unfortunately—and to nobody's great surprise—Freddie did not adhere to the behavioral ideals or the ethical code of the organization to which he now belonged. The activity for that first day was a nature hike in McKinney Falls State Park, where Freddie shoved a wad of raccoon droppings deep into a smaller boy's ear.

As the weeks passed, things continued to go poorly. Freddie had temper tantrums and sulking spells. He fought with his troop mates and sassed his scoutmaster. His behavior progressed from disruptive and impertinent to aberrant and antisocial.

When Freddie's troop learned the proper technique for building a campfire, he used those skills to set his neighbor's tool shed ablaze.

When they studied knot-tying, Freddie trussed an unsuspecting cat and tossed it into a storm drain.

At summer camp, when the other boys were striving for their woodcarving merit badges, Freddie used his knife to scrawl the words "Suck the big one" into the wall of the latrine.

For Freddie—and those around him—his membership in the

troop was a source of tension and unpleasantness. Then, on a crisp Saturday morning, when Freddie and his troop were picking up trash along Loop 360, something happened that made him happy to be a Scout.

He found a handgun.

It was there, hidden in some tall weeds in the median, just waiting to be discovered. A jolt of excitement rippled through Freddie's body. With his heart beating rapidly in his chest, he slipped the gun into his coat pocket.

Later, at home, he took it out and played with it, pretending to blast imaginary foes and tormentors. He liked the heft of the weapon, the feel of cold steel in his hands. It occurred to him that the gun vested him with a power he'd never possessed before. He was Arnold Schwarzenegger, Jackie Chan, and Clint Eastwood rolled into one!

I can do anything! he thought. *Anything at all!*

After careful contemplation, he realized there was really only one thing he wanted to do. So he waited until a Sunday afternoon, while his mother was at Wal-Mart. Then he removed the gun from his sock drawer and walked into the living room, where Dick was in the easy chair, watching football in his underwear.

"Well, if it ain't Freddie Martian," Dick said, his attention on the game. "Perfect timing, too. I need another beer, boy."

Freddie was amazed at how calm he felt. His voice came out loud and strong. "My name's Freddie *Martin,* you big asshole, and you can get your own damn beer."

Dick's head swiveled around, and his eyes were blazing—up until he noticed the pistol pointing at his forehead. Then his demeanor changed visibly.

That's right, Freddie thought. *I've got a gun. So you can shut your fat mouth.*

Dick's eyes darted back and forth several times, from Freddie's face to the gun. "Uh, that a toy? It don't look like a toy."

Dick was scared, no doubt about it, and Freddie was loving every minute of it!

"Take it easy, now, Freddie. Don't do anything stupid. Where'd you get that?"

"I don't like the way you talk to my mom," Freddie said. "You're such a jerk all the time."

Dick had his hands in front of him, making placating gestures. "That's understandable. I can see your point. Absolutely. Thing is, when a man comes home from a long day at work, it's normal to be a little grumpy. That's my problem. I'm just an old sourpuss. You can understand that, can't you?"

"I don't like the way you talk to me, either. You call me names and put me down. I'm tired of it."

Dick gave him a weak smile. "I don't blame you at all. And you know what? I can do better. Yes sir, most definitely. I can work on it. I'm glad you brought this to my attention. Now why don't you sit down and let's talk this thing out? Hell, the truth is, I wanna be your friend, Freddie. We can be buds, you and me. How 'bout that? Maybe go camping together. Catch a few fish. We'll start out fresh. Put all these nasty old feelings behind us. A whole new start."

Freddie knew Dick was lying. They'd never go fishing.

"Freddie?"

Dick was just saying whatever he could to keep Freddie from shooting. His index finger began to tighten on the trigger.

"Why don't you put the gun down?"

Freddie had the feeling that life would be much better if Dick wasn't around. His mom would be happier. She'd be mad at first, but then she'd be happier. And Freddie knew *he'd* be happier.

Sweat was running down Dick's temples. "Put it away, okay? Then we'll sit here and watch the game. Just us two men. Watching football. Maybe we'll make some nachos. Whattaya say? Can we do that? Please?"

Freddie said, "Shithead." Then he pulled the trigger.

PART THREE

Because handguns and other firearms are so easily accessible to many children, adolescents, and other family members in their homes, the risk of gun violence in the home increases dramatically.

—BRADY CAMPAIGN WEB SITE

Boys who learn about firearms and their legitimate uses from family members and who own firearms legally have much lower rates of delinquency than those who own firearms illegally and those who do not own firearms.

—NRA-ILA WEB SITE

As a rule we disbelieve all the facts and theories for which we have no use.

—WILLIAM JAMES

22

IN AUSTIN, DETECTIVE Paul Hebert was surfing the official Web site for the city of Missoula, Montana—they called it the Garden City because of the relatively mild winters, if you could believe the hucksters who were responsible for slogans like that—when Ramon showed up at his office door again. Operating on three hours of sleep and the kid looked as chipper as a spring foal. Homicide, Hebert decided for the hundredth time in the past year, was a young man's game.

Ramon had a purposeful expression on his dark face. "Remember that charge against Henley? Selling a gun illegally? He cut a deal to testify in a different case?"

Hebert remembered. It had happened seven years ago. Waste of time, he figured. "What about it?"

"I called the DA's office this morning, and they told me the prosecutor on that other case—guy named Roland Nichols—had retired up in Dallas. They gave me his number, but he didn't answer."

Probably out fishing, Hebert thought. Which made him wonder what kind of fishing they did in Missoula. He figured it was chiefly trout, because the Web site showed a guy knee-deep in a crystal-clear stream, probably the Bitterroot River, casting a fly. *I could be joining you real soon, buddy.* A man wouldn't even need an ice chest. Just tie a six-pack to your belt and drop it in the water.

Ramon wasn't finished. "The DA just called me back with some news. Dallas PD found Nichols dead in his garage about two hours ago."

"Homicide?"

"Yep."

Here we go, Hebert thought. He reluctantly closed his Internet browser. Bye-bye, Montana. For now. "When'd it happen?"

"Late last night or early this morning."

Hebert contemplated this new information. A prosecutor and one of his witnesses had been killed a day apart, with the crime scenes separated by a four-hour drive. The odds against those two incidents taking place independently of one another were high. That was good news, because if the crimes were linked, it might narrow the field of suspects. Then again . . .

"Let's not jump to any conclusions just yet," Hebert said. "They might be unrelated."

Ramon, despite his short time on the job, smiled the smile of a veteran, one who'd seen all the morbid shit this job had to offer. "Maybe so, but our guy yesterday was smothered with bumper stickers, right? *Gun-shop* bumper stickers. Well, Nichols was drowned with a bottle of gun oil."

"Say again?"

"Nichols was blasted with a stun gun, just like Henley, and force-fed a quart of Hoppe's."

"You're shitting me."

"For real."

Well, that sealed it. The murders were linked. Some nutjob was on the loose. "Forensics get anything?"

"No prints on the bottle—it was wiped clean—but they did get a partial on the cap. Didn't match Nichols. No hit on AFIS."

"Know what I'm worried about?"

"Who might be next on this guy's list."

"Exactly. That's our number-one priority. We need to know

everything about those two cases. Henley's original case, plus the one he was testifying in."

"Already on it. The DA's gonna fax some stuff over shortly, and they want what we have so far on Henley's murder. They've got their own investigation going."

"Ain't much, but let's give it to them. And set up a conference call with Dallas ASAP."

"Will do."

Hebert took a settling breath. "Who found him?"

"Nichols?"

"Yeah."

Another smile. "A neighbor. Their dog came home with his toupee."

John Marlin and Bill Tatum drove north on Highway 281 in the deputy's cruiser.

Finally, something to go on. Some hard facts. A complete name to go with the face. Background information, the works. And a pretty good lead, too, though it could fizzle as quickly as it had developed.

The caller—Natalia Dominguez—had told Garza that her brother, Rodolfo, had crossed illegally into the States about four months ago. He'd spent the majority of that time working day jobs in Del Rio, just across the border from his hometown of Ciudad Acuña. But things were tight. Money wasn't coming easily. So he'd traveled eastward, toward central Texas, in search of steadier work. Rodolfo had arrived in Blanco County, according to Natalia, about two weeks ago.

He hadn't really settled in. He was a loner of sorts, so he hadn't made any friends yet. He'd been sleeping in the state park because he hadn't saved up enough money to rent a place. Not after purchasing an old used truck. White, with a camper top. He was very proud of it.

She knew all this, she said, because Rodolfo had been phoning her every evening recently, like clockwork. Yes, they were a close family, but it was their mother's declining health that prompted the regular calls. She was gravely ill, and Rodolfo knew she didn't have much time left. He was a good son, Natalia said, checking in every night.

Until Sunday.

She hadn't heard from him on Sunday, and she figured, well, he's working late. But she didn't hear from him Monday, either, or Tuesday, and she grew concerned. Rodolfo would call if he could, she had no doubt about that. Natalia had had no way to contact him, so she'd fretted and worried and hoped he'd be in touch.

"She was afraid to contact the authorities," Garza said afterward, "because she thought we'd find him and deport him."

"So why'd she finally call?" Tatum asked.

"Because their mother died this morning. The funeral's on Saturday. Really, she didn't have a lot to tell me—except for one very interesting piece of information. The last time she talked to Rodolfo—Saturday night—he was excited about a new job he was starting the next day. He teased her, saying that while she was still down in Mexico, he'd be up in America rubbing elbows with a famous country singer." Garza grinned.

"Mitch Campbell?" Tatum said.

"She couldn't remember the name, but yeah, who else? He's the only one we've got." Garza looked at Marlin. "You talked to him?"

"Not yet. He was pretty low on the list."

"I'd say he just moved up. Let's see if he can tell us anything useful. Maybe he can open this thing up for us. We need to know if Dominguez showed at Campbell's place on Sunday morning."

So Marlin accessed Campbell's contact information on the tax-roll database, only to find a phone number with a Los Angeles area code. He called it and a young woman answered. He'd reached Campbell's manager's office, she said, but get real, there was no way she could give out the singer's home number. She'd be, like, totally fired. Marlin asked to speak to Mitch's manager, and she said he was in Nashville all week. He told her it was a police matter, and she asked how she was supposed to know that for sure. She said sorry, but it was amazing the humongous lies people would tell to get close to Mitch. She finally gave Marlin the manager's cell number, but when he called it, he was routed to voice mail. He didn't leave a message.

"Let's just drive out there," Tatum suggested.

So that's where they were headed—to ask an ultra-conservative nationally recognized gun-rights advocate if he knew anything about an illegal Mexican alien who'd been shot dead. The irony of it all needed no comment.

Along the way, Marlin pondered the phenomenon that was Mitch Campbell. He could understand why the singer rubbed some people the wrong way—not as a performer, but as the NWA's representative. He was just a little too . . . unctuous, that was the word. Smarmy. Cocky. Downright condescending at times. Enough so that Marlin had considered canceling his own NWA membership.

Campbell's negative attributes aside, he obviously had something going for him, or millions of gun owners around the nation wouldn't have responded to him as they had. They'd anointed Campbell as their crusader, and he seemed to wear that mantle with relish.

Strange, though. Where were all these new gun-rights proponents before Campbell came along? Marlin had to wonder: Do people choose their champions based on their beliefs, or do the champions elicit newfound "beliefs" from malleable people? Can a flashy marketing campaign with a glib spokesperson create a get-on-the-bandwagon effect?

They'd been riding along in silence, and now Marlin said, "You a member of the NWA, Bill?"

"Naw, I've never been much of a joiner. You?"

"My dad signed me up when I was fifteen. Been a member ever since."

Tatum nodded, but didn't say anything.

"How many guns do you own?" Marlin asked.

"Counting rifles and shotguns?"

"Yeah."

"Maybe a dozen."

"How old were you when you got your first one?"

"Twelve or so, but I'd gone hunting with my dad for several years before that. He taught me how to be safe."

"Ever wish there weren't so many guns around?"

Tatum laughed. "Yeah, every time some idiot points one at me. Then I always wish there was at least one less in the world."

"Would you outlaw them if you could?"

"Oh, hell no."

"Why not?"

"Because there'd still be millions of guns out there, which means they'd be in the hands of criminals. It seems awfully unfair to disarm everyone except the people willing to break the law."

Marlin nodded. "Okay. For argument's sake, if you could snap your fingers and make every gun in the world disappear, would you?"

Tatum didn't hesitate this time. "No way. They've got more positives than negatives. Law enforcement, hunting, self-defense. Besides, that'd be a cop-out."

"How so?"

Tatum seemed to search for the right words. "It's like that old cliché, letting a few rotten apples spoil the bunch. Our society is based on freedom, you know? The freedom to say what you want, to act and think however you want. But with that freedom comes a responsibility to behave like an adult. You have to conduct yourself in a way that doesn't hurt others, and if you cross that line, *that's* when you get your freedoms taken away."

Tatum slowed to take a right on Cypress Mill Road. "All right, what about you? Would you get rid of guns? I can't say anyone would blame you."

Tatum was making a subtle reference to the death of Marlin's father. Even thirty years later, Marlin felt a melancholy pang in his chest. His dad, Royce, had been the game warden in Blanco County for twenty-two years, until he was shot and killed by a poacher in 1976. Heartbreaking, yes. A tragedy that Marlin carried with him every day. But he blamed the poacher, not the rifle the man used. He'd felt a lot of guilt over the years because of that stance—as if he were committing a sacrilege against his father's memory—but he knew his dad had held the same views.

"I don't know what the answer is," Marlin said. "Sensible laws don't bother me. Background checks, waiting periods. By all means, let's keep guns away from felons. But flat-out banning them doesn't seem to work. They tried it in England."

Tatum gave him a sly glance. "Where's all this deep thinking coming from, anyway? Nicole?"

"No, I was just thinking about Mitch Campbell. Why'd you mention Nicole?"

"Well, considering what happened to her."

"What're you talking about?"

Tatum frowned. "When she was stationed in Mason. That domestic violence call."

Marlin stared at him.

"You don't know about that?" Tatum asked.

"Apparently not."

Tatum shrugged. "I don't know all the details. I just know some drunk asshole held a gun to her head for about thirty minutes."

Marlin's stomach tightened. He could feel his face flushing with heat. Nicole had never said a word. "When did she tell you about it?"

"She didn't tell me, Ernie did. Told me and Bobby, right after she came to work for us. I think it was his way of telling us she could handle herself. Not that we needed it. Nicole, on the other hand—she's never mentioned it."

Ernie was Nicole's cousin, so yeah, he'd know. *But why hasn't she told me?* Wasn't she comfortable enough to share that sort of thing with him? It appeared she wasn't.

He'd have to ponder the situation later, because they were approaching the entrance to Mitch Campbell's ranch. Tatum slowed the cruiser and pulled up to the gate, an ornate affair, flanked by immense walls of native limestone. Very impressive. As expected, the gate was fully automated, controlled by a keypad to the left of the driveway. Above the keypad was an intercom button; visitors who didn't know the code were buzzed in from the house. Tatum pressed it.

Marlin pointed out a small security camera mounted at the top of the left-hand column. Could be useful if it recorded video, but it might do nothing more than feed a monitor.

They waited thirty seconds, then Tatum punched the button again. No response.

"Think he's home?" Tatum asked.

"Who knows?"

"Any idea how far it is to the house?"

"More than a mile, I'd guess. Probably closer to two." Marlin had driven up to the homesite once, before Campbell had moved in. A poaching call, with shots fired. The "poacher" had turned out to be a construction worker with a bad muffler.

Tatum thumbed the button again, to no avail. Then he wrote *Please call me as soon as possible* on the back of one of his cards and slipped it into a seam along the keypad's housing.

23

RED O'BRIEN HAD always considered himself a world-class drinker. Beer. Whiskey. Gin. Top-shelf tequila or a four-dollar bottle of rum—it didn't matter. He'd drink it just the same. Years of alcohol abuse had built Red's tolerance to the point where he could sock it away better than most men twice his size—as evidenced by Billy Don, over on the leather sofa, his eyelids drooping, his jaw slack, an empty highball glass still clutched in his beefy paw.

Mitch Campbell, on the other hand—here was a man who could keep up. They'd been pounding Crown Royal, fast and straight, for two hours solid—Mitch telling all kinds of amazing stories about Nashville backstabbers and groupies and life on the road—and the singer didn't hardly seem tipsy at all. Well, maybe just a tad. Red was impressed.

And what a life Mitch led! He was the real deal, a modern-day cowboy, rambling from town to town, wowing the crowds, then riding into the sunset. As Southern as biscuits and gravy. Mitch's life was a nonstop thrill ride, full of fast times and faster women, and Red could feel the envy eating at him like a bad case of scabies. *Maybe someday,* Red thought, *I can be just like him.*

Right now, they were over near the Wurlitzer jukebox, studying a collection of photographs on the wall. There was Mitch, rubbing elbows with everybody from Dolly Parton to George Strait to Garth Brooks. Shots from concerts and award ceremonies and private parties. The photos went on and on. Mitch on the tour bus. Mitch at the Grand Ole Opry. Mitch signing some gal's sizeable upper tit. Mitch smiling as some silver-haired man handed him a platinum record.

Red noticed a shot of Mitch at the CMA Awards, climbing out of a limo with Brenda Graves, the Shreveport Sensation. The woman had the voice of an angel and the body of a certified homewrecker. Red would've given his eyeteeth just to lick the woman's shoes.

Mitch leered at him. "I know what you're thinking."

"What's that?"

"You're wondering, did I bang her?"

That was another thing that had surprised Red about Mitch. He wasn't all Mom-and-apple-pie, like his reputation. This old boy had a wild side, and he obviously enjoyed all the fringe benefits of his fame. Red couldn't blame him a bit.

"I guess that question crossed my mind, now that you mention it," Red said. He was doing his best to remain casual and composed. He didn't want to come across as a gushing dipshit.

"Oh, yeah," Mitch growled. "Big time."

"How was it?"

"Sweet." Mitch took a swig of whiskey and pointed to another photograph. "Sally Jane Murdock—now, she's a wild one. I got her from behind in my dressing room at Farm Aid." He continued along the wall. "Luanne Madison could deep-throat a microphone stand if she put her mind to it . . . and Mary Alice Meadows, well, let's just say she wears long sleeves to cover up the rope burns."

Rope burns? Red wasn't even sure what that meant. Something kinky, he figured. He was, quite frankly, a little embarrassed to be hearing all this intimate stuff. Red wasn't exactly tight-lipped himself when it came to girlfriends and such, but he generally stopped short of sharing hard-core details. It just wasn't gentlemanly. Besides, wasn't Mitch dating that young actress, Sheryl Hudson? Red didn't see any pictures of her.

He decided now would be a good time to steer the conversation toward more important things. He'd been biding his time, waiting for the right moment. He realized he wasn't even nervous; the booze had settled him down. He nodded toward a clipping from *Music Row* magazine: "COLD, DEAD HANDS" WINS SONG OF THE YEAR.

"That musta been quite a night, huh?" Red said.

"Hell yeah," Campbell replied. "After the show, I nailed Marcie Sommers in the elevator at the—"

"You know, Mitch," Red said, his impatience finally getting the best of him, "I wanted to tell you about that song I wrote."

Campbell furrowed his brow. "Huh?"

"'Member?" Red said. "Down by the road? I said I was a songwriter?"

The singer shook his head and grinned. "Shit, dude, everybody thinks they're a songwriter. Problem is, most of them aren't."

Dude? Did he just call me dude? Weird, but Red ignored it. "I can believe that," he said. "I surely can. But new songs gotta come from somewhere, right? I mean, if nobody was willing to listen to other people's songs, we wouldn't have no music at all, would we?"

Red didn't know if that argument made sense entirely, but Mitch didn't seem to notice. "Well . . ." he said.

"It sure would be a honor," Red went on, "if you'd listen to my song and give me your opinion." He took the cassette out of his breast pocket.

"You wrote a song, huh?" Mitch seemed amused by that fact. Not necessarily in a good way.

"Sure did," Red said proudly. "It's called 'Come and Take It.' You familiar with the Battle of Gonzales in 1835?" Red had been a poor student, but he remembered that particular subject because he'd written a paper on it in the eighth grade. Made a solid C minus.

"My history's a little rusty," Mitch said.

"Well, now, it's a hell of a story," Red said, rubbing his hands together with excitement. "Gonzales is where the Texicans—that's what they called the white boys—fired the first shot of the Texas Revolution. See, the Mexicans had given the Texicans a cannon to scare off the Indians. A few years later, the Mexicans wanted it back—but by then, the white boys was wanting to govern themselves, and they needed the cannon for their army. So they said, no way, we're keeping it. The Mexicans got a little nasty about it, so our boys had a flag made up that said . . . take a guess."

"Come and take it."

"Exactly! They wasn't about to give up that big gun, you know? And I think a lot of people still feel that way today. Like with all those Commies wanting to outlaw handguns and such. You know what we say? We say, 'Come and take it!' Don't that sound interesting?"

"Maybe," Mitch said. "But . . . my manager says I shouldn't listen to other people's material. Opens me up for a lawsuit."

"Aw, Mitch, you know I wouldn't do nothin' like that. Let me just play it once. No obligation or nothing. If you don't like it, I won't bother you no more about it. Promise."

Mitch stared at him for a long moment, then smiled and said, "There's a stereo over by the bar."

"Excellent!" Red hustled to the stereo and popped the cassette into the drive. He hit Play, and a few seconds later, he heard his own embarrassing voice.

> *Down around Gonzales*
> *Back in 1831*
> *Some Texas boys got their hands*
> *On a big ol' iron gun*
> *But four years later Santa Anna came calling*
> *And the Texicans took to cannonballing*
> *They said . . .*
> *Come and take it!*
> *But you'd better bring a lot of help*
> *Come and take it!*
> *We're gonna fire till the barrel melts*
> *Come and take it!*
> *You can see our flag is flying high*
> *And we'll live those words till the day we die*
> *So come and take it!*
> *Oh yeah, come and take it!*

Between the verses, Red snuck a peek at Mitch, looking for any sign of interest. He saw none. Now he was beginning to feel like a total fool. *He hates it! The song is horrible!* Red was sweating nervously. He cringed as the second verse began:

> *Things haven't changed much*
> *People still want my gun*
> *But in a way I'm a Texican too*
> *Like Stephen F. Austin's son*
> *So if you're one of those Washington types*
> *Who thinks you can step all over my rights*
> *I say . . .*
> *Come and take it!*
> *But you'd better wear a Kevlar vest*
> *Come and take it!*
> *You're walking right into a hornet's nest*
> *Come and take it!*
> *You can see my flag is flying high*
> *And I'll live those words till the day I die*
> *So come and take it!*
> *You've got your work cut out*
> *There ain't no doubt*
> *Come and take it!*
> *'Cause I'm red, white, and blue*
> *Through and through*
> *So come and take it!*
> *Oh yeeeah! Come and take it!*

Red turned the stereo off. This was the worst mistake of his life. He was afraid to look at Mitch, but he finally did. Poker face. Neither man spoke. Billy Don was snoring on the couch.

Finally, Red couldn't stand it anymore. "Well?"

Mitch smiled. "I can't believe I'm saying this . . . but that is a kick-ass song."

Holy shit! "You're teasing me."

"No, I'm not. It's really good."

Red was so excited, his head was actually buzzing. "Well, god-damn."

"It has a lot of potential."

"That's fantastic!" he said. "So . . . what happens now?"

"I think . . . it needs something," Mitch said.

"You mean, like, different words? A different tune?"

"Nothing that major. Let me think on it a minute."

Red sipped from his glass of whiskey. He could hardly sit still. This was amazing! He had written a kick-ass song!

Mitch finally said, "I can't put my finger on it. Maybe it needs a bridge."

Red heard the buzz again. A shrill sound, like a jumbo-size June bug diving headfirst into one of those electric bug zappers. Was it really in his head? He tried to ignore it. "A bridge, huh?"

"I think so."

"Fine by me, but, uh, what's a bridge?"

Mitch smiled. "You don't know what a bridge is?"

"No, sir. I never got formal training or nothing like that." Red heard the buzz a third time. He couldn't stand it anymore. "You hear that?" he asked, wiggling a finger in his ear, hoping to make it go away. "That infernal noise?"

Mitch placed his drink on the bar and said, "Somebody at the gate. Be right back."

Mitch didn't know which it was—the alcohol or the distraction of these two goobers—but he was feeling much better. Getting his confidence back. More on top of things. Yeah, so he'd shot a Mexican dead. Big deal. Accidents happen, right? Nothing he could do about it now anyway. In the bigger picture, was that really a reason for anyone to get upset? Mitch decided it probably wasn't.

As he walked down the hallway toward his office, he swayed toward the wall and had to put his hand out for support. Whoa Nellie, as the skinny one, Red, might say. Mitch was drunker than he'd realized. Felt fabulous, but the whiskey had gone straight to his head. Hadn't eaten all day. In fact, when was the last time he'd managed to keep something down? He couldn't remember. He had a hell of an appetite now. Could eat the ass end of a running mule, as Red might say. That Red. Had a way with words. Mitch couldn't help liking the guy. The other one, too.

Mitch's office door was open, so he staggered in and sank into the chair behind his desk. Punched a key and brought his computer screen to life. It was tied in to the security system. He'd be able to see who the visitor was.

Just click on this icon here . . . wait for the application to load . . .

He reached for his drink, but it wasn't there. Where had he left the damn thing?

Hurry up, computer.

Ah, he could see it now. The entrance to his ranch, in living black and white. Mitch chuckled. *Living black and white. Clever.* Might be a good song title someday.

There wasn't anybody at the gate. They'd left already. Moseyed on down the road, as Red might say. Mitch let out an audible whoop. Another good title! *Mosey on down the road.* Excellent. Where were all these lyrics coming from? Mitch scribbled the lines down on a notepad, then left the office, returning to host his visitors. Jesus, they were a couple of hayseeds. Still, it was nice to have somebody to keep him company. Somebody to drink with.

Mitch was halfway down the hall when he had a fantastic idea.

24

"COME TO WORK for you?" Red asked, his head spinning with the very idea. The wild proposition had—for the moment, anyway—pushed his song from his mind. "Here? On the ranch?" He glanced over at Billy Don, who was now in a prone position on the couch.

"Just for a couple of days," Mitch said. "Get the place ready for the rally. You know about the rally, right?"

"I think I heard somethin' about it," Red replied. "Ain't that supposed to be a big affair?"

Mitch was pouring them both some more Crown, saying, "Yeah, but that's all taking place down below, on the lower pasture. We've got a crew coming that'll set all that up. I just need somebody to get the area around the house in shape. I've got a few VIPs staying with me that night. My producer, some people from the label, my manager."

Red thought for one fleeting second about Advanced Technologies, Inc. He'd be kissing off the cushiest job of his life, and he realized it didn't bother him a bit. Not with the way Mitch had reacted to Red's song. Good-bye, software geeks! Hello, Nashville!

"Sounds like a winner to me. What kinda work are we talkin' about?" Whatever it was, Red figured he and Billy Don could handle it.

"Just do what you can in the next couple of days. Trim trees, pull weeds, shit like that. Just get the place presentable. There was supposed to be a Mexican guy handling the job, but he never showed."

Mitch had a funny look on his face, maybe testing the waters to see how Red felt about foreign laborers.

Red had no problem sharing his thoughts on that topic. He shook his head and made a *tsk-tsk* sound. "Ain't that just like a Mexican?"

After work, back in the apartment in Plano, Tricia sat quietly as Dieter listened to the one and only phone call Dale Stubbs had placed all day. Dieter had been anxious for her to return, to see if the Interloper 3000 had worked properly. It had. The recording was crisp and clear: Dale talking to Glenn Dobbins' secretary, making lunch plans with the congressman.

Dieter played the call three times, while Tricia, bored to tears, was wishing she was at home, drinking a wine spritzer and watching the previous Sunday's episode of *Desperate Housewives*. She'd TIVo'ed it. TIVo, as far as Tricia was concerned, was the absolute bomb.

Finally, Dieter turned the device off and stared at her. "So he came into the office early, made this one call, then left?"

It sounded tremendously mundane to Tricia, but she played it up, wanting Dieter to value her efforts. After all, he was paying her a buttload of money. "Weird, huh?"

"Then he was gone all day?"

"Yep. Flew to Austin, just like that."

"And it wasn't on his calendar."

"Nope."

"Does he usually tell you where he's going?"

"Always."

"But this time he didn't?"

"Just said he had some things to take care of." She couldn't understand why Dieter found it so mysterious. So Dale had gone to Austin for lunch. Big deal.

"I find this odd," he said. "Does he normally make his own calls to arrange lunch?"

"Never. He'll tell me who he wants to have lunch with, and then I'll call that person's secretary." She suppressed a yawn.

"Does he ever book his own travel?"

"Of course not. I do it. It's my job."

Dieter leaned back in his chair, his beret cocked jauntily over his left eye. "Interesting," he said.

The sun was sinking behind the caliche-capped hills west of Johnson City when Marlin and Tatum returned to the sheriff's department. Marlin looked for Nicole's cruiser in the parking lot, but it appeared she and Ernie weren't back from Ken Bell's ranch yet.

In his office, Bobby Garza said, "This case is really starting to piss me off. I feel like we're walking through quicksand."

"You and me both," Tatum replied. "Should we have gone over the gate? I have to tell you, I was tempted."

Marlin had been, too. He'd vaulted plenty of fences in the past two decades. But it was one thing when you were tracking down a poacher; it was quite another when you were attempting to access a potential witness in a homicide investigation. That meant following the rules to the letter. No mistakes.

Garza agreed. "No, you did the right thing. We'll get hold of him eventually. You left a note?"

"Yeah."

"Call his manager every hour until we get through. Leave a voice mail every time. Be a total nuisance."

"Gotcha."

"Meanwhile, John, you focus on J. B. Crowley for the time being. The truck was parked near Crowley's house, and I want to know if that was a coincidence or not."

It was full dark when Marlin left the sheriff's department.

At Crowley's house, nothing had changed. No vehicle in the drive, no lights on inside. Marlin's note was still wedged above the door-knob. He circled the house with a flashlight, looking for a broken window. There wasn't one, and all of the panes were too dirty to be new.

He went to the street, peeked into the mailbox, and found it half full. Wherever Crowley was, he'd been gone for several days. Marlin was tempted to sort through the mail, thinking he might find a clue to Crowley's whereabouts, but that would be a federal offense without a warrant.

The feed store had been closed for hours, so Marlin drove home, where he found half a dozen messages waiting on his answering machine: residents in the neighborhoods near Ken Bell's ranch, calling him back. He returned the calls—went six for six as far as reaching actual people—but none of them had any knowledge whatsoever about the murder of Rodolfo Dominguez. He called some of the other numbers on his list and got the same result. Nobody saw anything, nobody heard anything.

He sat for five minutes in total silence.

Then he dialed Nicole's home number. Got her machine and hung up without leaving a message.

He went to the refrigerator, grabbed a bottle of beer, and retreated to the couch in the living room. The Texas Rangers were playing on ESPN, but he couldn't focus on the game.

Some drunk asshole held a gun to her head for about thirty minutes . . .

It made his palms damp. Now some things made sense, though. Like why she'd made that crack about his NWA membership. Why she'd acted the way she had this afternoon.

He thought about calling her cell phone, but decided it was a conversation he'd rather have in person. Assuming she'd be willing to talk. Maybe she wouldn't be. Maybe their relationship hadn't progressed as far as he thought. If it had, surely she'd share a traumatic event like that with him. If the situation were reversed, he'd certainly have told her about it. Hell, the situation *had* been reversed; Marlin had had his share of excitement on the job, and she knew about all of it. He'd recounted each episode in detail. Why hold back?

Depressing.

Top of the ninth and the Cardinals were winning by five.

He flicked the TV off, put the cordless phone back into its cradle, and went to bed, where the scent of her shampoo lingered on his pillow.

25

IN PAUL HEBERT'S long career, he'd only dealt with one bona fide celebrity—a hotheaded, womanizing, hard-partying relief pitcher for the Astros. His old partner Vince had dubbed it the shishkabob case. Late eighties.

What happened was, the pitcher and his newly reconciled wife were enjoying a quiet afternoon at their minimansion in the high-dollar area known as West University. Beautiful day, and they were grilling steaks on an elevated deck in the backyard. Birds were singing in the trees and everything was just dandy.

Then one of the pitcher's love-struck groupies showed up and ruined the party. Turned out the pitcher had been giving the groupie one-on-one lessons on the proper way to grip a bat, so to speak. *Now I'm pregnant,* she said, pointing a finger, *and he's the dad.*

The situation, of course, became tense, words were exchanged, and the two women went at it like hellcats. Pulling hair. Slapping and scratching. Kicking and biting. Eventually, the wife got the upper hand, and she managed to shove the girlfriend over the deck railing.

If they'd all been lucky that day, it might have worked out differently. A ten-foot fall, the girl could have limped away with a few broken bones, or maybe even just a sprain.

But they weren't lucky, because she landed on the spikes of an ornamental fence and took one straight through the heart. Never even had a chance to whimper. The wife drew three years, and the pitcher was booted down to double-A ball, where he suffered a career-ending hand injury when he punched a mascot dressed as a woodchuck.

Fortunately, Hebert wasn't expecting that sort of drama tonight. He and Ramon arrived at Sabrina Nash's loft at a quarter after ten. They'd phoned ahead, but they hadn't given her any details. They wanted to be there to gauge her reactions.

Standing on her doorstep, Ramon cupped his hand to his mouth and checked his breath. Hebert smiled. The kid would've been in his early teens when Sabrina Nash's show was a big hit. Raging hormones and all that. Ramon might've even had her infamous bikini poster on his bedroom wall. Probably getting half a stiffie right now from the memories.

When she opened the door, Hebert couldn't help but be a little tongue-tied himself. Gorgeous lady, just like he remembered her. A little older, of course, but still a knockout, even wearing a simple V-necked top and purple silk pants. Her blond hair was pulled back with one of those stretchy headband gizmos, and she was wearing small rimless glasses that made her glorious green eyes all that more appealing.

"Miss, uh, Miss—"

"Nash."

"Yeah, I'm Detective Paul Hebert. Sorry for the late hour, but—"

"It's okay."

"This is my partner, Detective Ramon Arriaga. Thanks for seeing us."

"Come on in."

She led them inside, and Hebert took the opportunity to sneak a peek at her backside. Jeez. Like a goddamn sculpture. *How's a woman her age manage that?*

She offered coffee, which Hebert declined for the both of them. Then they sat on matching leather sofas in a living room that was tastefully decorated without being prissy. Comfortable, but nothing too extravagant. Expensive, sure, but not so it rubbed your face in it.

Something smelled nice, like a scented candle or a bowl of potpourri. Large watercolor paintings of flowers hung on one wall, and on another, framed prints of political cartoons. Soft jazz was playing, and a floor lamp cast muted light on a book—one of those larger paperbacks—on the couch next to her. They'd interrupted her reading. Hebert checked the title: *The Second Coming of Lucy Hatch*. Sounded kind of erotic.

Sabrina Nash sat on the edge of the sofa cushion, her back straight, her knees together. She looked at Hebert with expectant eyes, but she appeared to have no idea why they were there. He didn't ease into it, because he didn't see the point.

"Miss Nash, you read the *Statesman* today?"

"Call me Sabrina. No, I didn't. I don't read it every day."

"Watch the news on TV?"

She shook her head. "You're making me nervous. What's happened?"

"You remember a man named Wilber Henley?"

Her face clouded over, which told Hebert something right off the bat. "Of course I do. He sold a gun illegally to Duane Rankin," she said. "He skipped the background check. He didn't fill out any paperwork."

Exactly, Hebert thought. *He testified to that fact and helped put Rankin away, but you still hated the son of a bitch. And who could blame you?*

"We came here to tell you that he was murdered."

Her eyes opened wide. She looked at Ramon, then back to Hebert. "My God. How . . . ?"

"He was killed in his gun shop. Here in town."

"When?"

"Late Monday night or early Tuesday."

"What, a robbery?"

"No, ma'am. He—Well, let me cover a few other things first. I'm sure you also remember Roland Nichols."

"Yes." She laughed. "Why? Is he dead, too?"

Hebert stared at her.

"Oh my God, he *is* dead?"

Hebert nodded. "He was killed sometime between Tuesday night and Wednesday morning."

Her lips parted, but no words came out. Either she was a damn good actress—which meant she must've taken a *bunch* of lessons since *Holy Roller*—or she was genuinely surprised. Shocked, even.

Finally, she said, "I don't know what to say. That's horrible."

"So you can understand why we're here."

She frowned. "Frankly, no."

"The incidents are connected. I can't get into the details, but we think the same person killed both men."

She suddenly covered her mouth with her hand. "Oh my God."

"Yes, ma'am."

Then the actress asked an odd question: "Were they shot?"

"I'm afraid I can't say. Why do you ask?"

"I don't—It's just that the guy owned a gun shop. And with Nichols—I don't know—I guess it would just seem ironic if they were shot."

Hebert let the strange comment pass, because he wasn't sure what to make of it. "Can you think of anyone who might want to harm either of them?"

Like, say, Harry Jenkins?

Hebert and Ramon had put their heads together with the wise folks at the district attorney's office, and it seemed clear that everything revolved around the Duane Rankin case. The killer's motive, obviously, was vengeance. Wilber Henley had provided the gun that had indirectly led to the death of Sabrina Nash's son, and Nichols, citing a lack of physical evidence, had lowered the charge from murder to manslaughter.

Seven years later, somebody was still pissed about it. That theory seemed like a stretch until Hebert learned that Duane Rankin was up for parole. It was what a psychologist might call a catalyst. The triggering factor that got this whole shebang started. And the more they studied it, the more they realized they really had only one viable suspect.

Sabrina Nash shook her head and said, "No, I—I have no idea who'd do something like that. I can't imagine . . ."

"I'll be straight with you. We'd really like to speak to your ex-husband."

"Harry?"

"Yes, ma'am."

"Is he—Oh my God, you think *Harry* did it?"

"Do you?"

"Of course not. Get serious. That's ludicrous."

"Did you ever hear him make any threats about this sort of thing? Lately, or seven years ago?"

"Never. Not then and not now. Harry hates violence. He wouldn't . . ."

"Does he have a temper?"

"Well, sometimes, sure. He was angry about what happened. We both were. You can understand that."

"I can. Yes, ma'am."

Hebert got the sense that the actress was holding back. No, she wasn't lying; more like she was having suspicions of her own, and she was doing her best to hide them. Probably why she asked if the victims had been shot. She'd probably made the same leap that he and Ramon had: that Harry Jenkins, if he had to kill someone, would never use a handgun.

"On the other hand," Hebert continued, "I bet this parole hearing on Monday has stirred up some bad feelings."

"That's only natural."

"Yes, ma'am, it is. All the same, we'd sure like to speak to Harry. Has he been in touch lately?"

There was a pause. Not much of one, but enough that Hebert noticed it. "Not in a few weeks," she said.

Now she is *lying,* he thought. He paused for a moment, trying to decide how hard he wanted to press her. He stood and sauntered over to the collection of framed prints, buying some time.

"Hell of a talent," he said.

The cartoons were more complex and refined than most cartoons he'd seen. But Harry Jenkins, Hebert had learned, was equally known for his razorlike commentary, not just his artwork. Hebert looked at Sabrina, and she smiled, tight and forced.

He turned back to the prints. "Me, I can hardly draw a straight line. And those clever captions he comes up with? Knowing all the ins and outs of politics and big business and stuff like that? Sheesh. He must have a mind like a friggin' steel trap."

Behind him, she said, "Smartest man I've ever known."

There were nine cartoons in three rows of three. Black frames, gray mats. His eye naturally fell on the one in the center, and then he moved to the one next to it, and—

What the hell?

He went back to the one in the center.

He studied it longer and couldn't believe what he was seeing. His heartbeat picked up. "What's the story on this one?" he asked casually.

He continued to eye the cartoon as Sabrina Nash answered. "You've heard of Glenn Dobbins?" she asked.

"Sure. The congressman. Running for governor."

"Well, he got the bright idea that we should allow teachers to carry concealed guns in school—as a measure of protection for the students. This was right after Columbine. Anyway, Dobbins introduced a bill to that effect, and there was a protest outside his office in Abilene. A *peaceful* protest. Nobody was doing anything wrong or breaking the law. But Dobbins was friends with the police chief, who sent a bunch of cops down in riot gear. A couple of the protestors were beaten on the way to jail, but they couldn't prove it. Harry did a whole series on it—really stuck it to Dobbins—and it won him the Pulitzer."

Hebert remembered something about the controversy. The cartoon showed a skinny, wild-eyed kid holding a picket sign, with a sneering, barrel-chested cop bearing down on him from behind, nightstick drawn.

But that wasn't the interesting part. No, sir.

What had caught Hebert's eye was the fact that the kid had a DOBBINS FOR CONGRESS bumper sticker pasted across his mouth. What it showed was *modus operandi,* big time. The caption read GLENN DOBBINS' IDEA OF FREE SPEECH.

"When did this run?" Hebert asked.

"Seven years ago," she said. "Right before Jake died."

Hebert nodded somberly and let a moment of respect pass. He sat back down on the couch. He'd tell Ramon about his discovery later.

Sabrina Nash was waiting patiently.

"Any idea how we can get ahold of Harry?" Hebert asked.

"He mostly works from home."

Yeah, I know, Hebert thought. *We've already been to his house. Three days' worth of mail in the mailbox.* "We haven't been able to reach him there. You got his cell number?"

She gave him a small smile—a genuine one this time. "He doesn't own a cell phone. He's sort of . . . eccentric."

Hebert smiled back. "I can understand that. I wish I could throw mine in the damn lake. Pardon my French. Let me ask you this, then. Does Harry have family we can talk to? Brothers or sisters? Anyone who might've heard from him recently?"

"He has a brother in California, but they don't talk very often. His parents have both passed away."

"Friends? Someone he might be staying with?"

She shook her head. "Harry was never very good at making friends."

"Maybe a girlfriend, then? I hate to ask personal questions like this, but—"

"No, it's fine. Harry and I are still close. He'd tell me if he were dating someone special, and he hasn't mentioned anything like that. Have you tried Byron Gladwell? He's Harry's boss at the newspaper."

"Yes, ma'am. He wasn't able to help us." *But, oh, by the way, he did tell us that Harry's been acting really bizarre lately.*

Hebert knew his persistence would only underline how anxious he was to speak to Jenkins, maybe even cause her to clam up, so he tried to sound offhand. "Okay, if Harry decided to take a quick trip— maybe, you know, to blow off steam—where would he go? Anyplace special you can think of?"

In other words, where would he hide out?

Something flashed in her eyes—again, for just an instant. It was enough. *She knows something.*

But she said, "Harry just sits at home and draws. That's all he does. His cartoons are everything to him now. If he's not there, I have no idea where he'd be."

And that, Hebert thought, *is lie number two.*

The rednecks were long gone, and Mitch was passed out in front of the television when the cordless phone rang. He noticed it didn't even jangle his nerves. That was the nice thing about whiskey. Dulled the senses. Kept him from being jumpy. He checked the caller ID, saw that it was blocked, answered anyway. *Who gives a fuck?*

A voice said, "Hey, Norm, it's me again."

"You're a stubborn sumbitch, ya know that?" Mitch said. "I'm tellin' ya, ain't no Norm here."

"Laying it on a little thick, aren't you? Dude, your accent is thicker than it was earlier. You should try to be more consistent."

"You should try to be less of a jerkoff." Mitch giggled. Witty line.

"Been drinking a little, Norm?"

"I ain't Norm."

"But this *is* Mitch Campbell, right? Can we agree on that?"

"I got an idea. Why don'cha tell me who you are first?"

"I will. Eventually. But here's a hint. I was a photographer for the school newspaper. In fact, I was sorting through a bunch of old junk this evening, and I found a real doozie. An issue from April of our senior year. Remember that Al Gore rally on campus?"

"Yeah. I mean no. I wasn't there. What campus?" *Careful. Watch your tongue.*

"You know how it was. Most of the student body was pretty conservative. Bunch of spoiled kids from old East Coast money. But there was a handful of liberals, and you used to hang with that crowd now and then. Rebelling against, well, whatever. Mostly I think your friends liked to piss off their parents."

"Got a point?"

"Well, yeah. In this one particular photo, you're holding up a sign that says LICK BUSH."

Damn. I remember that. Vaguely.

"Face it, Norm. That's the kind of thing that could ruin you. Remember that mess with the Dixie Chicks?"

"They're still singing."

"Yeah, they got past it. But you? Dude, you created a whole new identity from scratch. You're not who you say you are. How do you think your fans would react to that?"

"I might give a fuck if I was this Norman Kleinschmidt you keep babbling about." Mitch knew there was something wrong with what he had just said, but he couldn't nail it down. The caller pointed it out for him.

"I never said the name Kleinschmidt."

Oops. There it was. *Well, shit.*

"Time to come clean, Norm. Time to fess up."

"You asshole."

"Hey, I'm not the one that's a fraud. You brought this on yourself."

"I ain't no fraud."

"You can drop the accent. It's kind of annoying."

"I'll drop something, all right. I'll drop you like a bad habit."

"God, do you know how stupid you sound? You need to quit fighting this and just hear me out."

Even in his inebriated state, Mitch knew he was trapped. This guy had him. "What do you want?" Mitch asked. This time, there was no twang. In fact, he sounded exactly like a kid from Middlebury, Vermont.

"You know what?" the caller said. "I think we'd better wait until you sober up a little. I don't want you changing your mind on me later."

"Let's just get this over with," Mitch pleaded.

"I don't think so. I'll call you back tomorrow."

Then a dial tone.

Mitch rose to his feet, swayed unsteadily for a second, then walked to the library. He scanned a shelf full of books. *Ah, there it is.* His senior yearbook. He began thumbing through it. He quickly learned that the caller wasn't *a* photographer for the newspaper, he was *the* photographer. There was only one. Now Mitch knew his name. Big deal. Didn't help.

26

A MONTH BEFORE the NWA held a rally in Houston—and a full seven years after an incorrigible Boy Scout named Freddie Martin sent a .22 round whizzing past Dick Angerman's right ear—Angerman parked his Camaro at the curb in front of a run-down duplex in Del Valle, just off Highway 71, southeast of Austin.

With the brim of his baseball cap pulled low, he crossed the lawn and knocked softly on the door of unit B. He was carrying a bottle of Tickle Pink in a brown paper sack. He had two joints tucked in with his Marlboros. Party time. He'd been looking forward to this all week.

Sometimes, when he was waiting on the doorstep like this, Dick wondered if the neighbors were watching him from behind darkened windows. *Goddamn prying bastards.* Were they in there, leering and snickering at him? The truth was, he didn't really care if anyone judged him. It had taken a long time to come to grips with the situation, but he had, and he thought he was a better man for it. Compassionate. Open-minded. So why did he feel so ashamed?

He knocked again.

A few seconds later, the light behind the peephole was obscured for a moment, then he heard the slide of the dead-bolt lock. The door swung open and Bonita was standing there in a long, lacy nightgown. Green. Dick's favorite color. *Lord have mercy, she looks good tonight.*

"Why joo late, baby?" she asked, pushing her plump bottom lip out in a mock pout. Her long black hair was in disarray, and Dick found it incredibly sexy. Her makeup was thick and colorful, like one of those soap-opera stars on the Mexican channel. She was absolutely mesmerizing. "I was falling asleep waiting for joo."

He smiled at her. "Had to work late. Backed-up toilet over in Westlake. You know I get time and a half on Saturdays."

"Why din't joo call?"

"I was on the road. I can't call you from my cell phone 'cause Irene might see it on the bill."

"Joo coulda used a pay phone."

"Aw, I didn't want to take the time. I was in a hurry to get over here. Don't be mad, 'kay?"

She frowned for a moment, then stepped aside and let him in. She closed and locked the door behind him.

As always, he couldn't contain himself. He wrapped his free arm around her and pulled her close. Her body was small and fragile. She resisted at first, then gave in. "Missed you," he whispered into her ear. "Missed you so much." He nuzzled her neck and was swept away by the smell of the body lotion she always wore. Mango.

Their mouths met and their tongues danced like mating snakes. The bottle of wine slipped from his hand and landed with a muted thud on the carpet. She removed his cap and ran long fingernails through his thinning hair. She playfully bit down on his tongue, then sucked on it— a hint at what was to come. He felt himself growing hard.

He ran his hands up her torso, cupping her breasts, which seemed to have grown even larger in the past few months. Excellent. The hormones were doing their job. Her voice had risen an octave since he'd known her. Laser treatment had taken care of the hair problem.

Yes, the transition was coming along nicely.

The truth was, Bonita was nearly the perfect woman—except for the penis.

* * *

Two hours later, lying in the dark, she said, "Joo awake?"

"Yeah, baby."

A long pause, then: "I'm sad."

"I know."

"I'll never have enough money."

Dick knew that, too. The surgery would cost a fortune. Less in Mexico, but still a hell of a lot. He patted her thigh, careful to keep his hand away from the danger zone. Last thing he wanted was a handful of man parts. "Some day you will. Just keep saving."

He didn't want to have the same conversation they'd had several times before. She had a scheme in mind, and it was too crazy. She was desperate and emotional—a side effect of the hormones, he guessed.

"I can get it sooner," she said.

He didn't answer.

"I don' wan' to wait," she said.

Deep down, he couldn't blame her. He wondered what he'd do in her situation. Thinking about it kind of creeped him out.

"It's too dangerous," he said.

"Not if I do it right."

He couldn't argue with that. With a little luck, she could get her hands on a major amount of cash with less effort than a trip to an ATM. On the other hand, if she got caught, things could get ugly fast.

"I'd worry about you," he said.

"I know."

"What if he catches you there?"

"He won'. I still have a key. I wait till he's gone."

"I bet he changed the locks."

"Nu-uh."

Dick flipped onto his side. "How do you know?"

He could tell she was afraid to say it, but she did. "I go there today and test it. The key still work."

"That was risky," he said.

"Nobody see."

"They could've."

"They din't."

The silence settled in. He could hear a toilet flushing in the adjoining duplex, followed by muffled voices. He wondered what kind of conversation they were having over there. Nothing like this one, he was sure.

"I don't want you to do it," he said.

"I don' want to, either. But I'm going to."

He sighed, but he had to admit there was something exciting about it all. He wondered if she was expecting him to help. She hadn't ever brought it up, and he wasn't going to offer. No way.

"You've made up your mind?"

"Jess." Neither of them spoke for several minutes. Then she said, "I wish I had a gon. Jus' to be safe." That's how she said it. Gon. *Gun.*

He struggled with it for a long time, then he said, "I've got one you can borrow."

Angerman had said adios to Patty Jo and her psychopath kid ages ago—but all these years later, he still had the gun he'd taken away from Freddie.

27

ONE OF THE things that had always intrigued and puzzled Marlin about investigating crimes—and one of the things that made it exciting and interesting—was the seemingly arbitrary and inexplicable ways in which elusive facts would suddenly present themselves in pairs or groups. Bits of information that had danced out of reach for days would, quite unceremoniously, fall into your lap in a neat little package. It was like watching for a shooting star during a meteor shower. Sometimes you'd strain your eyes for hours without seeing one—then you'd spot two or three in half a minute. They'd appear in front of you, seemingly of their own volition, often when you weren't expecting it.

Thursday morning was a good example of that phenomenon.

He had just turned off the shower when the phone rang. Out the window, the sun, still below the horizon, was beginning to pinken the underbellies of cirrus clouds to the east. Geist was snoozing quietly on the bathmat, directly in front of the shower stall. Marlin stepped over her, wrapped a towel around his midriff, and made his way to the phone in his bedroom.

"This is Marlin."

"Hey, it's Mike Winters. Hope I'm not calling too early."

"Not at all."

"Sorry I missed you yesterday. I was making deliveries most of the afternoon."

"Well, thanks for calling me back. Quick question."

"Shoot."

Of course, just then, Marlin heard the beep of call waiting.

"Can you hold for a sec, Mike?"

"Sure."

Marlin switched to the other line, and Bill Tatum, sounding satisfied, said, "Mitch Campbell's manager finally called me back. He said Mitch is at home and we should go see him. Wants this whole thing cleared up."

"He give you a phone number?"

"Yeah, and one better: the code for the gate. Do the numbers six-seven-nine-one ring a bell?"

The numbers on the slip of paper in Rodolfo Dominguez's truck. "Oh, hell, we should've put that together."

"No doubt, but now we know. Let's just move forward. Ready to take a ride?"

"You coming this way?"

"Yep. Be there in ten."

"I'll be ready." Marlin clicked back over to Mike Winters. "Sorry about that, Mike."

"Not a problem. You had a question?"

"You know J. B. Crowley?"

A strained tone came into Mike's voice. "Unfortunately, yeah. Not real crazy about the guy. Sort of a jerk."

"So I've been told."

"You didn't hear it from me, okay? He's a big customer."

"So you know where he works?"

"Oh, sure. He's the foreman on Mitch Campbell's place."

Marlin thought, *Why doesn't that surprise me at all?*

After Marlin disconnected, he turned toward his closet, then stopped to make another call instead. In the excitement of learning Rodolfo Dominguez's identity the previous afternoon, he'd forgotten something. When the dispatcher answered at the sheriff's department, Marlin said, "Darrell, I need you to run a guy's history for me. Last name is Crowley."

"I've been thinking about this," Congressman Glenn Dobbins said. "Maybe we could spread some money around. Like last time."

"I don't know if that would work," Dale Stubbs replied. "Depends on how it plays out. Who gets involved."

"If worse comes to worst, it'll be our only option."

"Let's hope it doesn't come to that."

"I'm counting on you, Dale. The bad press could kill us. No governorship, that's for damn sure. Hell, I might even lose my seat in the House."

"Whatever needs to be done, I'll do it," Stubbs replied. And he meant every word of it.

"I feel a little weird about this," Byron Gladwell said.

"It's the best thing for him," Paul Hebert replied. The three of them—the third being Ramon—were standing outside Harry Jenkins' office. According to Gladwell, Jenkins didn't use the office much, but undisturbed fingerprints had a long shelf life. They could compare Jenkins' print to the partial from the gun-oil bottle cap.

"I feel like I'm betraying him," Gladwell said. He was a pear-shaped man with thin hair and a weak chin. Meek. Didn't come across as a newspaperman. He blinked a lot. Big eyes behind corrective lenses.

"Look at it this way," Hebert said. "We get his prints and it'll probably clear him. You'll be doing him a favor."

Gladwell looked at him skeptically. "I'm sorry, and don't be frustrated with me, but I'm inclined to say no."

Hebert said, "I notice you didn't print anything about Harry in the paper this morning."

"As far as we're concerned, there's nothing to print. We don't deal in speculation."

"Hey, I understand. Smart move, keeping it quiet like that. It won't be so quiet if I have to get a warrant."

Gladwell blinked some more, thinking it over. "I want you to know, Harry is going to be very upset."

Waiting for his flight at LAX, Casey Walberg found a quiet corner and made a phone call. It rang five times, then went to voice mail. He dialed a cell number. Same thing—five rings and out. He smiled. Was Mitch Campbell trying to avoid him? Maybe. More likely, he was still sleeping it off.

"We need blood," Stubbs said.

"Blood?" Mitch replied. "Why?"

"You know."

Suddenly they were in Mitch's truck, which had a sturdy grille guard, made from welded pipe, protecting the front end. Bouncing around in the pasture where the rally would be held.

"So you're getting married, huh?" Stubbs said.

"Yeah. Right after the rally."

"Love her?"

"Who?"

"Sheryl."

"I guess. It's good publicity. That's what Joe says."

Stubbs pointed at a huge deer. It was the size of an elephant. "That fawn'll do. Nail her."

Mitch tried to hit it, but the deer was nimble and leapt over the truck on legs like pogo sticks.

"This field is full of weeds," Stubbs said. "You should do something about it. Fire hazard in this drought."

"J. B. is gonna mow it for the rally. Or maybe he already did." Mitch turned the truck around for another pass. "Why don't we just shoot it?"

"Too loud."

"I'm scared."

"Deep breaths, son."

"What do you want?"

"We'll talk about it after you sober up."

The fawn was all the way across the pasture now. Mitch pointed the truck right at it. The deer was back to its normal size. It was rooted in place, its eyes bulging with terror, watching the truck zoom closer. Mitch floored the accelerator.

Right before the impact, Stubbs said, "I can't even begin to tell you what a monumental fuckup this is."

Mitch was crying now. He said, "I know," and then he felt a small jolt, and the deer flew through the air, hooves over tail, and now the horn was blaring and blaring and ringing and ringing, and Mitch sat up in bed in a cold sweat. His heart was thumping. Christ, what a nightmare.

Another ring. And another. Then it stopped. Ten seconds later, his cell phone, over on the dresser, started ringing. He ignored it. It stopped, and then the landline started again. Mitch couldn't handle it anymore. He answered.

Joe Scroggins said, "Know anything about a dead Mexican?"

"Jesus, a what?"

"A dead Mexican."

"No. I mean, yeah, I've been hearing about it on the news, but—"

"Blanco County cops called me just now. Said the dead guy was supposedly working on your place."

"Wait, it's the same guy? J. B. mentioned hiring somebody, but he never showed. That's all I know."

"Cops're gonna wanna ask some questions. They's headed your way."

"Now?" Mitch was out of bed, holding the phone with his shoulder, struggling to pull some jeans on.

"Right now. I gave 'em the gate code."

"Ah, Jesus, Joe . . ."

"Sorry 'bout that, but you been damn hard to get hold of lately. I had to give 'em something. Best to put this whole thing to rest right quick. Just be right up front with 'em and they'll be outta your hair."

"Of course I will. I'll tell them everything I know, which is nothing."

"Good boy. They agreed to keep it low profile. We don't need the media gettin' hold of this, makin' a big deal outta nothin'."

"I agree."

"Okay, then, this J. B.—what sorta character is he?"

"What do you mean?"

"He wouldn'tve done something stupid, would he? Like shooting a Mexican?" Joe said it like he was half-kidding, but Mitch could hear a trace of concern.

Mitch laughed, and it sounded surprisingly genuine. "Get serious, Joe. He's not even here. He's been out of town since Saturday."

"Excellent. That's what I wanted to hear. All right, then. Sounds like everything's under control. Lemme know if you need anything. You all set for the shoot?"

"The shoot?"

"The chili commercial, son. Remember?"

Mitch had completely forgotten. "Of course I do. I'm ready. What time are they getting here?"

"Around two. Let me know how it goes. I'll see you at the rally."

And then Joe was gone. And then the doorbell rang.

Seven miles from the nearest town, near the end of an isolated county road, Sabrina Nash stopped at a long caliche driveway that was cordoned off by a chain strung between two wooden fence posts. But, as she remembered after all these years, one side of the chain wasn't locked; it simply hung from a nail on the back side of the post. As Harry used to say, "At least it keeps the honest people out."

She navigated slowly down the rutted, sloping road, her undercarriage scraping occasionally, until, two hundred yards in, she came to a modest cabin on the banks of a river. Sabrina saw no sign of activity. Good. No Volvo. No other vehicles, either, which didn't surprise her. Sure, it was summertime, but with the drought, the river had been reduced to a meager, dirty trickle. Who would want to sit out here and bake in the sun, especially when swimming wasn't an option?

Around the perimeter of the cabin, tall native grasses—brown and thirsty for water—indicated that there hadn't been regular visitors for several months, probably since spring break. She recalled that the local man who maintained the property only came out if someone was going to be using the place.

She cut the engine, stepped from her Lexus, and paused, listening. Nothing but the incessant buzzing of cicadas. There was no wind, and the heat, even at eight in the morning, was beginning to build.

The humidity pressed against her like a warm washcloth, and she immediately began to perspire.

She looked left, then right, and saw nothing but trees. The cabin sat on fifteen wooded acres, and the adjoining tracts, both much larger, had nothing on them at all—no houses, no cabins, no structures of any kind. The nearest actual neighbor was a good half mile away.

Yep, if Harry needed a place to get away, this was the perfect spot. *But Harry doesn't need to hide,* she reminded herself. *It's ridiculous that I'm even out here. This is a fool's errand.*

On the other hand, she decided, now that she was here, she might as well have a look around. She walked to the cabin, the gravel crunching under her feet, and knocked on the front door. *Why the hell am I knocking?* She tried the knob. Locked. Of course it was. There wasn't anybody inside, and there hadn't been for quite some time. She put her face to the dusty glass and studied the dim interior. She could see the entryway and part of the small living room. She didn't see anybody. There weren't any shoes near the door or clothes strewn about.

She circled to the left side of the cabin, peering through miniblinds into the first bedroom. Queen-sized bed, mattress stripped, no pillows. Visitors had to bring their own linens. The top of the nightstand was bare. There was no other furniture.

She moved to the next window, the second bedroom, where she saw the same two sets of metal-framed camp-style bunk beds that had been here ages ago. Again, no sheets or pillows. The room became blurry, and she realized she was crying.

She remembered that Jake always chose one of the upper bunks, because he liked to pretend he was sleeping in a treehouse in the middle of a jungle. In the morning, over scrambled eggs and bacon, he'd tell elaborate stories about tigers and elephants and other exotic creatures he'd encountered around his "campground." She hadn't thought about that in years. Strange how snippets of buried memory could leap out at you, as clear and detailed as if they'd happened days ago.

She wiped her eyes and continued to the rear, where four wrought-iron chairs and a barbecue grill sat on the covered concrete patio. A tire swing, which had been suspended from an oak limb as thick as an oil drum, had fallen to the ground, its rope rotted through.

She could see Jake in that swing, giggling wildly, Harry pushing him higher and higher. She shook the image out of her head and stepped onto the patio, and then she froze.

The back door was open.

Just four inches or so, but it was open. She stepped closer and saw splintered wood along the doorjamb. The door had been forced. Suddenly the cabin didn't seem so abandoned. She felt the urge to return to her car, but she didn't.

She pondered the possibilities. Maybe Harry *had* been here. Or partying teenagers. Or a group of harmless illegal immigrants seeking shelter. On the other hand, maybe it had been a psychotic mask-wearing axe murderer straight out of some gory horror flick.

"Hello?"

What if someone—not Harry—is inside? What if they're watching me right now? Waiting for me. Nobody knows I came out here.

She called more loudly. "Hello?"

Her shout caused the cicadas to stop buzzing, which only made the situation creepier. The sudden silence was just too much. She was fully prepared to run. She decided that if anyone other than Harry poked his head out, she'd put those grueling hours on the treadmill to good use and haul her toned ass into the hills. Just abandon the car and scoot.

"Hey, Harry? You in there?"

Nothing.

"I'm coming in!"

She didn't budge.

I'm letting my imagination get the best of me. Nobody is in there.

Then she had a terrible thought. What if Harry was inside, and he wasn't answering because he couldn't? He'd been despondent and depressed. He still blamed himself. Had he been suicidal? In her opinion, no, but with Harry, you never knew what might happen next.

Christ, why did I let that idea enter my head? Stupid!

She knew she'd never be able to leave now without checking the interior of the cabin.

She debated calling the police, but she'd already decided against that route, hadn't she? In truth, she'd lied to the two cops last night. A lie of omission. She'd had an idea where Harry might be, and she hadn't told them. It had surprised her the way she'd kept her mouth shut.

"Hey, Bill, I'm going inside. You wait out here." Yeah, real slick. An imaginary companion, to make the axe murderer think twice about attacking her. Like anyone would fall for that. Before she lost her nerve, she stepped to the door and pushed it open. It gave a long, slow squeal as it swung inward, and now she could see into the small kitchen. Again, no signs of an occupant; no dirty dishes on the Formica countertop, no coffee mugs on the round wooden breakfast table.

She stepped inside, leaving the door open behind her. The air was muggy and still. Dust motes floated in thin rays of sunshine that sneaked through the blinds like lasers. The cabin smelled vaguely of rodent droppings. One last time, she said, "Hello?"

All was still.

She checked the kitchen sink and found it dry. The refrigerator had a six-pack of beer in it, but there was no telling how long that had been there. Then, in the trashcan under the sink, she found a bunch of beer cans and several plastic trays from frozen dinners. She could tell from the remnants that the food had been eaten recently. Someone had been here, but it wasn't necessarily Harry.

I should leave right now.

But she didn't. Instead, she took a hallway to the right and inspected the bedrooms more closely. They were as empty as college dorm rooms between semesters. The shared bathroom showed no signs of recent use.

That left the living room. Sabrina found nothing in there except a worn couch, an easy chair, and a small TV on a metal stand. She remembered that the reception out here was surprisingly good, picking up stations from both Austin and San Antonio. She'd find Jake in here on Saturday mornings, watching cartoons, trying to be quiet as his parents slept late.

The fireplace was clean of ashes. A stack of old newspapers rested on the hearth, something to start kindling with. There was nothing to indicate that Harry had been the one in the cabin, and that lifted her spirits. Maybe the detectives were off target.

Okay, then. Good. She turned to leave, but stopped. Something wasn't right.

She gave the room another look, and her eyes settled on the stack of newspapers. That's what it was. They were all aging to a muted yellow—except for one copy right on top of the pile. It was as crisp and white as if it had been printed last week.

She pulled it from the stack and saw that she was wrong. It hadn't been printed last week, it had been printed yesterday. Her heart sank when she saw a below-the-fold headline on the front page:

GUN SHOP OWNER KILLED

Her knees went weak and she dropped into the easy chair. There was no more denying it.

Oh, God. He's lost it.

Her eyes welled up again, and she began to sob. The tears came freely—for Jake, for Harry, even for Wilber Henley and Roland Nichols. Ten minutes later, she was numb. She didn't know what to believe. She couldn't decide if she should alert the detectives or keep her mouth shut. There was an ugly part of her that wanted to applaud Harry for his actions, and she had to remind herself that violence wasn't the solution.

She rose and returned to the kitchen, where she found a pen and paper in a drawer.

The note was simple and to the point:

H—

Call me! Important!

—S

She left it on the breakfast table in the kitchen.
She took the newspaper with her.

28

WHEN THE DOOR swung inward, Marlin was taken aback by what he saw. Mitch Campbell was known as a good-looking guy—a certified heartthrob—but this man looked like he might be Campbell's haggard, unhealthy older brother.

His eyes were sunken and bloodshot, and he was skinnier than he looked in his videos. His feet were bare. He was wearing faded jeans and a pearl-snap shirt with the sleeves torn off—the latest in slacker-country fashion, but it made Campbell look more like a derelict than a trendy Nashville performer. Marlin knew that Campbell had recently finished an extensive tour, and he decided that life on the road must be hard on a man.

The first thing Campbell said, smiling, was, "Well, a lot of critics have said my guitar-playing is a crime, and I guess they were right. I wondered when y'all would track me down."

He chuckled, and his teeth—the ultra-white, capped dental work of a celebrity—looked out of place on his tired face.

"Mr. Campbell?" Bill Tatum said, returning the grin.

"Yeah, how are y'all doing? Joe just called and said you were on your way." He stuck his hand out, and Tatum and Marlin introduced themselves. Campbell's eyes lingered on Marlin's badge for a few seconds.

Tatum said, "You got a minute to talk?"

"Sure, come on in."

He led them to a large, expensively furnished living room, and Marlin, following behind, smelled whiskey. Not fresh whiskey, but the soured scent that seeps from a man's pores after a bender.

Campbell gestured toward a pair of overstuffed armchairs. "Y'all want coffee or anything?"

"No, thanks," Tatum said, and looked at Marlin.

"I'm fine." They were both anxious to get down to it.

Campbell sat on a black leather couch, one bare foot tucked under his butt. "Okay, then. I'll help in any way I can, but I'm afraid you're in for a letdown. This is about that dead Mexican man, right?"

"Yes, sir," Tatum said. "His name was Rodolfo Dominguez. Did you know him?"

"Never heard of him, never met him. If I had, I would've called you folks. I saw it on the news."

"Did you recognize him?"

"Sorry, no. What happened, anyway? They said he was shot?"

"Yes, sir, he was."

"Right across the road from me, huh?"

"Not far from here."

"They were saying at first you thought it was a hunting accident."

"They?"

"The news people."

"Something like that."

Campbell nodded. "Sucks either way, I guess. Hate to see somebody killed with a gun."

Marlin wondered what that meant. That it was a tragedy because someone had died? Or that a death by gunfire brought discredit to the gun-rights community? He supposed the distinction didn't really matter.

"We spoke to his sister in Mexico," Tatum said, "and she told us Rodolfo was supposed to start working here this past Sunday. Know anything about that?"

Campbell's brow furrowed. "Joe said something about that, too.

All I know is that J. B. was gonna hire somebody to get the grounds in shape for the rally, and the guy never showed. Whether or not it's the same guy, I have no idea. I ended up hiring a couple of men myself."

Just like we figured, Marlin thought. *Crowley, not Campbell, had hired Rodolfo.*

"Has J. B. hired men to work out here before?" he asked.

Campbell nodded. "Yeah, sure, a couple times, especially right after the house was built. J. B. hired a crew to cut cedar, and to build the rock entrance at the gate. But that was six or eight months ago."

"Were they illegal aliens?"

Campbell shrugged. "Well, they looked like Mexicans, but I don't know if they were illegal or not. J. B. handled all that stuff. I never even spoke to them."

"So, you don't know for sure whether Dominguez ever set foot on your ranch?"

"I really don't."

"We noticed that you have a security camera at your gate. Does it shoot video?"

"No, it's just a monitor, so I can see who's down there."

"Where is J. B. now?" Tatum asked.

"On a trip with his son."

"So he's married?"

"Divorced. Takes the kid on vacation in the summer."

"Where were they headed?"

"On a camping trip, I think. Fishing. I wish I could tell you where, but he didn't give me any details."

"Somewhere nearby?"

"I would assume so, but I'm not sure."

"You know the ex-wife's name?"

Campbell paused, thinking. "Jesus, I feel bad; you're asking me all these things I don't know. If J. B. mentioned her name, I don't remember it. He doesn't talk about her much. He doesn't talk about anything much. J. B.'s a quiet guy." He suddenly snapped his fingers. "The ex-wife lives someplace in East Texas. Does that help?"

"Maybe so. When did they leave?"

Campbell brightened, apparently happy for a question he could answer. "Saturday morning—that was the plan."

"Did you talk to him on Saturday?"

"No, the last time I saw him was Friday afternoon." Now Campbell appeared concerned. "I have to ask this: Is J. B. a suspect or something? I figured you just wanted some information from him."

Tatum fudged. "We're just gathering as many facts as we can. If we could talk to J. B., it would really help us out. He tell you when he was coming back?"

"A week or ten days or thereabouts. We have a pretty loose arrangement. What he does for me—it's not a nine-to-five type of job. As long as he takes care of things, I just let him come and go as he pleases. It works out fine."

"He have a cell phone?" Marlin asked.

"Yeah, I've seen him with one, but I don't even know the number." Campbell smiled again. "Man, I'm sorry I'm not being much help. I feel like an idiot."

"No, you're doing fine," Tatum said. "Any chance he'll call you while he's gone?"

"I really doubt it. He has no reason to."

"What about the rally? Isn't he helping you get ready for it?"

"Oh, J. B. won't be involved with that. Besides, it's a pretty simple process. It's all trailers nowadays. The bathrooms, the concession stands, the stage—everything. All they do is pull the trailers in and unhook. Generators provide all the power. Shouldn't take but a day to get it all set up. The Alliance hired a bunch of people to take care of all that. All I've gotta do is show up and sing."

"I'm a little confused," Tatum said. "Didn't you say J. B. was hiring someone to get the grounds ready for the rally?"

"Well, kind of. What I meant was, the grounds up around the house. Some VIPs are spending the night, so J. B. said he'd find somebody to get the place in order. But the rally itself will be held on the lower pasture. You drove right past it."

"How many people you expecting?" Marlin asked. Coming onto the ranch, he and Tatum had noticed at least forty acres of mowed pastureland on either side of the driveway. Parking on one side, he figured, and the rally on the other.

"About five thousand. Either of you planning to join us?" The singer was smiling again, knowing that he was putting them on the spot. He was fishing for information, wanting to see if they were members of the NWA.

"Uh, family picnic that day," Tatum said. "Sorry."

"I imagine I'll be working the lake," Marlin said. "Fourth of July—lot of people on the water."

Campbell pointed at Marlin's shirtfront. "Yeah, I was noticing that you're a game warden. How did you wind up working on something like this?"

Marlin offered his standard sardonic explanation. "Hey, it's Bobby Garza's county. I just do what he tells me."

"Well, if you get a chance, come on by. Just show your badge and you'll get in free, whether you're a member or not. The NWA treats cops right. And I guarantee it'll be a lot of fun. Good food. A lot of nice, conservative ladies. And the music won't be half bad, either. Hey, I'll put you both on my guest list so you can get backstage."

"That'd be nice of you," Tatum said.

"Bring a friend, if you want."

"We appreciate it."

There was a moment of silence, and Marlin wondered if Tatum had decided against a direct approach. Now was the time to end the interview or take it to a different level. Tatum chose the latter by saying, "Mr. Campbell, were you aware that J. B. Crowley once killed a man?"

Campbell sat stock-still, pure puzzlement on his face. "Pardon me?"

"In Houston, eight years ago, he shot a black man. This was after they'd had some sort of dispute on the highway."

Darrell Bridges had run Crowley's complete criminal history, as Marlin requested. It revealed a few interesting facts—namely, one charge of aggravated assault, for which Crowley had spent eighteen months in Huntsville, and one charge of second-degree murder, for which he'd been acquitted. Marlin made a few phone calls, and an assistant district attorney named Weiser shared the pertinent details. The sole eyewitness said he'd seen the black man brandishing a gun, but only after Crowley had fired the first of his two shots. The media immediately insinuated that it was a racist killing by a gun fanatic, and gun-control advocates were prepared to have a field day. Lawyers for the NWA offered to represent Crowley "in the best interest of law-abiding gun owners everywhere." But then the witness suddenly became forgetful. Maybe the black man *had* fired a shot first. The jury had no choice but to find Crowley not guilty. Crowley had been suspected of several other crimes since then—including two cases of arson and the severe beating of an outspoken anti-gun crusader—but he was never indicted.

"He's a bad dude," Weiser said. "We just haven't been able to nail him yet."

"You think he threatened the witness?"

"Personally, hell yes. And he's been loosely affiliated with the NWA ever since. We think he's unofficially on the payroll, if you know what I mean."

"Doing what?"

"Bag man, strong-arm tactics, whatever."

Mitch Campbell, on the other hand, obviously hadn't known about his foreman's past. His complexion had gone pale. "Jesus. I didn't . . . I had no idea."

"How long have you known him?"

"Just about a year now. Ever since he came to work for me."

"How did that come about?"

"A friend recommended him for the job. I have to say, this really throws me for a loop. I've never seen any signs that J. B. was a violent man. None at all. He just does his work without complaint."

"Who was the friend?"

Campbell was staring into space, stunned by what he'd heard. "What?"

"The friend who recommended J. B."

"Uh, Dale Stubbs. You know who that is?"

Tatum nodded. Then he leaned forward to give his next words extra weight. "I shared all of this with you because I wanted to stress how important it is that we speak to J. B. Hopefully, he'll tell us something that will clear him. If he was traveling, he'll probably have receipts from a motel or a gas station. All we want to do is rule him out. Chances are, he had nothing to do with it. But if he calls you, it's important that you not spook him. Understand?"

Campbell blinked several times, still processing everything. "Absolutely. Of course. But I really think you guys are barking up the wrong tree. I'm pretty sure J. B. left on Saturday morning, before all this mess got started."

*   *   *

They walked in silence to the cruiser, and the moment they closed the doors, Tatum said, "Did you hear what I just heard?"

"Absolutely."

"So I'm not crazy. He just made a major slip-up there at the end?"

"Oh, yeah."

Tatum took a deep breath. "I can't believe it. Christ, he had me going until then."

"Me, too. I was surprised you didn't call him on it."

Tatum started the car and headed down the driveway. "I wanted some time to think this through. We need to double-check—make sure it really was a slip."

"It was, Bill. We never released that information. Not specifically. He knows more than he should."

Neither of them spoke again until they reached Cypress Mill Road. Then Tatum said, "If this pans out, you got any idea what a serious can of worms we're about to open?"

This wasn't the way it was supposed to work out. Not at all. Everything was getting all screwed up, and now the cops were on the trail of an innocent man.

Mitch hurried to the bar, poured a shot of bourbon, and downed it in a quick, practiced motion. He repeated the process three more times. Then he called Dale's direct line.

"The cops were just here," he blurted. "About the dead Mexican!"

"Goddamn, now, take it easy."

"I'm freaking out, Dale! They know he was supposed to be working here. They were asking about J. B."

"Don't worry about it. He was out of town. That's why it was the perfect place to leave the truck."

"But Christ, I'm just—"

"Worrying for no reason. Did they point the finger at you at all?"

"No."

"Did you manage to keep your wits about you?"

"Yeah, I think so."

"Didn't say anything stupid?"

"No."

"I assume you acted ignorant about everything."

"Right."

"Attaboy. I'm proud of you."

Mitch couldn't help but feel comforted by the remark.

"And you gotta remember," Stubbs continued, "it was all a big mistake. You didn't mean for it to happen, but it did, and you feel awful sorry about it. But there really ain't no point in punishing you for it now, is there? That's like closing the barn door after the cow done got out. Focus on that and it'll get you through."

It occurred to Mitch that what Stubbs was saying went against one of the NWA's basic tenets: that guns wouldn't be a problem in America if those who committed crimes with them were adequately punished. But now was not the time to quibble.

"Thanks, Dale," Mitch said.

"You just lie low, son. Everything'll be fine."

Dale Stubbs knew that everything would *not* be fine. He realized that he'd been deluding himself all along. Mitch Campbell was too panicky, too much of a weak sister, to make it through an extensive police investigation. He'd eventually cave, and then everything would be ruined. Stubbs could not allow that to happen. But what could he do?

An attorney? Send an NWA lawyer in and tell Campbell to keep his mouth shut? No good. The cops would say, *What do you need a lawyer for? You haven't done anything wrong, have you?* They'd apply pressure by leaking choice information to the media, and reporters from the major networks, newspapers, and magazines would descend on Mitch like flies on a deer carcass. And the scumbags at the tabloids would blow everything out of proportion, as they always did, or they'd tell complete lies. They could make a goddamn hangnail sound like brain surgery. No lawyers, then.

Stubbs sat quietly in his office and tried to come up with something—*anything*—to avoid impending doom. As far as he could see, he had no options at all.

Well, that's not exactly true . . .

There was one way. But it was completely outrageous. Way too radical. Surely there was a better solution. He wracked his brain for alternatives and drew a total blank. And his mind meandered back to the one and only answer.

I can't believe I'm even considering this.
Quit thinking about it.
It would work.
It's crazy.
But it's the only way out.
Don't do it.
Fuck you. Desperate times call for desperate measures. Dobbins is counting on me.

He left the NWA offices and used a pay phone at a nearby convenience store. No record of the call that way. After three rings, a man answered, and Stubbs said, "I need your help again. Right now."

29

THE FIRST TIME Sabrina met Harry, he was smoking a joint, naked, in a hot tub.

She was high in the hills above Hollywood, on the back deck of a spacious home owned by a well-known producer. Her first New Year's Eve away from Texas. Inside, it had been as loud and hot as a cattle car. The crowd was jammed elbow to elbow—actors, writers, pop stars, agents, managers—and it was one of those nights when everyone was letting their hair down. B-list starlets with low-cut dresses, stiletto heels, and dilated pupils giggled on every side of the room. Normally businesslike directors slurred their words and occasionally groped the aforementioned starlets, who squealed with mock indignation.

Sabrina's date—an assistant to the assistant programming director at one of the networks—had already made five visits to the bathroom, sniffing and wiping his nose vigorously each time he returned. He chattered incessantly about his ex-girlfriend and the time he played golf with Lee Majors and the value of a good boob job in this town. As the evening wore on, he couldn't keep his manicured hands off Sabrina's ass. She was glad she'd driven herself to the party, because she couldn't stand the thought of him attempting to give her a good-night grope on her doorstep.

An hour before midnight, she excused herself and stepped outside for some fresh air. There were plenty of people on the deck, too, but they were in smaller groups, holding low-key conversations.

The air was cool and crisp, and Sabrina could feel the four glasses of wine she'd drunk in the past two hours. *I'm twenty years old and I'm at one of the hottest parties in the country. So why aren't I having a good time?* The truth was, she was homesick. With the production schedule on *Holy Roller,* she hadn't had time to make any new friends or keep in touch with her old ones. And she hadn't met anybody in this crowd that she'd want to "do lunch" with anytime soon.

The host, a producer named Derek, came by with a bottle of wine in each hand and refilled her glass. His eyes were unfocused, he seemed to be leaning to the left, and the cadence of his speech was seriously out of whack. "Hey . . . there you having . . . fun?"

"Sure. I—"

"What's a pretty . . . girl like you all . . . alone for?"

"I was just—"

"C'mon . . . over here I wantcha . . . meet my brother."

He swayed unsteadily through a throng of partygoers toward a far corner of the deck, where the crowd was sparse. Sabrina, following behind, could smell marijuana and chlorine, and then she saw the hot tub, hunkered in the dark beneath a trellis. There were three people in it, and as Sabrina's eyes adjusted, she saw that two of them were women, and they were topless. One of them appeared to be sleeping, her head back, her arms extended along the top rim of the tub. Sabrina recognized the young woman as an actress from *Knight Rider.*

Derek said, "Hey guys this . . . is the iniminable . . . the initimable . . . this is Sabrina Nash. You can't copy her." Then he abruptly turned and levitated back the way he'd come, leaving Sabrina standing there, feeling intrusive.

"How are y'all?" she said. A quick hello, and then she'd go back inside, sober up with some coffee, and go home. Settle in with Dick Clark and a bottle of champagne.

"'Y'all,'" the one conscious woman snickered, drawing the word out, making fun of it. She was tucked up against the only man in the tub.

"I'm Harry," the man said. A joint was glowing in his hand, barely above the waterline. His shoulders were strong, his arms sinewy, but he had the round baby-faced look of an adolescent.

"Derek's brother," Sabrina said.

"Much younger, I might add. And more talented."

Sabrina smiled. "You in the business?" She felt pretentious using that phrase, but, well, everybody did.

"Seen the poster for *Cyborg Invasion?*"

"Sure. I went to the premiere last weekend."

"I drew the illustration."

"Really? It was excellent. So you're an artist."

Harry shrugged. "They paid me. I'm an ugly slave to commerce." He took a hit from the joint. He offered it to her; she shook her head. He said, "You're in one of Derek's shows. I wouldn't forget that face. Which one is it?"

"*Holy Roller,*" Sabrina said.

"That's the one," Harry said.

"It's a horrible show," his companion added.

"Pardon?" Sabrina said.

"Be nice, Beth," Harry said.

"It objectifies women, that's all I'm saying." Beth drank deeply from a fluted glass. Her hair was wet, her makeup smeared, and her eyes mere slits. She was a little heavy, and she was easily ten years older than Harry.

"You're missing the satire, Beth."

"Satire? Get real."

Harry winked at Sabrina and said, "Her show mocks social norms. She's skewering the stereotype of the blond bimbo. It's a powerful message. She's working for change from the inside."

"Yeah, right. The next Gloria Steinem."

"I thought you were all sisters in the battle against oppression. Maybe you should take it easy on her."

"Maybe you should quit flirting with her."

Harry shook his head. "Man, you're drunk."

"I'm not *drunk,* I'm just not a fan of little miss hot-pants over there."

How did I get in the middle of this? Sabrina wondered.

"Beth studied sociology at Berkeley," Harry explained. "Which means she thinks she knows everything."

Beth erupted with a "Ha!" Followed by: "You'd sleep with her in a heartbeat, wouldn't you? I know that much."

"Oh, great. I'm so glad you joined me tonight."

Sabrina started to turn, saying, "I'll think I'll go—"

"That's right, run away," Beth said. "Go back inside with the beautiful people."

Sabrina didn't think before she spoke, she simply spoke, and what came out was, "Jesus, lady, who put the bug up your ass?"

"Hey-o!" Harry called. "The sexpot strikes back!"

Beth wasn't pleased at all. "You did! You're reaffirming the notion that women are sexual commodities. You should be ashamed. If you even understand what I'm talking about."

"I understand just fine," Sabrina said, "but my career choices are none of your business." *Just go back inside.*

"Sorry, honey, but they are, because that little prick-tease you play every Thursday night reflects on all women. You may think you're simply flouncing around in a pair of tights, but what you're really doing is whoring us out."

"Oh, I see, *honey.*"

"Do you?"

"I do, and maybe you're right. Or maybe it's because you couldn't fit into that same pair of tights without a gallon of Crisco."

"Ouch," Harry said.

"What's that supposed to mean?" Beth huffed.

"It means you shouldn't hit the junk-food aisle every time you get the munchies. That's why you're chubby." Sabrina was on a roll now, and it felt great. "It wouldn't hurt to shave your armpits, either. Believe it or not, it's not inherently demeaning, it's simply good hygiene. A woman can be sexy without being an object. You should try it sometime."

Harry, who was chuckling, stuck the joint into his mouth and began to applaud. "Bravo! Well said!"

"You bitch!" Beth spat.

"Tight-ass," Sabrina replied.

"Slut!"

"Ballbuster."

"Hear, hear!" said Harry.

Beth pulled away from him. "I'll have both of you know that I'm proud of my body! I'd rather look like a natural woman than . . . than a porn star!"

"Mission accomplished," Harry muttered.

There was a sharp intake of breath as Beth expressed shock at Harry's betrayal. Sabrina tried to stifle a giggle, because, oddly enough, she was starting to feel sorry for Beth, who was now clambering clumsily over the side of the tub.

"Both of you are so immature I can hardly stand it!" she shrieked. She grabbed a towel from a nearby table and wrapped it around her torso. "Harry, I'm leaving. I don't know why I even came to this stupid party."

"Drive safely."

"I mean it!"

"There are nuts on the road tonight," Harry said. "What's one more?"

"Well, then . . . screw you!" Beth attempted to swirl dramatically, but lost her footing and crashed to the deck. Sabrina went to help her.

"Stay away from me!" She rose awkwardly and scurried into the house through a side door.

Everything was strangely quiet. Sabrina turned and saw that all of the guests on the deck had been watching the commotion. They quickly pretended to go back to their conversations.

"Oh, God. I'm, uh, really sorry about that," Sabrina said.

Harry gave her a don't-worry-about-it wave. "I should be apologizing to you. Beth is a judgmental pain in the ass."

"But that's not like me at all. Normally, I wouldn't have—"

"No, you did good. It was nice to see somebody unload on her like that."

There was a moment of silence, punctuated by snores from the *Knight Rider* actress, who had slept through the confrontation.

"You aren't really mocking social norms, are you?" Harry asked.

Sabrina smiled. "Not quite."

Harry smiled back, and it was the most genuine expression Sabrina had seen in months. "But you would if you had the chance?"

"In a heartbeat."

"Okay, then." He took a massive hit from the joint—held it, held it, held it—finally exhaled, and said, "Any chance you could give me a ride home?"

30

"GOOD, I WAS just looking for y'all," Bobby Garza said, sounding not quite urgent but definitely focused. Marlin and Tatum had come straight to his office. "How'd it go?"

They closed the door and took the two chairs in front of the sheriff's desk. Tatum then recounted the Mitch Campbell interview, with Marlin chiming in on occasion, filling in the details about J. B. Crowley's criminal past.

"Everything was going along just fine," Tatum said. "He was helpful, cooperative—happy to answer all our questions about Crowley. But then, as we were wrapping it up, Campbell said . . ." He turned to Marlin, who had jotted down the singer's remark verbatim.

" 'I really think you guys are barking up the wrong tree. I'm pretty sure J. B. left on Saturday morning, before all this mess got started.' "

Garza kept a poker face. He crossed his arms in front of his chest and said, "Read that back to me again."

Marlin recited the quote a second time.

Garza nodded. "We held back the estimated time of death.

Nobody knows that but us and Lem Tucker." The sheriff didn't appear nearly as intrigued as Marlin had expected him to be.

"All we told the media was that Dominguez had been dead for less than a week," Tatum said. "Which means it could've happened as far back as the middle of last week. Campbell had no way of knowing we'd narrowed it down to Saturday after midnight."

"Did you press him?"

"No way. Not yet. I wanted to, you know, have some semblance of a plan."

"Good, because there's something else y'all need to hear." He grabbed his phone and dialed an extension. "Nicole, grab Ernie and come back in here, please."

He hung up.

Marlin hadn't seen or spoken to either deputy since the afternoon before. "They ever find anything at the scene?"

Tatum said, "Nope. First thing this morning, I asked them to start calling glass repair shops." He looked at Garza. "They get something?"

Garza's smile was enigmatic. "I'm gonna let her tell you."

There was a rap on the door, and the two deputies came in. Ernie Turpin closed the door behind them and they both stood to the right of the desk. It was the first time Marlin had seen Nicole since he'd learned about the situation in Mason. He tried not to think about it. He noticed that she wasn't making eye contact with him.

"Nicole," Garza said, "please tell them what you told me ten minutes ago. Just the good part."

"Happy to." She faced Tatum and Marlin but spoke to the chief deputy. "I've been asking glass companies about recent customers with Blanco County addresses. When I reached a place in Austin called Instaglass, one of the salesladies got all excited and told me Mitch Campbell bought a sheet of glass yesterday afternoon. She's a big fan, so she asked for his autograph. He laughed and said he wasn't Campbell but people made that mistake all the time. He was wearing sunglasses, but she was certain it was Campbell."

"Security camera?" Tatum asked.

"No. She did watch him all the way to the parking lot, so she was able to describe his SUV. Dark blue Ford Expedition, which matches Campbell's registration."

"Don't suppose she got the license plate?" Marlin asked.

"If only. She had no reason to. But she did say there was some kind of large, round decal on the rear window, passenger side. She couldn't get specific about the design. She thought maybe it was blue and black."

Marlin knew where this was going. "An NWA sticker," he said.

Nicole nodded. "I printed a JPEG from the NWA Web site"—she laid a sheet of paper on Garza's desk—"and this is the decal you get when you sign up as a lifetime member."

The decal was round, with black letters on a blue background.

"It's the largest sticker they offer—ten inches in diameter," Nicole said. "You get a smaller version if you join as an annual member."

"You see an SUV when you were at his place?" Garza asked Tatum and Marlin.

Tatum said, "No, we parked in front. I think the garage was around the side, with its own driveway."

"Okay, we'll work on that. Now, your turn. Tell these hardworking deputies what you've learned."

Tatum and Marlin ran through it all again. The two deputies' faces became particularly animated when Tatum mentioned Campbell's verbal miscue.

Ernie said, "Christ, that's good stuff. How's he know the TOD?"

"Good question," Garza said dryly. "Almost as good as 'Why did he want to buy a sheet of glass anonymously?' Here's a question of my own: Does everybody realize what we're digging into here? If Campbell was mixed up in this, it'll be huge, and I want everybody to treat it accordingly. Nothing is to leave this room unless I clear it. Questions?"

"Where's this leave us on Crowley?" Turpin asked.

"Theories?" Garza said to nobody in particular.

"It all depends on his alibi," Marlin said. "Was he out of town or not? And I keep wondering about motive."

"Could've been something simple," Tatum said. "Maybe they had a dispute about money. Or maybe Dominguez had a smart mouth. Judging from his record, Crowley is a first-class asshole. Sounds like it doesn't take much to set him off."

"Then how does Campbell figure in?" Nicole asked.

"Maybe he's covering for Crowley," Tatum said.

"Meaning Dominguez was killed at Campbell's place?"

"That'd be my guess. Whatever the case, I'd agree with Bobby—something's up with Campbell. He's in this somehow. Maybe he's in it alone, but I'm betting he's not. Maybe the two men Mrs. Buell saw hanging around Dominguez's truck were Campbell and Crowley."

Marlin finally caught Nicole gazing at him. What was that look on her face? Self-satisfaction that Campbell might be involved?

The moment was broken when Garza said, "Here's how we'll move on this. Nicole, I want you to drive to Austin and interview the gal at Instaglass, plus any other employees who saw this guy. Get it all on tape—what he was wearing and everything he said, as far as the witnesses can remember. Have her repeat the description of the truck and the decal. Play it cool, though. If she asks whether it was Campbell, tell her no. Downplay it. Say you're investigating someone else."

"Will do."

"Ernie, I want you to get both Campbell's and Crowley's phone records."

Marlin said, "We've got both of Campbell's numbers now—home and cell—but all we have for Crowley is a home phone."

"Well, let's run what we got. Go back two weeks. Bill and John, y'all work on Crowley's whereabouts. Just keep talking to people and see if you can find out where the hell he is. Work on finding the ex-wife. Surely she'd know where her boy is."

Red rolled up to the gate at ten o'clock, on the dot. Mitch had told them not to start working before ten. Late sleeper.

"What I'll do," Red was saying to Billy Don, "is make about ten or twenty dubs to hand out to Mitch's people after the rally. Sorta get the ball rolling."

He punched in the gate code.

"Dubs?" Billy Don said.

"That's what us musicians call a cassette copy of a song. A dub."

"You think that's a good idea?" Billy Don asked.

The gate didn't open.

"Aw, hell, Mitch won't mind. You've seen what a nice guy he is. He likes us. We're in what they call the inner circle."

Red punched the code again. Six-seven-nine-one.

"I don't know, Red. Sounds a little pushy."

Billy Don clearly didn't understand how the music industry worked. The gate still wasn't moving.

"Saturday's my big chance," Red said. "Gotta take advantage of it."

He tried the code a third time.

"That's the thing," Billy Don said. "I don't remember Mitch inviting us to come on Saturday."

The gate remained firmly closed. "You was passed out."

"You sure?"

"Yeah, I saw you on the couch with—"

"No, I mean are you sure we're invited on Saturday?"

Red stared through the windshield, trying to recall what Mitch had said. "Well, shit, I think so."

"But you don't remember?"

Red drummed on the steering wheel. Why wasn't the gate opening? "You know what? You're ruining my damn day."

He leaned out his window and pushed the intercom button. After a moment, he heard Mitch say, "Yeah?"

"Howdy there, Mitch. It's Red, down at the gate."

A long moment of silence, then: "Yeah?"

"The code ain't working."

"Had to change it."

"Oh. You wanna give me the new numbers?"

"Five-six-six-two."

Red punched the numbers in, and the gate swung open.

"Hey, Mitch?" Red said.

"What?"

"We got some doughnuts if you—"

"Just get to work, okay?"

"Uh, okay, Mitch. Sure thing."

Red pulled through and started the long drive to the house. "Jeez, who pissed in his oatmeal?"

Billy Don was looking at him. "That what it's like in the inner circle?"

*   *   *

Marlin caught Nicole in the parking lot before she left for Austin. She was seated in her cruiser, the door open. The sunlight was angling through the windshield, sparkling her auburn hair with diamonds.

"Nice work," he said.

"You, too." She was looking off at the horizon.

"Weird thing about Mitch Campbell, huh?"

"No doubt."

A block away, an eighteen-wheeler downshifted as it rumbled toward the center of town on Highway 290. The temperature was still low yet—only eighty-five or so.

"Okay, I'll just say it. What's bothering you?"

"How do you mean?"

"What was that in my office yesterday?"

"Nothing. I'm fine."

"If I did something wrong, could you just tell me what it was?"

"I was bitchy, I know. It was the heat. My fault." She grabbed a pair of sunglasses off the passenger seat and slipped them over her eyes.

Without thinking it through, he said, "Is it about that thing in Mason?"

She leaned her head back, then let it fall forward. A gesture of exasperation. "Mason? I . . . goddamn, are y'all talking about me behind my back?"

"We weren't *talking* about you. We were talking about guns and it came up in conversation. Bill told me about it. But it sure makes me wonder why I never heard it from you."

She rested her chin on her chest, and a single teardrop slid down her cheek.

"Nicole, I—"

She held a hand up. "Not now, okay? I can't talk about it right now." She turned the key and cranked the big engine. "I've gotta go."

He could smell her perfume on the light breeze, and it made his heart heavy. *We can't have secrets.*

"Dinner tonight?" he said.

She nodded, but she didn't say a word as she pulled the door closed.

31

BRIAN AND MAURICE had just left Brian's house, heading for the IHOP near the airport, when Brian slapped the dash and said, "Shit, turn around, I forgot my nine."

Maurice looked at him. "You fuckin' kidding me?"

"No, man, turn it around."

"A night this important, how you forget your fuckin' piece?"

"Shit, man, I don't know. But I ain't going without it."

It was a stupid mistake. Nerves. Brian was keyed up, because this was their biggest deal ever.

"Be late," Maurice said.

"We ain't meeting till midnight. Take five minutes. We got plenty of time."

So Maurice whipped a U at the next light, and they went back to Brian's place. It was a crummy rental house on the south side, but Brian was planning to move to nicer digs after tonight's score. Nothing too flashy, though, because the cops would start to wonder where a twenty-year-old got the money.

Maurice pulled in behind Brian's RX-7, and Brian trotted to the front door. He unlocked the dead bolt, hurried into the living room, and found his Glock on the table, next to the scale, right where he'd left it. It was a nice piece. He'd traded five grams of coke for it. He turned to leave when something stopped him. It took him a moment to figure out what it was.

What the fuck?

The light was on in his bedroom, down at the end of the hallway. He was pretty sure he'd turned that light off. He was almost certain that he had.

He stood absolutely still. He heard nothing except the sound of the air conditioner. He waited until it shut off. Complete silence. Still nothing.

Bonita had locked the front door behind her. She nearly wet herself when she heard the dead bolt turn and the door open. She froze immediately.

She had already retrieved the cardboard box marked SCHOOL PAPERS from the shelf in Brian's bedroom closet, and she'd seen that it was crammed full of cash. Enough for Mexico, most likely. She'd dropped Dick's gun on top of the cash, ready to carry everything out the door. Now she was stuck, both hands holding the box, and she didn't dare move. The house was quiet. Whoever was out there had stopped moving.

She hoped it was Brian. She hoped he was alone. If he was alone, there would be less trouble.

Was somebody raiding his stash? Nobody knew where he kept it—not even Maurice.

Brian knew he'd have to check it out. He started slowly down the hallway, staying close to the wall, to avoid the squeaky floorboards in the center. He noticed that his hands were moist around the butt of the Glock. Near the doorway, he paused and listened again. Not a sound. He was fucking paranoid, that's all it was. Maybe he *had* left the light on.

He had to decide whether to peek around the jamb or jump through it, with the Glock out and ready.

He jumped—and *holy fuck!*—there was a person standing in the middle of his bedroom. Brian's finger tightened on the trigger, this close to pulling it, when he recognized her. He lowered the gun.

"Jesus!" he said, catching his breath. "What are you doing here? I almost shot you!"

Then he saw that she was holding his money box.

"Oh, you little fucking whore!"

"What we gonna do wit' her?" Maurice asked. He seemed amused by the situation, Brian's old poke ripping him off. Real funny. Brian had called and pushed the meeting back by an hour. Blamed it on a flat tire. They went for it.

Now the bitch was on the bed, tears running down, telling Brian how sorry she was. Brian kept telling her to shut up. But what now? He damn sure couldn't call the cops.

"I got a idea," Maurice said.

"Yeah?"

"She fine. She a good piece of ass?"

Bonita looked at Brian now, shaking her head, her eyes pleading.

Brian wasn't willing to take it that far. He wasn't a goddamn rapist. Besides, he didn't want to admit that he'd never actually had sex with her. She had always put him off. Blamed it on being Catholic. Always went down on him instead. "Hell, no," he said. "Ain't even worth it."

"Shee-yit. It all worth it."

"No way, Mo."

Maurice was disappointed. "Cain't jus' let her go."

"I know."

"Gotta make her pay somehow."

"Let me think." He was walking a fine line. He didn't want to be too hard on Bonita, but he didn't want to appear soft in front of Maurice. He had to land somewhere in the middle. Something cruel, maybe. Or embarrassing. Get her back without actually hurting her. Brian's cell phone was still in his left hand, and it gave him an idea. "I say we take some pictures of her. Put 'em on the Net."

"Nudie pictures?" Maurice asked.

"Yeah."

Maurice chuckled. "That'll work."

Brian figured it was a reasonable solution. She couldn't go to the cops and gripe about it. Not unless she admitted to burglary. Besides, he wouldn't have to actually post the photos. Maurice would never check.

Maurice stepped toward her and said, "Bitch, drop yo drawers."

Brian saw a different look on Bonita's face now. That pissed-off Latina shit going on. Proud and angry. Stubborn as hell. Christ, he'd dealt with that before. She didn't budge. She stared at the wall with her arms crossed.

Maurice snapped his fingers in front of her face. "Yo. You hear me?"

What happened next changed Brian's life. For the worse.

Bonita said, "Joo want to know why I need the money? I show you!" She suddenly stood, unbuttoned her jeans, and lowered them to midthigh. She wasn't wearing panties, and—

And—

Oh, sweet Jesus.

Maurice nearly tripped as he took several steps back. "Mothafucka," he said.

Brian couldn't believe his eyes. He felt nauseous.

Maurice said, "I heard about shit like this on Springer, but I ain't never seen it."

Brian was hyperventilating. His face was hot with shame. *What if Maurice told people?*

"Girl got herself a willie," Maurice said, pointing. "You see that?"

"Shut up, Mo!"

Bonita pulled her jeans back up and marched out of the room. Neither man moved to stop her.

Maurice was starting to laugh. "She one a them she-males. You was banging a she-male."

"Shut up!"

Brian heard the front door open and close.

"Dog, she got a dick the size of a—"

Brian swiveled and pointed his Glock at Maurice's face. "I swear to God, Mo, you ever tell anyone about this, I'll fuckin' kill you. You hear me?"

"But she hung like a—"

"Not another fuckin' word! I'm not kidding!"

Maurice held his hands up in surrender, still smiling. "Chill out, man. She fool me, too. You think I want that getting 'round? Be our little secret."

"All right, then."

"It's cool."

Brian looked at the gun in his hand. "I shoulda fuckin' popped her, you know?" he said. "Little goddamn freak!"

Maurice shrugged.

Brian felt gross all over. "I shoulda fuckin' popped her," he said again.

"Don't you mean *him*?" Maurice said.

Brian raised the Glock and shot Maurice twice in the chest.

PART FOUR

Gun control laws help stop crimes before they happen. For example, background checks, required by the Brady Act, have helped prevent potentially dangerous people from owning guns.

—BRADY CAMPAIGN WEB SITE

The Wright-Rossi survey [of imprisoned felons] shows clearly that gun laws affect only the law-abiding, and that criminals know it. Eighty-two percent of the sample agreed that "Gun laws only affect law-abiding citizens; criminals will always be able to get guns."

—NRA-ILA WEB SITE

The humble suffer when the mighty disagree.

—PHAEDRUS

32

CASEY WALBERG HAD been immersed in the slimy underbelly of Hollywood for so long, he'd almost forgotten how different the rest of the country was. Here in Texas, for example, he'd discovered that people were authentically friendly—even when they didn't have anything to gain from it.

The woman at the car-rental counter, for instance, had actually whispered, "Make sure you fill the car up when you return it, because if we do it for you, it's a big rip-off. Save yourself some money." *Why,* Casey wondered, *would she say something like that to a total stranger?* She'd never seen Casey before, and she'd likely never see him again. So what did she care if he spent too much on a tank of gas? Strange, but refreshing.

Driving through Austin on Ben White Boulevard, there'd been a construction zone, and the right lane ended abruptly. Casey was screwed, his path suddenly blocked by orange traffic cones. Now he'd have to bull his way over. Then a man in a rusty Buick slowed and waved Casey into the middle lane—and goddamn if the man wasn't smiling when he did it. Bizarre, but in a good way.

Now Casey was experiencing the same kind of outgoing hospitality in a small hardware store in Johnson City. He'd just picked up a pair of heavy-duty wire cutters when a man said, "I had some just like 'em. They'll go through a fence like warm butter."

Casey turned and saw a man of medium height, as bony as a runway model. He was wearing a cap that said POACHERS DO IT AT NIGHT. He had yellow teeth, and his hair was an inch away from being classified as a mullet. And he wasn't alone. Behind him was one of the largest men Casey had ever seen. Had to be six and a half feet, maybe three hundred pounds. Made Schwarzenegger look small. *God help me,* Casey thought, *he's wearing overalls.* In L.A., if someone wore overalls, there'd be a reason behind it. Trying to appear folksy. Wanting to set a trend. Hoping to give the impression that he didn't care what other people thought, precisely because everybody cared so damn much about what other people thought. But this monster of a man wore overalls simply because he was an overalls-wearing kind of guy. It was who he was. Casey loved it. He loved them both. The best casting director in Hollywood couldn't find a match for these two yokels.

Casey hefted the wire cutters and said, "So these are pretty good, huh?"

"Worth every dollar," Poacher said. He smiled. "The game warden took my last pair. Along with my two-seventy."

Casey nodded, even though he didn't know what a "two-seventy" was. Then he said, "Okay, well, thanks for the recommendation."

Before he could turn and head for the checkout counter, Poacher said, "We're just picking up a new chain-saw blade ourselves. Plumb wore out the old one."

Back in L.A., Casey, at this point, might've said something snarky—perhaps "You've mistaken me for someone who gives a shit." Here—he just couldn't do it. He didn't know why, but it struck him as purely American—somehow Rockwellian—to exchange a few pleasantries with a stranger in a small-town hardware store. Good karma, maybe. Whatever, he couldn't resist it. So he said, "That so? Guess you're from around here?"

"We sure are," the man replied, starting to laugh. "And from the way you talk, I'm guessing you're not."

Casey grinned with him. Six years in California and he still hadn't shaken his New England accent. "No, you caught me. I'm just, uh, visiting some relatives. But man, it's beautiful in this area."

"Yup. God's country," Poacher said. "Come to Texas once and you don't never wanna leave."

"Which ain't always a good thing," Overalls said, glaring. "Yankees come down and we cain't get rid of 'em. They's like cockroaches. 'Cept they got money to spend."

Casey decided it was good-natured ribbing—the closest thing to an unkind word he'd heard during his visit.

"Then again," Poacher said, "sometimes folks move out here and we're glad to have 'em. Like our new boss. Maybe you've heard of him." He leaned closer and lowered his voice. "Mitch Campbell."

Hold on a minute.

Casey looked left and he looked right. This had to be a gag. Someone, maybe one of his friends back home, had figured out what he was doing in Texas and had staged an elaborate practical joke. He expected Ashton Kutcher to come bursting out of the back room, the camera trailing behind. But no. There was no sign that the two men were putting Casey on.

"You work for Mitch Campbell?" he asked.

"Yessir." Poacher was plainly proud of it. In fact, Casey had a suspicion that Poacher had initiated the conversation merely to share that fact.

Regardless, Casey could hardly believe his luck. "In what capacity?" he asked.

"Huh?"

"What do you do for him?"

"Groundskeepers, you might say," Poacher replied. "We're helping him get his place ready for the rally on Saturday."

"Really? That sounds cool." Casey's mind was racing as he tried to determine how he could use this information to his advantage.

"Oh, yeah, Mitch is great. The three of us is good friends. We go way back."

"I understand he lives on a ranch."

Casey had done his research. Thanks to a feature story in an on-line hunting magazine, he knew that Mitch Campbell's property was surrounded by an eight-foot fence—hence the wire cutters. He'd also accessed the NWA Web site and downloaded driving directions to the ranch for the rally. A few more details wouldn't hurt, though. Casey didn't want to get arrested for trespassing before he had a chance to approach Mitch.

"Yeah, it's more'n two thousand acres," Poacher was saying. "Bought the old Reimer place. They was some of the early settlers around here. Built a cabin out there in eighteen hundred and something. When was it, Billy Don?"

"Hell if I know."

Casey didn't care about settlers. All he heard was the part about two thousand acres. Big place—more than twice the size of Central Park. *I'm gonna need a jug of water,* he thought. *Good thing I ran into these guys.*

Casey, thinking fast, said, "If I owned a place that big, I'd put my house smack in the middle of it. More privacy that way. Is that what Mitch did?"

"Naw, he's way in the back near the fence line. The highest hill on the ranch. Helluva view. He butts up against another big place anyway, so it's plenty private."

Just follow the fence, Casey thought. *Cakewalk.*

"I heard he's a dog lover," he said. "Out in the country like he is, I bet he has a whole passel of dogs." He got a kick out of using the word "passel."

Poacher said, "I ain't seen no dogs. I thought he had one named Buster, but I guess it died or something."

"How about security guards?"

"Ain't seen none of them, either. Just Mitch, all by his lonesome."

"That's surprising," Casey said. "Very surprising."

The entire film crew had arrived in one vehicle, an SUV the size of a river barge. Behind them came a truck towing a livestock trailer with two horses inside. The animal wrangler. Mitch remembered that phrase from his days in the ad biz.

Now they were all out in a large field behind Mitch's house. The two horses were standing in the shade of an oak tree, staring into space, twitching their tails occasionally. *Strange beasts,* Mitch thought. *Don't they get bored?*

The director was a small Jewish man with rimless glasses, a shaved head, and a Brooklyn accent. He was sweating profusely in the afternoon sun, but that didn't dampen his enthusiasm. He swept his arm in a wide arc, saying, "Then you'll gallop across this open space, right up to the camera, and say, 'Cougar Brand Chili! It's always a number-one hit!'"

"Love it," said the account executive from the ad agency.

"To die for," said the marketing VP from the chili company.

"I'll, uh, be riding?" said Mitch. He'd ridden a horse exactly once in his life. A geriatric pony, really. Back at summer camp, when he was ten years old. These horses were much bigger. They'd be harder to drive. Mitch wouldn't know what he was doing. He'd look like an idiot.

"Problem?" asked the director.

"Well, you know I love to ride," said Mitch. "Live for it. But I twisted my ankle last week. Still a little tender."

"Oh. I see. Not good. Frankly, your manager, uh . . ."

"Joe."

"Yes, Joe. He should've called me. If you can't ride, well, it's . . ."

"Unfortunate," said the account exec.

"Disappointing," said the marketing VP.

Mitch shrugged, meaning *Sorry about that.*

"But not insurmountable," said the director.

"Idea?" asked the account exec.

"Solution?" asked the marketing VP.

"I think so," said the director. "Can you *sit* on a horse?"

"Just sit on it?" Mitch asked. "Yeah, sure, I can do that." He was wearing the outfit they'd brought for him: ostrich-skin boots, well-pressed jeans, and a starched button-down shirt. His Resistol hat kept the direct sun off his face, but that didn't help much. It was one hundred and four degrees, and Mitch was sweating like a whore in church.

"Okay, then. We'll use Warren as a stand-in for the riding shots," the director said, nodding toward the animal wrangler, a tall, lean man with a weathered face. "Then we'll cut to Mitch sitting on the horse. Everyone okay with that? Warren?"

Warren was sucking on the stem of a weed or something. "Fine with me. Which'n you wanna use?" This man, Mitch could tell, was an authentic cowboy. He could see it in the way Warren carried himself.

"Let's start with the paint," the director said. "Mitch, if you don't mind, please go stand beside the paint. I want to see how you two look together."

The paint? What the hell did that mean?

Mitch hesitated, and Warren, at Mitch's elbow, muttered, "That's the splotchy-looking one."

Mitch looked at Warren, who smiled and shook his head. *You ain't fooling me,* he seemed to be saying.

"That's a fine paint," Mitch said loudly. "Good-looking mare."

"We'll need a matching outfit for Warren!" the director called.

"He's a gelding," the wrangler said quietly.

Paul Hebert didn't really give a shit about Duane Rankin, but he called a guy at the Board of Pardons and Paroles anyway and gave him a heads-up, saying hey, if you let that scumbag out next week, you should warn him that somebody might want to stick a rifle-cleaning rod up his butt or something. Hebert figured that might be fatal if the killer shoved it up there far enough—especially if he used one of those wire-bore brushes. The guy at P&P agreed to discuss the situation with Rankin, if he were in fact released.

Hebert had just hung up when Ramon popped into Hebert's office again. "Good news and bad news," he said.

"Start with the bad," Hebert said.

"Jenkins' prints don't match the one from the bottle cap."

"Damn it."

"Doesn't rule him out. That partial might not be from the killer."

"Yeah, yeah. What else? Cheer me up."

Ramon grinned. "We just got a hit on Jenkins' credit card."

"Where?"

"Johnson City. At the Super S."

"When?"

"Nine fourteen this morning."

"What'd he buy?"

"A bunch of frozen dinners and a case of beer."

Hebert nodded and put one foot up on his desk, thinking. "What the hell's he doing in Johnson City? Nothing but shitkickers out there. He'll stand out like a turd in a fruit salad. It'd be a lot easier for him to keep ducking us in Austin or San Antone."

"That's what I was thinking," Ramon said, handing Hebert a sheet of paper, "and then I remembered a poster I saw in Henley's gun shop. I printed that from the NWA Web site."

Hebert saw that there was an NWA rally on July 4—two days from now—in Blanco County. Hebert could picture it: a bunch of blowhard, flag-waving, conservative white guys, squawking about their rights as Americans. Like they—or we, really—had anything to complain about. Then Hebert noticed that the rally was in support of gubernatorial candidate Glenn Andrew Dobbins, who was to be a special guest.

He looked at Ramon and said, "I just had a bad thought."

"Thinking maybe Dobbins is his next target?"

"That about sums it up."

Until now, it hadn't occurred to Hebert that Jenkins might go after someone unrelated to the Rankin case, but it made as much sense as anything else. Jenkins and Dobbins already had bad blood between them. Plus, Dobbins was as rabidly pro-gun as they come. What could be more symbolic than killing him?

33

MITCH LEARNED SOMETHING in the scant twenty minutes he sat atop the paint (which, he learned, was the English version of *pinto*): horses have a peculiar odor about them. Not necessarily a bad smell, not at first, but a pungent one that becomes tiresome. Strong, especially in the heat. Flies apparently liked it, because they had quickly swarmed all over the place. Big, mean, biting ones that descended on Mitch as if he were an all-you-can-eat buffet. Plus, when a horse takes a dump, it's not an insignificant affair. Must be four or five pounds he's cranking out like sausage from a grinder.

Mitch delivered his lines with a smile, though, and the ordeal was over in less than an hour. The film crew departed, and Mitch retreated to his house. He was hot and sweaty and smelled like a stable, so he went directly around back to the pool. Stripped naked and jumped in. The cool water was fabulous. He stayed under, holding his breath, enjoying the brief respite from his hangover. When his lungs began to burn, he surfaced. A young man was standing poolside, staring down at him.

"Fuck! You scared me."

"Hiya, Norm."

He was Mitch's age, wearing hiking boots, shorts, and a T-shirt damp with perspiration. He was holding a plastic jug, half full of water.

"Casey Walberg," Mitch said.

Casey smiled. "I'm touched. You remembered."

"You're trespassing."

"Sorry about that. You can call the cops if you want."

"And how the fuck did you get my phone number?"

"Not important."

Mitch realized he had no leverage. "What the hell do you want?"

"Climb on out of there. We need to talk."

"How much do you want?" Mitch asked. They were sitting in patio chairs beneath a large umbrella. Mitch had a towel wrapped around his waist. *He can ruin me if he wants to,* he thought. *Or bleed me dry, like those goddamn horseflies.*

"Not much for small talk, are you?" Casey said.

"Oh, I'm sorry. Where are my manners? You're looking good, Casey. How've you been? Want something to drink before you blackmail me?"

Casey laughed, a quick, sudden snort. "Dude, you think I want money? Well, actually, I do want money, but not from you. Come on, I wouldn't do that to an old pal."

We were never pals, Mitch thought. *I barely remember you.*

"What, then?"

Casey seemed not to hear the question. He was studying the hot tub, the tennis courts, the house itself. "You've got a sweet setup here, Norm. I'm happy for you."

"Uh-huh."

Casey shook his head, grinning. "Dude, I recognized you the first time I saw one of your videos. I said, *I know that guy from somewhere.* Took me a while to place the face, though. Boy, you've changed. Much taller. No more babyface. The blond hair is a nice touch. And the goatee. Oh, and that drawl! Cracks me up. But my question is: Are you fucking crazy? How long did you think you'd get away with it?"

"You'd be surprised. Nobody seems to care much about my past. All they care about is what I am *now*."

"But they had to ask questions. Like 'Where were you born?' 'Where did you go to school?'"

"I'd just change the subject. Said I wanted to protect my family's privacy."

"The whole thing is just ballsy as hell."

"My manager's idea," Mitch admitted. "Figured I'd sell better if I was from the South. It's about marketability. It's about image."

Casey appeared amused. "It's about bullshit."

Mitch was starting to sweat again. The heat was oppressive. "Yeah," he admitted. "It is."

Casey took a long drink from his jug of water. "I figured it out about six months ago. I was just flipping through the channels, not thinking about it, and there you were, and I'm like, *Holy shit, that's Norm! That's who it is! Norm Kleinschmidt is a goddamn celebrity!*"

Mitch was thinking, *Six months ago? Then why is he just now showing up?*

"To be honest," Casey continued, "I've thought about putting the squeeze on you. Obviously, you could spare a few bucks to keep your little secret."

"What's stopping you?"

Casey frowned. "Man, I work for a living. I'm not some goddamn leech. I don't need your money."

Mitch could feel his shoulders relaxing. "But you want something."

"Well, yeah. A favor. Let's talk about your wedding on Saturday night."

Mitch saw no reason to deny the rumors. "What about it?"

Casey took a long drink from his water jug. "Goddamn, the tabloids will eat it up for weeks. The country superstar marries the Hollywood princess. And we both know how this publicity thing works. You act like you want to keep the whole thing hush-hush, but you sell the photo rights to a single publication. *People*, maybe. *Us Weekly*. So, instead of being swarmed by a bunch of damn paparazzi, all you're dealing with is a single photographer. And they've *paid* you a shitload to be there. That sound familiar?"

Casey was in show business. That much was obvious. "Maybe," Mitch said.

"Doesn't really matter," Casey said. "Because as of right now, I'm your wedding photographer. That's the deal."

Mitch stared at him, trying to look angry and conflicted. Truth was, he was getting off easy. The situation could've been much worse. "And you'll turn around and make a fortune on the pictures," he said.

Casey's eyes lit up. "Naturally."

John Marlin laid six small venison cutlets on a cutting board and pounded them vigorously with a meat mallet. The secret to tenderness. Then he submerged them in a bowl of milk, where he'd let them sit for fifteen minutes before dredging them with flour and sprinkling them with pepper and garlic powder. Then they'd go into a quarter inch of hot oil for just a few minutes on each side. He washed two large potatoes and cut them into medium chunks, unpeeled. He and Nicole both liked their mashed potatoes with the skin still on. With lots of salt and butter. A festival of cholesterol, but as long as it wasn't a nightly thing . . .

At six thirty, he heard a key in the front door. Geist immediately rose from her spot on the kitchen floor and bustled into the living room. Marlin heard the door open and close, and the gentle murmurs of Nicole's voice as she greeted Geist.

"In here," Marlin called. He picked up a dish towel and began to wipe his hands.

Geist led the way, the tags on her collar jangling, her tail thumping wildly against the door frame. She dashed over to Marlin, then turned and rushed back to Nicole, who was just entering the kitchen. She knelt and petted Geist some more. "Okay, okay. Settle down."

Marlin stayed where he was, near the stove. "How's it going?"

Geist was squirming and wriggling and putting on a show of utter excitement. *Nicole is here! Nicole is here!*

"Fine," Nicole said, giggling, as Geist assaulted her with canine kisses. Then, all at once, the dog turned, walked to the center of the kitchen, and settled down onto the floor with a grunt. The official greeting was complete.

"Smells great in here," she said. She was wearing her standard summertime civvies: sneakers, khaki shorts, and a well-fitting tank top. She was an absolute vision.

"You want a beer?"

"Sounds good."

He poured a couple of Shiner Bocks into frosted mugs and handed her one.

"Can I ask you for a favor?" she said.

"Sure."

"Can we forget about this afternoon? Just for a few hours? Can we just not talk or think about it?"

"Fine with me."

She nodded, then leaned against the countertop and watched him work. He began to shred lettuce, tossing it into a large wooden bowl for a salad.

"So?" he said. "How'd it go in Austin?"

"Nothing new. This woman I talked to . . . she has no doubt it was Mitch Campbell. She said he wasn't quite as handsome in person—almost like he'd been sick lately. But she was adamant that it was him."

"No real way to prove it."

"If we're lucky, his phone records, or Crowley's, will show a call to that store. Where is Ernie on that?"

"Records should start coming in tomorrow. If not, then we're looking at Monday."

He rinsed a plump tomato and began cutting it into wedges.

"How about you?" Nicole said.

"Bill managed to track down Crowley's ex-wife in Woodville, and she said Crowley picked up his son on Saturday afternoon. Assuming she's telling the truth, that means his alibi is solid."

"Think she's lying?"

"Who knows? She said Crowley and the boy were camping at Lake Fork, so I called the warden up there and asked him to keep an eye out."

"That's a big lake. What're the odds?"

"Pretty slim. He's got a couple of other wardens working the lake, too. They might stumble across him."

Lake Fork had been the premier bass-fishing spot in Texas for more than twenty years, with more than three hundred thousand anglers visiting it annually. Realistically, Crowley was a needle in a haystack.

"The ex-wife gave us a cell phone number," Marlin said, "but we got routed to voice mail. Didn't leave a message. We want to talk to a live human. Besides, the ex says he doesn't always carry it."

Nicole took a long drink of her beer. She watched as he diced a cucumber.

"You know, you're gonna make somebody a wonderful wife some day," she said. "Not just a pretty face—you can cook, too."

He smiled. "You're just after my gravy recipe."

She leaned close, got up on her toes, and whispered, "Oh, I'm after more than that." Her breath was warm on his ear. She kissed his neck while he attempted to slice a carrot.

"Ah . . ." he said.

She moved behind him, sliding her hands under his shirt, along his rib cage. He gave up on the carrot.

"I'm pretty sure this never happens to Emeril," he said.

She slid her hands over his backside, then down his thighs, and then up around the front.

"Bam!" she said. She began to unbuckle his belt.

"Maybe I should turn this skillet off for a while," he said.

"I think that's an excellent idea."

34

TRICIA WOODBINE'S CELL phone rang at seven o'clock, and she ignored it. It was Dieter calling again, as he had every ten minutes in the past hour. Jesus, he was persistent. Like a frat boy trying to get laid. But Tricia didn't care. She was in the driver's seat now, and she intended to take full advantage of it.

Earlier, on the way to Plano for her six o'clock meeting with Dieter, she'd listened to Dale's recorded calls. First, there was a conversation on there between Dale and Glenn Dobbins. Tricia didn't really understand it; the congressman said something about spreading money around. Sounded kind of shady, but nothing she could really use.

Then Mitch Campbell had called—and Tricia knew she'd hit the mother lode. She'd been absolutely amazed at what she'd heard. She listened to the conversation three times, and there was only one way to interpret it.

Mitch Campbell had killed someone. Some Mexican guy. It was totally surreal, like something you'd see on TV.

But she didn't have any details. Who was this person Mitch killed? Why did he kill him? Tricia didn't have a clue. That's why she was in her apartment, surfing the Internet, attempting to sort it all out. She was tingling all over, and she wondered whether the man who'd captured the Kennedy assassination on film had felt this way. This was *big*!

She went to Google and searched for *dead mexican blanco county*. Wow. A quarter million hits. She looked at a few, but they were all unrelated. She tried *murder in blanco county*. Again, way too many hits. Random stuff. Oh, duh. Why was she making this so hard? She typed in *blanco county newspaper*, and she found the home page for the *Blanco County Record*. She clicked on it.

Oh. My. God. It was the lead story. She scooted her chair closer and began to read about the unsolved murder of an illegal alien named Rodolfo Dominguez.

Midway through, she had a delicious thought. SNATCH would doubtlessly pay her a ton for the recordings—even more than she and Dieter had agreed on. But wouldn't Dale, and the NWA, be willing to pay her even more than that? She would totally have an auction!

Later, after dinner, they washed the dishes together, then sat on the living room couch. Her hand was clasped in his, and he studied her slender fingers. The ring would fit, he knew, because, a few weeks earlier, Melinda had discreetly sized one of Nicole's rings while "admiring" it. It would fit—when the time was right.

"Thanks for dinner," she said.

"My pleasure. Want another beer?"

"No, I'm good."

They sat without speaking. There was a tension to it, but Marlin let it be. He could hear his metal roof creaking as it cooled. Geist was sacked out on the floor.

"I think I'm ready to talk now," she said.

"You sure?"

"No, not really, but I will." Her lips formed a tight line, and her eyes seemed to grow emptier somehow. "It's not like I was keeping it from you, it's just that I don't like to talk about it. With anybody."

He waited.

"But you need to know, don't you?" she asked.

"I'd like to."

"Why?"

"Because I want to know every part of you. I want to know what makes you *you.*"

She gave him a small smile, and that was encouraging. "Good answer," she said. He waited some more, until she said, "I think that's fair. What did Bill say?"

"That you answered a domestic violence call and got into some trouble. A man was drunk."

"He said I *answered* a call?"

The question took Marlin by surprise. "That's what he said."

She shook her head, but not at his answer; more like she was trying to rid herself of a ridiculous memory. "I wasn't there as an officer, I was the victim."

Marlin could feel the heat beginning to rise in his face. *The victim.* He kept his voice low and calm. "What happened?"

She looked down at her lap. "I'd been dating this guy for about three months. Not long. Nothing serious. At least, *I* wasn't serious. There was something . . . a little off about him. He seemed fairly, I don't know, normal, I guess—but then he'd have these tremendous outbursts of anger. Not at me, but in traffic, screaming at other drivers, or he'd yell at a waitress. Ugly scenes, especially if he drank too much. It was enough to make me decide I didn't want to be around him. We'd been seeing just enough of each other that I felt I should tell him in person. Stupid mistake, but, like I said, he'd never directed his anger toward me. So anyway, I dropped by his place one afternoon on my day off. Wasn't carrying my gun. He'd been sitting around with his roommate watching baseball all day. And drinking. He was pretty drunk. The roommate went to the store when I got there—giving us privacy, I guess. I should've left, too—done it at another time—but I wanted to get it over with. So I just told him, 'Look, it's not working out. I don't want to see you anymore.' He acted completely surprised. He asked me why, and I said he had a problem with anger, and with drinking, and that I didn't want to be in that type of relationship. I had the speech all planned out in my head. He listened, and then he started telling me how he'd change. He'd control his anger, he'd quit drinking. The truth was, even without those flaws, he wasn't the guy for me. He just wasn't, you know? So I told him, no, it was over, and that he should go ahead and work on his problems on his own, that he'd be a happier person for it. He started crying and pleading and saying he loved me and that he was hoping we'd get married some day. Let me tell you, that was news to me. We were so far away from that sort of step, I was just completely dumbstruck. I mean, *three months.* He was already thinking about *marriage?* I kept putting him off, saying, no, really, this is it, it's over. Then, big surprise, he starts to get angry. He calls me some names and says I'm a manipulator and that I'm cruel and mean and a bunch of other shit. I get up to leave, and so he swings back in the other direction, apologizing all over the place, telling me how much he cares for me and what a great person I am. I'm like, okay, fine, let's just leave it at that. He says, 'I have a few of your things here. I'll go get them.' I should've just left right then, but I didn't. He goes into his bedroom and comes back with a gun. An automatic. I never even knew he owned one. He—"

She paused, and Marlin sat in silence, his heartbeat thrumming in his ears. He didn't even know the man she was talking about, but he wanted to kill him. Her hand was tight around his, but she showed no other sign of emotion. Then she continued.

"He starts screaming at me, the same old bullshit we always hear about in these cases. He can't live without me. If he can't have me, nobody else will. Like that. He puts the gun against my head, and I fucking hate this, but I start begging him not to shoot."

Her eyes began to well.

"I see movement through the window, and I realize that the roommate is out there, seeing everything that's happening. He runs off, and I know he's calling it in. But I'm thinking they'll be too late. So I start to tell him whatever he wants to hear. I say we can still be together, but he needs to calm down and put the gun away. He calls me a liar and a bitch and it just goes on and on. He's acting like a raving lunatic, completely off the deep end, and I can't even understand half of what he's talking about. Finally, I hear a car out front, and then another. The phone rings, but he won't answer it. He knows who it is. I try to talk to him, but he tells me to shut up. He's getting panicky, and I'm thinking, well, there's no good way out of this one. I'm screwed. If I'm lucky, he'll just shoot himself. Then I hear a bullhorn. The negotiator outside is making contact. They want him to answer the phone. And that's when he got this look in his eye . . . I can't even explain it. Total resignation, I guess. Defeat. He shoves the gun right under my chin and asks me why I did this to him—and then he pulls the trigger."

Marlin noticed that her hand was hot and moist.

"His roommate," she said, "didn't like having a loaded gun in the house. He'd unloaded it a few days before."

"Christ."

Nicole's face was flushed, and she had to take a deep breath to compose herself.

"What'd you do?" Marlin asked.

"I broke his fucking nose with the palm of my hand. Then I ran out of the house. After that, he just gave up. He was on suicide watch for a week."

Marlin reached up with his free hand and stroked her hair. The air in the house was dense and warm. "I'm sorry."

"Not something I like to replay in my head."

"I don't blame you. Did you talk to anyone afterward?"

"A shrink?"

"Well, yeah."

She nodded. "The department sent me to see someone for a few months. It helped."

"Did you testify at the trial?"

"Hell yes, I testified. He spent three years in Huntsville, then he got out and moved to Amarillo. I have no idea where he is now. Dead, in jail, I don't care."

"*Three years?*" Marlin asked, incredulous. How could they let a man like that out after only three years?

"His story was that he knew the gun was unloaded and he was just trying to scare me. I guess the judge bought into it when he sentenced him. But that's not even what pisses me off the most. Yeah, I wish he'd been put away for the rest of his life, but the thing is, I never should've been in that position to begin with. Guys like that shouldn't have access to guns."

Marlin tried to choose his words carefully. "Did he have a record? Any previous history?"

"No."

"Hard to see it coming, then, I guess. The question is: How do you keep guns from dangerous people—before they've proven that they're dangerous?"

She pulled her hand free from his. "How about licensing gun owners, like they do in California? And take it a step further. Before you get a license, you'd have to pass some sort of mental-health test."

Red tape, he thought. More bureaucracy that would fail miserably.

She wasn't done. "The gun laws in this state are so lax, it scares me. No registration, no safety training. Jesus, you have to take a safety course to get a hunting license—but not when you buy a gun. Doesn't that strike you as a little backward?"

"I can understand why you feel that way."

"But?" She was getting heated up.

"But what?"

"I'm not feeling a lot of support from you."

"Nicole . . . let's not talk about it, okay?"

She stood up quickly and walked across the room. She picked up her empty beer mug and set it back down. "Just use your head, for God's sake!"

"You have every reason to be angry about what happened," he said, "but please don't take it out on me."

She wouldn't make eye contact. "You know what? I think I'll just go home now."

"Come on, Nicole, you don't—"

"No, I think I should. I'm not mad. I just need to be alone. This wore me out."

"You *seem* mad."

She came over and kissed him on the cheek, but her lips were cold and dry. "No, I'm not, I promise. I was out of line. I'll talk to you tomorrow."

Then she was out the door, and the clap of her car door slamming sounded like nothing so much as a distant gunshot.

35

THE PERSISTENT WHINE of a chain saw was driving Mitch up the wall. He couldn't concentrate. No matter where he went in the house, he heard it—right up until dark, which was nearly nine o'clock this time of year. He'd been dulling the noise with a glass of Crown now and then—quite a lot, really—but it wasn't helping much.

Then, at nine fifteen, after the chain saw had finally stopped, Mitch heard a knock on the door. Had to be the two bumpkins. Nobody else was on the ranch. Mitch wasn't in the mood for company, so he ignored it. They knocked again, and then, a few minutes later, he heard their truck start and drive away. Finally.

Peace and quiet. Now he could think.

What he'd been contemplating was this: Would it really be so bad if J. B. got blamed for the dead Mexican? J. B. had already killed one man, and it sounded like he hadn't really paid his dues for that. Didn't he still owe a debt to society? Mitch figured he probably did.

The more Mitch thought about it, the more he became convinced that there was a sort of poetic justice to the situation. By God, J. B. *deserved* to take the fall.

So fuck J. B.! Let J. B. hang! Give J. B. the needle!

Someone buzzed at the gate.

Holy shit. It was J. B.

"How ya doin', buddy!" Mitch slurred over the intercom. "Come on up."

Mitch met J. B. at the front door. He wished he hadn't had so much to drink; he needed to keep a clear head. "J. B., you ol' dog. I didn't expect you back so soon."

J. B. was his usual self. Stoic. Not unfriendly, but stiff. He was wearing dirty Wranglers and a faded denim shirt. His yellowed Stetson rested on his head. The expression on his face was unreadable. Was that a grin? A smirk?

"Came back early," J. B. said. "Got some friends over, Mr. Campbell?" He was eyeing the glass of whiskey in Mitch's hand.

"No, just a little nightcap. Come on in. Have one with me." Mitch wondered if that was a mistake. He'd never opened his bar to J. B. before. J. B. followed him in, and Mitch said, "How was your trip?"

The foreman shrugged. "Hooked a couple. Nothing to brag about."

Mitch's mind was racing. *I have to play this right. Tell him about the cops, but act like the Mexican was never here. Don't get confused! Don't say anything stupid! Keep my story straight!*

"Boy, we sure had some excitement around here while you were gone," Mitch said, leading the way down the hallway.

"That right?" J. B. said. A man of few words.

"Yeah, a wetback was killed on the ranch across the road. The weird thing is, the cops say you hired him to work here."

Mitch could hear J. B. walking behind him, but there was no answer.

"You remember anything like that?" Mitch asked. "Hiring a Mexican guy?" He stepped into the large recreation room and headed for the bar.

For no reason that Mitch could discern, he was getting goose bumps on the back of his neck. That's when he heard a soft, peculiar sound. Not loud, but well defined.

Click! Something made of steel, snapping into place.

Mitch glanced at the mirrored wall, and through his alcoholic haze, he saw something in J. B.'s hand. For a moment, Mitch was totally perplexed. It made no sense at all. It looked like J. B. was holding a knife. A lock-blade hunting knife. And now he was coming up behind Mitch, raising his arm.

Acting on instinct, Mitch lunged to his right, diving under the pool table, just as the knife came swooping down, slashing the space where Mitch had just been standing.

"What the fuck are you doing?" Mitch screamed.

He'd come out on the other side of the pool table and was now facing his foreman. Mitch thought his heart was going to explode in his chest. "Put that goddamn knife down!"

But J. B. came around the table after him. Mitch had nothing on his feet but socks, and he couldn't get good traction on the tile floor. He slipped and slid as they circled the table three times. J. B. was no faster in his boots.

"J. B., come on, tell me why you're doing this!"

The cowboy wouldn't answer. His face was as hard and emotionless as limestone.

Mitch picked up a pool ball and winged it, but J. B. ducked, and it sailed high. Mitch threw another, but J. B. bobbed to the right. J. B. came at him again, three more times around the table, and now Mitch was gasping for air. He couldn't keep this up much longer. "Stop! Please stop!"

J. B. showed no sign of quitting. Mitch grabbed another ball and bounced it smartly off J. B.'s torso. It seemed to have no effect whatsoever. Mitch launched another, aiming for the head this time, but his arm was already getting weak and his accuracy was for shit. He hit the Wurlitzer instead, shattering the glass.

Mitch reached down and hastily removed his socks. A pool cue was lying on the green felt tabletop. Mitch picked it up and grasped it firmly with both hands. "Stay away from me! I'm warning you!"

J. B. began circling the table again, as fast as he could move. Mitch ran, too, his lungs on fire, his head spinning. J. B. was gaining on him, turning one corner as Mitch turned the next. If only he could get to the phone, or better yet, to the bar. There were knives back there. But he'd never make it. He had to keep the pool table between him and J. B.

Mitch could feel J. B.'s presence a few feet behind him. Any moment, the cold steel of the knife would sink into his flesh. He had to do something. He had to take a stand. He whirled, swinging the pool cue with as much strength as he could muster.

Contact. Major contact. The cue shattered, the heavy end spinning away like a baseball player's broken bat. He'd caught J. B. right above the ear, and now blood was pouring down the side of his head. His knees buckled, he swayed, but he managed to keep his feet.

J. B. shook his head—and then he kept coming. Mitch had nothing now but the slender end of the cue. No heft. No length. The other cues were in a rack on the wall, too far away. He was fucked.

Another loop around the pool table. Then another. Then the worst thing possible happened. Mitch slipped on his own sock and went down.

That's it. I'm dead. It's all over.

In an instant, J. B. scrambled around the table, taking advantage of Mitch's fall. Mitch lay on his back, holding the half-cue like a spear in front of him, knowing it was futile. He was sapped, his will gone, and now J. B. would slash his throat.

But J. B., coming around the last corner, stepped directly on a loose pool ball. He pitched forward, coming down right on top of Mitch—and the shattered pool cue. It went straight into J. B.'s chest. Mitch held the cue firmly as it plunged through bones and muscle, exiting between J. B.'s shoulder blades.

Mitch could feel warm blood flowing over his hands. J. B. let out a coarse grunt. He moaned softly, his face just inches from Mitch's. Then the knife fell from his hand, landing on the tile beside Mitch's head.

Ten o'clock rolled by, and Dale Stubbs was starting to get butterflies. He vanquished them with a large tumbler of scotch. *Take it easy,* he thought. *It's still early.*

At eleven, he was pacing his den, *willing* the phone to ring. *Christ, where is he? What the fuck is happening?*

By midnight, he was in a full-blown panic. J. B. had had more than enough time to drive to East Texas, drop off his son, and make it back to Blanco County. The deed should be done by now. Why hadn't he called?

At twelve thirty, Stubbs got into his truck, drove several miles from his home, and stopped at a pay phone.

He dialed J. B.'s cell. Got voice mail.

This ain't good. Ain't good at all.

He called again. Same thing.

Maybe J. B. had changed his mind. Maybe the son of a bitch had decided that the NWA could go to hell.

Stubbs waited ten minutes, then tried one more time. No luck.

He began to smash the phone against the housing until it came apart in his hands.

36

"BOARDING PASS AND ID, please."

It was early Friday morning, and a paunchy fertilizer salesman named Sam Shelton was on his way to Lubbock. God, he hated traveling. Parking way the hell out in Bumfuck, Idaho. Waiting in the god-awful heat for the damn shuttle. Standing in line with a bunch of morons at the ticket counter. All of it was a tremendous pain in the ass. Now he had to show his driver's license yet again—to a guy who looked a hell of a lot more like a hijacker than Shelton did. Coffee-colored skin. Black eyes. Big, furry eyebrows, and a nose the size of a ripe zucchini. Young, too, like those Islamic nuts that were always blowing themselves up. The only thing missing was a turban. Working security, for Chrissakes. Talk about the fox guarding the henhouse.

"I just showed my ID to the guy at the Continental counter," Shelton snapped. He was sick of this unchanging routine.

"I'll need to see it, too, sir."

The guy spoke with no accent, but Shelton wasn't fooled. Didn't mean the man wasn't a foreigner.

Shelton sighed as loudly as he could and dug for his wallet. Sure, keeping the airports safe was important—he could get behind that—but couldn't these people get their heads together and run things a little more efficiently?

"Here's a concept," he said loudly, for the benefit of the fellow travelers around him—to show that he wasn't afraid to speak his mind. "How about if y'all worked this thing out so we only had to show our damn license once? Would that be too much to ask?"

"Sorry for the inconvenience," the guy replied. Smug. A hint of a smile. Wearing a white shirt with a stupid gold emblem on the sleeve. He was enjoying this, exerting his power, making Shelton jump through hoops.

Shelton handed his ID over. The dark-skinned man eyeballed it for five seconds and said, "Thank you, sir. I notice that it expires in three weeks. You might want to get it renewed if you're traveling again anytime soon."

The passengers behind Shelton were shifting impatiently, but he couldn't resist saying, "As a matter of fact, I'm flying next month. You telling me I can't use that ID?"

"Afraid not."

"What the hell does it matter if it's expired? It's still *me*. It's still an official ID." Shelton was having visions of waiting in another long line at the Department of Public Safety. More bureaucratic bullshit.

"Sorry, sir. It's standard policy at every airport in the nation."

Shelton snatched his driver's license from the man's hand and said, "Ridiculous. Absolutely ridiculous."

The smile again. "Have a nice day, sir."

"Yeah, sure."

Shelton grabbed the handle of his carry-on bag and proceeded toward the next stage in this gauntlet from hell. The X-ray scanner. People were stacked up like sheep, placing everything on the conveyor belt, removing shoes and jewelry, trudging like zombies through the metal detector. The greatest country on the planet, and a regular guy like Shelton had to practically strip naked to board a plane. What a fiasco. Didn't anybody realize how insane it was? Couldn't somebody come up with a better way?

The line crept forward, and Shelton checked his wristwatch. His flight left in twenty-five minutes. Cutting it close. There wouldn't even be time to get a Bloody Mary at the bar. "Can we hurry it up, please?" he called out to nobody in particular. Nobody in particular responded.

Shelton grabbed a gray plastic tub and placed his keys and cell phone in it, followed by his watch and his sunglasses. He kicked off his Florsheims and dropped them in, too. Slid the tub down the line.

Nobody was moving. What the hell was the holdup?

An elderly woman—eighty years old if she was a day!—was being asked to remove a necklace. Shelton could hardly stand it. Apparently they were accosting grandmothers nowadays. Like she was really some sort of threat. Like she had explosives in her orthopedic shoes. "Got a flight to catch," Shelton sang out, which earned him a glare from the large black lady working the metal detector.

Finally, the idiots determined that Granny wasn't a terrorist, and the line moved forward. Two more passengers, and then Shelton was waved ahead. He plopped his bag on the conveyor belt. He passed through the metal detector without setting off any alarm bells.

The black woman—her name was Clarita Maddox, according to her name tag—was still frowning at him as he passed by.

"Great system we got here," Shelton muttered. "Put us all through a friggin' cattle chute."

"We're doing the best we can, sir," Clarita said to his back, but Shelton ignored her.

Now he stepped to the other side of the X-ray machine and waited for his bag. Another damn delay. The guy that examines the luggage as it passes through had brought the conveyor belt to a halt.

"Someone packing an emery board or something?" Shelton said loudly. "Ooh, scary." In his mind, he added, *Hurry the fuck up, pinheads.*

At least his gray tub had made it through, so he balanced on one leg at a time, putting his shoes back on, feeling like a stork as he did it. He grabbed his cell phone, his watch, his keys, his sunglasses—and that's when he realized it must be his own bag that the guy was studying so intently. What was up with that?

Then he felt a firm hand on his elbow. He turned and saw that he was surrounded by four security guards. Clarita and three new ones, all men. The one holding Shelton's elbow was a young guy, small, slope-shouldered, face like a weasel. "Please step over here for a moment, sir."

Shelton groaned. "Jesus, what now? I gotta get to the gate."

The security guards formed a tighter knot around him. "Sir, I need you to exit the line and come with me."

Shelton had had enough. He swatted the man's hand away and said, "I'll miss my flight! God damn it, I'm sick of all—"

Shelton was never able to figure out exactly what happened next. Weasel Face was no more than five-six, maybe one-forty, but he did . . . *something.* Too fast to see. Some kind of martial arts move, and the next thing Shelton knew, he was headed for the floor. His back hit the carpet with a thud and the air exploded from his lungs. He couldn't breathe. People were shouting and scrambling away from the area. The four guards collapsed on top of him, pinning him to the floor. Shelton struggled, but they held his arms and legs. Someone had a firm grasp around his throat.

For a brief moment, Shelton wondered, *Nail clippers? Is this about my nail clippers?*

From his vantage point on the floor, he saw three uniformed cops sprinting this way. Before the cops arrived, Weasel Face took the opportunity to lean down and whisper into Shelton's ear. "You don't ever—*ever*—bring a gun into *my* airport." He jammed an elbow into Shelton's ribs. "We clear on that, asshole?"

37

MARLIN WAS AWAKE before dawn, tossing and turning, knowing he'd get no more sleep, wishing he'd handled things differently.

I should've kept my mouth shut. She'd had a gun to her head, for Chrissakes, and what did I do? Defended her ex-boyfriend's rights. What an ass I was.

Nicole was pissed, and he couldn't blame her. And yet—

He didn't mean to be cold, but didn't he have a right to his opinion? He hated to hear what Nicole had gone through, but couldn't he be compassionate without having to change his beliefs?

Now Marlin was starting to get worked up. *Why am I thinking about this?*

He climbed out of bed and let Geist into the backyard. He showered and shaved, then filled a thermos with coffee. For an hour he drove quiet county roads, his windows down, enjoying the relatively cool morning air, contemplating what he knew so far. Or what he thought he knew.

Rodolfo Dominguez had been shot through a window. Mitch

Campbell had bought a pane of glass and denied his identity to the store clerk.

Dominguez had been hired by J. B. Crowley to work on Campbell's ranch. Crowley had a violent past, including a homicide that had been ruled justifiable.

Mrs. Buell had seen two men hanging around Dominguez's truck on Sunday afternoon—but it appeared that Crowley had been four hours away at Lake Fork.

Campbell knew more than he should about the time frame of the murder. Was he involved? He had to be. Had he parked the truck along the roadway simply to get it off his ranch? Sounded like a reasonable theory.

But what about Crowley? If he was at Lake Fork, who was the second man Mrs. Buell had seen? What if the two men at the truck had simply been interested buyers?

Marlin was on Sandy Road, approaching Highway 281. Head south to the office? It was early yet. He turned left, going north, then took a right on Cypress Mill Road. He'd make a swing past Crowley's house, just for the hell of it. Maybe Crowley was home by now.

What they needed was something more against Campbell. It was too early for a search warrant. Not because they couldn't get one—they might be able to—but because they didn't want to tip their hand just yet. If they came up empty, Campbell would know they were looking at him. A guy like him would involve a lawyer in a heartbeat. The NWA would insist on it. That would really screw things up. Marlin had learned a lot about homicide investigation from Bobby Garza and the deputies. Contrary to stereotypes, you didn't rush out and grab a suspect and sweat him under a bare bulb. In a perfect world, what you did was interrogate a suspect *after* the case had been built, when you'd gathered every scrap of evidence you could possibly find. When guilt was damn near undeniable. Or when you had no other options.

He passed Crowley's place, but he didn't stop. The brush was thick, but Marlin could see that the driveway was still empty, the porch light still on. Nobody home. He continued up the road, passing the entrance to Campbell's ranch. The gate was closed. No sign of the singer. Friday was garbage day, and Campbell's rolling trash cart was outside the gate, waiting to be emptied.

Marlin smiled. *Hello there.*

He continued to a slight curve in the road a few hundred yards away. He could still see Campbell's gate. He made a three-point turn, pulled to the shoulder, and grabbed his microphone. Couldn't raise Garza or Tatum. Too early. He asked the dispatcher to call the sheriff and tell him to contact Marlin on the radio.

Then he waited. This was one of the rare instances when he wished he had a cell phone. He'd avoided owning one so far, mainly because the phones seemed to turn normal human beings into roadway hazards and self-important idiots. The radio would work though. Marlin would simply be discreet about it.

Two minutes passed, then Garza said, "One-fifty-three to seventy-five-oh-eight."

Marlin keyed the mike again. "Hey, Bobby, refresh my memory on something. Do we need a warrant to collect a person's garbage?"

If this were a poaching investigation—if Marlin wanted to check the trashcan for duck feathers or a deer hide—he wouldn't need a warrant, as long as he had probable cause. A recent state law had given game wardens extra latitude in search-and-seizure that other officers did not have. But what about a case like this?

Garza said, "You mean at the curbside?"

"Yeah."

The sheriff was chuckling when he said, "No, sir, we do not. Where are you?"

"Right where you think I am. Care to join me?"

"On my way."

"Can you bring a clean tarp? And some duct tape?"

The phone jolted Mitch awake. He didn't know what time it was, but it was light outside his window. He had a vague sense of doom, but he couldn't remember why. His thoughts were muddy. Something bad had happened last night. What was it?

He answered. Dale Stubbs said, "Hey, buddy. They setting up for the rally yet?"

Mitch cringed as bits and pieces came back to him. The hunting knife. The pool table. The cue stick. J. B. was dead. Stubbs had to have sent him. It was the only thing that made sense. Stubbs wanted

Mitch dead, so he couldn't reveal what had happened last Sunday.
Sacrifice Mitch to save the precious NWA.

"You summunabitch," Mitch said. "I know whatcha did." He noticed that his words didn't come out very clearly. He was mumbling,
like he was still drunk.

"Jesus, son, what the hell're you talking about?"

"Don' fuckin' deny it, Dale. Rat bastard."

"I got no idea what—"

Mitch hung up. He was still so tired. He just wanted to go back to
sleep, but he knew he couldn't. His memory was like Swiss cheese.
He remembered drinking a shitload of whiskey while J. B. was still lying on the floor. Had he cleaned up the recreation room? Something
told him he had driven J. B.'s truck, but where had he taken it? Holy
fuck, what had he done with the body?

The swimming pool. He had a vague recollection—something to
do with the swimming pool.

"Yeah, Miss Nash, it's Paul Hebert. The detective?"

Bad news? Sabrina wondered, gripping the phone tighter. *Have
they caught Harry? Is he in jail?* "Yes?"

"I'm just, ah, checking in. Have you heard from your husband?"

Thank God. Not bad news.

"My *ex*-husband. No, I have not. If I had, I would've called you,
like you asked."

"Never hurts to check. Listen, we have indications that he's been
in Blanco County recently. Might still be out there."

Sabrina started to reply, but her voice froze in her throat. Had the
detectives been to the cabin? If so, they'd found her note, and they knew
she'd lied on Wednesday night. "Blanco County," she managed to say.

"Yes, ma'am. We've checked all the motels, and we can't find him.
I was wondering if—"

"I knew where he might be staying."

"Exactly. Maybe a friend you forgot about?"

Sabrina was at a threshold. Come clean, or cross the abyss into total deception? "I have no idea," she said firmly.

The line was silent for several moments, and Sabrina just knew
that she'd been caught. Now Hebert would come to her house and

arrest her. She wouldn't make it to the hearing on Monday. She couldn't testify. Rankin would go free. *Damn you, Harry.*

"That's disappointing," Hebert said. "I was really hoping you could help us out."

"Sorry."

"See, the thing is, we were kinda wondering why he might be hanging around in that area, and my partner pointed out that there's an NWA rally at Mitch Campbell's ranch tomorrow. Buncha gun nuts out there. Congressman Dobbins, too. I'd hate for there to be trouble."

Sabrina felt sick. She understood the implications. "If I hear from him, I'll call you immediately."

"Yeah, you do that. Or if you have anything else you want to tell me. Anything at all."

Hebert hung up and thought: *She's lying. She's got an idea where Jenkins might be, but she ain't sharing. Not a lot I can do about it, either.*

He reached for his cigarettes, intending to go outside for a smoke, and just then Ramon showed up at his office door. Seemed the kid was always popping in, grinning, ready to share some new piece of information. Tenacious bastard. Showing himself to be a fine cop. Good thing Hebert was retiring, otherwise he'd feel the need to keep up.

"Byron Gladwell just called," Ramon said. "The *Statesman* owns a cabin out on the Pedernales River. Ten minutes from Johnson City. A weekend place for the bigwigs."

"Well, fuck. Why didn't he tell us that yesterday?"

"Said it slipped his mind because nobody's been out there lately on account of the river being dry. Plus, Jenkins hasn't been out there in ages, ever since the kid died, and Gladwell doubts he's out there now."

"But you got directions anyway."

"I did."

Hebert slipped the pack of cigarettes into his breast pocket. "Let's go."

Garza drove past Marlin, made a U-turn, and came up behind him. He'd brought Bill Tatum with him. The three of them met between the vehicles, two hundred yards from Campbell's gate.

Garza was smiling, shaking his head. "Damn, John, you think of everything."

"Worth a shot, right?"

"Definitely," Tatum said. "You got a plan?"

They couldn't afford to get sloppy. They had to collect the evidence, if there was any, cleanly. No claims of contamination later. "I say we dump everything on top of the tarp in the back of my truck and seal it shut. But I'll need one of y'all to help me lift the cart."

Marlin could hear the deep drone of a large engine coming in their direction. "Man, I hope that's not the garbage truck."

They all turned and watched for the vehicle.

"If it is," Garza said, "we're gonna have to let this go. We can't have anyone talking."

Marlin heard the slow squeal of brakes, then the engine idled steadily. The vehicle had come to a stop. Crap. Marlin listened for the familiar clatter of trash being dumped, but he didn't hear it. Maybe the driver was simply lost. Then the engine huffed, and the vehicle was once again coming this way.

Finally, it came into view. Marlin relaxed. It was an eighteen-wheeler, and it slowed as it approached Campbell's ranch. It pulled to the shoulder, and a man emerged from the cab. He crossed the road and stopped in front of the keypad, and a second later, the gate swung open.

"Setting up for the rally," Marlin said. "There'll be more trucks coming."

"We gotta be slick about this," Garza said. "I don't want anyone seeing us."

The man climbed back into the truck, dropped it into gear, and swung it carefully through the gate. He proceeded up the driveway, and the gate closed behind him. Marlin could hear the engine long after the rig was out of sight.

Marlin said, "How about if one of y'all drives back to 281 and keeps an eye out for traffic?"

Garza gestured east. "What if someone comes from this side?"

"We'll have to chance it. We'll make it quick."

Garza nodded in agreement, but smiled at Tatum and said, "I'll be the lookout. Bill's the one with all the muscles. Perfect for hoisting garbage."

"Gee, thanks. I knew there was a reason I worked out."

"Remember," Garza said. "Discretion." Tatum nodded, and Garza drove away in the cruiser.

While they were waiting for Garza to get in position, Marlin said, "Any phone records yet?"

"Nope. Maybe this afternoon. I sent Nicole up to the Verizon offices and Ernie over to T-Mobile. Records always seem to appear faster when there's a cop waiting in the lobby."

Marlin climbed into the back of his truck and spread the tarp evenly across the bed. Five minutes later, Garza's voice came over the radio: "Seventy-five-oh-eight, you're all clear."

Tatum and Marlin hopped into the truck and drove the short distance to Campbell's gate. Marlin passed the entrance, then backed in. They stepped from the cab, and Marlin glanced east for oncoming vehicles. All clear. Marlin felt the need to hurry, like a schoolboy pulling a prank.

He wheeled the cart to the rear of the truck, feeling its weight, wondering if the remnants of a windowpane were discarded inside. "This sucker's full."

They each grabbed a side and hefted it over the tailgate. Some of the trash was in garbage bags, but some was not. Beer and liquor bottles rattled and bounced. There were scraps of food and empty tin cans and soiled paper towels.

And Marlin thought he heard the tinkle of broken glass.

38

TRICIA WOODBINE HAD decided that the first thing she'd do, after she got the money, was take a monthlong trip to the Caribbean. Jamaica. Belize. The Caymans. Barbados. Wear a thong bikini and make wives slap husbands for ogling. Enter wet T-shirt contests. Get a massage every day and take a different cabana boy to bed every night. What's that, José? You don't speak English? Not a problem. The Virgin Islands would be a little less virgin by the time she got through. Eat mountains of seafood and drink gallons of rum. Lounge on the beach, getting a deep, dark tan. Maybe even read a few good books. Maybe.

But first things first.

She arrived at the SNATCH apartment at nine thirty. She knocked twice, waited three seconds, and was about to knock twice more—her secret code—but she didn't. *Screw it,* she thought. *We're doing this my way. Today, I'm hell on three-inch heels.*

"Who is it?" The red-haired guy.

"Cameron Diaz." Tricia stifled a giggle.

"Who?"

"Charlize Theron."

No response.

"Would you believe Jennifer Aniston?" It was a lousy imperson- ation of Maxwell Smart. She'd been watching too much cable.

The door opened a few inches, then swung wide. The redhead was standing there, looking even more stern than usual. "You think that's amusing?"

"Oh, absolutely. Don't you?"

"Dieter has been —"

She strolled right past him, into the apartment, and down the hallway, saying, "Yeah, I know. I bet the poor boy has a blister on his dialing finger by now." She knocked on Dieter's door, then opened it.

Dieter was behind the desk, his beret in place, the phone mashed against his ear. He glared at her and hung up. "Where the hell have you been?"

She didn't reply right away. First, she stepped into the room and closed the door behind her, leaving the redhead scowling in the hall. She circled her usual chair and sat, crossing her legs with an exagger- ated motion. She smoothed her skirt. She cleared her throat. *This is going to be fun.*

"Dieter, sweetheart, I have something for you. Well, more accu- rately, something for *us.* But before I reveal what it is, I want you to think long and hard about the contributions I've made to your little spy ring."

Small patches of pink were showing on his cheeks. "So far, you have contributed nothing."

Tricia sniffed. "Oh, I don't think that's true at all. And even if it is, it's about to change." She reached into her purse and removed a small digital voice recorder. The kind busy executives use to remind them- selves of important crap because they think they're too cool to use a paper and pen. "I recorded a very intriguing phone call yesterday, and I thought you might want to hear it."

She looked at him. He looked back. "Well?" he said.

"It's from Mitch Campbell," she said. "He must've called Dale's direct line, because it didn't go through me."

She held up the voice recorder, and Dieter said, "That's not the Interloper 3000. Why are you using that?"

She gave him her killer smile, the one that could lure men across barroom floors like zombies. Soften him up a little. Or maybe harden him up. "I'll get to that in a minute. For now, just listen." Tricia pushed the Play button, and the conversation ensued:

This is Dale Stubbs.
The cops were just here. About the dead Mexican!
Goddamn, now, take it easy.
I'm freaking out, Dale! They know the Mexican was supposed to be working here. They were asking about J. B. . . .

She watched Dieter's face closely, and by the time the recording was finished, she knew she had him hooked. He displayed no emotion whatsoever—but still, Tricia knew. He was trying so hard *not* to react that it was a dead giveaway. Dieter stared into space for a long while, then said, "Who's J. B.?"

"No idea. But really, does it matter?"

The important thing, Tricia knew, was the dead Mexican. She removed an envelope from her purse and unfolded the two pages inside. She'd printed the newspaper article off the Internet. She handed the pages to Dieter, and he began to read about Rodolfo Dominguez. He didn't smile or nod or sit up with enthusiasm. He was a total blank. After he was done, he said, "Where is the Interloper 3000?"

"In a safe place." *My lingerie drawer.*

"I want it. Now." He actually *growled.* He was seriously pissed.

She reminded herself: *I am in charge!* So she blurted it out. "I want more money. I deserve it." She didn't sound as assertive as she'd hoped. More like a whiny little girl.

"You're already being well paid."

"This is worth more. A lot more." She didn't have the nerve to mention the auction angle.

"You little fucking traitor."

"Dieter!"

"Double-crossing whore."

"Hey!"

He leaned forward and held out his hand. "That recorder will be enough. Give it to me!"

Tricia had prepared for this. She'd practiced. Before Dieter could react, she pushed the appropriate buttons. "I just deleted the message," she said. "Now you've got nothing."

Dieter rose to his feet—he was much taller than she'd expected—and began to come around the desk. Tricia had prepared for this, too. She removed her handgun smoothly from her purse.

"Stay back!" Her hands were trembling.

"What, you're going to shoot me?"

"If I have to."

He stared at her for a long moment. She'd never seen a face so consumed by anger. "Get out," he said.

She kept the gun pointed at him. "I'll be back at noon tomorrow. Have an offer ready."

"Get the fuck out!"

She yanked the door open, and the redhead was lurking in the hall. He saw the gun and moved aside, letting her pass. She tried to move with grace and dignity, but she found herself scrambling to get out of the apartment.

"Have either of y'all listened to Mitch Campbell's CD?" Bobby Garza asked.

Marlin, Bill Tatum, and the sheriff were in Garza's office. Making small talk. Drinking coffee. Waiting.

"Yeah," Tatum said. "If that's country music, which country are they talking about?"

"It's all going that way," Marlin said. "Crossover pop."

They'd been tempted to hang around and watch as Henry Jameson made an initial inventory of Campbell's garbage, but Henry had said he'd let them know ASAP. *Maybe an hour,* he'd said. There were protocols to follow. For now, they were in limbo.

"Give me Merle Haggard any day," Tatum said.

"Johnny Cash," Marlin said.

"Conway Twitty," Garza said. His feet were propped on his desk. The soles of his boots were as worn as an old baseball.

Marlin laughed. "I didn't know you were a Conway fan."

"Everything but the hairdo," Garza said.

Marlin checked the clock on the wall. Quarter of ten. The room was so quiet, he could hear the clock ticking. There was nobody else in the building except for Darrell, the dispatcher, out front.

"*Hello darling,*" Garza sang. "*Nice to see you . . .* "

"What'd you do with the money?" Marlin asked him.

"What money?"

"That your mom gave you for singing lessons."

"Boy, I walked into that one. No good?"

"You could torture suspects. Make 'em confess."

Garza snorted. They waited some more. Marlin was starting to get restless.

"My brother plays the steel guitar," Tatum said after a while. "Has a band called the High Plains Drifters. They get a lot of gigs around Beaumont."

"Beaumont?" Garza said. "I figured with a name like that—"

"I know. Doesn't make much sense."

"Maybe they like the movie."

Tatum looked at him.

"With Clint Eastwood," Garza said.

"Oh, right. I'll have to ask him."

Marlin sipped from his coffee. Not enough cream.

Tatum's cell phone chirped, and the chief deputy answered it on the first ring. Marlin decided it wouldn't be Henry; he'd call Garza's direct line. Maybe Ernie or Nicole. Tatum listened, then said, "What time exactly?" Another pause, then: "Okay, good. I appreciate you telling me. Was he on his way back home?" Marlin could faintly hear the reply over the cell phone's tiny speaker. It sounded like a woman's voice, but he couldn't make out the words. "Okay, thanks again," Tatum said. He hung up. "That was Crowley's ex. He dropped the boy off in Woodville at about three o'clock yesterday afternoon. She didn't know for a fact that he was coming back home, but she assumed he was."

Garza started to say something, but then *his* phone rang. He answered, listened, then dropped his feet to the floor. "Excellent." He gave them a thumbs-up. "How much?" Garza asked. "Okay, good. Nice work. Let us know the moment you're done." He hung up, and his face was taut. "We've got loose glass in the bottom of one of the trash bags. Plus blood on a bunch of paper towels. A lot of it."

"Son of a bitch," Tatum said. "We've got him."

"Looks that way. Henry will send it all to the lab in Austin to be sure, and that'll take a few days. Meanwhile, Henry's gonna run a few tests of his own. He can at least tell us if the blood types match. And he'll take a closer look at the glass. Give him a few more hours."

For reasons Marlin couldn't quite pinpoint, he was having a tough time wrapping his mind around this one. They had evidence, sure—but what possible reason could a man like Mitch Campbell have for shooting Rodolfo Dominguez? How could he do something so stupid? It was beyond comprehension—but then again, many homicides were. "What next?" he asked.

"We search his place," Tatum said flatly. "The sooner the better. Campbell said some people are staying at his house tomorrow night. Visitors could destroy evidence."

"Definitely," Garza said. "So start working on an affidavit. For Campbell's entire ranch, not just the house. We'll wait on these other tests Henry's running, but I want to be ready. This'll be the most important affidavit either of y'all will ever write, so it's gotta be bulletproof. Don't leave anything to the imagination. Put everything in there, and I mean everything, and tie it all together with a pretty bow."

Tatum was nodding, saying, "Let's say Judge Hilton signs off on it later this afternoon. You sure you want to go in that late in the day? We'll need to do some searching outdoors. And we'll need a big crew. There's not much time to get organized."

"Good point."

"Tomorrow would be much better."

They all knew what that meant. The rally would have to be canceled or postponed.

"Unfortunately for Mitch, you're right."

"A bunch of higher-ups from the NWA are gonna be there," Tatum said. "They're gonna be pissed if we ruin their little party."

Garza grinned. "Well, they understand the Second Amendment pretty well. We'll just have to remind them how well we understand the Fourth."

Marlin wanted to try another call to J. B. Crowley, so he retreated to his office—the first time he'd been there all morning. On his desk was a vase of flowers, and a small envelope was tucked under the vase. Inside, on the card, in Nicole's elegant handwriting, it said: *How about a cease-fire?*

He stared at it for a long time.

Then he dialed the phone. When a young woman answered, he gave his name and asked for Melinda.

A few minutes later, Melinda came on the line and said, "So, I heard you like one of the rings."

"I do."

She laughed. "Just keep practicing those words. That's all you have to remember. Are you wanting to look at some different sizes in that same cut, or . . ."

His forehead was damp. "No, this is the one. I called to give you my credit card number."

"Excellent!" Melinda said. "I'm so happy for you. Let me grab a pen."

39

"THERE IT IS," Paul Hebert said. "Pull over on the grass and we'll walk in."

They'd found the driveway, with a chain stretched across it, just as Byron Gladwell had described. Now they needed to use some stealth. The last thing Hebert wanted was for Harry Jenkins to hightail it into the woods before they got a chance to talk to him. Hebert wasn't in shape for a foot chase. The last time he did a sit-up, he was reaching for the remote control. The only weights he lifted nowadays were twelve ounces. He could barely even jog his memory. And Ramon? He was three decades younger, but he'd smoked for fifteen of those years. He wouldn't do much better than Hebert.

So they closed their car doors quietly and began walking slowly down the rough caliche road. Ultimately, if Jenkins ran, Hebert and Ramon had no authority to stop him; they had no arrest warrant. Jenkins was merely a suspect. He could take off or sit mute or tell them to go fuck themselves, and Hebert couldn't do a damn thing about it. *Life sucks when you don't have any evidence.*

Hebert kept moving, Ramon following behind. After a few minutes, the cabin came into view, a hundred yards away, in a small clearing on the riverbank. No car out front. No signs of activity. Hebert gestured to Ramon, and they veered into the tree line. They'd sneak right up on the bastard. It was already ninety degrees, and Hebert wished he'd left his suit jacket in the car. They walked under a canopy of huge oak trees, a bed of leaves and sticks crunching beneath their feet. Now they were thirty yards away.

Hebert whispered, "You circle around back and watch the door. I'll enter in the front."

Ramon continued through the trees, and he was quickly out of sight. Hebert waited a full minute, then he simply strode from the woods and walked directly toward the cabin. If Jenkins bolted now, at least they'd see or hear him. They'd know where he was, and that was progress.

But as Hebert approached the door, all was quiet. No shouts from Ramon. Nobody peering from the windows. Hebert stepped onto the concrete porch and listened. He heard nothing. Maybe Jenkins was asleep. It'd be perfect if they caught him napping. Talk some sense into him before he got all worked up.

Hebert tried the knob. Locked. Gladwell had told Ramon where a key was hidden, but Hebert didn't want to go in unannounced, Jenkins maybe thinking he was an intruder. The cartoonist would be the last person to carry a gun, but jeez, it wasn't like the guy had been thinking clearly lately. So Hebert knocked, loud and firm. Nothing. He knocked again. More of the same. "Mr. Jenkins?" No reply. No sound of movement inside.

The key was above the door, resting on the upper trim—right where fifty percent of the "hidden" keys in America could be found. The other fifty percent were under doormats. Hebert slid the key into the lock and eased the door open. "Jenkins?"

Hebert rested his hand on his revolver and stepped inside. He stood motionless, listening again. Back in his days in uniform, Hebert had entered a thousand different domiciles. After the first few hundred, he'd developed a sixth sense. Hebert knew right away the place was empty. He called Ramon in, and they searched the cabin anyway, but Hebert's intuition was right. No Jenkins. The garbage can in the kitchen was filled with TV dinner packages and dozens of beer cans. So, yeah, Jenkins had been here—he had, in fact, forced the back door—but now he was gone.

There was a pen and a notepad on the round wooden table. The pad was blank.

"Red, let me ask you somethin'," Billy Don said.

It was ten till ten, and Red was driving north on Highway 281. He didn't reply because he'd been in a piss-poor mood since yesterday, all because of the way Mitch had acted. He couldn't get over it. *No wonder it's so hard to break into Nashville,* he thought. *Everybody's a two-faced asshole. They treat you like a friend one minute, vermin the next.*

"Hey, Red?" Billy Don wasn't giving up.

"What?" It was the least inviting *What?* Red could manage.

"Are you happy?"

"Happy about what?"

"You know, 'bout life in general. Are you a happy person?"

"What the hell kind of question is that at ten in the morning?"

"I was just wondering, is all."

"Well, stop. I don't want to talk about it."

Red glanced down at the Pedernales River as they crossed over it. Even here, near the small dam, the water was hardly more than a big brown puddle. Depressing.

"It's just that you're always trying to come up with some big scheme," Billy Don said. "A million-dollar idea. Something to make your life better. But the way I look at it, we already got it pretty good."

Red did *not* want to get drawn into this conversation. Sometimes talking to Billy Don was like talking to a senile lobotomy patient. But Red simply could not let that comment pass. "You gotta be shittin' me. We got it good?"

"I think we do, yeah. Ain't never been on food stamps. We get hungry, we go out and shoot somethin'. Got steady work most of the time. A roof over our heads."

"My trailer? Jesus Christ, Billy Don, it's a friggin' dump."

"It ain't so bad."

"The roof leaks, the septic's always backing up. The carpet's so nasty, I take my shoes off when I step outside so I won't get the grass dirty. Half the furniture I found at the dump. A raccoon would be embarrassed to live there."

"Well, I ain't embarrassed. You know, some people ain't even got homes."

Red shook his head and turned right on Cypress Mill Road. What was the point in discussing it? Argue with a simpleton and you both lose.

"I just think you oughta try to be happier," Billy Don muttered. "Life's short, you know. You don't have to be rich or famous to enjoy it."

Red snapped. He couldn't help it. He said, "Well, goddamn, Billy Don, maybe I'm not trying to get rich. Maybe I just wanna hang around a better class of people."

He immediately regretted it. Billy Don had a pained look on his face, like when he'd eaten too much pie. He turned and stared at the window.

Red drove in silence for a minute, then said, "I didn't mean that, Billy Don. You know that. You're my best friend."

The big man kept his face turned away. "Funny way of showing it."

"Well, I apologize, okay? My temper, you know. If I was to become a famous songwriter and move to Nashville, I'd take you with me. No question about it."

Another minute passed.

"And if it don't work out," Red said, "we'll just keep living in that damn trailer until it falls down around our ears. Okay?"

"Yeah, okay." Mumbling like a six-year-old.

Red pulled up to the gate, entered the code, and drove onto the ranch. Half a mile in, he came to the pasture where the rally was to be held. He stopped the truck. The field was a beehive of activity. Red counted a dozen cargo trailers, most of which had been unhooked from their trucks. He saw one that had been converted to a portable men's bathroom, with metal stairs at each end. There was another just like it for the ladies. Six more appeared to be concession stands, and one was a first-aid station. On the far side of the field was a flatbed; Red figured that one would be the stage. At least fifty men were hard at work, unspooling thick electric cables, assembling bleachers, moving huge speakers around on dollies, erecting a six-foot chain-link fence to keep people from wandering off during the rally. Red—knowing how much manual labor was involved—was impressed at what they'd already accomplished.

"Damn, they don't mess around, do they?" Billy Don said.

They sat and watched for several minutes, and in that time, two more trucks arrived. The rally crew was working like a well-oiled machine.

"Tomorrow," Red said, "Mitch is gonna sing his number-one hit song right out there on that stage. The ladies are gonna go wild and start throwing panties and such at him, screaming, lifting their shirts, blowing kisses. Afterwards, he'll hang around and drink beer and listen to everyone tell him what a great guy he is. Then he'll go up to his million-dollar house on his ten-million-dollar ranch and go to bed with his girlfriend, who happens to be one of the purtiest movie actresses I ever seen. Now . . . are you telling me you wouldn't switch places with him? Are you saying Mitch doesn't have some pretty good reasons to be happier than you and me?"

Red knew he'd made his point. But all Billy Don would say was, "Maybe so. But he sure didn't seem too happy yesterday."

They'd spent most of the previous day trimming the towering live oaks around Mitch's house. Lots of deadwood. They'd hauled the limbs and branches away in Red's sixteen-foot trailer, dumping them illegally along an unpaved county road in the dark of night.

Today they'd mow, edge, and weed, and then they'd be done. So Red spent the remainder of the morning pushing his junky old Toro around Mitch's enormous front lawn, which, even in the drought, was as flawless as a putting green. A sprinkler system—that was the key. Billy Don buzzed here and there with the string trimmer, which looked like a child's toy in his arms. By one o'clock, the temperature was well over a hundred, and their shirts were drenched with sweat. They took a break for lunch and decided to eat in back, by the pool.

Rounding the rear corner of the house, Billy Don stopped in his tracks. He pointed. Mitch was stretched out in a lounge chair by the diving board. He appeared to be sleeping. "Maybe we oughta eat in the truck."

Red shook his head. "Not me. You go on back if you want, but I'm kicking back in the shade." In truth, Red was hoping Mitch might wake up and be the same friendly guy he was two nights ago. Red could steer the conversation toward the rally, maybe wangle an invitation.

He walked across the grass and stepped onto the concrete apron around the pool. Billy Don hesitated, then followed. They grabbed a couple of chairs a few yards away from Mitch. Red cleared his throat, but Mitch didn't budge.

"Oh, man," Billy Don whispered. "He's really gettin' burnt."

The singer was wearing a T-shirt and shorts, but his legs, arms, and face were bright pink.

"Think we should wake him up?" Billy Don asked.

"If we don't, he's gonna look like a lobster in a couple hours." Red spoke louder now, saying, "Hey, Mitch. Time to wake up."

No movement.

"Yoo-hoo, Mitch. You're getting awful red."

Still nothing. Billy Don grinned and made a drinking motion with his hand. Red figured he might be right. Mitch wasn't just sleeping, he was passed out. Red stepped over to him and jostled his shoulder. It was like jiggling a bag of potatoes. "Hey, Mitch! Rise and shine!"

The singer's eyelids fluttered and slowly opened. His eyes were glassy and dull, and there was no recognition in them at all. "Wha' the fuck. Who is it?"

"You was gettin' burnt. Figured we'd better wake you."

Mitch propped himself on his elbows and looked around. Then he laid back down and covered his face with both hands. Red could hear him saying, "Oh, fuck. Son of a bitch. Jesus Christ."

Must be a bad hangover. Red could relate. He'd once had a hangover so intense, he'd almost had to baptize it. "Want some aspirin?" he asked. "Maybe some whiskey? Hair of the dog?"

Mitch, with his hands still on his face, said, "Water."

"Billy Don, run inside and get the man some water."

Billy Don didn't argue. He retreated into the house and came back a few minutes later with a large glass. Mitch sat up and drained it in one long pull. Then he stood and shambled toward a wooden shed thirty yards away, tucked in some trees. The pump house. The pressure tank for the well was probably in there, along with chemicals and other supplies for the pool.

Red watched as Mitch steadied himself with one hand against the small building, opening the door a few inches with his other hand.

Mitch peeked in, then immediately slammed the door. He bent over, his hands on his knees, and Red expected him to retch. But he didn't. After a long moment, he righted himself and walked back to his chair. Strange scene.

"More water?" Red asked.

Mitch shook his head. He had a glazed expression on his face, like a man who'd almost gotten his arm caught in a combine.

"You all right, Mitch? Something bothering you?"

Mitch glanced at the pump house again. Then he looked at Red and said, "I need you to do something for me."

"Hell, that's what we're here for. Name it."

40

SERGEANT MURRAY WHEELER didn't like being assigned to the airport, because so many people—including his friends and family—kidded him about it. Forget the fact that Wheeler was on the front line in the battle against terrorism, they still teased him.

"Murray had to handle a crime wave today," they'd say. "Someone stole a snow globe from the gift shop." Ha-ha. Hee-hee.

"Hey, Murray, have you pulled any pilots over for speeding lately?" Get the irony? A real knee-slapper.

"Ever get into a high-speed chase in one of those little golf carts?" Hilarious.

So whenever he got a chance to work off-site, on an interesting case, he took advantage of it. Big time. That's why he was sitting in an interview room at the county jail, waiting to talk to a scumbag. Kid named Brian Foster, busted late last night, possession with the intent to distribute. Not his first time, either. Finally, after fifteen minutes, a guard brought him in. The punk sat, glaring, with his arms crossed.

Acting tough. Skinny little bastard. Probably snorted as much speed as he sold.

Wheeler didn't shake hands or introduce himself. He simply slapped a photo on the table and said, "Recognize this gun?"

The kid didn't want to look at it, but he couldn't help himself. Curiosity.

"Nope," he said. Lying little shit.

"Your stepdad is Sam Shelton, right?"

"Yeah. What about him?"

"We found this gun in your stepdad's luggage when he tried to board a plane for Lubbock this morning. We're holding him until we get this cleared up. He's plenty pissed off."

That seemed to interest Foster. "Sam's in jail?" He was smiling.

Well, technically speaking, it wasn't jail. Just a holding room. "Damn right," Wheeler said, "and he told us you were the last person to use that suitcase. You borrowed it from your mom when you went down to Mexico two weeks ago. What'd you go to Mexico for, Brian?"

Foster laughed. They both knew what he went to Mexico for. Meeting with his wholesaler.

"No comment?" Wheeler asked. Foster glared. So Wheeler said, "Funny thing is, the piece comes back as stolen. Even funnier, the man who owned it is a fairly important guy. I'm gonna do everything I can to bust the shitwad that took it. You got yourself into a world of hurt, kid. Possession of stolen property."

Now Foster wasn't smiling. He had that same panicked expression that the air-traffic guys got during a tornado warning. "You can't prove nothing. I've never seen it before."

"Then why did we find your fingerprints on it?" Wheeler said, pulling a bluff.

Foster had no answer for that. He sat silently. Wheeler let it go for thirty seconds.

"We might be able to work something out," he said, "if you didn't steal it. If you got any brains at all, you'll tell me where you got it. Otherwise, your stepdad walks, you go down for it. With your record, you're looking at prison."

The boy did exactly what Wheeler knew he would. He said, "What about this possession charge? Can you help me with that?"

"I can put a good word in with the prosecutor," Wheeler replied. "Tell 'em you cooperated." Which didn't mean crap. They'd still nail him.

"I can trust you?"

"Sure."

Foster considered it for a long while, then said, "I got it from my girlfriend. Ex-girlfriend. About a month ago."

"Where'd she get it?"

"No idea."

"What's her name?"

"Bonita Salazar."

"Where can I find her?"

The kid gave Wheeler an address and a phone number. Then he said, "Only thing is, I come to find out that Bonita ain't her real name."

"Okay, then, what is it?"

The kid shook his head, grimacing. "Promise not to laugh?"

"Yeah."

"Her name's . . . Arturo."

Wheeler smiled. But he didn't laugh.

41

SABRINA WORKED IN her garden all morning, trying to get her mind off Harry. In the early afternoon, she came inside, had lunch, then took a shower. When she got out, there was a message on her answering machine. It was Harry. He did not sound good.

Hey Brina, it's me . . . I found your note. I can't believe you found me. I just couldn't stay in the house anymore. Maybe you're right. Maybe I need to get out of there. Anyway, I need to talk to you about something . . . I, uh . . . Shit, this is hard for me to say . . . I've . . . I've been having some unhealthy thoughts lately . . . And I've been drinking way too much . . . I'm just having a really tough time keeping it together . . . Thinking about Jake, you know, and the parole hearing, getting angry all over again . . . So I did something drastic . . . Maybe you'll be proud, or maybe you'll think I'm crazy . . . I probably am, but I had to do something . . . I couldn't let things keep going the way they were . . . So . . . I . . . Well, hell, I'll just say it . . . I checked myself into rehab . . . I don't know whether it will help or not, but wish me luck, okay? . . . What this means is, I don't know whether I'll make it to the hearing or not. Please don't hate me for that. It's probably better that I won't be there . . . I'll be in touch to see how it went. I gotta go. I'll talk to you later.

Sabrina played the message two more times, wanting very much to believe it.

Marlin and Bill Tatum were working on the affidavit together when Bobby Garza came into the chief deputy's office, closed the door, and sat down next to Marlin. He seemed pensive. Or incredulous.

Tatum, sitting behind his computer, said, "Something?"

"Yeah. Nicole just called. She's on her way back with Campbell's home phone records, but I asked her to go ahead and tell me what she had." Garza glanced at a note in his hand. "Keep in mind, the estimated time of death for Rodolfo Dominguez was sometime between midnight on Saturday and noon on Sunday. What Nicole tells me is that there were no outgoing calls from Campbell's house after six P.M. on Saturday, and only one all day on Sunday, placed at eleven forty-three in the morning. Care to guess who he called?"

"J. B. Crowley," Tatum said. His voice was hopeful.

But Garza shook his head and dropped a bombshell. "Dale Stubbs."

Tatum had had his hands poised over his keyboard, but now he crossed his arms and leaned back in his chair. "The NWA guy."

"Yep."

"What about incoming calls?" Marlin asked.

"There were a handful, but none that lasted longer than a minute," Garza said. "I'm guessing he didn't pick up. Those calls probably went to his answering machine."

"Maybe Crowley was already at Campbell's place when Dominguez was killed," Marlin said.

"Could be."

"Or maybe Campbell called Crowley on his cell phone."

"We'll have to wait and see," Garza said. "In the meantime, let's go back to Campbell's outgoing calls again, just for grins. There weren't any on Monday, or on Tuesday or Wednesday. Weird, huh? Like maybe he was avoiding all contact. The next call he made from his home phone was on Thursday morning, at eight fifty-two—which, if memory serves, is right after y'all finished interviewing him."

Tatum grabbed a manila folder and consulted his notes. "Yeah, we left his house at eight forty-five."

"And being the diligent interrogators that you are, you left him in a state of great anguish and discontent. Guess who he called to share his pain?"

"Dale Stubbs."

"You're a quick learner, Bill. That's why I love you." He turned to Marlin. "Mrs. Buell said one of the men she saw was about sixty."

"Yeah, with a lot of gray in his hair."

"Let's pull up Stubbs' latest license photo and see—"

"Hell, don't bother," Tatum said. "I've seen him in magazines. That's what he looks like."

Marlin let out a low whistle.

But Tatum was frowning. "Why would Campbell call Dale Stubbs? If he was alone when it happened, why would he call anyone?"

"He was scared," Garza said. "He wanted help. And can you think of anyone who'd be more interested in keeping the situation quiet than the NWA?"

The room fell silent for several moments as they all pondered this new information. Then Garza said, "When you talked to Crowley's wife, what kind of vibe did you get?"

Tatum said, "You mean, was she telling the truth? Sure seemed that way."

If they could verify Crowley's alibi—that he had picked up his son on Saturday afternoon and gone directly to Lake Fork—they could eliminate him as a suspect.

"What do you want to do, Bobby?" Tatum asked.

The sheriff didn't answer for a long time. When he finally did, he said, "Y'all keep working on the affidavit. I'm gonna have a chat with Dale Stubbs."

"We could get in trouble for this," Billy Don whined, shaking his head. "Serious trouble. Like, prison time."

They were in Red's truck, driving away from Mitch's house. They had a gruesome load in the back. Red wished Billy Don was liquored up, because he cared about stuff a lot less when he'd been drinking.

"We done it before without any problems," Red replied.

Several years back, they had buried a body. A drug-addicted veterinarian. They'd disposed of the corpse as a favor for a rich man. Red hadn't felt too bad about it because the moron had overdosed on horse tranquilizers. Anybody that stupid deserved an unmarked grave.

"Yeah, it was dumb then and it's dumb now," Billy Don said. "If it all happened like Mitch said, he should just call the cops."

"What, and ruin the rally?"

"Screw the rally. I ain't goin' to prison for Mitch Campbell."

Red didn't want to hear "Screw the rally." Not now. Not after what Mitch had promised him. Things were finally coming together.

"What if he called and they didn't believe him?" Red persisted. "You know how cops are. Never believe nobody. Might ruin his career."

Sitting poolside, Mitch had told them the whole story. The foreman of his ranch had attacked him, out of the blue, with a hunting knife. Mitch had no idea what had brought it on, except that the foreman was a mean son of a bitch with a history of violence. Killed a man in Houston. Maybe Mitch had said the wrong thing, or the foreman was jealous of Mitch's success. In any case, Mitch had fought back and managed to defend himself with a pool cue. Sounded like a hell of a brawl.

"Besides, this ain't even a felony," Red said, although he had no idea if that was the truth. "We're talkin' county jail, at the very worst." He had to calm Billy Don's nerves.

Billy Don squinted at him and said, "Since when do you know anything about the law?"

"All them real-life murder shows on cable TV. Better'n law school. Even if they found out what we did, we could ask for a flea bargain."

"A flea bargain?"

"Yeah, I know, weird name, but that's what they call it. And from what I can tell, it usually means a slap on the wrist, like maybe probation. Happens all the time. I mean, shit, it ain't like *we* killed the guy. We're just moving him from one place to another. But you're worryin' about nothing anyway, 'cause Mitch said he'd keep us out of it if the cops came snoopin' around."

"And you believe him?"

"Ain't got no reason not to."

Red studied Billy Don from the corner of his eye. Right now, Billy Don was nothing but a three-hundred-pound roadblock between Red and his shot at success. He needed the big man's cooperation, more than he'd ever needed it before. Because Mitch had offered Red something in return for their help. It was nothing short of a dream come true. Red was getting chills just thinking about it.

Mitch had promised to perform Red's song at the rally.

Writing an affidavit for a search warrant was a lot more complicated than most people would imagine—far from a rubber-stamp process. Even a relatively simple one—say, to search a suspected marijuana dealer's home—could run to five or six single-spaced pages. In this case, Marlin and Tatum were up to fifteen pages, and they were crafting every paragraph with painstaking care. It wasn't enough to simply recount a plethora of details and observations; they had to succinctly explain their findings, and meticulously argue the conclusions one could infer from those findings. They couldn't leave it to the magistrate, or the judge at a pretrial suppression hearing, to connect the dots. If they did, the case would be scuttled.

So they labored over every word, avoiding nuance, shoring up every statement with cold, hard fact. They were down to the final page when Bobby Garza stepped into Tatum's office. He let out a sigh and said, "Y'all aren't gonna believe this."

"You talk to Stubbs?" Tatum asked.

"Worse. I talked to Henry."

"Are we going where I think we're going?" Billy Don asked, scowling.

Red had turned off the driveway and was following an overgrown caliche road toward the northwestern corner of Mitch Campbell's ranch. "You'll see," he said.

"Aw, Red, not the Reimers' place. That ain't right."

"You got a better idea?"

Billy Don braced one hand on the dashboard as they bounced over a huge rut in the road. "That's sacred ground."

"If I 'member my history right, old man Reimer was a undertaker. So it won't bother his spirit none."

Billy Don grunted with disapproval.

Red recalled that the Reimers were one of the families that had petitioned to move the county seat from Blanco to Johnson City back in the late 1800s. Their original cabin still stood on Mitch Campbell's land. Red had last seen it during a poaching excursion ten or twelve years ago, and it was in sad shape then—the roof collapsing, the walls buckling, all the windows gone. Even so, some locals had gotten their panties in a wad when Campbell had bought the ranch, worried that he might tear the cabin down. In a newspaper interview, Mitch had promised not to, and had even made some comments about maybe having the place restored some day.

But Red didn't care about the cabin. Not specifically.

He slowly pulled around an oak grove and the structure came into view, cloaked in the shade of a towering pecan tree. The cabin was in worse shape than ever. One entire side had fallen to the ground, leaving nothing but a crumbling chimney. Weeds had wormed their way through the rotted pine floors. Red thought it was sad in a way, if you cared about stuff like that.

He parked as close as he could and killed the engine. It was still and quiet and brutally hot.

"This is kinda creepy," Billy Don said.

"Don't be a wuss."

"Why put him in the cabin?" Billy Don asked. "Why not just bury him in the woods?"

"We ain't doin' neither."

"What, then?"

Red opened his door and climbed out. There wasn't a bird or a squirrel or even a field mouse in sight. It *was* kind of creepy. He closed his door and said, "There's gotta be an old well around here someplace."

"Hazy Hills Treatment Center, may I help you?" The woman's tone was curt and efficient. It didn't match the image of compassion and concern that oozed from their television ads.

"Can you tell me if you have a patient named Harry Jenkins?"

"No, ma'am, I'm afraid not."

"No, you can't tell me, or no, you don't have a patient by that name?"

"The former. If we did have a patient by that name, I couldn't tell you. All of our records are confidential, as per federal and state regulations."

The woman recited the line by rote.

"Could you tell me if you *didn't* have a patient by that name?"

"No, ma'am. Otherwise, you could simply call all the centers in town until you found one that *didn't* tell you the patient *wasn't* there."

Sabrina spotted a flaw in the system. "What do you do when a patient receives a phone call?"

"We discourage phone calls, except during the appointed hours."

"But when people call, what happens?"

"At check-in, the patient provides us with an approved list of visitors and callers. If the caller is not on that list, we don't put them through."

"What exactly do you say?"

"I just told you. I would ask for your name." The woman's patience was wearing thin.

"Yes, I know. But after you've asked my name, then what?"

"I don't know how I can be any more clear. If you were on the approved list, I would put you through. If you weren't on the list, I would not put you through."

"But what would you say exactly, when you came back on the phone, after checking the list?" The question was: How did they get rid of unapproved callers without providing a tip-off? Whatever they said was bound to give some indication as to whether the patient was or was not at the facility.

There was a long silence. Then: "Oh. I see what you're doing. You're looking for a loophole."

Sabrina didn't deny it.

"I think that's sneaky," the woman said.

"I'm sorry. I don't mean to be. I just really need to reach my ex-husband. He left me a message, but he didn't tell me which treatment center he was checking into."

The woman softened a bit. "In those cases, when a caller isn't on the approved list, we route them to a recorded message. Would you like to hear it?"

"Please."

"One moment."

There was a click, then Sabrina heard:

Thank you for calling Hazy Hills Treatment Center, the home of brighter tomorrows. Unfortunately, we cannot put your call through. Confidentiality laws prevent us from revealing whether the person you are calling has or has not been admitted to our facility. Have a nice day.

Sabrina hung up, and realized that she hadn't given her name. Jesus, this was getting complicated! She called back and got the same woman.

"Me again," Sabrina said.

"So nice to hear from you."

"Sarcasm doesn't suit you."

"Ma'am, if you'd like—"

"Okay, I'm sorry. Let's start over. I'd like to speak to Harry Jenkins. Please."

"One moment."

"Hey, wait, aren't you going to ask my name?"

"Oh. Yes. Your name?"

"Sabrina Nash."

"One mo—uh, Sabrina Nash?"

"Yes."

"From *Holy Roller?*"

"I'm afraid so."

"Well, this is a surprise. I recognize your voice now. I'm sorry if I was brusque earlier."

"I don't blame you. I can imagine the calls you get."

"You have no idea. Anyway . . . I'm a big fan. Your show was hilarious. I still watch the reruns."

"Thank you very much."

"You're calling for Harry Jenkins."

"I am."

"Um . . . well, do you want to hear the recorded message again?"

"Not really."

The woman whispered: "Between you and me, wouldn't he put you on his approved list?"

She was saying, *Harry isn't here.*

"Yes, he would. I appreciate your help."

"My pleasure. Good luck."

After she hung up, Sabrina closed the yellow pages. If Harry hadn't checked into the largest, most well-known clinic in town, then he could be anywhere, and she didn't have the energy to call them all and go through the same rigmarole. For that matter, Harry might've gone to a different city—Houston, Dallas, or San Antonio—looking for a place where they'd be less likely to recognize his name.

Or he might not be in a treatment center at all.

42

MUCH TO SERGEANT Murray Wheeler's surprise, Arturo Salazar—aka Bonita—didn't look like a man at all. For starters, he, or she, weighed about one-oh-five. Her features were soft, her skin smooth, her demeanor feminine. She was the kind of girl that, if Wheeler passed her on the street, without knowing what he knew, he'd think, *Yowzah, there goes a nice piece of tail.* Truth was, it was troubling him that he was having a tough time keeping his eyes off the tops of her breasts. She was wearing a low-cut blouse, and the merchandise appeared as authentic as any he'd ever seen. Bigger than his wife's, in fact. Supple, yet firm. Round and perky and—

Jesus, get ahold of yourself, Wheeler. Her shlong is probably bigger than yours is.

They were in the living room of Salazar's small duplex. She hadn't offered coffee, or even a glass of water. She was plainly on edge—probably wondering what fresh hell was about to enter her life.

"Miss Salazar," Wheeler said, "as I mentioned on the phone, I need to talk to you about Brian Foster."

She frowned. She looked scared. "What about heem?"

"He said he got a gun from you," Wheeler said. "A Ruger twenty-two. It was stolen property. And I need to know where you got it."

"Am I in trouble?" She was beginning to cry. She was staring at the floor, hugging herself as if she were cold, and Wheeler couldn't help noticing that her cleavage was—

Goddammit, focus! There was a box of Kleenex on the table. He handed one to her.

"That depends on, uh, on where you, uh, got the gun," Wheeler said. He couldn't concentrate.

She wiped her nose and looked at him. "Joo jus' wan' to know where I got it?"

"Yes."

"This isn't about Maurice?"

"Maurice who?"

"Brian's frien'."

"What about him?"

"I don' know."

"Is there something I should know about Maurice?"

"Like what?"

"Did you get the gun from him?"

"No."

"Then why did you bring him up?"

"I don' know."

Odd. "Where *did* you get the gun, Miss Salazar?"

"I din't steal it. I din't know it was stolen."

"That's good. Then you probably won't get in trouble."

That lifted her spirits. She smiled. Wow. Her eyes were amazing. Wheeler had been to Cancún a few years ago, and her eyes were as blue as the waters that lapped at the—

Son of a bitch! Quit thinking about her! Him!

"But I need a name," he said.

"Deek," she said.

"Deek?"

"Jess, Deek. Short for Reechard."

Oh. *Dick.* What were the odds of that?

43

DOBBINS' CHIEF OF security—guy named Coyt—was about Ramon's age, which, in Paul Hebert's opinion, was awfully damn young to be heading up such an important detail. Coyt wore a gray suit with a white button-down shirt and a red-and-blue-striped tie. His black shoes gleamed. He smelled like one of those cologne ads in men's magazines, the kind you unfold for a free sample.

"What you've told me," Coyt said, "does not concern me a great deal." The three of them were in an office near the capitol. Lots of big oak furniture and dark paneled walls. "We take very good care of Congressman Dobbins."

"I'm sure you do," Hebert said. "But at an event like that . . . there's gonna be a lot of people carrying."

Coyt smiled. "Including me, and five of my colleagues."

"Hard to stop someone who's got his mind set."

"But you said the person who killed Henley and Nichols didn't use a firearm." Coyt's hair was trimmed meticulously. The barber had probably used calipers.

"Not so far," Hebert said. "Doesn't mean he won't change his MO. My opinion, Dobbins should skip the rally."

Coyt shook his head. "Out of the question. Simply not possible."

"Then he should wear a vest."

"Not practical. It's July. One hundred degrees out."

Hebert hadn't mentioned Harry Jenkins' name yet, because the theory that Jenkins was a killer was still purely speculation, but now he felt obligated. He removed a photo from his jacket. "This is the man you want to keep an eye out for. Harry Jenkins."

Coyt scowled at the picture. "The political cartoonist?"

"Yep."

Coyt smiled again, smug as hell. "What's he gonna do? Jab the congressman in the neck with a fountain pen?"

Hebert smiled. "He might do exactly that."

Citizens were allowed to write letters in support of inmates who were up for release. Loved ones wrote them. Friends. Even former bosses. Every letter went into a file, and each was given due consideration by the appropriate members of the Board of Pardons and Paroles.

On Friday afternoon, two days after his meeting with Sabrina Nash, Marcus Roark opened one such letter.

Dear Sirs:

My name is Cynthia Stein. I got married when I was nineteen years old. Too young, my mother said, and she was right. Neither my husband nor I were ideal spouses, but we tried to make it work. We failed, and our divorce became final three weeks ago. That's why I'm writing to you now. When the police contacted me seven years ago, I was hesitant to speak to them. At the time, I certainly didn't need any extra stress placed on my marriage. The detectives told me that Duane Rankin was suspected in a shooting, and that he was claiming to have been with me at the time. He said that we worked together, and that we had slept together a couple of times. I said that the work part was true, but the rest wasn't, and I wasn't with him. There's only one problem. I lied.

"Holy shit," Roark said softly.

* * *

When Marlin got home at a little past six, he changed into shorts and a T-shirt. He walked barefoot into the kitchen, popped the cap off a bottle of Miller High Life, and went out the back door, where Geist was waiting on the porch. Marlin sat on the top step, in the shade, and Geist leaned against him, sluggish from a day in the sun. He took a big gulp of beer. It was still ninety-three degrees, but Marlin's house sat at an elevation of fourteen hundred feet and, as usual, there was a nice breeze; the humidity wasn't getting a chance to do its damage.

Marlin owned seven acres, but he'd fenced half an acre behind the house for Geist. This small patch was the only part of the property that he hadn't left natural. No bluestem or sideoats grama. No caliche. Instead, he'd hauled in some rich loam and planted Bermuda grass, which, thanks to the drought, was now a sickly yellow. Marlin wasn't big on lawn sprinklers. In hindsight, maybe the Bermuda hadn't been such a good idea.

Geist wandered lackadaisically into the yard and came back with a tennis ball. Marlin tossed it to the fence. Rather than trotting after it, Geist gave him a look that said, *What'd you go and do that for?*

The beer was good and cold. Marlin drained it and went inside for another. He came back out and sat in the same spot.

What now?

The blood in Mitch Campbell's trash hadn't matched the blood of Rodolfo Dominguez. One was O positive, the other A positive. The shards of glass hadn't matched the microscopic fragments in Dominguez's wounds. No way they could get a warrant now. The fact that Campbell had bought a pane of glass wasn't nearly enough. The fact that he seemed to know the time of death was helpful to the investigation, but a judge wouldn't see it as grounds for a search. Without the blood and the glass, they had virtually nothing.

In fact, they had worse than nothing. Now they had another riddle to unravel: Whose blood was in the garbage? Someone had obviously been injured, but was the wound fatal? For Christ's sake, just what in the hell was happening at Mitch Campbell's place?

What's more, how did Dale Stubbs figure into it? Garza hadn't been able to reach him. The secretary Garza had spoken to—who impatiently pointed out that she wasn't Stubbs' regular assistant—said she thought Stubbs had already left for Austin. No, she didn't know if he'd be checking in for messages. No, she didn't know where he was staying. Yes, of course he'd be at the rally tomorrow.

Marlin heard a vehicle pulling up his driveway. Geist must have recognized the pitch of the engine, because she ran to the back door, whining and wagging her tail with excitement. *Nicole.* Marlin went through the house and opened the front door just as she was preparing to knock. She gave him an uncertain smile.

"Lose your key?" he asked.

Geist was on the porch, rubbing against Nicole's calves, begging for affection. Nicole leaned to pet her.

"No. I just thought I'd better . . ."

She wasn't sure she was welcome anymore. He opened the door wider and gestured her inside. It felt awkward. He hated awkward. "Beer?"

"Sure."

He went into the kitchen and got two more bottles out of the fridge. He returned to the living room and handed one to Nicole. They sat on the couch, at either end. Geist sat on the floor by Nicole's feet and rested her massive head on Nicole's thigh. Heaven.

"Ernie called Garza a few minutes ago," she said. "Campbell's cell phone records were worthless. He hasn't used it since Saturday."

He nodded. No real surprise there.

"You think Stubbs was involved?" she asked.

"Somehow, yeah. I figure he helped Campbell stage the scene on Ken Bell's ranch. The trick'll be proving it."

Nicole had stopped petting, so Geist nudged her hand with her muzzle. Spoiled rotten. The house was too quiet.

"Thanks for the flowers," he said. "They're in the kitchen on the windowsill."

She didn't look up. She was gazing at Geist, but even from this angle, Marlin could see a wet shine in her eyes. "Are you mad at me?" she asked.

"Of course not. Last night, I thought it was the other way around."

She shook her head. "I wasn't mad, exactly. I . . . I don't know what I was. Messed up, I guess."

"Understandable. Think you still have some, uh, unresolved issues?"

"Probably."

"Maybe it's worth talking to somebody about it?"

"I think so." She sniffed, but she wasn't crying. "I know I don't want to lose you. I couldn't stand it."

Geist whimpered softly. She'd always had an ability to sense discord. It made her uneasy.

"You won't. I can promise you that. But we do have to work this thing out."

Nicole nodded. "I want to. If we can."

"Of course we can. But we both need to be able to have our own opinions."

"I know that. I think that my, uh, situation blinds me a little."

"Nothing wrong with that."

"Except there are times when I need to keep my mouth shut."

"Not many, but some. That's true for everybody. If an atheist and a priest were having lunch, they'd probably be wise to avoid the topic of religion."

She smiled weakly, but still didn't look up. She was rubbing Geist's ears, but Geist was staring sideways at Marlin. *You two need to make up,* she seemed to be saying.

"Can you explain it to me?" Nicole asked. "What we were talking about last night. Why you feel the way you do."

"I'm not sure that's a good idea."

"It would be good for me to hear. I'd like to know."

Marlin hesitated, but he decided he should do it. A test of sorts. For both of them. He said, "Okay, here goes. I think it's a bunch of bullshit when people blame guns for crime, instead of blaming criminals." That seemed to sum it up. Short and sweet. He saw no reason to say more.

"Even considering what happened to your dad?" she asked.

"Yep."

"See, I have a tough time understanding that."

"Well, the truth is, you don't have to. It's just my opinion. You're free to have your own. In fact, I *know* you have your own opinion, and it's different than mine, but it doesn't bother me. That should work both ways."

"I know it should. Sometimes I have trouble keeping my anger in check."

He wanted to move toward her, but he thought it would be best if he stayed put. "You went though something terrible. But what it comes down to is this: Can we disagree without it screwing up our relationship? I say we can. What do you think?" He was thinking about the diamond ring, currently locked in his gun safe.

She took a deep breath. "It's bound to come up now and then."

"Maybe. But so what? You gonna harass me when I go hunting? Maybe picket outside my deer blind?"

She was shaking her head, grinning mildly, like, *Don't be ridiculous.* "You gonna get mad if I change the channel when an NWA commercial comes on?"

"Not at all," Marlin said. "But last I knew, the darn remote was acting up. I think the batteries are dead."

She laughed. A big, authentic guffaw, and Marlin knew they were getting somewhere. Geist opened her mouth and let her tongue loll, panting happily. She seemed to sense the easing of tension in the room.

Marlin moved closer to Nicole and grasped her hand in his. She leaned into him, wrapping both arms tightly around his torso. They stayed that way for several minutes, just holding each other close, while Geist tried to join in.

Mitch poured the last few drops out of a bottle. Opened another. Filled his glass. Took a gulp. Felt the burn in his throat, the fire in his belly. His eyes watered. Jesus, that was good. He wished he could always feel like this. The liquor made everything go away. Nothing was important right now. Nothing was scary. No worries. No guilt. Everything was just fine.

He'd go to the rally, even though Dale Stubbs had tried to have him killed. He had no other choice. Pretend everything was fine. Business as usual. The show must go on.

His guitar was on the couch beside him. He picked it up. Had to practice Red's song. He strummed the strings, but his fingers felt thick. Clumsy. *Come and take it.* Not bad.

When the phone rang, it was nearly midnight.

"Were you sleeping?" Bill Tatum asked.

"Yeah, but I had to get up anyway. The phone was ringing."

"Funny. I drove past Crowley's place earlier. Still no sign of him."

"You called to tell me that?" Marlin could feel Nicole's bare hip pressing against his own. Geist, curled on the floor, had raised her head at Marlin's voice.

"No, I called to tell you I saw several vehicles with NWA stickers in the parking lot of the Best Western. Turns out that's where all the muckety-mucks are staying. The clerk said they reserved the entire place before the location of the rally was announced."

"Let me guess. Dale Stubbs is there."

"I'm looking at his truck right now."

"You gonna wake him?"

There was a long pause. Tatum finally said, "I don't think so. I have something better in mind."

"Heaven forbid. A plan?"

"The beginnings of one."

"Is it any good?"

Tatum laughed. "You'd better hope so. Because you're the one that has to carry it out."

44

"YOU AND BONITA Salazar are, I take it, intimate?"

"Huh?"

"You're lovers."

"What? No, of course not. We're just friends."

It was Saturday morning, and Murray Wheeler was pleased with himself for stretching his investigation into a second day—even if it was Independence Day. He had to work anyway, inside the airport or out.

Now he was sitting with Dick Angerman in a coffee shop in south Austin, a few blocks from the body shop Angerman owned. He was an oily-looking guy with bad teeth. He smelled like nachos. Murray didn't like him. Bonita deserved better.

"She said you're her boyfriend."

"Hell, no," Angerman said, making a disgusted expression. "Her vocabulary ain't so good, bein' a Mexican and all. I'm a *boy* and I'm her *friend*. See? Boyfriend."

"Right." Murray sipped his coffee. He hated a liar. "Where'd you get the gun you gave her?"

"Gun?" Angerman was frowning. Overdoing it.

"Yes, Dick. The gun. A twenty-two."

"I don't know nothin' about it."

How could Bonita have fallen for this toad? A real piece of work. "The gun was stolen. One way or another, I'm gonna find out who stole it."

Angerman shrugged. "Like I said, I don't know nothin' about it."

Murray went in a different direction. "I hear you tied the knot recently."

Angerman smiled, but only because he was supposed to. "Sure did."

"Congratulations. What's her name?"

"Uh, Irene."

"Does Irene know about Bonita?"

"Oh, Christ. I'm telling you, there ain't nothin' to know."

The waitress stopped by, and Murray ordered a piece of pie. Pecan. With whipped cream. They sold pie at the airport, but it was like eating a piece of cardboard.

"I need to track this gun, Dick. Bonita says she got it from you. Now, she may be lying, or maybe she's confused, but I'll have to check into it, you understand? That means I'll have to talk to Irene, and all your friends, and all your employees at the shop. I can't promise to keep Bonita out of it." It was extortion, pure and simple. The threat of exposure. You use what you've got.

Angerman held it together for ten more seconds, then he cracked. "Okay, goddammit, I'll tell you. But I didn't know nothin' 'bout it being stolen."

"Of course not."

45

DALE STUBBS LAY in his motel room, alone, the bedspread pulled up to his chin. He pushed the panic from his mind long enough to ponder the possibilities.

First off, and most likely, Mitch had probably killed J. B. Crowley. That would explain why J. B. hadn't called. It would also explain why Mitch had said the things he'd said yesterday morning. *You summunabitch. I know whatcha did.* Stubbs was having a tough time picturing it, Mitch getting the upper hand on J. B., but it could happen. Stubbs had told J. B. not to use a gun; the last thing Dale had wanted was the spokesman for the NWA to be killed by a firearm. If Mitch was strangled or bludgeoned or knifed, the NWA could officially blame it on the anti-gun kooks. It was a supreme irony, but the anti-gunners were known to get violent now and again—like with Henley and Nichols. Mitch had figured it out. *Don' fuckin' deny it, Dale. Rat bastard.* But he couldn't exactly tell the cops, could he? Not without fessing up to the dead Mexican.

Then Stubbs had another unsettling thought. *What if Mitch doesn't show for the rally?* No, that was ridiculous. Mitch, like Stubbs, had to play along as if nothing strange was happening.

Stubbs shivered. The motel room felt like a meat locker. The air conditioner seemed to have two settings: Hades or Arctic Blast. But the cold air seemed to ease his pounding head. He'd been up late, going from room to room, shaking hands, patting backs, drinking scotch, trying to act as if his world wasn't coming unglued. Maybe it wasn't. Maybe there was still hope.

There was only one other possibility Stubbs could imagine: J. B. had turned traitor. He'd told Mitch everything. Maybe Mitch had even paid him off. The kid had a ton of money—more than enough to satisfy a two-bit redneck like Crowley. What would J. B. have done then? Taken the money and run, naturally.

Stubbs heard a car door slamming outside, followed by the roar of an engine. He glanced at the clock. Nine thirty. He was supposed to be at Campbell's ranch at eleven. The rally started at noon. It was going to be a strange day, no doubt.

Stubbs climbed from the bed, shut the AC off, and noticed an envelope on the carpet in front of the door. He stepped over it and peered through the peephole. Nothing but trucks and SUVs. Nobody lingering near the door.

Stubbs' name was neatly written on the envelope in block letters, along with the word CONFIDENTIAL. He had a sense that nothing good was going to come of it. He picked the envelope up, opened it, and removed the single sheet of paper inside. The typewritten note read:

```
Listen up, because there isn't much time left.
I am the game warden in Blanco County. I am
also a member of the NWA, and my loyalty runs
deep. I hope you understand what I mean by that
last remark. I know what happened with M. C.
and the wetback. I know that you helped him re-
solve the situation. Some of the deputies are
starting to figure it out. We need to take ac-
tion now to contain this thing. Call me at 556-
3950 before the damage is irreversible. I can
help.
```

Stubbs' knees went weak, and he sagged to the floor. *Oh, Lord.* He lay on his back. It felt like a heavy man was sitting on his chest.

It was a replay of the morning before, except this time they were in Marlin's office. Waiting. They'd been there since six. It was now nine forty-five. They spoke occasionally. They'd already discussed college baseball and Garza's son's fourth birthday party and the price of beef.

Dale Stubbs hadn't called.

At the moment, they were sitting quietly, drinking coffee. Marlin was thumbing through an old issue of *Texas Parks & Wildlife* magazine. He found an interesting article about melanistic deer.

"If we're wrong about this," Garza said, smiling, "can't you just picture the guy's face when he reads the note?"

"Utter confusion," Marlin said.

"Think we're wrong?" Tatum asked.

Garza said, "Nope. I think we're right on."

"Then why hasn't he called?"

Nobody answered that one.

According to the article, there were more melanistic deer in an eight-county area in central Texas than in the rest of the world combined. Marlin hadn't known that. He closed the magazine and said, "I'd say we're right, but Stubbs doesn't want us to know it. He senses a trap. He's playing it safe, keeping his mouth shut."

"Or maybe he's not alone," Garza said. "He hasn't been able to make the call yet."

Tatum said, "The clerk said Stubbs' wife wasn't with him."

"Doesn't have to be his wife."

They waited some more. It was five after ten.

"This was a risky move," Tatum said. "If it doesn't work, it's all on me."

Garza smiled again. Marlin had always admired the sheriff's ability to remain cool. "Second thoughts?"

Tatum shrugged. "Maybe, yeah."

"What's your backup plan?"

"Give me a few minutes, I'll come up with one."

A tape recorder was resting on Marlin's desk, next to his phone. A black line ran between the two devices. One end of the black line was plugged into the microphone receptacle of the tape recorder. The other end of the line featured a small suction cup, which was affixed to the back of the phone's handset. It was the most primitive method of recording phone calls Marlin had ever seen, and yet the performance was nearly flawless. The total cost: about seven dollars at any electronics store. Legal, too, even without a warrant. In Texas, a call could be taped as long as one party was aware of the recording. Now all they needed was for the phone to ring.

At ten fourteen, it did.

Paul Hebert felt like a bumpkin as he drove over to Ramon Arriaga's house.

The night before, he'd walked into an Academy store, found a sales guy, and said, "I need some hunting clothes."

"What sort of hunting?"

"I don't know. What do people hunt this time of year?"

"Not much. It's July."

"When's the next season start?"

"September first. Whitewing and mourning dove."

"Okay, dress me like a dove hunter."

The guy gave him a strange look. "You don't really, ah, hunt, do you?"

"Nope."

"Then why—"

"Costume party."

The salesman smiled. "Gotcha."

So now Hebert was wearing the complete ensemble. An olive-colored shirt with huge pockets (for dead birds, he guessed) and ventilated panels over the shoulders. Camouflage baseball cap with the Remington logo above the bill. Wrangler jeans. Hiking boots with high cuffs for ankle support. A modern-day Elmer Fudd, complete with amber-tinted shooting glasses.

Even so, when Ramon came out his front door and climbed into the car, Hebert had to smile. His partner had out-rednecked him. The kid was wearing a white Resistol hat and a pearl-snap shirt with dancing green cows printed all over it.

"Holy fuck," Hebert said. "Where'd you get that thing? It's hideous."

"Christmas gift from my wife."

"Oh. I, uh . . ."

"Don't worry about it. Ugliest shirt I own."

Hebert was backing the Crown Vic out of the driveway. "What the hell, we'll blend right in."

He followed Lamar down to 290 and went west. Mitch Campbell's ranch was an hour away.

Marlin pushed the Record button and answered his phone. "This is John."

There was a long silence, then, "I got your note."

Marlin felt a tingle in his belly. He gave Garza and Tatum a thumbs-up, then cupped the phone and lowered his voice. "I'm glad you called. I'm worried about, ah, recent events."

"I need your name." The voice was wary.

"John."

"Your full name."

"John Marlin."

"I'll call you back."

Before Marlin could reply, Stubbs hung up. Marlin dropped the phone back into its cradle and recounted the brief conversation.

"He's checking you out," Garza said. "Wants to make sure you're who you say you are."

"Probably double-checking that you're an NWA member," Tatum added.

"But this is good," Garza said. "He's biting."

"Play it cool," Tatum said. "Remember, *you're* doing *him* a favor."

"At this point, you're his only option."

"But he'll still be suspicious."

"If he gets skittish, don't push too hard."

"Yeah, because you're putting your own career on the line, right? Play it like you'd just as soon back out."

"He'll want to know what you know."

"But don't share anything unless he offers something first."

"Just draw him out slowly."

"You nervous?"

Marlin laughed. "I wasn't, but y'all are making me that way."

"That's okay," Garza said. "Showing some nerves is good. It's what he'd expect."

Seven minutes later, the phone rang again.

Way up on Mitch Campbell's back patio, Casey Walberg could see a long line of vehicles on Cypress Mill Road. Cars, trucks, SUVs, motorcycles.

The party was already starting. Casey would've loved to be down there, just out of morbid curiosity, but this was part of the deal. Casey had to stay up here and wait. Casey figured it was Mitch being overly cautious. Probably thought Casey would change his mind and spill the beans in the middle of the rally. But no, this arrangement was just fine. Casey could sell the wedding photos for a small fortune. And, in the future, there'd be other opportunities. Say, for instance, when Mitch and Sheryl had their first child. Casey would call up and say, "Hey, Mitch, congratulations. Sure would like some exclusive photos." If Casey played it right, Mitch Campbell could be a cash cow.

Jesus, even from this distance, Casey could hear the distorted sounds of "My Cold, Dead Hands" blaring from someone's stereo.

Red turned his stereo down as a man in a neon-orange safety vest waved him through Mitch's gate. He followed the line of vehicles in front of him into a large field, where more men in vests were directing traffic, making sure everyone parked in an orderly fashion.

"You nervous?" Billy Don asked.

Red tried to chuckle, but his stomach was in a knot. He was about to jump out of his skin. He'd had four beers for breakfast to calm himself down. "Am I nervous? Hell no, I'm not nervous. Why would I be nervous?"

He was wearing his best jeans, which had very few holes, along with his cleanest pair of work boots. One had a big stain near the toe—oil from a chain saw—but other than that, they looked pretty spiffy.

"If Mitch was performing *my* song," Billy Don said, "I'd be shittin' my britches."

"Maybe you should be the songwriter, Billy Don. You got such a lovely way with words."

One of the orange-vested guys pointed to a spot beside a Hummer, and Red pulled in next to it. Then a Chevy parked next to Red, followed by an SUV next to the Chevy, and so on. The field was large, but it was already half full. Red and Billy Don stepped from the truck and joined the flow of people crossing the driveway to the field on the other side. After a few hundred yards, the rally-goers funneled toward a temporary gate, where three security guards in blue NWA shirts were stationed. One was sitting at a table with a computer. A sign on a pole read:

NWA MEMBERS ONLY. HAVE ID READY.
NOT A MEMBER? JOIN TODAY AND GET A FREE SHIRT!
SUPPORT THE SECOND AMENDMENT!
No recording devices of any kind.
In accordance with state law,
handguns must remain concealed at all times.

People were flashing their NWA cards and sailing right through. When Red and Billy Don got to the gate, one of the guards—a fat man with a bushy mustache—said, "NWA ID, please."

"Don't have one," Red mumbled. "We're, uh, on Mitch's guest list."

The fat guard raised an eyebrow and looked at them doubtfully.

"He ain't kidding," Billy Don said, putting a hand on Red's shoulder. "This here's one of Mitch's best songwriters."

"Don't embarrass me, Billy Don," Red said, but he kind of liked the attention. People in line were looking at him with respect.

The fat guard said, "Names."

"I'm Billy Don Craddock and he's Red O'Brien."

The young guy at the computer started tapping on the keyboard. "Craddock and . . . ?"

"O'Brien," Billy Don said. "Red O'Brien. Soon to be a Nashville hotshot. Won't be long before *he'll* be the one banging Brenda Graves."

Red heard some giggling. He was blushing, but it felt good.

The computer guy was frowning, staring at his screen. For a moment, Red's heart sank. What if Mitch had forgotten to put them on the list? Then the man said, "Okay, yeah, here they are."

Now the fat guard was all smiles. "Come right in, gentlemen. Glad you could join us today."

Marlin lifted the phone and said, "This is John."

"Why should I trust you?" Stubbs asked.

"Because we're all fucked if you don't. And because you don't have any alternatives."

"I have plenty of alternatives. Always do."

"Then use one of them," Marlin replied. "I'd just as soon stay out of it."

Stubbs didn't say anything for a long while, and Marlin wondered if he'd blown it. Finally, Stubbs said, "Maybe we should talk."

"That would be good."

"But not on the phone. You going to the rally?"

"Yeah."

"You know what I look like?"

"Yeah."

"Find me there. I'll be around."

"Will do. Or you look for me. I'll be in uniform."

Silence. Then, "You, uh, think we can fix this thing?"

There was no remorse in the question. Stubbs sounded, instead, like a man concerned about a faulty transmission.

"I think so," Marlin said. "Depends on what 'this thing' is. Depends on whether I've read the situation right. I'll need to know some details."

"You got a plan?"

"A loose one. A work in progress."

Stubbs made one last remark: "You seem like a good man—but if this is a goddamn setup, I'll personally shoot you between the eyes. That's a promise."

Marlin already hated the son of a bitch. He said, "If I were in your shoes, I'd do the same thing."

46

SABRINA NASH HAD already vacuumed, done three loads of laundry, and scrubbed the grout in her bathroom shower. Now she was watching one of those home-improvement shows; this one was teaching her the finer points of hanging Sheetrock. She had never hung Sheetrock, and never intended to, but she was doing what she could to keep her mind off the gun rally in Blanco County.

What if Harry was lying about the treatment facility? What if the detectives were right, and Harry was intending to harm Congressman Dobbins?

Maybe I should let him do just that. Ah, Harry.

The phone rang, and she expected it to be him. But when she answered, a voice—somewhat familiar, but not Harry—said, "Mrs. Nash?"

"Yes?"

"This is Matt Mergenthaler."

"Oh my God! Matt! How are you?"

"I'm fine, thanks."

"You sound all grown up, Matt. This is such a nice surprise!"

"Yeah."

"How are your parents?"

"They're well. They moved to Georgetown about five years ago."

"Yes, Harry told me. How are they liking it there?"

"They play golf almost every day, so my dad's in heaven. Is Mr. Jenkins, uh, still in the same house?"

"He is. A nice family moved into your old place, except they have a son who plays the drums. Drives Harry crazy. What's going on with you nowadays? Are you living here in town?"

"No, I moved to Richardson two years ago. Got a new job."

"Excellent. What line of work?"

"I'm teaching political science at the community college. Just part-time, because I like to have some free time for my own projects."

"Well, good for you. You were always an excellent teacher."

There was a momentary pause, and Sabrina knew the small talk had come to an end. "The reason I'm calling," Matt said, "is that Duane Rankin's lawyer contacted me a week ago. He told me Duane has a parole hearing this coming Monday."

"Yes."

"He wanted me to testify on Duane's behalf."

"Oh." Sabrina was at a loss for words.

"I told him to go to hell. I just wanted you to know that."

"Thank you, Matt. That means a lot to me."

Now there was a second pause, and it stretched into an awkward silence.

"There are some other things I want to say," Matt said. "I've always felt like, well, if only I hadn't introduced Duane to your family, maybe—"

"Don't think that way, Matt. You couldn't possibly know what would happen."

"Still, I . . . I blame myself sometimes. For Jake. For the things that happened afterward."

The divorce.

"It wasn't your fault, Matt. None of it."

"I still think about him all the time. I've always wanted to find a way to make up for my mistakes."

He's carrying as much guilt as Harry.

Christ, Harry. She knew she couldn't just sit and wait to hear from him. Or from the cops. She had to find him.

A man in an orange vest directed Marlin to a small reserved parking lot, closer to the rally site, where he pulled in next to a Mercedes SUV.

He took a deep breath. "Okay, guys. Here goes nothing."

He locked his truck and walked across the gravel driveway to a gate, where three security guards nodded and waved him through. Inside the fenced pasture, the atmosphere was that of a carnival. The crowd was thick—people standing in groups, talking, laughing, milling to and fro. There were long lines in front of every concession stand. Marlin could smell cotton candy and hot dogs and peanuts. He saw people eating corn dogs and fajitas and funnel cakes, drinking beer and iced tea and lemonade. The sun was intense, but it didn't seem to dampen the spirit of the NWA faithful.

Marlin strolled slowly through the crowd. Mostly white people, young to middle-aged, dressed fairly well. Lots of sports shirts in khaki and camo, blue jeans and boots, though most of the women and a few of the men wore shorts and running shoes. Plenty of colorful western-style clothing and straw cowboy hats and sporty sunglasses. Marlin noticed an abundance of modified fanny packs—he'd heard them called pistol packs—the easiest way to conceal a weapon when you weren't wearing a coat. The truth was, the guns weren't really hidden; at an event like this, everybody knew exactly what was in those packs, but they met the legal requirements for concealment. Marlin saw a cute teenage girl wearing a T-shirt that said YOU CAN'T OUTRUN MY COLT. A clean-shaven Hispanic man wore a Resistol and a god-awful shirt with dancing green cows on it.

Marlin saw Nicole and Ernie Turpin, in uniform, standing in the shade of the portable men's room. It was the best place to loiter. Sooner or later, every male at the rally would make a trip to the john. Marlin caught Ernie's eye, and the deputy responded with a discreet head shake. *No luck so far.* Nicole spotted him, too, and gave him a wink. Any other woman could do that and it'd be corny. With her, it worked.

He wandered toward the far end of the pasture, where a flatbed trailer had been converted to a stage, complete with a skirt of red-white-and-blue bunting. Steel poles around the perimeter of the trailer supported a lightweight metal roof, from which hung the U.S. flag, the Texas flag, and an NWA banner. On each side of the stage was a tower of speakers stacked four high, and country music floated gently on the breeze. Lee Greenwood singing "God Bless the USA." An Independence Day standard. Ol' Lee probably got more royalties from July Fourth than all the other days of the year combined. Shrewd move, recording that song.

Down here, the crowd was sparse. There were several rows of bleachers that formed a triangle with the stage, with a large open area in the center. Some people had already staked out choice spots with lawn chairs and blankets. Later, when the rally officially got under way, this area would be jammed. For now, the bulk of the crowd lingered near the concession stands and portable restrooms. Marlin watched as three young stagehands ran wires and adjusted speakers and tested wireless microphones. These guys were hired hands, definitely not NWA material. They had shaggy hair and scruffy faces. One was wearing a tie-dyed shirt. Another had on flip-flops. They went about their business with unhurried efficiency.

It was eleven fifteen. Marlin had a portable radio clipped to his belt, with the mike attached to his shirt, above the pocket. He pretended to depress the mike button and said, "Seventy-five-oh-eight to one-fifty-three. You read me?"

A few seconds later, he heard Garza say, "One-fifty-three to seventy-five-oh-eight. Ten-four on that, loud and clear."

Excellent. The wire under Marlin's shirt was working. Garza and Tatum were sitting in the sheriff's cruiser on Cypress Mill Road, past the entrance to Campbell's ranch. They'd be able to record the conversation.

He turned and headed away from the stage, back toward the masses. Time to track down Dale Stubbs.

The twenty-three-year-old named Bernie liked his job a lot, chiefly because it was easy and he could do it stoned. They called him a sound technician, but how hard was it to string speaker cable? Plug this one in here, plug that one in there. He'd done it hundreds of times, and it wasn't exactly rocket science. Made good money, too, for a dropout. Met a lot of interesting people.

It was twenty after eleven when he met another one. A guy standing below the stage said, "How's it going?"

Bernie looked down and saw a tall dude wearing a cowboy hat. He was an older guy, like maybe thirty or forty, wearing an NWA T-shirt with fresh creases in the sleeves.

"It's going," Bernie replied. "We're almost done." He figured the man was worried about the rally starting on time.

"Excellent," Cowboy Hat said. "We like to run a tight ship."

Bernie kept working, and the man kept standing there. After a few minutes, the man said, "Hey, listen. You know who Dale Stubbs is?"

"Yeah, sure. He's, like, your grand poobah or something."

The man smiled. "That's a good way to put it. Dad would get a kick out of that. Oh, hey, I'm being rude." He stuck his hand up toward Bernie and said, "I'm Danny Stubbs."

Bernie had to lean over to shake hands. "My name's Bernie."

"Nice to meet you, Bernie," Danny Stubbs said. "We really appreciate all your hard work."

"Not a problem."

"Hey, Bernie, guess what. It's my dad's birthday today."

"Oh really? That's cool." *Why are you telling me this?* Bernie wondered.

"Yeah, it is. He's gonna be running the show today, and I've got a little surprise in store for him. Something to show him how much I love him. He's a hell of a guy, you know? The thing is, I need your help. I need a favor."

Bernie hesitated. He didn't have time to fool around with some stupid birthday shit. He had work to do.

"Uh, well . . ." Bernie said.

Danny Stubbs took a hundred-dollar bill out of his pocket and folded it in two, lengthwise. "Won't take but a minute or two," he said.

Paul Hebert hooked up with Ramon over near the first-aid station, which wasn't a bad thing, since Hebert was about to keel over. Jesus

Christ, the heat. Brutal. His shirt clung to his back, and his damp jeans were chafing his thighs. His boots seemed to weigh about ten pounds each, and his hair, under his baseball cap, was wetter than a drowned rat. On the other hand, he figured it was about seventy degrees in Missoula right now. The bastards.

Ramon was eating a hot dog with salsa and jalapeños on top. The kid looked fresh and dry.

"Goddamn, don't you beaners ever sweat?" Hebert asked.

Ramon shrugged. "When it gets hot."

Hebert drank deeply from a liter of cold water. There was a man pushing a cart around, handing out free bottles. Who says the gun nuts don't have hearts?

"You seen anybody that looks remotely like Harry Jenkins?" Hebert asked.

"Nope."

"Keep in mind that he might've changed his look some. Maybe cut his hair to fit in. Or dressed like a rube."

Ramon nodded and popped the last of the hot dog into his mouth. Hebert was getting queasy just thinking about food. He didn't know how much more of this he could stand. If he spotted Jenkins, it would likely turn out to be a mirage.

Joe Scroggins banged on Mitch Campbell's door at ten till twelve. The little dickhead was AWOL.

"Mitch! Goddamn it, are you in there?"

He banged some more. Nothing. He tried the door and found it unlocked. He stepped inside. "Mitch! Hey, Mitch!"

He went straight to the bedroom, where he found his star performer snoring loudly. There was a pool of vomit on the pillow, an empty bottle of bourbon on the nightstand. This boy was worse than George Jones in his heyday. It was hardly worth the aggravation. There'd have to be some changes. For now, tough love.

Scroggins went into the bathroom for a glass of cold water, returned to the bedroom, and dumped it on Mitch's head.

Mitch sat bolt upright, sputtering, saying, "Fuck! Shit! What is it?" His eyes were dull and sunken. His face was bloated and red. Not even thirty years old and Mitch Campbell looked like a washed-up alkie.

"Up and at 'em, kid. You got a show to put on."

He gazed at Scroggins for a long moment, as if he couldn't quite place the face. "Joe? What the hell's going on?"

"The rally. Remember? Get your ass out of bed."

Mitch cupped his head with both hands. "Oh, man. Yeah. I'm okay. What time is it?"

"Time to get ready. Come on, now. Let's get you into the shower."

"I don't need any help."

"You do, son. Lots of it. Believe me."

At five till twelve, a gentle murmur rippled through the crowd, and then the murmur turned into an excited buzz, and people began to cheer and applaud. Marlin, taller than most of those around him, could see the upper torso of a tall, tan, attractive man in a well-pressed khaki shirt. He was shaking hands, waving, smiling with a blinding set of white teeth. The gold watch on his wrist glinted in the sun. He was escorted by half a dozen serious men with short haircuts, golf shirts, and identical Ray-Ban sunglasses. Security. The honorable congressman from West Texas had arrived. Marlin clapped, too, just in case Dale Stubbs was somewhere watching him.

At precisely twelve o'clock, the song on the sound system—the newest George Strait single—cut off in midchorus. There was a brief pause. Then Marlin heard the familiar opening notes of "God Bless America." In unison, like a school of fish moving as one, the crowd turned and proceeded toward the other end of the pasture. They'd done this before. Some were singing. Everyone was smiling. Marlin went with the flow, thinking there was something vaguely cultish about it. Courtesy was observed; nobody rushed or jostled or shoved. By the end of the song, five thousand bodies had assembled in an orderly fashion near the stage. The bleachers were packed, but the bulk of the audience was standing, giddy with excitement.

After another pause, Marlin heard an extended drum roll, followed by a big, brassy arrangement of "The Star-Spangled Banner." Hats came off. Hands were placed over hearts. Some older men saluted. Small U.S. flags were waved. Marlin could understand how easy it would be to get swept away in the fervor. There was a sense of genuine purpose in the air. Marlin got a chill, as he always did, during the last line of the anthem.

Then, with no introduction, Dale Stubbs ascended a set of stairs behind the stage and strutted toward the microphone stand. The audience erupted.

47

MURRAY WHEELER FOUND Freddie Martin living alone in a well-kept one-bedroom apartment near the UT campus. The kid was a sophomore, working his way through, pursuing a degree in psychology. He was medium height, thin, with sandy hair and a fair complexion. There was something sad about him. And maybe a little effeminate.

"Dick Angerman gave me your number," Wheeler said.

"Jesus, there's a name I was hoping I'd never hear again."

"I understand he dated your mother."

"For a while, yeah. Long time ago. She suffers from a serious lack of self-esteem, you know?"

"You and Dick didn't get along."

"Is he in trouble or something?"

"Maybe. Probably not."

"Damn."

"So you didn't get along?"

"You met him. Can you imagine putting up with that asshole when you're twelve years old?"

Wheeler didn't say anything.

"No, I hated his guts. The son of a bitch was abusive."

"You took a shot at him."

Freddie Martin's jaw dropped open. "Is that what this is about? That was ages ago."

The door to the bedroom opened, and a pretty brunette girl wearing a long nightshirt scurried into the bathroom without looking their way. *Way to go, Freddie.*

"I'm only interested in the gun," Wheeler said. "Specifically, where you got it." Wheeler realized his case was coming to a rather unspectacular conclusion. If the kid stole the gun, he was twelve years old when he did it. There wouldn't be any charges at this point. Wheeler might get a pat on the back from the gun owner. Maybe a story in the newspaper, which would be nice. But then, he'd be right back at the airport.

Freddie Martin said, "I found it."

Wheeler snorted.

"No, really. Swear to God. I'll take a lie-detector test or whatever. I found it."

Wheeler believed him, and now the case was really coming apart. Wheeler wouldn't even be able to nail the thief.

"Where'd you find it?" he asked. Might as well follow it through to the bitter end.

"I was a Boy Scout," Freddie Martin said. "We were picking up trash along Loop 360."

"One of those adopt-a-highway deals?"

"Exactly."

"When was this?"

"About seven years ago."

Something was starting to register in the back of Wheeler's brain. "Where on Loop 360?"

"Man, I don't remember. I was a little kid."

"North or south of the river?"

"North, I think. Oh, wait, this might help. I remember one of the other kids found part of a taillight. There'd been a wreck along that stretch a few days earlier. Some old sitcom actress. I think her boy died or something."

48

THE CHEERING AND clapping and whistling went on for a good thirty seconds. Within this group, Dale Stubbs had attained the celebrity status of a rock superstar. Marlin watched it all with puzzled amusement.

Stubbs smiled and waved and nodded, eating it up. He was obviously in his element, poised and practiced. He was well dressed, wearing the obligatory khaki shirt and blue jeans, both items starched and pressed to perfection. His snakeskin boots matched his snakeskin belt, which held his pistol pack in place. If he was nervous about his upcoming rendezvous with Marlin, he showed no sign of it.

Finally, Stubbs held his hands up, palms outward, and the crowd quickly quieted. He removed the mike from the stand and said, "I wanna welcome y'all to Blanco County, where great Americans still recognize the value of freedom!"

That's all the audience needed to hear to start hooting and hollering all over again. With great enthusiasm. For a long time. Marlin figured

Stubbs' speech was going to be similar to a State of the Union address, with prolonged bursts of applause throughout.

This time, as the audience began to settle down, an attractive blond woman in a clingy T-shirt and short shorts appeared at the foot of the stage, carrying a bouquet of roses. Stubbs noticed her and made a *For me?* gesture. She nodded. He knelt down to accept the offering, and the mike picked up the woman saying, "These are for you, Dale! They're from all of us!"

"Thank you, darling. That is just so sweet."

The blonde perched on tiptoes to give Dale a kiss on the cheek. Then she sashayed back to her spot in the crowd, with several men wolf-whistling in appreciation. More applause and chuckles and playful slaps on upper arms from watchful wives.

Stubbs held the roses up and said, "I'm touched. I really am. Thank you very much. But honestly, I should be giving flowers to all of *you*. My friends, you are the lifeblood of our great nation—the cornerstone on which our democracy is built!"

The audience seemed to agree. They cheered for themselves and thrust fists proudly in the air.

"Yes," Stubbs said. "Yes, indeed. Well deserved. All of you." As he spoke, he strolled to the rear of the stage and passed the roses off to a young female assistant, then came back to center stage. "Boy howdy, folks, we've got a real treat in store today. Later this afternoon, we'll hear from a close personal friend of mine . . . a remarkable man and a tireless foe against those who threaten our personal liberties . . . the next governor of our great state . . . Glenn Andrew Dobbins!"

A manic cheer rose up: *Daw-bins! Daw-bins! Daw-bins!* It went on for half a minute.

"But first . . ." Stubbs let loose with a hundred-watt smile. "Well, it's no secret—y'all know who our host is today, and we'll get to him real soon. I know you came to see him, not me, so I'll keep my opening remarks short."

He then proceeded *not* to keep it short. He spoke in broad terms about the threats posed to our society by liberal politics. He lambasted despotic leaders in the Middle East, he expounded on the role of America as a beacon of hope, and he submitted that the only good terrorist is a dead terrorist. He pontificated on the merits of harsher prison sentences and stricter parole guidelines and an increase in the use of capital punishment. He was pompous and smug, self-righteous and absolutely certain of himself. Marlin could understand why Nicole held the man in such disdain. Marlin began to work his way to the front of the crowd. He wanted to be nearby when Stubbs was finished with his diatribe.

Joe Scroggins said, "The florist and the caterer are coming at five. Sheryl arrives at five thirty."

Mitch grunted.

Scroggins shoved another cup of coffee in front of him, although the first two hadn't done much good. The kid was a basket case, but at least he was dressed. Thank God this wasn't a serious gig. Mitch could sleepwalk through a couple of songs, then call it a day. Or maybe he shouldn't bother at all.

"We could pull the plug, kid. Say you're sick. Nobody would complain much. Fans'd be disappointed, but they'd understand."

Mitch had his elbows propped on the breakfast table, both hands around a mug. He needed both hands to keep it from spilling.

"Can't do it," Mitch said. "Got a new one to perform."

"Do what? You got a new song?"

"Yeah. I wanna break it out today."

Scroggins smiled. New material? Mitch hadn't written anything since before the tour. This was excellent news. "It any good?" he asked.

Mitch nodded, and for just a moment, Scroggins saw vibrancy and enthusiasm in his eyes. "Best one yet."

"That's great to hear, son. How come you haven't told me about it till now?"

"I, uh, I just wrote it in the past few days."

Joe's cell phone rang. A member of the NWA crew, wondering where they were. Scroggins said they'd be down in ten minutes.

Mitch took a big drink of his coffee. "This'd be a lot better with some bourbon in it."

"Not a good idea, kid."

"Okay, then, *I'd* be a lot better with some bourbon in *me*. Come on, Joe. Just a little? Something to clear my head."

"Goddammit, Mitch."

"Please?"

Near the back of the crowd, Paul Hebert's cell phone vibrated. He checked the caller ID and then ignored it. Didn't recognize the number. Not anybody from the office.

A minute later, it vibrated again. Same caller. Whoever it was, he'd have to leave a message.

Then it vibrated again. Man, this guy was a pest.

Stubbs' words carried on the southerly breeze, and Casey Walberg had to laugh.

There's only one way to deal with scum like Osama bin Laden and Saddam Hussein! Hunt 'em down and exterminate 'em like the cockroaches they are!

If the leftist show-biz crowd could hear this speech, the outrage and indignation would be palpable. They'd be frothing at the mouth.

Alec Baldwin, in the name of anti-violence, would want to stone Stubbs to death.

Susan Sarandon would rant about body bags and imperialism disguised as patriotism, but conservatives would be too busy picturing her naked to listen.

Martin Sheen would mistake *playing* a politician for *being* one, and presume to know how the gun issue should be settled.

Janeane Garofalo would ramble about the mainstream media's failure to reveal the truth in America while nobody paid her much attention at all.

Casey was enjoying himself. Better than prime-time television. This guy Stubbs was as ignorant as a box of hammers. Hell of a show.

"Makes sense to me," Billy Don said, sitting in the bleachers.

Red nodded, even though he wasn't really paying attention to the speech. He was too busy scanning the backstage area, anxious for a sign of Mitch. If he got any more excited, he was going to need an adult diaper.

* * *

"What a moron," Nicole Brooks whispered to her cousin, Ernie Turpin. Her skin was crawling. Dale Stubbs was a creep. She would have loved nothing more than to pull her revolver and park a round squarely between his eyes. Of course, she recognized the hypocrisy in that fantasy. Plus, it would be awfully hard to place an accurate shot from sixty yards.

Ernie smiled. "Maybe not the best place to voice that opinion."

Nicole grinned back. "Freedom of speech, baby. These guys believe in the First Amendment, don't they?"

"Sure they do. In fact, they'd say it's the Second Amendment that keeps all your other rights safe."

"You sound like John, you know it?"

Ernie raised an eyebrow at her. "And that's a bad thing?"

The crowd cheered at some remark Stubbs had just made.

Nicole felt a pang of remorse in her stomach. "No, it's not," she said. "Not at all."

Joe Scroggins chaperoned Mitch Campbell through the employee gate to the backstage area, where they quietly greeted several execs from the label, then shook hands with Congressman Dobbins. Mitch appeared amiable and in control. Joe felt guilty about it, but three fingers of bourbon had made a world of difference. It was a whole new Mitch, with a light in his eye and a spring in his step. Sunglasses, a big white hat, ready to wow the crowd.

Steering with one hand, Tricia Woodbine felt around in her Kate Spade handbag until she found what she was looking for. Oops. That wasn't it. That was her diaphragm case. Okay, there it was. Her snub-nose .38. Tricia could understand why Dale was so infatuated with these things. Such power! Such an advantage! Yesterday, she wouldn't have been able to get away without it. Now it gave her just enough confidence to go back.

At precisely twelve o'clock, she knocked on the door to SNATCH headquarters. She had her gun in her hand, held tightly at her side.

She'd have preferred to call, but she'd been too flustered yesterday to ask for a number. Besides, wannabe spies don't give out phone numbers. So she'd come in person, knowing it was risky. Dieter had a temper, she'd seen that much. So much so, that she'd been too nervous to go home. Just to be safe, she'd taken a suite at a luxury hotel. Put it on her credit card, of course.

She waited. Weird. Normally, the grumpy redhead answered the door very quickly. She knocked again. She could hear traffic on Preston Road, but back here, to the rear of the complex, nothing was moving. No sound from behind the door. Maybe it was a trick. Well, she simply wouldn't go inside the apartment. If Dieter wanted to negotiate, he'd have to do it out here, on the concrete walkway. She wasn't going to be as idiotic as one of those girls in those slasher movies, the ones who wandered into damp basements or darkened sorority houses while the killer lurked under the stairs. Tricia hated those girls. Like, get a clue.

She knocked a third time, more firmly. Maybe they were huddled in his office, deciding how much to offer. *Better add another zero, boys.* If they didn't cooperate, she didn't know what she'd do. She'd abandoned the auction idea. Dale had a lot of money, but Jesus, if Dieter had gotten so hostile, just imagine how the NWA would react.

Okay, this was getting silly. Where were they? Surely they hadn't gone to lunch. Not right now. They knew she was coming at noon. Against her better judgment, she reached out, grasped the doorknob, and turned it slowly. The door wasn't locked. She eased it open a couple of inches and listened. She heard nothing. She swung the door wide and couldn't believe what she saw. Rather, what she didn't see. The living room was empty. No computers. No televisions tuned to CNN or MSNBC or Fox.

"Dieter?"

He didn't respond. But why would he, if it was a trap?

Well, fudge! She didn't have any choice but to check it out. She held her gun in front of her and stepped inside.

Dale Stubbs was on autopilot, reciting his usual gun-rally spiel, but all he was thinking was: *This is the strangest thing I've ever done. I'm about to introduce a man who knows I want him dead.*

* * *

"Well, I guess you've listened to me ramble on long enough," Dale Stubbs said.

Marlin was up close now, ready to make his move as soon as Stubbs left the stage.

"So let's have some fun. Let me ask y'all something. Can anybody think of a better way to celebrate Independence Day than a live rendition of 'My Cold, Dead Hands'?"

The audience cheered enthusiastically. Clearly, they were ready for the star of the show.

"Okay, then! Ladies and gentlemen, I'd like to introduce a wonderful American and an amazing talent, a national treasure, a one-of-a-kind advocate for gun rights, our own Mitch Campbell!"

The singer came up the steps to the stage, waving genially, his guitar slung behind his back, and the frenzy reached near-hysteria. Elvis had probably received less animated receptions. In the heart of Memphis. When he was thin. A middle-aged woman near Marlin was one adoring shriek away from a nervous breakdown.

Mitch walked toward Dale Stubbs, trying his best to appear comfortable and relaxed. Stubbs stuck out his hand, and Mitch shook it without hesitation.

Stubbs leaned in, covering his microphone, and said, "I'm not sure what you were talking about on the phone yesterday morning, but I think you got the wrong idea." The smile on his face said, *You can trust me. We're still buddies, right?*

Mitch smiled right back and said, "You're a liar. Now get the hell off the stage."

When the phone vibrated a fourth time, Hebert answered it.

A man said, "Is this Hebert?"

"Yeah?" Dale Stubbs was introducing Mitch Campbell.

"My name's Murray Wheeler. I'm on the job at the airport. Your CO told me to call you."

The connection was poor. Lots of noise.

"Yeah?"

"Look, I got a weird situation here. I got a stolen gun that I traced back to the kid who found it seven years ago."

"Stolen gun? Well, why don't you call—"

"Hold on a sec. You'll want to hear this. The kid picked it up along Loop 360, two days after a shooting not far from there. The Sabrina Nash accident. I was on traffic detail back then. I worked that scene. You remember it?"

That doesn't make sense, Hebert was thinking. *They already got Duane Rankin's gun.* "Yeah, I'm familiar with it," he said. "Gotta be a coincidence."

"No way. Not when you hear who owned the gun."

Wheeler said something else, but it was drowned out by applause as Mitch Campbell strutted to center stage.

Dale Stubbs was receding discreetly toward the back of the stage, to the stairs, leaving the singer alone in the figurative spotlight.

The crowd was beginning to surge forward—still well behaved, but excited as all get-out—and Marlin decided now was the time to move. He began working his way sideways. He'd catch up with Stubbs in the backstage area.

Campbell had a microphone in his hand, and now he said, "My Lord, I've died and gone to heaven. Thank you! Thank you so much! Y'all are too kind. Today is the birthday of our great nation, and there's no place I'd rather—"

The speakers emitted an ear-splitting squeal of feedback, causing people to cover their ears and scrunch their faces with displeasure. Campbell looked around, then grinned and shrugged, as if to say, *Technical problems. What can you do?*

Mitch Campbell said, "My Lord, I've died and gone to heaven."

"You there?" Hebert asked.

"What?"

"You there?" The connection was getting worse.

"Yeah, Jesus, where are *you*? The circus?"

"Long story. Who's the owner?"

"What?"

"Who's the goddamn owner?"

Wheeler spoke, but a whine of feedback obliterated the words.

Bernie had warned Danny Stubbs there'd be feedback, but all Danny had said was, "That's okay. That'll be your cue to turn Mitch's microphone off."

"Turn it off? I won't get in trouble?"

"No, I promise. This is going to be hilarious."

Finally, the feedback faded, and Campbell spoke into his microphone. There was no sound. He shook his head and tapped on the end of the mike, to no effect.

Then Marlin heard a voice, and Stubbs and Campbell heard a voice, and the vast NWA audience heard a voice, and what that voice said was:

Attention!

Attention, please!

Attention all you ignorant gun-loving hillbillies . . .

49

TWENTY MILES AWAY, at New Horizons Rehabilitation Center in the small town of Fredericksburg, Texas, Harry Jenkins was patiently working his way through the lunch line. The cafeteria itself was surprisingly well appointed and comfortable, with crisp white tablecloths, fresh-cut flowers, and decent flatware. Less like a school cafeteria and more like an upscale Luby's.

"Fish or chicken?" the perky woman behind the counter asked. She had a benign smile plastered on her face. *Isn't life just dandy?* the smile seemed to ask.

The young guy behind Harry said, "Stick with the chicken. The fish'll give you the squirts."

The woman, holding a pair of tongs, said, "Oh, that's not true. Don't tell stories." She was still smiling widely, though not as warmly.

"Swear to God it's carp," the young guy said. "Bottom feeder."

Harry looked at the tong lady, who rolled her eyes and said, "It's whitefish. Flown in from Alaska."

"I'll, uh, try the chicken," Harry said.

"Oh, pooh," Tong Lady said.

Casey was confused. What was going on down there? Mitch Campbell had been speaking, then feedback, and now someone else was addressing the crowd.

. . . ignorant gun-loving hillbillies . . .

What the hell? Instinct took over. Casey grabbed his best camera and sprinted downhill, through the trees, toward the pasture.

Marlin stopped where he was. The audience had gone strangely silent. People were frowning. Heads were turning, searching, puzzled.

Thank you so much for coming! What a wonderful day! It turns out, I have a treat in store for you, too. Today I will introduce you to the most powerful weapon known to man . . . the weapon of truth!

"Can you hear me?" Wheeler asked.

"Yeah." Something weird was happening onstage. Campbell's mike was dead. Now somebody else was speaking. Taking over. *Jenkins is making his move!* Hebert looked around for Ramon but didn't see him. "Tell me! What's the name?"

"You still there?"

"Yes, the name! Who owned the gun?"

Today I will introduce you to the most powerful weapon known to man . . .

Wheeler spoke again. This time, Hebert heard him just fine.

. . . the weapon of truth!

Down near the stage, to the left, Red said, "What the hell is this?"

"Got no idea," Billy Don replied. "But if it's supposed to be a joke, it ain't funny."

"No, sir. Ain't funny at all."

* * *

Marlin saw Dale Stubbs bound back up the stairs. He was plainly fu-
rious, looking left and right, trying to locate the source of the voice.
But it seemed to be coming from the skies or the trees or from the air
itself. The crowd was starting to grumble with displeasure. Stubbs
jerked the microphone from Mitch Campbell's hands and tried to
speak into it. It was still dead. He slammed it to the stage.

The apartment was absolutely empty. Not a stick of furniture or a
stray issue of *The Nation*. It was as if SNATCH had never been there.
But why would they flee? Why would they suddenly pull up stakes
and—
   Oh, bitch!
   Tricia realized she'd made a colossal mistake. She'd made sure of
her own safety all night long—but it wasn't *her* they wanted.
   She hustled back to her car and raced home. She jerked her car
into a parking spot and sprinted to her apartment. Her hand was unsteady as she turned the key in the lock. When she opened her door,
she knew her dream had just died. She saw a jumble of dumped drawers and overturned furniture. She hurried to her bedroom and dug to
the bottom of her lingerie drawer, only to confirm what she already
knew. The Interloper 3000 was gone.

Dale Stubbs knew who was behind it. The goddamn anti-gun kooks,
pulling one of their stunts! Those sons of bitches! He grabbed the mi-
crophone from Mitch, spoke into it, but the damn thing was useless.
He threw it down.
   Then the voice came again:
   *Your spokesman, Mitch Campbell, is quite the performer! In fact, I'd like
to play his latest recording. This is a little number I call, 'How I Murdered an
Immigrant and Almost Got Away With It.'*
   A cold bolt of fear pierced Stubbs' chest. *Oh sweet mother of God.*
   He recognized his own voice over the speakers: *This is Dale
Stubbs.*

* * *

This is Dale Stubbs.

The cops were just here. About the dead Mexican!

Marlin couldn't believe what he was hearing. It was clearly a phone call between Stubbs and Mitch Campbell.

Goddamn, now, take it easy.

I'm freaking out, Dale! They know he was supposed to be working here.

There was a low murmuring in the crowd, with an undertone of shock and surprise, but most people were listening with rapt attention. Dale Stubbs let out a moan of anguish, ran to one side of the stage, and began to jerk at the speaker cables. They held fast. He flailed and kicked at the speakers, but they were large and blocky and durable. Marlin had never seen anything quite like it.

Marlin's radio squawked. "One-fifty-three to seventy-five-oh-eight."

Garza and Tatum, wondering what was going on. They could hear it all over the wire. "Better get over here," Marlin said. "We've got a meltdown."

Stubbs finally tipped the tower of speakers over, jumped on top of one, and began to stomp the front grille. But it played on.

Did they point the finger at you at all?

No.

Did you manage to keep your wits about you?

Yeah, I think so.

Mitch Campbell, who hadn't moved an inch since the spectacle began, swayed unsteadily and collapsed onto his butt, with his head down and his shoulders sagging, a picture of total defeat. The audience was starting to simmer now, like water building to a boil.

I assume you acted ignorant about everything.

Right.

Attaboy. I'm proud of you.

Now the crowd had heard enough. They began to shout and boo and hiss, and Marlin could hardly hear the amplified words.

But there really ain't no point in punishing you for it now, is there?

People began to throw things at the stage. At Dale Stubbs and Mitch Campbell. It was a mutiny. Beer cans and paper plates and assorted half-eaten items of food were flying through the air. Most of them fell short, and Marlin and everyone else near the stage was getting pelted.

You just lie low, son. Everything'll be fine.

The recording seemed to have ended, and Stubbs gave up on the speakers. Now he was facing the audience defiantly, his face bright red, his chest heaving.

"Goddamn hypocrites!" he yelled. "I did what needed to be done!"

A flying corn dog knocked Mitch Campbell's hat off. He didn't budge. The audience had surged forward, pressing against the foot of the stage, and several men began to pound on it in anger. Marlin noticed that Stubbs' hand was resting on his pistol pack. Not good. Marlin needed to get up on the stage. He began to press forward, but the mass of humanity was like a brick wall.

He had gambled that there wouldn't be anyone in the men's bathroom during the speech, and he had been right. Now he exited, the wireless microphone in one hand, the Interloper 3000 in his pocket. He had shed his NWA T-shirt, revealing the shirt underneath. He discarded his cowboy hat and let his ponytail fall loose.

Marlin made it to the left side of the crowd, below the remaining tower of speakers. There wasn't a security guard in sight. If the audience decided to swarm Stubbs and Campbell, there'd be very little he could do.

"Don't you judge me!" Stubbs yelled. "I'm a goddamn patriot!" A beer can bounced off his knee. "Stay away from me!"

Then Marlin heard the voice again.

Quiet, please!

The audience heard it, too.

Please settle down!

The shouts and boos began to subside.

Please, let me speak.

A hush began to fall over the pasture. Now something was happening in the middle of the crowd. The audience was shifting.

Thank you very much! I hope you've enjoyed my little show.

The stage was shoulder height. Marlin attempted to hoist himself up, but he couldn't get a grip. He recognized a face. A local poacher. A huge man named Billy Don Craddock.

"Help me up!" Marlin said.

"What?"

"Lock your fingers together and let me—"

"Screw that," Craddock said. He put both hands around Marlin's waist and lifted him onto the stage like a rag doll.

Marlin scrambled to his feet, and now he could see everything. A ring had formed in the center of the crowd, and a lone man in a white T-shirt stood in the center of it. He was holding a wireless microphone.

The man said, "And now, for today's final event . . . a test of marksmanship!"

He spread his arms wide, like Jesus on the cross, revealing a red target on his chest. He bent one elbow to speak into the mike. "Go ahead, Dale! Take your best shot!"

Marlin instantly understood the man's intentions. "Stubbs!" he yelled. "Don't move!"

Still at center stage, Stubbs had a crazed grin on his face. He wouldn't look Marlin's way. Between Marlin and Stubbs, Mitch Campbell was still sitting, unmoving, seemingly catatonic.

"Don't do it, Stubbs!" Marlin unsnapped his holster, but he knew there was nothing he could do.

The amplified voice said, "Show us how it's done, Dale! Impress us all with your expertise!" Taunting. Cajoling.

Marlin got down on one knee, his hand poised over his revolver. "Stubbs, listen to me! Lie flat on the stage!"

"I promise not to move, Dale! Think you can hit me? I don't think you can."

It all happened in a matter of seconds.

In a quick and practiced motion, Dale Stubbs unzipped his pistol pack, slid his hand inside, and emerged with a nine-millimeter automatic.

The audience instantly began to flee from the man in the ring. There were high-pitched screams of panic. If Stubbs fired, there was no telling who might be hit. At the same time, closer to the stage, guns—hundreds of them—appeared from everywhere. They came from fanny packs and purses and ankle holsters. Forty-fives and thirty-eights and twenty-twos. Barrels of carbon steel and alloy and chrome, grips of walnut and rosewood and mother-of-pearl. They were all aimed at Dale Stubbs, who now had his Glock extended in front of him.

Marlin sprang from his knee and rushed forward. Stubbs fired, and the nine-millimeter kicked in his hands. Marlin dove, slamming into Mitch Campbell, driving him flat onto the stage.

And then it was as if the heavens had opened up with the most violent bolt of thunder ever unleashed—crackling and rumbling, booming and rolling, roaring and crashing. The volume equaled a locomotive and a jet engine and a hundred fireworks displays combined.

Marlin, with his head down and covered, didn't witness it. But Dale Stubbs abruptly ceased to be.

50

SABRINA KNEW SHE was too late. Something had already happened at the rally. On Cypress Mill Road, a steady line of vehicles was zipping past, the drivers obviously anxious to put some mileage behind them. Sabrina rounded a curve, and a truck was coming right at her, in the wrong lane. She jerked to the grassy shoulder, narrowly avoiding a collision, and skidded to a stop. More drivers followed the truck's lead, and now both lanes were being taken by westbound traffic.

She jumped from her car and broke into a trot.

"You ready to speak now?" Bobby Garza asked.

It was one hour later. There were no more honking horns or racing engines or tires throwing plumes of dust. All was relatively quiet. Marlin, Garza, Tatum, and the singer were sitting on metal folding chairs in the fenced backstage area.

Mitch Campbell shook his head. He was unharmed, although his emotional state was questionable. "Shell-shocked" would be a good descriptor. Marlin felt a little of that himself. Hands still trembling, mouth dry. Too many bullets flying too close. Nicole had hugged him, then scolded him for what he'd done. Risking his life for Campbell. He couldn't blame her.

"We really need you to answer some questions," Garza said. "Clear this thing up for us. If that recording was misleading, now's the time to tell us. Give us the facts. Set us straight."

A lot had transpired in the previous sixty minutes.

For starters, virtually the entire NWA crowd, including Congressman Glenn Dobbins and his entourage, had vanished. They had scurried en masse to their vehicles and hurriedly departed, rats from a sinking ship. Garza and Tatum had made some efforts to halt the exodus, but it was futile. Besides, it would be nearly impossible to identify all of the shooters who had blown Dale Stubbs to bits. Further, they had all been within their rights to do so. When Stubbs had lifted his weapon and fired, endangering the lives of so many, he had effectively declared open season on himself. Stubbs' body—what was left of it—was still on the stage, behind yellow crime-scene tape.

Garza had made some phone calls, and a slew of other law-enforcement officials were on the way. A Texas Ranger from Llano. A mobile crime-scene unit from the Department of Public Safety. Even a supervisor from the ATF field office in Houston. The sheriff had decided it would be best to let these other agencies assist in processing the scene and in documenting what had taken place; that way, there would be no second-guessing from political organizations on either end of the spectrum.

The still-unidentified man with the target on his shirt was being loaded into a helicopter for transport to Austin. Stubbs' slug had caught him through the upper right chest, and he had lost a lot of blood. The EMTs had said his prognosis was poor. Once he had been airlifted, the entire pasture would be sealed off and preserved, such as it was, for the crime scene investigators.

"Mr. Campbell," Garza said softly, "we have plenty of reasons to believe you killed Rodolfo Dominguez. We think Dale Stubbs helped you cover it up. If that's not what happened, you need to tell us your story."

Campbell stared into oblivion, his eyes glazed. He shook his head and finally spoke. "I think I need a lawyer." He looked at Garza, and the expression of fear and confusion on his face was almost pitiable. "Think the NWA will help me?"

Yeah, good luck with that, Marlin thought.

"Something tells me you'll have to get your own attorney," Garza said. He looked at Tatum, who rose wordlessly and helped Campbell out of his chair.

"To the station?" Tatum asked.

Garza nodded, and Tatum led Campbell away.

Nicole came through the gate and said, "Bobby, those Austin cops are still waiting . . ."

Earlier, a couple of men had identified themselves as homicide detectives. They said they wanted to have a word with Garza when he was done with Campbell.

Casey Walberg scrolled through the photos on his digital camera for a third time. Unreal. Absolutely unreal. Somehow, he'd captured it all. The wacko standing with his arms spread, the target on his chest. Stubbs up onstage, drawing his weapon. The wacko getting shot. Then the massive hail of gunfire that had turned Stubbs into hamburger meat. At the time, swiveling back and forth between the two subjects, Casey had simply taken photos as fast as the camera had let him, hoping for the best. The best was what he got. The best series of photos he had ever snapped. Crisp. Dramatic. Gut wrenching. These weren't cheesy shots of wardrobe malfunctions, this was real news. True photojournalism. *Time* magazine kind of stuff. The opportunity for a fresh start, if he wanted it. He wasn't even sure how to go about it.

As Sabrina dashed through the front gate of Mitch Campbell's ranch, she heard the distant *whump-whump-whump* of helicopter blades. She flagged down a truck with two middle-aged men in it.

"What's going on?" she screamed.

The truck was still rolling, with Sabrina walking beside it.

"A shooting," the driver said. He wasn't going to stop.

"Who?"

"Dale Stubbs and some other guy."

"What other guy? Who was it?"

"That's all I know, lady." He hit the gas and left her in a cloud of dust.

The older one was named Hebert, the younger one Arriaga. They introduced themselves, and then Hebert told a remarkable story that began with a crime seven years ago. Marlin remembered it, because it had been all over the news. Sabrina Nash, a sex symbol from the early eighties, had been involved. Her vehicle had been fired upon, and her son had died in the resulting crash. Hebert described a stalker named Duane Rankin, who was still in jail for the shooting, but was up for parole. He gave them details about two bizarre murders, which had also made the news recently. One of the victims had sold a gun illegally to Rankin; the other had been the prosecutor in the case. Revenge killings, Hebert called them. Harry Jenkins, Sabrina Nash's ex-husband, had become their primary suspect.

"Until forty minutes ago," Hebert said.

"What happened then?" Garza asked.

"The guy in the chopper? We got a good look at him before they lifted off. It wasn't Jenkins."

"You sure?"

"Absolutely."

Marlin heard a commotion on the other side of the stage: Nicole speaking to a woman who sounded upset.

Hebert stood up. "That's her. That's Sabrina."

What a real news photographer would do, Casey decided, was turn the photos over to the police. The shots were, after all, evidence. Casey would still own the rights to them. He could still sell them to a newspaper or magazine. With luck, he could use them to launch a career as a legitimate photographer. No more booby shots. No more lurking in alleys or accosting drunken starlets.

Okay, then. Most of the cops seemed to be gathered near the stage, and behind it. Casey approached one of them.

* * *

Sabrina Nash was still a stunningly beautiful woman, despite the red face and swollen eyes. She'd been crying, but now she wasn't. She was seated next to the older detective, Hebert.

"You're absolutely certain?" she said.

"Yeah," Hebert said. "I know what Jenkins looks like. It wasn't him. This guy was much younger."

"But Harry looks—"

"It wasn't him. Trust me."

She leaned back and let out a long breath, but she didn't seem convinced. "What about those other men? Henley and Nichols? Did Harry . . . ?"

"I can't say for sure right now," Hebert said, "but my gut tells me no. It was this other guy. The way he did it . . . it fits with the others."

Ernie Turpin was walking through the gate, carrying a camera, just as Garza said, "We didn't find a wallet on him. Hopefully we can ID him off prints."

"We'd like a copy of those prints," Hebert said. "We've got a partial from the scene at Roland Nichols' place."

Garza nodded, and Turpin leaned down and spoke to him quietly. The deputy was showing him something with the camera. Garza took the camera and said, "Miss Nash, I think I can set your mind at ease. I've got a photo of the guy."

She sat forward. "That would be good. I would very much like to see it." She turned to Hebert. "No offense, but I . . . I just want to be sure."

"I don't blame you."

"I'm only going to show you one of these," Garza said. "Because the rest are . . . well, this should do it." He stood and stepped over to the actress and squatted beside her chair. The two detectives loomed behind her. Garza held the camera for her to see the small viewing screen.

She began to smile—her eyes saying, *No, it isn't Harry!*—but her smile turned into an expression of shock. Her hand covered her mouth. "Oh my Lord! Oh no."

Hebert was leaning closer. "What? That's not Harry, right? I've seen pictures of him."

"Oh my Lord," she said again. "I don't believe this."

"What? What is it? Do you know him?"

She nodded. "You're right. It's not Harry. It's Matt. Jesus, it's Matt Mergenthaler."

That evening, Tricia was drinking her fifth vodka and Sprite, flipping through two hundred channels of pure crap, when the story hit the airwaves. She sat forward in disbelief. A shootout at the rally. Dale Stubbs was dead. They showed his photo. Then came another face she recognized. Dieter. She finally knew his real name. Matthew Mergenthaler. He wasn't wearing a beret this time. He was dead, too.

51

TWO DAYS LATER, Hebert had all his ducks in a row. He and Ramon were ready to move forward. But carefully. They hadn't shared what they'd learned with Sabrina Nash or their lieutenant or anybody at all. Not just yet. Not until they'd confirmed their suspicions. After all, things weren't always what they seemed. Hebert still felt pretty stupid about the mixup with Harry Jenkins. Way off base on that one.

Right now, he was sitting in a plush reception area outside an important man's office. Ramon was on Hebert's left, Murray Wheeler was on his right. Yep, Hebert had asked Wheeler to come along. Good cop. He was the one who'd put the facts together. He deserved a break from the airport.

The receptionist, an attractive middle-aged woman in a blue dress, gave Hebert a placating smile. "I'm sure he'll be with you shortly. Things have been sort of crazy around here since Saturday."

"I can imagine," Hebert said.

"Sure you don't want coffee?"

"I think we're all set."

She smiled again and busied herself with some paperwork.

They waited. Finally, after twenty more minutes, the receptionist's phone rang. She picked it up, listened, and said, "They'll be right in." She stood, made an escorting-type gesture toward the office door, and said, "Gentlemen?"

When they entered, Byron Gladwell was behind a massive oak desk. His office was large and well decorated. He greeted Hebert and Ramon, introduced himself to Wheeler, and they sat in four chairs around a small conference table. There were, of course, several copies of that morning's *American-Statesman* on the tabletop. The editor, showing off his wares.

Gladwell had a hurried demeanor about him—rushing to meet a deadline, no doubt—but he managed a solicitous smile. After yet another offer of coffee, he said, "Okay, what can I do for you today?" Friendly. Cheery. No idea what was coming.

Hebert immediately removed the .22 automatic from his pocket and placed it on the table. There was an evidence tag affixed to it. "I believe this is yours," he said.

A frown. "Really? My old gun?"

"Serial number matches the one you reported stolen."

Gladwell didn't touch it. He made a show of examining it from several angles. Then he shook his head, acting confounded. "I guess it is. I'm really surprised. After all this time, I . . . where did it turn up?"

"Kid found it," Wheeler said. "In some weeds along Loop 360."

"Is that right?" Gladwell said. "It still looks good. No rust or anything. You'd think it would've—"

"He found it seven years ago," Hebert said. "It didn't have time to rust."

There was a small tic in Gladwell's left cheek. Hardly noticeable. Hebert noticed, though. "Well, I'm just amazed to be getting it back," Gladwell said. "Wow. Seven years later." He came forth with a meager laugh. "Who says you can't count on the cops, right? Hell, maybe we should even do a piece on it. *Editor reunited with stolen gun.* Could be interesting. Any idea how it ended up on the median?"

"Yeah, we've got a theory about that," Hebert said. "We think you threw it there."

Gladwell attempted to smile. "You, uh . . . what?"

"We think you tossed it after you shot at Harry Jenkins. Probably when you saw the patrol car coming up behind you."

Poor liars tend to overact. The look on Gladwell's face was almost comical. He sputtered a few times, starting to say different things, going for flummoxed, and finally settled on "Is this some sort of joke? You can't be serious."

Hebert opened a manila folder and removed a sheaf of paper. "The Nash incident occurred on a Saturday. April tenth. You reported the weapon stolen three days later, on a Tuesday."

"That sounds right. My memory is sort of—"

"You told the responding officer that the burglary occurred on April third or fourth. Someone kicked your back door in."

The tic in Gladwell's cheek was steady now. "Yes, that's right. I didn't bother reporting it until I discovered my gun had been stolen. They didn't take much else."

"So where were you on that weekend, the third and fourth?"

"Lost Pines. I was camping."

"With who?"

"Nobody. Just me."

"You went on a camping trip by yourself?"

Gladwell was tapping a pencil rapidly on the conference table. "Look, I really don't understand why—"

"When did you leave?"

"Early Saturday morning."

"When did you come back?"

"Sunday evening."

"You live alone, Mr. Gladwell?"

"What's that got to do with anything?"

"So you live alone."

"I do."

"And obviously, since you were burglarized, there wasn't anybody staying at your house that weekend, right?"

"No, there was not."

Hebert stared at him for several seconds. Then he removed another sheet of paper from the folder and laid it on the table. Phone records. "Then can you explain why there were seven calls to and from your residence during those two days?"

Gladwell picked up the paper, his eyes darting wildly over it. "I . . . I don't know. All I know is I wasn't there. This can't be right."

"You used to own a black truck. Correct?"

"Yes."

"Might even look blue at night."

"I don't know what that means."

"It was your only vehicle, so I assume you drove it to Lost Pines."

"I . . ."

"You sold it on April sixteenth."

"I want all of you to leave now."

Hebert had plenty of circumstantial evidence. What he wanted was an outright confession. It was up to Wheeler to get it. He had told Hebert he was good at bluffing, and now he had to prove it. The airport cop leaned forward, solemn, even angry. "I was a traffic cop seven years ago," he said. "I worked the accident. I pulled Sabrina Nash's son from the wreckage. And I was the one who started to pull you over on Loop 360."

"No. No! Not me."

"I had a dashboard camera in my unit, but it didn't record your license plate clearly. Let me tell you, we had some of the computer wizards at the station work on it. The technology wasn't quite there yet. Things have changed since then."

Hebert removed one last sheet of paper from his folder. It appeared to be an authentic photograph from Wheeler's dash cam. It wasn't.

Wheeler said, "There's your truck, Mr. Gladwell. Your license plate. Driving north on Loop 360 on the evening of Saturday, April tenth."

Gladwell's face began to contort. Pain. Fear. Guilt. It was all there. He was beginning to cry. He didn't speak. Nobody did for several minutes. Hebert finally broke the silence.

"I can only imagine what it's like to work with Harry Jenkins. From what I understand, he's a, well, a bit of a prick. Condescending. Insubordinate. Basically, you've had to put up with his bullshit for fourteen years."

That gave Gladwell an out. He took it. He was nodding, his nose running. "He's an asshole," he said.

"I'm sure he is. Doesn't ever listen to you. Undermines your authority."

"Yes! He's arrogant and egotistical and . . . and overbearing."

"That's what everybody says. Pushy and vain. Thinks everyone else is a moron."

"I hate the son of a bitch. I hate him!"

I feel like I'm betraying him. That's what Gladwell had said when they'd collected prints from Jenkins' office.

Hebert said, "I'm guessing you only wanted to scare him. Shake him up a little." Hebert didn't think anything of the sort, but he didn't want to frighten the editor into silence with talk of premeditated murder, and the penalty it would carry.

"I . . . I'd been drinking. I couldn't take it anymore. The putdowns, the disrespect. I didn't . . ."

"You didn't what?"

Gladwell covered his face with his hands. He was sobbing. "The windows were tinted. I didn't know his family was with him."

The following day, Sabrina Nash parked her car and checked her makeup in the mirror. Not bad. Her eyes were still a little puffy and red, but nothing too obvious. Not that it mattered. She'd be crying again shortly.

The funeral had been lightly attended. Matt's parents had been there, of course, and a handful of relatives, but his friends, apparently, had stayed away. Maybe it was the rain, which, finally, was coming down in sheets. Or maybe they found it hard to mourn a person who'd killed two men. Sabrina didn't. To some degree, she could understand why Matt had done what he had. She couldn't condone it, but she could understand it.

"Matt loved Jacob," his mother had said after the services, hunched under the tent, her face as dark and troubled as the sky. "Probably as much as you and Harry did."

"He never quite got over . . . what happened," his father added.

"I'm so sorry," Sabrina replied. What else was there to say?

Now . . . Harry. Now she had to go in there and tell him the truth. Not Duane Rankin. Byron Gladwell. For God's sake, it was Byron Gladwell. Harry, of course, would blame himself. Gladwell's hatred for Harry had been the root of it all. Well, if Harry was going to have a breakdown, at least he was in the right place for it. Cynical, but true. Someone had to be strong.

She locked her car and trotted through the downpour to the front door of the facility.

"Hebert just called me," Bobby Garza said, sitting behind his desk. "Duane Rankin is a free man. Walked out of Huntsville two hours ago. Figured you'd want to know."

"Story of the decade," said John Marlin, holding a cup of coffee, leaning against the doorjamb. He could hear the rain booming on the rooftop of the sheriff 's office. " 'Innocent man spends seven years in prison.' "

"Rankin comes out and Campbell goes in. Byron Gladwell, too. It's going to be a media circus."

It already was. So far, the sound bites had been hilarious.

The National Weapons Alliance had put out a press release stressing that Campbell's side of the story hadn't been heard yet. Suddenly they appeared to value the Fifth Amendment as much as the Second. On the other hand, they said, Campbell's contract as their spokesperson was coming to an end, and they felt it best if all parties involved went their separate ways so Mr. Campbell could focus on defending his respected name. Mighty big of them.

Sheryl Hudson, Campbell's rumored fiancée, refuted the gossip altogether. She said they were just friends. Acquaintances, really. She didn't know him that well. Certainly not the kind of man she'd marry. She'd already been spotted in the company of the drummer from a heavy-metal band called Sow's Udder.

Mitch Campbell, conversely, was the only one keeping silent. No matter; the evidence spoke for itself. Small shards of glass had been found in the grass outside Campbell's bedroom window. They'd found a slug, which was matched to a commemorative .45 given to Mitch by the NWA. They also discovered traces of deer blood in the barrel of one of Dale Stubbs' hunting rifles. Marlin had been correct about the blood splatter.

In addition to the Rodolfo Dominguez homicide, Campbell was facing a second count, this one for J. B. Crowley. A day earlier, an anonymous caller had tipped Garza to the location of Crowley's body: in an abandoned well on Campbell's ranch. Found with the body was a bloody, broken cue stick. Crowley's truck had also been found on the ranch, with more blood in the bed, and Campbell's prints on the steering wheel. Add that to the evidence they'd taken from Campbell's garbage—the glass from Campbell's broken juke-box, the blood that had matched Crowley's—and Marlin figured the case was a slam dunk. Unreal.

"What's going on with Dobbins?" Marlin asked.

The recording device that had been found on Matt Mergen-thaler's body had contained an extra surprise: a call between Dale Stubbs and Congressman Glenn Dobbins.

"Pretty obvious that Dobbins was involved in the cover-up," Garza said. "But there's no way to prove it."

"What was that bit about 'spreading money around'?"

"Weiser has a theory about that," Garza said, referring to the as-sistant district attorney in Houston. "He thinks Dobbins was refer-ring to Crowley's homicide case. Maybe the witness wasn't threatened. Maybe he was bribed instead, by NWA lawyers."

"Has Weiser talked to the witness again?"

"Yeah. He's sticking with his original story. But the Dobbins cam-paign is history, that's for sure. The rumor is, he's gonna pull out."

That's not enough, Marlin thought, *but it'll have to do.*

"Meanwhile, a guy from *Newsweek* is coming down tomorrow," Garza said, shaking his head at the ridiculousness of it all. "They're writing an article to go with those photos that . . . what's his name?"

"Casey."

"Yeah, Casey Walberg. They're writing a story to go with those photos he took. I don't really want to talk to them, and I thought maybe—"

"Forget it," Marlin said.

Garza was starting to laugh. "Come on, you were the big hero and—"

"No way."

"At least say a few words. You gonna be around?"

Marlin was already backing out of the doorway. "Taking a few days off," he said. "I'll see you next week."

The next day, the rains had moved on, but a thick white blanket of clouds blocked the sun. Turkey vultures drifted effortlessly on cur-rents, like fish suspended in water. The temperature was mild, mideighties, with a gentle breeze from the west. Low humidity. Perfect day for a picnic.

Nicole, ahead of him, uphill, said, "Getting tired?" That smile. She looked healthy and strong in shorts and hiking boots. Hair in a braid. No uniform. No badge. No gun. Marlin's heart fluttered.

"Just pacing myself."

"We should do this once a week. Great for the heart." Her breath came easily.

"Only if you carry me."

She reached back and took his hand.

Fifteen more minutes and they'd be at the top of Enchanted Rock, forty miles west of Johnson City. It was one of nature's oddities: a massive, domelike batholith of pink granite that loomed hundreds of feet in the air and covered more than six hundred acres. The view from the top was astounding. Best of all, they'd have it to themselves. Marlin hadn't seen another visitor to the park all morning.

He had a pack on his back. Sandwiches and fruit. Energy bars. A jug of water. Sunscreen. A camera.

And a small velvet-covered box.

Epilogue

THE WORLD OUTSIDE Red O'Brien's trailer was gloomy. Cold and drizzly. Gray and muddy. Early November.

Four months had passed since Mitch had been revealed as a murderer and a fraud, and Red had been in a foul mood ever since. Jesus Christ. *Middlebury, Vermont?* What sort of country singer comes from Vermont? The articles proved that it was all lies. Mitch Campbell was not a bull rider. Not a trophy-winning bass fisherman. Not a Copenhagen addict. Not a former short-order cook who managed to shed his grease-stained apron and become an American icon.

Red was doubly crushed. Not only had he watched one of his idols fall in disgrace, Red had lost his one realistic chance at success as a songwriter.

"Come dark, we could go shinin' for hogs," Billy Don said. They'd intended to hunt dove today, but the weather had interfered. Typical. Don't make plans, because you'll only be disappointed. Red knew all about it. A fat drop of water fell from the ceiling and hit the bucket below with a loud *ploink!*

"Ain't in the mood," Red said.

"It's gonna let up."

"Don't care."

Red was sitting in his easy chair, a bottle of beer within easy reach. His shotgun was leaning nearby. A Sara Evans video was playing on CMT, and even *that* didn't cheer Red up. She was one fine-looking babe, singing about sparks flying in the dark, but Red couldn't get into it.

Ploink!

"You're gonna have to get over it," Billy Don said.

"Get over what?"

"Shit, you don't think I know what you're stewing about? You came *this* close. And now you think the world is against you. But you gotta just keep tryin'."

Next up, the veejay said, *is Clyde Crawford, who is fresh out of prison, hoping to make a comeback with his latest single . . .*

Billy Don pointed at the screen. "See, that's a perfect 'zample. Man gets out of jail and gets right back on the horse that threw him."

. . . and this is an interesting one, a song written by Clyde's manager . . .

"You gotta do what he's doing," Billy Don said. "Pick yourself up and dust yourself off."

. . . some troubles of his own after that debacle with Mitch Campbell . . .

"It's like my granny always said. If you think you can—"

"Hush up," Red said, leaning forward, listening closely. He couldn't believe what he was hearing. Clyde Crawford was standing in front of an enormous U.S. flag, plucking the opening notes on his guitar.

"But, Red, if you—"

"Hush!"

Then Clyde Crawford sang the first line.

> *Down around Gonzales,*
> *Back in 1831 . . .*

"Son of a bitch!" Red said.

> *Some Texas boys got their hands*
> *On a big ol' iron gun . . .*

"Sheep-screwing bastards!" Red said.

But four years later Santa Anna came calling . . .
Red reached for his shotgun.
And the Texicans took to cannonballing . . .
He leveled it at the television.
They said . . .
Come and take it!
Red was giggling maniacally as he pulled the trigger.